# PINE CREEK

## KAMILLE ROACH

First published in 2023 in Australia
ISBN: 9798395448736

Copyright © Kamille Jane Roach, 2023

The moral rights of the author have been asserted.

All rights reserved. Except as permitted under the Australian Copyright Act 1968 (for example, fair dealing for study, research, criticism or review), no part of this book may be reproduced, stored in a retrieval system, communicated or transmitted in any form or by any means without prior written permission.

The characters in this book are fictitious, and any resemblance to real persons, living or dead, is purely coincidental.

Edited by Michele Perry, Wordplay Editing Services.

10 9 8 7 6 5 4 3 2 1

*For Jemma*

## *Prologue*

Sara would remember how cold it was the day Alec went missing. Grey, seal-skin sky, lonely highway, road slick with wet. Anything living wrapped deep into itself; sheep and cattle huddled close; birds nestled together with their eyes shut.

# Part One

*Chapter 1*

**Saturday morning, June 1989**

She'd never come before.

Wearing a red scarf and clutching something two-handed to her chest, Sara's neighbour, Lillian Stynes, strode across the highway toward the Hamilton farmstead.

The movement had caught Sara's eye as she stared glumly at the wintry sky above the solid dark green pine plantations slotted between the cleared farmlands of Pine Creek.

At their gateway, Lillian paused, her face turned in the direction of the sign: *Hamilton's* bolted to the front fence.

Slippers on, Sara raced into the kitchen and warmed her bum in front of the pot-belly stove. She went to the window and pulled back the curtain.

Eating toast at the dining table, Sara's sister Anne, older by two years, squinted in the sudden light. Her dark hair had been similar to Sara's until Sara massacred hers with Mum's sewing scissors.

'Anne, it's Alec's mum!' said Sara. She imagined Lillian was carrying an injured kitten as she watched her use one hand for the garden gate while she cradled the other against her body. Lillian cast a wary look at the huge radiata pine tree some idiot had planted near the front door. Sara pulled one of Anne's scarves off the back of the chair and tied it around her head.

Anne frowned. 'Jesus.' She patted her hair down and tried to see through the window.

Lillian knocked, but there was no barking.

Dad must have taken the dogs out already.

'Mum?' Sara called.

Mum hurried out. She was fine-featured with hazel eyes and always stooped as if she expected the roof to fall in. She rolled off her rubber gloves, untied the bow at the small of her back and placed her apron over the back of a chair. After a deep breath, and a habitual check of the pins which suppressed curls above her ears, she slid the front door open. 'Hello? Oh, Mrs Stynes?'

Wind gusts pulled at Lillian's coat and scarf as her mauve-tinged lips were hidden by breath fog.

The huge pine sighed, and holly leaves rattled as though shaken by a hidden hand.

Mum hugged herself. 'Oh, my gosh. So cold, isn't it?'

'My son, Alec, is missing. Have you seen him?' said Lillian. Her large blue eyes swept the room.

Sara's stomach did a small flip the same way it did when she was asked to speak in class. 'I saw him running near our boundary yesterday.'

Mum twisted around.

Lillian nodded, her expression a pale mix Sara recognised as fear and hope.

Sara noticed how hollow Lillian's cheeks were and could see that despite the two coats she wore, she was very thin. Lillian had a beanie pulled down over her hair and wore no makeup, but Sara still thought she looked beautiful. Only once had Sara seen Lillian walk down the main street of Parkwood, and when she'd passed a group of teenaged boys, they'd pumped their hips and grabbed their balls behind her back.

'That's right. He got home before the rain,' said Lillian. 'Then ate dinner and went to bed.' Her hands sprang out from her chest. In them was a man's wet dress shoe, dirt stuck in the dotted pattern.

'I've looked everywhere. This was next to the highway.'

Sara's stomach grumbled. She was sure she'd seen Alec wearing that type of shoe.

'We were at the hospital last night,' said Mum. 'Robbie had a bad appendix.'

'Is he alright?' Lillian asked.

Sara thought Lillian looked genuinely worried.

'Yes. He's still in hospital.'

'Can you help me please?' said Lillian.

Mum nodded. She had her palm pressed against her cheek. 'Here, I'll get you the local fire brigade's number so they can let people know what's happened, or they can help you look for Alec, okay?'

After Lillian had left, Mum allowed Sara and Anne to check the Workers' House in case Alec had sheltered there. Sara rushed through the cold morning with her sister, wearing a coat, beanie and gloves. Each of their breaths clouded the air. Sara wiped her nose on the back of her glove.

Sara checked the bathroom and small bedrooms, while

Anne checked the lounge and master bedroom. Sara watched Anne walk into the darkened room. She remembered the thunderstorm the night she'd visited Ryan. Sometimes she could still feel his big hands gripping her hip bones, his lips wet against her throat.

When they got back, the phone rang. A search had been organised for Alec. Everyone was meeting in the Stynes' front paddock.

Dad came in for morning tea. 'Steer clear,' he said, indicating the gathering crowd that could be seen through the window. 'It's none of our business.'

Anne rolled her eyes and shut herself in her room.

Sara jogged down inside the front boundary fence and watched from behind the Workers' House gate.

Over in the Stynes' paddock, yellow vests were scattered through the crowd like glow-worms. There was no sign of the few sheep and two Alpacas that lived there as the group split. A handful went left into the pine forest, and the rest fanned out and moved slowly towards the front of the property. They trickled down the drive and then walked along the highway. Someone pointed to the nearby embankment where scuffed mud had rolled down the slope.

A man in a yellow vest crossed the road and began walking along the channel that ran parallel to the highway. He stopped suddenly.

'Here!'

Heads began flicking back and forth before people ran over in twos and threes. They gathered around the man, but he stuck his arms out, indicating everyone stay back.

'Alec?' Lillian called. Sara saw her breaststroking through the crowd.

The man turned with both hands held up and his head shaking from side to side.

The group closed in around Lillian and netted her with their arms.

'No!' Lillian cried and twisted to break free. A woman fat with coats enveloped her. They both sank down out of sight.

A crow cawed for several long seconds. In the tall gum tree above Sara, several more joined in, the drone stretching out as the big birds launched up and cloaked the air with coal-black wings. Sara thought of the grim reaper.

She felt sure, Alec — the boy brave enough to wear a wild, colourful jacket — was dead.

## Chapter 2

**Friday – Four weeks before Alec's death**

Sara had a good view of the neighbour's driveway from the kitchen window. She knew that the lady who'd rented the place six months previous collected her son Alec from the Coltan train station every fortnight on a Saturday. Pine Creek was smack centre between the cities of Coltan and Parkwood, but it was smoky Coltan, thirty kilometres east, where the train from Sydney terminated.

There were lots of kids who hung around the station on their bicycles, the boys wearing their hair shaved on top and long at the back. They rode around and spat on the footpath.

Alec's hair was long enough for him to be mistaken for a girl. Several times Sara had seen him walking along their eastern boundary to the forest. He wore short trousers, dress shoes and a colourful patchwork jacket, which made it obvious he wasn't local. At their school, a kid could get a hiding for wearing clothes like that.

Alec and his mother rented Old Dave's cottage, which was

surrounded on three sides by pine forests. The five acres of grass and bracken fern was a permanent home to two alpacas and a handful of sheep with overgrown fleece. In the past, Sara's dad had sneered and called it a 'hobby farm'.

Within a fortnight of the Stynes' arrival, the Country Women's Association president, Cherie, had dropped in to visit. Afterwards, she shared the news that Lillian was a single mother with one child, Alec, who was fourteen and visited alternate weekends because he lived with his dad in Sydney. Alec was in a program for gifted students ... music or arts, or something. Lillian was a bookkeeper and had moved to Pine Creek so she was close to her mother, who was in aged care in Milton; a tiny place fifteen minutes away.

Dad said he'd guessed the new neighbour didn't have a husband. 'Don't you go over there,' he warned. 'Divorcees are worse than spinsters.'

*Another Len Hamilton 'fact'.*

'Yes, Dad,' Sara had said to herself.

A few weeks after the Stynes moved in, there was a grass fire next to the highway. It happened all the time when the weather was dry because people threw lit cigarette butts out of their car windows. From the house, Sara had seen the smoke and then a thin tide of flames spread up into Old Dave's front paddock. Then she saw a familiar white ute. Her dad there, slapping a wet hessian bag along the flames, which were headed towards the house. Dad took ages to come home, even though Lillian was a divorcee. Mum had to reheat his dinner in the oven.

Afterwards, Lillian had sent a 'thank you' card. Dad said it was nice to be appreciated and gave Mum his critical side-eyes; a similar look to the one he used when he'd told her to smarten herself up. Lillian's card did wonders, because Dad didn't make any more comments about her, except to say that sometimes one had to be generous to those less fortunate.

The weekend before, Sara noticed Alec had arrived on Friday afternoon instead of Saturday morning.

And now Sara was waiting to see him turn up at his house, not because she liked him – he was weird and only fourteen – but because she'd heard a rumour.

Anne stood in front of Sara, breaking the view with cleavage, necklaces, and teased hair. 'What are you looking at?' she said, hands to the jut of her hips.

They had been home for long enough to get bored while Mum made a start on the weekend housework.

Sara shifted. 'Nothing. Go back to your love affair with the mirror.'

Anne huffed through her nose. At school, when Anne walked along the corridors, the boys' heads turned. Sara admitted she was impressed by her sister's slow, rolling walk which turned her buttocks into two rocking melons. Sara had tried to replicate the walk behind Anne on the driveway one afternoon, but she almost twisted her ankle.

That afternoon, Anne's hair was perky in a high side ponytail, fringe tortured with a comb and lacquer, orange scarf knotted at the top of her head. She wore dangling earrings, several necklaces, and numerous bracelets, obviously determined to look like Madonna from her music video 'Like a Virgin'.

Through the window, Sara saw the Stynes' little red Suzuki crawling up their driveway like a ladybug.

Anne swivelled and peered through the window with a jangle of bangles. 'I wonder when Ryan's due back?' She probably thought Sara was watching the Workers' House.

'Tomorrow night. He has TAFE exams, remember,' said Sara.

Her sister grinned, tongue between her open back teeth. 'God, you're naïve.'

Sara blushed.

Anne leant over and spoke into her ear. 'Want me to give him a kiss for you?'

'Shut up!' Sara elbowed her sister and twisted away.

'Don't swear. Your father will be here shortly.' Mum checked behind them, and Sara copied, as did Anne.

Sara thought to an onlooker, the three of them must look like they all suffered from a similar tic. She headed for the pantry. 'You're jealous because I've lost weight.'

Mum came over, stroked Sara's ponytail and kissed her on the head.

Sara squirmed away. 'I just want to go walking,' she complained.

'Just a walk? Back for dinner?'

Sara nodded. 'Course.'

It wasn't exactly a lie.

She'd heard the rumour on the bus Wednesday morning.

'Alec Stynes is a homo!'

Meredith dropped it casually like a snake on the floor between Sara and the other three kids who lived at the beginning of the bus run. One kid ducked; another drew back.

There were usually five of them, but Anne had taken the morning off.

Meredith, a private schooler, had her hair permed and suffered from eczema. She scratched the back of her knee.

Suddenly possessive of her neighbour, Sara folded her arms. 'You don't even know him,' she said.

'I know people from his school in Sydney,' said Meredith with a sniff.

The four of them exchanged raised eyebrows and huddled in.

Meredith leant into their circle. 'He held a boy's hand!' she whispered, clearly eyeing the pink shock on their faces. 'Have you seen the way he dresses? There are heaps of homos in the city.'

'Gangs beat them up down there ... my brother lives in the city,' Cameron rushed. He was about thirteen, always seemed desperate to get his head inside a gossip circle. His greatest asset was his brother, an apprentice mechanic who'd moved out of home. He launched into the details of gay gang bashings.

Sara felt pinpricks down the back of her arms.

'Stop it!' Pip cried into her hands. Pip was small with her blonde hair in two plaits. Sara noticed the part down the centre of her scalp had gone strawberry red.

'Idiot,' Meredith reprimanded the boy. 'She's only eleven.' She patted Pip's back.

Cameron drew back, cheeks ruddy, crossed his arms hard and thudded back against the seat. They all stared out the windows.

Sara searched her bag for a drink but there wasn't one. She found an orange, but the thought of eating made her feel sick.

## Chapter 3

### 1982 Pine Creek, N.S.W.

In 1982, when Sara was eight, the black cloud of AIDS came to Australia. At first, Dad said it was just a rumour. But every night it was on the news, with a count which went up like numbers spinning on a poker machine. Dad went quiet for a bit and then started saying angry things about it, so Sara knew it was true. Until then, she'd never heard of an 'epidemic'.

AIDS soon inundated the news, current affairs and talk-back radio. Mum and Dad leant in to catch every bit of information, checking each other as though to confirm what they'd heard.

Before Dad got in from work one night, Mum had the TV on. Sara had heard that AIDS was spreading quickly among homosexual men, prostitutes and IV drug users. One weekend at a local dance, a group talked about it in a corner of the hall. Sara heard them say AIDS was a gay disease that was killing innocent women and children. Sara imagined the virus as an evil black octopus with long, deadly tentacles reaching up from the darkness. She'd heard people who caught it were dying horrible deaths. She imagined blood coming from their mouths, skeletal bodies covered in sores.

Often, Sara, Anne and Robbie weren't allowed near the loungeroom at news time.

Before AIDS, Dad had sometimes yelled at the TV, then AIDS came, and he yelled all the time. His eyes turned to slits, and the skin snarled along his nose. Sara had never seen him hate something so fiercely.

'You dirty paedophile perverts! Don't bloody deserve rights, scum poofters!' He'd shake a knuckled fist at the screen, white drop of spittle on his lower lip, then jump to his feet in front of his chair, chest squared. 'See that, Ellen?' he'd say, pointing at the TV. His voice high-pitched. 'Those disgusting faggots have spread AIDS, and now they want rights! Did you hear that?' He choked out a horrible laugh, face reddish purple.

Sara thought he might need someone to slap his back to help him breathe.

Mum had scuttled into the kitchen as soon as she heard Dad come home. She was preparing dinner.

Mum's real name was Elena, which she had told them when they were old enough, but Dad thought it sounded too Italian. Sara knew Mum was adopted from Italian people and that Dad didn't want a bar of them. Mum had been a twin, and her parents had kept her brother.

'Bloody disgusting! Terrible isn't it, Ellen?'

'Mm-hm.' Mum nodded, but she'd kept her eyes on the carrots she was cutting. Sara knew Mum understood. It was an answer she used with Dad, which was neither a 'yes' nor a 'no'. Her way of staying out of strife.

'Speak up, Ellen, for Chrissake, woman! Disgusting, isn't it?'

'Yes, Len.'

The right words.

*Yes, Len. Yes, Dad.*

At Sara's school, groups of boys pretended to be gay to get laughs. They spoke with lisps and affected tones, like they were reading a fairytale.

Towards the end of 1982, Dad went to a meeting in the Pine Creek Hall. He'd been talking more and more about the lack of rainfall and said that they were in a drought, which meant farmers were going to suffer.

On the bus to primary school, Sara saw neighbours feeding grain and hay to their sheep and cattle, just like her family had been doing. Dad growled about steep feed prices.

The paddocks grew bald as cows searched the dirt with their tongues. When Dad loaded the ute with hay and they bumped across the brittle ground, the cattle bellowed and ran towards them – a stampede of rust brown and white. Mum said a weed with purple flowers which grew around Pine Creek had two names: Patterson's Curse and Salvation Jane, because it was drought-resistant. Sara scanned the paddocks until she found the mauve hue, relieved there was something they could count on if Dad stopped buying feed.

Gradually, week by week by month, it felt to Sara as though the weather held them hostage. Her dad frequently scowled up at the sky as he scratched the necks of their kelpie, Rusty, and red-heeler, Jack.

In their house, everyone quietly followed Dad's rules, cautious of everything they said. Sara knew, like Mum, Anne and Robbie, that she had to be careful. She imagined herself a ghost who floated from room to room.

April 1987, just after Sara turned thirteen, the drought was over, but AIDS was gaining momentum. The grim reaper advertisement appeared on TV – the scythe-bearing reaper bowling a black ball at a group, including children and a mother with a baby. Sara watched in horror as the people were knocked to the ground. Their dead bodies were then swept up by the gate. She left the light on at night.

## Chapter 4

### Friday – Four weeks before Alec's death

Ten minutes after she'd seen the red Suzuki, Sara slipped out with muesli bars shoved in her pockets.

Beyond the front gate, she walk-ran along the crumbly bitumen of the old highway beside their front fence where potholes oozed gravel and road base.

Everything on her right was theirs, though Dad hadn't boasted since the drought. In the dry cold, stunted sage-green coated the cleared paddocks bordered by ringlock fences topped with two threads of barbed wire that fooled sheep and most cows unless spooked and seeking freedom. Further away were rolling hills with grey piles of granite rock, fawn tussocks, dark-trunked gums and oval-shaped dams. She walked through the tunnel of gums and pines and past a brook popular for dumping unwanted kittens. The kittens usually escaped to nearby haysheds to quarrel over warm corners and soon have their own kittens.

Hoisting herself to the top of the gate, Sara jumped over.

The Workers' House, an old three-by-one, capped with a corrugated iron roof, sat squat in the middle of an unkempt garden.

Workers occasionally stayed during shearing, hay baling and jobs that lasted more than a day, but the only regular visitor was Ryan. Almost eighteen, he drove his navy Ford Escort from Sydney's western suburbs each Saturday fortnight, and then to Sara it felt as if everything about the farm warmed.

Sara let herself inside, walked into the bathroom, which doubled as a laundry, and yanked open the dryer. She pulled out the bedsheets and carried the high bundle through the house to the double bed. She opened the curtains, fitted the bottom sheet over the mattress, laid a flat sheet on top, then shook out a doona, put it on top and neatened the corners. She slapped the pillows and placed them at the head of the bed and then grabbed one and lifted it to her face. Eyes closed, she inhaled.

It had been Sara's turn to do the sheets following Ryan's last visit. She'd discovered if she didn't wash the pillowcases, Ryan's smell, a mix of shaving foam and woody sage, stayed on the fabric.

After a moment, Sara sighed, walked out and hurried across to the gate. There was movement to her right. As she'd expected, Alec stood at the bottom of his driveway beside the highway.

Sara ran over to the corner post, which led to the front paddock, pulled herself up, walked over the top wire and jumped down to the ground.

Sara watched as Alec crossed the road and then turned east. Using trees for cover, she moved closer and fell in behind him, as he walked with his shoulders seesawing. Sara was close enough to hear him clear his throat a few times and start humming.

Sara was aware that the news about Alec being gay would spread across Pine Creek like Christmas beetles through the eucalypts. If it was true, the Stynes would be lucky if they were simply evicted.

Sara's family occasionally attended a dance at the local hall, which was held every few months. The last time had been about six months ago. The band always played the same music, mostly for progressive dances, followed by the 'Chicken Dance', and then slow music for the married couples. Suddenly Lillian, who had arrived a few weeks before, had walked in. Sara became aware that people had stopped talking. Several women stared at Lillian while they talked with their heads close together. Most of the men were looking at Lillian too, but with happier expressions. Sara could see why. She thought Lillian looked lovely. Lillian wore a lemon-coloured dress, red lipstick, and her short blonde hair was in waves. She joined in the progressive dance but then sat down on her own, with a drink, until an old man sat with her. Then she seemed to relax and smiled as she talked and laughed. At one point she looked up and suddenly her face fell.

Sara noticed Dad looking at her, his eyebrow raised. He smiled to himself and turned his back. Lillian got up, made her way through the tables and went outside. Sara thought she must have left the dance, because she didn't see her again.

Sara ran her hand over the top of the dry grass and wild oats.

Dad said wild oats were something men sowed, but women didn't. When Sara asked her English teacher what her dad meant, she said that it referred to high spirited young men having lots of sex.

In class, they had studied a play called *The Crucible*, about the Salem witch trials in the 1600s. It riled the girls, while the boys shifted in their seats and smirked uncertainly at one another. To Sara it seemed an easy equation; young men had lots of sex and got congratulated. Young or single women had sex and were seductresses, whores and witches and burnt or drowned. The teacher pointed out books on the suffragettes, in case anyone was interested in the history of women's rights.

The teacher was the sort of woman Dad would call a 'women's libber'. He always said it with a disgusted look on his face, like they were cockroaches.

Up ahead of Sara, Alec's skinny legs were visible between his colourful socks and his short trousers, his oversized dress shoes kicking to the sides. He turned sharply right into the firebreak, which ran between the forest and the Hamilton boundary, and then he disappeared into the trees.

Sara stopped at a big red gum in the middle of the paddock. She slid down, back against the tree trunk. She was hungry and wasn't sure how far Alec would go or when to approach him. A flock of their merino sheep had spread out near the opposite fence. Late sun on the side of her face, Sara squinted up at magpies that talked high in the branches.

Sara ate a muesli bar and eyed the sheep. They were ewes who'd been joined by the rams a month or two ago. They now had slightly rounded bellies, and lambing was expected in spring. She remembered a lamb from a previous season with a tiny patch of black wool on its shoulder. Dad had said the damn thing was obviously not purebred. He'd caught it, cut out the dark wool with a knife and then sewed the edges together while it bleated and struggled.

Sara peered around at the edge of the forest. She really needed to go over and tell Alec about the rumour. Warn him to watch his back.

She wondered if people were gathering the lynch squad. But what if Meredith was wrong, and Alec was just into weird clothes?

Sara knew her dad wasn't the only one who hated the homos, especially because of those violent gangs in the city. People said the gay men should die of AIDS because AIDS was their fault and their punishment, like God had ordered a virus to specifically eradicate them.

Dad made them sound like a different species, inhuman, like their blood was green or their brains mis-wired. He also said a relationship was between a man and woman, and he was backed up by God, and the Bible.

Dad said a lot of things. Brought God into it when he needed.

Sara rolled her body around the tree. Maybe Alec was ashamed. Maybe he cried alone in the trees. If they roughed him up at school, he'd be scared and sad and carry the burden of it on his thin shoulders. Maybe Alec just needed to be alone. Like Sara did sometimes when the glare of people's eyes cut her up, and she didn't feel good enough.

It had been three days since Meredith had told them. Three days was plenty of time for the Pine Creek grapevine to pass the news around.

'Shit,' Sara mumbled. She then ran quickly to the boundary fence, climbed over and dropped down.

To the right, movement caught her eye. About fifty metres down the firebreak was Alec wearing a white shirt. He jumped, landed with bent legs and then spun around like he was in a sword fight, hair flying out from his head. Instead of a weapon, he held a sheaf of papers. Sara heard talking. Alec turned around and spoke like there was someone there, but no one was.

Alec did this again, changed his voice, moved dramatically from one side of the track to the other, arms swooping through the air. He stopped and consulted his papers, hair falling forwards.

Sara shaded her eyes. At school, the drama class had been practising for the school play. There had been posters advertising for extras and stage crew.

Suddenly, Alec dropped his arms to his sides, tilted his face upwards and sang. A high, strong note came from his mouth and fluttered upwards, like a beam shone directly from his heart. Sara got a shiver down her back as if her shirt had moved. Hairs stood up along her arms.

The sound turned and wound into itself; strands caressing each other, forming a wave that lowered and poured back down into Alec's mouth like honey.

He dropped his hand and tipped forwards at the hip. He swept his arm, trunk-like, side to side before he straightened.

*Not just a play, a musical.* Sara lifted her hands to clap, realised what she was doing and froze. She suddenly saw a snapshot of herself spying.

Alec grabbed his jacket off a nearby tree stump and threaded his arms into the sleeves.

Sara spun into action, jumped the fence, barrelled towards the red gum in a crouch-run and pressed herself into the trunk. After a moment, she peered over the tops of the grass.

Alec was about a hundred metres away and had turned left towards his house. He did a little skip. A few steps later, he did another one. Sara had missed her chance, but her task now seemed straightforward.

She hurried home, went into her room and closed the door behind her.

Alec was an actor and a singer, an artist. Artists could be eccentric, and people might be okay if they thought he was just different. She'd simply warn him, and they might even become friends.

Sara grabbed paper and pen, sat at her desk and breathlessly wrote his name. Holding the pen nib above the white, Sara's hand trembled slightly. Dad's stony eyes loomed in her mind. Sara bit her lip and exhaled for a long time.

She screwed up the paper and put it into the bin.

## Chapter 5

**Friday evening – Four weeks before Alec's death**

'Sara, c'mon!' Anne called from the kitchen.

Sara jumped, thoughts chasing each other. The rumour about Alec was just a rumour. Kids were always saying things. Parents often didn't take any notice. Probably too busy fighting their own battles. 'Coming!'

Anne was in the kitchen wearing an apron over her Madonna clothes. She grinned. 'He's gone.'

Sara checked out the back through the laundry door. The light had fallen, the air thick with dusk. There was a space in the machinery shed where Dad's ute was usually parked, rear in.

From inside the shed, Robbie kicked his bike stand down, saw Sara and waved. He strode downhill towards her. 'Hey!'

They walked down to the house together.

'Where'd you go?' Sara held the door open.

Robbie grinned. 'I sketched Pine Creek where it cuts through the back paddock.' He pulled a bowed sketchpad out of his shirt and opened it carefully. The paper crinkled. 'It's hard to draw movement. See how I've used the smudging and strikes here?' He pointed. The sketch was of a stream running between granite rock and reeds.

Sara swatted at a mosquito sailing through the open door. 'It looks like a black and white photo, Robbie.' She stepped inside and closed the door behind her brother, slapping a mosquito against the wall. It stuck there for a moment and then fell off.

Inside, Elvis' 'Heartbreak Hotel' started.

Robbie grinned and patted her shoulder. 'Hey, it's Friday night!' He kicked off his shoes, leaving them scattered.

Sara pulled off her shoes and placed them in the line against the wall. Near the speakers, Mum clapped and swirled in little backwards and forward steps, face lit like she'd had new batteries put in.

Sara walked into the kitchen and looked over Anne's shoulder. 'What are you making?' she said.

'Cacciatore,' said Anne. 'You say it like catch-a-tory.'

Sara practised.

Anne winced. 'You're a terrible Italian! Go dance with Mum!' She waved the wooden spoon, which sent a splat of something red onto the bench.

Mum's records were spread out across the top of the stereo. Elvis, The Seekers, The Carpenters, and The Beatles. Robbie plonked on the couch until Mum hauled him up. She waltzed him around to 'Love Me Tender', and he laughed and tried to go where she wanted him to go. Sara watched from the table, enjoying how her mum's body moved in disorganised circles, overcorrecting, staggering like a wheel on the gravel. Not the straight, nervous lines that made everything perfect so that Dad wouldn't yell.

\* \* \*

After dinner, Mum turned off the music and stacked the records down the bottom of the cabinet while Anne wiped the kitchen and took the scraps outside, where she would throw them directly into the chicken coop. While Robbie fed the dogs, Sara washed and wiped the dishes, tidied up, and then all four of them stood back and checked everything.

Sara and Robbie sniffed the air.

'Garlic?' Anne said. 'If he asks, we'll say it was sheep shanks with garlicky potatoes, agreed?'

Sara and the others nodded.

'Alright.' Anne took a deep breath and sighed. 'I'm off to bed.' She embraced Mum.

Sara, then Robbie, hugged Mum and kissed her cheek.

'We love you,' said Robbie.

Mum nodded, mouth closed; silence pulling her inwards.

Sara knew that next morning Dad would wrap his arm around Mum's legs after he'd eaten breakfast then whistle as he walked out. It had made Sara queasy to see Mum caught by his arm; her face plastered with the nervous smile of someone receiving a dubious gift. Mum's eye contact seemed to convey that Dad's good mood was proof that everything was fine. Sara reminded herself to be grateful for small mercies – something Mum had taught them.

## Chapter 6

### 1987 – Hamilton Farm

On weekends, farm work was done to the backdrop of Dad's yelling. Sara felt like they could never do things fast enough or good enough for him.

Still, Sara enjoyed riding the motorbikes or running with the dogs behind a flock of sheep during musters across the flats, scanning the rocky hillsides for strays, and watching the sheepdogs swing great arcs to drive the flock forwards. She didn't mind lamb marking either; lifting the stiff, gangly lambs up and holding their legs for Dad to give them a needle, nick a small Hamilton sign into the edge of their ear and put a tight rubber ring around their tails, and testicles, if they had them.

'Hold it still, for Chrissakes!' Dad yelled as the lambs struggled in their arms, the tight, short woollen backs of their bodies and heads wedged against their chest. Sara was always bruised after marking days, her shirts spotted with blood from the lambs' ears.

When it was hay season and the baler had turned the rows of dried grass into rectangular bales, she liked walking along beside the flat trailer. Dad had trouble finding willing workers, so all three of them were enlisted to throw bales up to him, and he would catch and stack each one. Even with gloves on, Sara's hands were red and stinging from grabbing baler twine, her forearms and thighs scratched from hours of levering stalky, 25-kilogram weights.

The bigger jobs – or 'the important work', as Dad called it – were kept for contractors.

One weekend, Dad shook his head when Sara and Anne offered to go out and help.

'Did you want the blackberries down at the creek sprayed?' Anne said. 'I could use some money for new shoes.'

'Your shoes are fine.'

At fifteen, Robbie had put in half the cost for his dirt bike, a red, yellow, and blue Honda CR 500 (earnt from his work at the servo pumping petrol and mopping floors) and now spent his spare time on the screaming two-stroke engine. This was effective in keeping him clear of their father. No one mentioned the sketchpad Robbie shoved into his shirt, or the pencils he tucked behind his belt before he rode off.

While they were talking at the kitchen table, the dogs began barking as a ute rolled up the driveway. Dad peered out. Two men were in the cab, each with an elbow on the open windowsill.

Dad got up from the table, lifted his hat from a hook inside the laundry above the boots and placed it on his head. 'We're making some new sheepyards,' he said. 'You girls are nothing but a bloody distraction.' He bent over, pulled on his leather boots and strode out. Sara heard him whistle. 'Rusty! Jack! Up! Good dogs.'

Anne followed Sara into her bedroom and sat on the end of Sara's bed, picking at the chipped polish on her nails. 'Can't go out, can't have anyone over, can't even work. Bloody dictator. It's like prison.'

Anne was different now she was older. There was an aura around her which made it hard to tell her things.

Sara heard the vehicles drive away. She had her knees bent beneath her chin, arms looped around her legs. 'It's not that bad ... Let's play Monopoly,' she suggested.

Anne shook her head and sighed. 'Sara, you never do anything. You never fight back.'

'There's no point. It just makes it worse.' Sara stared out the window away from Anne's eyes. 'I'm just waiting till I get out.'

'You're fourteen, Sara. That's three more years!' Anne jumped off the bed. 'Way you're going, you'll end up like Mum.' Anne stuck her face in Sara's before she walked out and slammed the door.

'Don't slam the door!' Sara said. She rested her forehead on her knees. 'Eight hundred and ...' she said.

First school term had started. Sara closed her eyes. She'd need a calculator to count the days before she was old enough to leave. But last time, the number had seemed to pull freedom further away, and made her sad.

That night, after Dad had fed the dogs, he joined them at the dinner table. First, he made eye contact with Anne and then her. 'Great day. Men work better without women hanging around. Isn't that right, Ellen?'

Chewing hard, Mum looked up. Eyes everywhere but settling on nothing, she offered the butter dish to Len.

Sara noticed Anne's knuckles, gripping a fork, turn white.

'Thank you, my dear.' Dad scraped his knife along the top of the butter and transferred it to his bread roll like he was performing surgery.

Shoulders high and tight, Mum stopped chewing and stared at Dad. Sara saw a solid block of something in her mother's face. Something that disrupted the Hamilton order. It scared Sara enough to stare at her peas. When she looked back, it was gone.

## Chapter 7

### Saturday – 27 days before Alec's death

No one Sara knew had been near Alec.

Dad said he would know if any poofters came to Pine Creek and promised, like any decent man, he'd get rid of them. He didn't say how.

Sara wanted to tell Anne what she'd heard about Alec, ask what she thought they should do.

Sara had finished her Saturday chores when she remembered to check the letterbox. As she jumped the grid between the gate posts, down the road, the Stynes' red car turned into their drive. Alec's unmistakable shape was in the passenger side.

Sara wandered slowly along the old highway.

She pondered the maths test she'd probably failed from the day before. How she would hide it from Dad. Mum said you either had a maths or a science brain, which Sara thought was true. Maybe she could tell Dad that.

Alec appeared on the hill near his front gate. Sara stood in his line of sight as he walked in her direction. But he faced down like he was watching the ground. When he got to the bend in his drive near the road, Sara willed him to look over. She could wave. It would be so easy then. She imagined telling him her name, and then what people were saying about him.

Sara's attention snagged on a slowing vehicle that had just driven past her.

Alec had noticed too; his head turned towards it. The ute was the type of one-tonner that every second farmer's son drove once they got their licence. It had a metal tray.

Alec's face was half blocked from view by the ute's thick antenna. Sara saw a long arm come out of the passenger side window. It pulled the air in a gesture for Alec to come over. Alec looked one way then the other and walked towards it.

Sara got an uneasy feeling. She suspected they weren't there asking for directions.

Suddenly, the ute's passenger side door sprang open, and Alec reversed a few steps and almost stumbled. Sara froze as she saw a man surge towards Alec with his arms out, like he wanted to trap him against the fence. Alec turned and sprinted up the driveway. The man ran after Alec, but one foot slipped out behind him, and he staggered forwards before he could right himself.

Alec was already halfway up his driveway and moving fast. The man stooped to pick something off the ground and then lifted his straight arm and sliced it down like a bowler.

Alec's elbows pinched his sides and his head flipped back. It reminded Sara of a movie where someone got shot in the back. Alec stumbled, then kept running. He was soon at the top of the driveway with one hand on the gatepost. He launched his body over the top and disappeared.

At the bottom of the driveway, the man stood with his hands on his hips. He turned, walked back to the ute and climbed inside. The wheels spun with a roar of acceleration as the vehicle surged back onto the highway and drew into the distance.

Sara's chest banged. What would the man have done to Alec if he'd caught him? What would Sara have seen; what could she have done?

Sara remembered Cameron on the bus, detailing what the gangs did to gay men, until Pip had started crying.

*They beat them, chase them over cliffs, hit them with slugs of wood that have nails hammered into the top. They mess up their faces, break their jaws, knock their teeth out and rape them with bottles, with the handles of things, and sometimes, just rape them.*

Sara swallowed. It hadn't happened. Alec had been fast.

She noticed movement. Alec reappeared. Hands on the top of the gate, his head turned one way and then the other as he stared down the road for a minute. He then hooked his foot into the wire of the gate, slung his other leg over, and slid to the ground on the other side. He leaned forwards and looked down the highway.

Alec removed his jacket and held it up in front of him, then bent his neck over and brushed the back with his hand. He cast another glance down the highway and, holding his jacket by the shoulders, he swept it one way, turned the other, knees slightly bent and swept it the other way. Alec looked like he was imitating a matador.

After a minute, Alec pushed his arms into the sleeves and climbed up on top of the gate. He slid down on the inside, did a jump with his knees tucked high, body twisting to the side as though completing a performance. He dropped out of sight.

Sara gazed down the road. The width of bitumen gleamed mean-navy between the dark, shadowy pine forests hemming its sides. Sara felt Pine Creek settle into its former stagnancy, but sensed something had stirred below the surface.

She was sure they knew about Alec.

## Chapter 8

### 1983

Mum said she loved Australia. She had always made a fuss of Australia Day by preparing a picnic with lamingtons and Anzac biscuits. Dad never came.

One Australia Day, when Sara was ten, Mum showed her something special after their picnic.

Dad had gone into town to celebrate the day with two contract shearers. Robbie and Anne had left for a party held in the primary school grounds for the over tens. Sara followed Mum around, sighing and twisting her skirt.

After cleaning the kitchen, Mum stopped and turned around. 'Come with me.' Her eyes glowed with secrets as she held out her hand. Mum led her to the master bedroom and closed the door behind them. She rustled around at the back of her wardrobe and then pulled something out.

Sara was transfixed as Mum carefully unwrapped an old scarf and revealed a silver box. It was the same size as a block of butter, the lid and four sides engraved with swirls and flowers. The box had four little decoratively curved legs. Mum handed it to Sara.

Surprised by the weight, Sara lifted the lid. Inside was lined with red velvet. 'It's beautiful,' she whispered.

'It was my mother's jewellery box. My brother had it sent to me when I found him a little while ago.'

'Your brother?'

'Yes. Shh, honey.' Mum glanced at the door, rewrapped the jewellery box and put it back in the wardrobe. 'That's enough for today. We've got chickens to feed and dinner to make.'

When Mum led Sara out of the bedroom and shut the door, Sara felt like the aperture to Mum's otherness closed, and once again, she belonged only to them.

## Chapter 9

**Saturday – 27 days before Alec's death**

As Sara walked back into the warm air of the house, she heard Dad whistling in the shower. She exchanged a glance with Mum and saw the slight lift in her expression. 'Is he going to the pub again?' whispered Sara.

'Seems to be,' said Mum.

Sara wondered if she should mention what she'd seen happen to Alec. Serious questions made Mum's eyes flicker, and sometimes she couldn't help telling Dad. Dad made all the decisions because he said Mum stuffed things up. Sara knew that anything about Alec should never be mentioned to Dad.

After Dad had grabbed a few cans of beer, he drove away into the sunset.

Mum waited a minute and then put her record on. Sara, Anne and Robbie looked at each other. Mum shrugged. 'May as well,' she said.

As Anne chopped things in the kitchen, the dogs started

barking and a car came up their drive.

Through the gloom, Sara could see Jacki's yellow Volvo. Elvis' black coffee baritone rolled out 'Heartbreak Hotel'.

Jacki was Mum's friend. She sold homemade formal wear cheaper than the shops. Anne's year twelve formal dance was a few months away, and Jacki was making her dress.

Mum and Anne had been to Jacki's a few weeks ago, but Dad had forbidden the use of the car when he found out they'd been there. He said he refused to 'cough up' his hard-earned money for petrol to *that* woman's house.

It had always been difficult to invite people over. Dad didn't seem to like anyone, especially Mum's friends and, because they were adults, Dad didn't say anything until they'd left. Then he'd emerge suddenly like he'd been lurking just out of sight, and shout about it. How dare Mum invite that dreadful woman! He couldn't relax in his own goddam house! He could not and would not put up with it! A man could be pushed too far. They didn't want to see that!

'His father was a hard man too,' Mum once explained, very quietly. 'Probably why his mother ran off. At least he doesn't hit us.'

'Knock, knock!' Jacki wiped her feet on the mat and let herself in. She exchanged quick cheek kisses with Mum then pulled blue satiny fabric out of a bag and held up a dress by the shoulders.

Mum covered her mouth. 'Oh, it's gorgeous! Thank you so much, Jacki.'

'I love it!' Anne called from the kitchen, grinning and bouncing on her heels.

Jacki squinted at something on the waistline. 'Just needs a fitting before we can close the zip. Then it's ribbon along here, and you're all set.' She looked around and smiled.

'Elvis!'

Mum took the dress and raced to put it in another room. She re-emerged, smoothing her hands down her thighs.

Jacki gave everything an approving type of nod. She did a hip wiggle. 'We used to call him Elvis the pelvis,' she said and laughed.

Mum covered a giggle behind her hand and opened the fridge. 'Would you like some tea ... or ah ... we have beer.' She squeezed her hands together like she was juicing lemons.

Jacki's eyebrows went up. 'Well, that would be—' She was suddenly illuminated by headlights which strobed through the window. She twisted to look.

Robbie went to the door and peered through. When he turned back, his face was pale. 'It's Dad.'

Elvis' 'Jailhouse Rock' started.

With a collective gasp, everyone except Jacki sprang into action. Jacki watched from the centre of the room, turning a little as everyone else raced around her.

Sara ran over to the record player, lifted the tone arm and clicked the power button. Silence.

The light came on.

Anne got a large pot, scraped the vegetables off the board into it, frowned as she chose dried herbs and then held the fridge open. After a moment, she grabbed chunks of meat from leftover roast beef, went to the pot and dropped them in. She screwed the lid back on a jar of olives and put it into the pantry, behind some cans.

Mum filled the sink and put some dishes in the water.

Jackie made a face. 'What happened? Is everyone okay?'

'Dad's home,' said Robbie, his hand on the light switch.

Jacki nodded slowly. 'How about I get going? You let me know if you need anything, Elena?' She walked over to Mum and grabbed her by the hands. 'You call me?' She shook Mum's hands until she looked up.

Mum's eyes flickered like she'd been whizzed around too fast.

'Anything, you hear?' Jacki frowned hard.

'Yes, oh. Yes.' Mum freed her hands, her face intent as she went to the dining table. She brushed something off and then looked at the floor. She hurried to the side of the fridge where the brush and shovel were kept.

Jacki backed away and let herself out the front. 'Bye now.' She cast an angry look towards the laundry, shook her head and closed the door.

The back door slammed.

Anne and Robbie flinched and then quickly walked out. Rooms that had been open, closed – like a fox had walked across a rabbit warren.

Mum lifted a wooden spoon and put it in the pot Anne had placed there. The spoon shook a little. Slowly, Mum stirred the meat and vegetables, her face slightly yellow as though the blood had drained away. 'Hello, Len. Not going out, then?' Mum's smile was shaky.

Dad grunted. 'Have the dogs been fed?' He looked at Sara.

'Not yet ... I was going to do it after dinner, but I'll do it now,' she said.

Dad put his hand out with an impatient wave. 'Poor buggers look hungry. Hand me the dog food.'

Mum rushed over with a can and spoon.

Dad disappeared and then the door whacked behind him.

Sara listened to Dad telling the dogs how good they were as she set the table with knives and forks.

When Dad got back in, he turned the television on. Sara heard the creak and pop of the lounge chair as the footrest was extended. 'Ellen, was that Jacki? What's she here for?'

'Anne's dress. She was just dropping it off.'

Sara noticed there was a cold look to the vegetables that Mum was stirring. Quietly, she handed Mum a box of matches.

Mum stared at the box for a moment, jerked like she'd been bumped, and then she moved the pot so she could light the burner beneath it. Sara filled a measuring jug at the hot tap, carefully carried it over to the stove and slowly tipped it over the meat and vegetables. After a moment, Mum raised her hand, so Sara levelled the jug and set it down on the bench.

Sara was aware that from where he sat in front of the TV, Dad's face was turned towards them.

'Ellen.'

Her back to Dad, Mum closed her eyes for a moment like she was gathering herself. Then she turned and walked over to him, hands clasped. 'Yes, Len?'

'Are you going to show me Anne's dress. Since I paid for it?'

'It's not finished, Len.' Mum sounded like hands were closing around her throat. 'Another fitting first and then Jacki —'

'What? For Chrissakes! Why'd you have to enlist Jacki bloody Shannon to do it?'

Sara backed out of the kitchen and hovered.

Mum said something Sara didn't hear.

'I don't give a shit about some bloody ribbon, for Chrissakes! It's not a bloody wedding dress. Just get it done yourself. You've got a machine.' His tone dropped into murky water. 'I can't stand that woman. You know I can't. Bloody Catholics with their smug bloody superiority. You're different when you've been with her, Ellen. You are, you bloody are! I should know, woman. I see it in you. You'll be just as bloody annoying as she is. I won't have it! I won't have Catholic rubbish stuffed down my neck.'

Mum made a reasonable sound. It could have been appeal or apology. Sara knew it wouldn't matter. Dad was like an Airforce Hercules which had taken off and wouldn't land until its mission was complete.

Behind Sara, Anne and Robbie emerged from their rooms.

'What's he on about?' whispered Anne. Sara felt her sister's elbow in her ribs.

'Shh. It's about Jacki, I think.'

Anne groaned softly. 'Knew it! May as well not go to the dance.' She retreated to her room, as did Robbie. The doors clicked shut.

Dad's voice went on a volume incline until the sound of it filled the house. He ranted about what was wrong with Jacki, including that she was a Catholic, and how fat her bottom was. Then he switched to yelling about the terrible decisions Ellen always made, to what an embarrassment she was, what poor judgement she had, and how she did things behind his back.

Mum wasn't to see Jacki again but finish the dress herself.

Later, after they'd all gone to bed, Sara could hear Mum using a low, soothing voice from the master bedroom. Shortly after, the heavy breathing started. Sara folded the pillow up around her head and squeezed it tight.

She tried to focus on the fact Ryan would be arriving down at the Workers' House sometime that night. Feel the warmth that infused the house when he was there.

ra fell asleep before she heard his car arrive. She dreamt

about the lamb with the small patch of black wool. Black turned to red as Dad's blade glinted and he sliced it out.

## Chapter 10

**1987**

When Sara turned thirteen, her body became less predictable. When Ryan made his usual visits to the farm, his presence seemed to expand and entirely fill her sphere. Inside her body, a twisting and pulsing thing began to stretch upwards. She imagined a mung bean unfurling, the sprout reaching and growing. Simultaneously, Sara's breasts became so sore she once cried during a strong breeze. Then her skin developed its own hunger, and Sara had to pinch her arms and bite her fingernails to control it.

Ryan's gaze created a buzzing in Sara's body that made her itchy. The minute he arrived, she had to drag her eyes away from his hips, his mouth and the silver belt buckle above his groin. Impolite places she'd been taught never to stare at. Sometimes, she'd shower in order to calm down after they'd shared morning tea.

After school, Sara dealt with her restlessness by running. She ran faster and faster until she was dripping with sweat.

Then she would stand beneath the shower before the water warmed and stay there until it got hotter than she could bear. It hurt, and then it felt good. In bed at night, she drew her fingers lightly across her lower belly, which made something clench and her face grow hot as she tried not to breathe too loud.

Dad had always alluded to something wild and untrustworthy which existed inside women. Something which had to be controlled. Sara began to wonder if Dad was right.

Sara asked her mum about the feelings.

Mum checked over her shoulder before she answered. 'Ladies don't discuss that sort of thing.'

Late one night, Sara saw a documentary on spontaneous combustion. An old man had disappeared from where he sat on his chair in the loungeroom. In the morning, a black scorch mark was left on the ceiling above the burnt wire and springs, a scatter of ash on the floor. 'A chemical reaction caused enough heat to initiate a fire inside his body, which destroyed him entirely.'

Sara knew what it meant.

In the right circumstances, with the necessary chemical reaction, it could happen to anyone.

Despite being younger, fresher, and containing more liquid than an old man, Sara became convinced that she was a candidate. The program suggested night was the riskiest time.

The next night, Sara got into bed after a fast run, a cold shower and an icy drink, but when she lay down, she burned. She wanted to feather her fingers across her stomach to make her belly clench, but instead, she held her arms by her sides like a soldier and forced her eyes to stay open. Despite her efforts, she fell asleep. Later, she woke in a panic. She raced to the kitchen and drank two glasses of water. This happened several times, and she was forced to get up to pee.

Mum took her to the doctor, where she was tested for a urinary infection and diabetes. The tests came back negative.

Sara reduced her water intake but kept a full glass by the bed. She was tired of getting up so much anyway.

During sport class, a week after the tests, Sara was wracked with abdominal pain. In the privacy of the girls' toilets, she found blood in her underwear. Hobbling, and sure her hip bones were collapsing inwards, she was escorted, tearful and shaking, to the sick bay. The school nurse calmly explained how to put a long white pad into her knickers, with the adherent strip on the back to hold it in place.

Just before Sara's fourteenth birthday, Mum brought a stack of books home and left them in the second lounge. Sara picked one up. It had a windswept lady and a man in uniform on the front cover.

Mum was a regular at the town library. Sara noticed reading about romance and adventures caused her mum to smile. When she read, Mum stopped fidgeting and looking over her shoulder.

'Steamy,' Mum once said.

Instructional, Sara discovered.

That afternoon, Dad came back early.

Sara was already well into the story, curled up on the couch by the fire, next to a rack of drying laundry. She was vaguely aware of the back door slamming.

Dad walked in. Sara jumped. He grabbed the book out of

Sara's hand and squinted at the pages she had been reading.

Sara began to stand. 'I was just about to go and help Mum.'

'Sit back down!'

Sara sank down. Her armpits prickled with sweat.

Dad shook his head slightly, wandered closer to the window, book open in his hands. Eyes glowing, he began to read. '*He stared at her as she ate the ice-cream, with a look which suggested he'd like her to take him into her mouth the same way.*' Smiling, Dad made an incredulous sound and flicked forwards a few pages.

Sara tried to slow her breathing, but her heart beat hard, and her face was blistering hot.

Dad used a louder voice. '*He gripped her slender waist with his strong hands and moved so she felt him deep in her soul as the light became blinding, and they both rose to meet it like birds into the sunset.*' He rolled his eyes.

Robbie and Anne walked in. Their eyes checked the room, clocking Sara huddled on the couch and Dad with the book.

Without looking up, Dad waved his hand at them to stay. 'This is what your little sister was reading. You must be so proud of yourself, Sara.'

Sara and Robbie exchanged a glance. Sara swallowed bile.

'Ellen! Come and have a listen,' called Dad.

Mum walked in, mouth frozen halfway open like she'd breathed all the way in, but not out.

Sara stared down at her hands. At the edge of her vision, she could see the others along the far wall, fidgeting.

'Wow, this is so good.' Dad chuckled as he turned a page. 'This quality reading you bring into our home, Ellen.' Dad re-read the passages using an animated voice. Suddenly, he slammed down the book. Its pages lifted slightly, and then closed like it had breathed its last. Bent on an angle from his waist, Dad glared into Sara's face, so close she could smell his sour breath. 'You know nothing, girl! You think that trash will teach you?' Spit flecked Sara's cheek. She was too scared to wipe it off. Dad threw up his arm.

Everyone flinched.

Mum looked like a scared turtle, head between her shoulders.

Dad kicked the book across the room, and it disappeared under the couch. He pointed at the couch. 'That dirty rot won't teach you about sex and marriage. Your husbands will!'

Sara looked at Mum, and then Dad. Dad's eyes flashed. Mum's eyes faced down in the natural curve from her rounded shoulders.

Dad stomped out through the door and down the hall towards the master bedroom. 'What've you got in here, Ellen?' he called.

Mum looked up, her eyes frozen in a drowned stare.

Sara could hear doors creaking and drawers sliding in and out.

'Ha! I can't trust you as soon as kick you!'

Mum's hands went to her mouth.

Dad appeared at the doorway to the loungeroom with a bundle in one hand and a fistful of photos scrunched in the other. He went down on one knee in front of the stove, opened the door and tossed in the photos. Dad unwrapped Mum's old scarf, grabbed the silver box from within and threw it into the fire.

Sara saw the flash of red as sparks flew up around the jewellery box.

Dad shoved himself up to his feet and stormed out.

'Oh!' Mum wailed and went down on her knees. She stuck her hand into the flames, yelped and retracted it. She grabbed a damp towel off the drying rack and wound it around her hand. Staring into the fire, her chest went up and down.

The back door slammed.

Everyone closed in around Mum.

Anne placed her hand on Mum's back. 'We can get more photos, Mum. I'm sure your family would have copies,' said Anne. Sara could hear a wobble in her sister's voice.

'It wasn't just photos, you idiot!' Sara cried. 'I hate him!' She sobbed against her mum's back. 'I'm so sorry, Mum.'

'You're burnt!' Anne cried. She raced into the kitchen.

Sara lifted her head. A black and red mark branded the back of Mum's hand. 'Oh, Mum!'

Robbie covered his eyes with his hand and then squeezed his finger and thumb into his eye corners, which showed the wet, pink inside his eyelids. 'God!' he growled.

Anne came back in with an ice brick. Robbie helped Mum to her feet. Mum got up, put the rolled towel beneath her arm and held the ice brick onto the back of her hand. 'Let's go to the doctors to get some cream,' she said.

Anne got the car keys, and they all watched as she put her driver training plates on the car.

Milton, just fifteen minutes away, had a small medical centre.

They waited in the car outside for more than half an hour before Mum emerged with a white bandage on one hand and the towel in the other like she'd caught a mouse inside it. She climbed back into the car.

Sara held out her hands to take the towel but Mum shook her head – red-rimmed eyes, her face damp as though she'd walked through mist. She rested it down on her lap.

They all sat in silence.

Sara's eyes followed a wattlebird weaving through a bright pink azalea, a tight feeling beneath her ribs. No one had said it, but Sara knew it was her fault.

Anne put the key in the ignition.

'How about we go to the ice-cream parlour?' said Mum quietly. Her mouth pulled into a small, dazed smile. 'I know it's a bit of a drive into town.'

'Yes!' said Sara, even though she didn't think she could eat anything. Emilie's Ice-Cream Parlour had hot-pink seats, a juke box and brightly coloured walls which might ease the tightness in her.

Anne drove them out of Milton, back past the Hamilton farm and all the way into Parkwood. Almost an hour, but no one complained.

Anne had to circle around until she found a parking space. When Sara opened the car door, she could smell something biscuity and sweet.

Emilie's was teeming with people, the tables crammed with families. There was one large boy at a two-seater opposite an empty chair, gazing at his thickshake adoringly. A group stood and moved from a large round table in the centre of the room, creating the only vacant seats.

Anne hurried over and began stacking plates and decorative glass bowls smeared with chocolate sauce. Sara joined in, and the two left a neat pile on the edge of the table.

A slim, red-faced girl with a blonde ponytail over one shoulder smiled slightly as she pulled a cloth from the pocket of her frilly white apron. 'Hi Robbie,' she said as she wiped the table.

Sara realised she'd seen the girl at school.

Robbie cleared his throat and quickly drew his gaze off the girl's chest, the soft rounds of her breasts having swelled in the V of her blouse as she leaned over. 'Hi, Amanda. Busy day?'

The girl straightened and tucked hair behind her ears. 'Hectic.' She pulled out a small writing pad and pencil. She noticed Anne and flinched girlishly. 'Oh, hi, Anne.'

Anne's eyes went up without her head moving. 'Hi,' she said dryly and picked up a menu.

After brief consideration Anne ordered the Emilie's Special. She handed the menu to Sara, who noted the Special consisted of six different scoops of ice-cream, with nuts, cream, and chocolate sauce. According to the picture, it came with triangular waffle sails plunged jovially into the top.

'Okay,' said Amanda, biting her lower lip as she wrote on her little note pad. 'Coming right up!' She rolled her eyes as she said the compulsory jingle, which was written on the front window and on the menu. She shot a grin at Robbie, who returned the attention with a smirk. Amanda then took the armful of sticky dishes and supported them with her chest. She slid sideways through the crowd, apologising when a woman with a toddler shoved her with the back of her chair suddenly and Amanda ran into it. Amanda disappeared quickly.

Anne cuffed the back of Sara's head without looking at her. 'Don't ever call me an idiot again.'

When Amanda delivered the plate of ice-cream, which looked insurmountable even for the four of them, Anne started eating straight away. Sara and Robbie took spoons. They dug at the oozy, glossy strawberry blitz and choc-chip ice-cream again and again, trying to taste each flavour before it melted together in the heat of the small, crowded room.

Mum watched, smiling slightly.

The Beatles 'She Loves You!' blared from the jukebox. Music, whining children and someone clapping over the top of an ice-cream cake created a roar which filled every space.

'Have some, Mum,' Anne said, offering a shiny spoon as the table nearby burst into an upbeat rendition of 'Happy Birthday!'

Mum shook her head. 'I enjoy it more when I watch you.'

Sara got an ache in her throat. She crammed her mouth with Supreme Mango and swallowed past it.

Robbie elbowed her. 'Make yourself sick.'

Sara elbowed him back. 'Shurrup.'

Mum put the towel that she'd been holding on the table. A small kid of about three ran for the door with a woman close behind.

'Sorry! Excuse me! Chloe! Not near the road!' Just outside on the footpath, the woman caught the child by the arm as a man wearing joggers shepherded her away from the verge. 'Thank you!' The woman swung the little girl up and wrapped her in a hug. 'Don't ever do that to me ever again!'

At their table, Anne moved the dessert to the side. The other customers, watching the frantic mother and waving child as they found their seats again, didn't appear to notice.

Slowly, Mum peeled the edges of the towel open and revealed the jewellery box.

Sara gasped. 'You saved it!' Feeling immediately lighter, she exchanged tentative smiles with Anne and Robbie.

Mum's brow creased as she picked up the box and checked it over. Sara realised only one of the four legs had been blackened by the flames.

'I'll polish that off,' Robbie offered.

Around them, people had resumed eating and talking and

wrestling children with ice-cream smeared mouths.

'It was my mother's. Isn't it beautiful?' Mum slowly turned the box to show them. The natural tarnish in the pattern highlighted the intricate swirls. She pulled it into her chest, alone with it for a moment. Then she rewrapped the box and held it in her lap. 'Silver doesn't burn easily,' she said.

When they got home, Sara went to the bathroom, stuck her fingers into the back of her throat and vomited in the toilet. She washed her face and pulled the scales out from the bathroom closet, stood on them, sighed and put them back.

In bed that night, as Dad's angry whispers came from the master bedroom, Sara's stomach hurt. She remembered what Dad had said about their husbands teaching them about sex and marriage.

Mum had been just nineteen years old when she'd met Dad, who'd been in his thirties. Mum told Sara he'd been quite charming. Bought her flowers and took her to a fancy restaurant. She hadn't had a boyfriend before and had left home because Jo, her adoptive mother, didn't need her to babysit her real children – two daughters – anymore. A few months after she met Dad, he told her they were getting married, and Mum said she'd been very happy.

Sara heard Dad's rhythmic murmurs, and Mum's heavy breathing. Sara pushed her fingers into her ears so hard they hurt. Shortly after, she heard the gentle gurgle of water in the pipes, indicating Mum showering quietly. Tears squeezed out as Sara remembered Mum kneeling – a pauper in front of the fire.

To Sara, a husband seemed a dark, distant shadow. Maybe someone like Dad. She clenched her hands and bit her lip and promised herself she would never, ever marry a man like him.

## Chapter 11

### Sunday – 26 days before Alec's death

When she met Ryan, Sara had been twelve. She remembered feeling as though the champion racehorse Phar Lap had been miraculously installed on their farm. Then fifteen, and at the Hamilton's for work experience, Ryan had glossy hair, muscular forearms and was already taller than Dad. If Ryan spoke to Sara, she encountered the whole-body chaos she got before a swimming race when the start gun cracked.

She noticed early that Ryan's handsome face wore a permanent smirk, which confirmed to Sara his subtle mockery of her. It helped her to decide not to let her heart burn with useless wanting.

Three years later, the effect had evolved into a more practical situation where Sara could work with him in apparent equality. Unfortunately, the useless wanting persisted.

With Ryan, on errands Dad had allocated them, Sara had laughed about the stupidity of sheep and the scourge of cockatoos that feasted on the newly seeded paddocks. She'd start giggling and end up howling, hands gripping her stomach. Ryan didn't once make fun of her, just laughed too, unlike the boys at school who had to check they each remained within the bounds of fragile social toughness which glued them. After being with Ryan, Sara always felt like she was floating above her life.

Ryan told Sara that he had been born on a farm, but his father had gone broke, sold up, and then his parents got divorced. From quite young, Ryan had lived in Sydney's western suburbs with his dad, but he told Sara he'd always wanted to return to the land.

When he left school for his electrician apprenticeship and a regular wage, Ryan sorted out payment for his continued services with Dad, which suited them both. Every fortnight, he had caught the train to Pine Creek until he earnt his driver's licence. Then one day, he arrived in a blue, second-hand Ford Escort, which always shone. He once told Sara he cleaned the hubcaps with an old toothbrush.

Ryan was older than Anne by a year. In the past Sara had noticed Anne give Ryan her special low-lash look; a look that Sara thought showed she was aware of her woman power. At almost eighteen, Ryan now held himself tall, like a man also aware of his power. She thought Ryan looked a lot like Elvis from Mum's album covers.

As far as Sara was aware, Ryan had had a couple of girlfriends, but only one whom she had met. Ryan brought Rachel to the farm with him one weekend. She was small with a sharp way of speaking and had long dark hair, which she wore in a high ponytail. The whole weekend, they alternated between kissing and arguing, which gave Sara a sharp feeling in her belly. She couldn't stop thinking about them staying together in the Workers' House overnight.

Sara concocted a whole argument with Ryan about his lack of professionalism. Fortunately, the argument never occurred because the pair left, Ryan didn't mention Rachel afterwards, and hadn't brought her back.

Sara was relieved Ryan's TAFE exams were finished. She knew he'd arrived late at the Workers' House the night before because this morning there was smoke coming from the chimney.

Waiting in the garden before he arrived, she quickly ran inside when she heard his car. She watched through the window as he pulled up and jumped out of the Escort then loped up the front step with his slow, graceful athleticism. In the bright sunshine, his black hair shone, and blue eyes twinkled. He wore his dark-blue jeans, which had creased to his exact shape, a tucked-in black t-shirt, and a leather belt with a big silver buckle.

Sara took a long drink from her glass of water.

Ryan smiled as he let himself through the door. 'Hey, Sara.'

'Hey.' Sara hurried into the kitchen to put the kettle back over the flame. She'd boiled it twice already and had to top it up. Her hand shook as she scooped tea leaves into the pot. The dining table was set with plates, cups and saucers. Sara carried over a serving tray loaded with scones, jam, butter and cream.

Dad came through the back door and cleared his throat. 'G'day, mate,' he said to Ryan.

They shook hands and then sat down at the table. Each took a scone.

Anne's door clicked. She melted into the room and sat a chair away from Ryan without looking at him.

'Anne,' he said.

'Hi.' She took a scone and waited for the jam, which Dad was using.

Dad handed it to Ryan, who offered it to Anne, but Anne shook her head. Ryan shrugged and used it first.

Sara took the full teapot to the table and carefully placed it on a cork mat. Once she'd brought the milk over, she sat next to Anne.

'Thanks, Sara.' As Ryan's scone fell in halves beneath the blade of his knife, Sara noticed the frown knotted between his eyebrows. 'Len, how would you feel about me having some friends down at the Workers? It's my eighteenth,' he said.

Anne began to do everything very slowly, eyes on her plate.

Ignoring the question, Dad watched Sara use the jam and cream. 'Cut it out, Sara. You're getting fat again. End up like that bloody CWA woman, Cherie.' He took his second scone and buttered it thickly.

Ryan cast Sara a sympathetic look.

Sara, face smarting, put the knife down. She lifted her teacup and took a sip. Outside the window, Sara could see Mum gazing upwards at the huge pine tree with a deep frown on her face.

Dad inhaled with deep authority. 'Nah. Make a mess of the place.' He took a big bite of his scone, and his jaw clicked as he chewed.

Sara was reminded of snakes who dislocated their jaws to cram entire goats into their mouths. She took another sip of tea.

Before Ryan had arrived, Mum had set the table and then gone outside to wage her war on weeds. The weekend previous, Sara had donned gardening gloves and helped Mum pull out the stinging nettles from beside the failed vegetable patch. Then they'd pulled out the vegetables. Despite Mum's best efforts, the broccoli and brussels sprouts were always soggy or covered in black spot and grubs. Sara didn't believe it was the fault of the nettles but went along with the eradication anyway.

In the shadows beneath her nemesis, the pine, Mum now rubbed her forearms. Towering over the house like a dark-green monolith, the tree chilled everything with its gloomy shade. Beneath, the grass was stunted, and the ground became bare and slimy when wet. In frosts, sharp ice teeth grew on the frozen clay.

'If Len would agree to having it chopped down, we'd get some more sunlight,' Mum said once.

But Dad hadn't agreed.

'I'm sure it's on a lean,' Mum had insisted.

Dad had stood to the edge of the tree and tilted his head. 'You're on a lean, more likely,' he said, and closed the matter with a quick brush of his hands.

Mum had stared at the tree with her head tilted until she finally sighed and walked back inside.

'Fair enough,' said Ryan to Dad.

Anne rolled her eyes and picked at some crumbs. Sara looked wistfully at her own plate. Anne's body seemed to distribute weight to her boobs and backside, making her waist look tiny and the boys unable to look anywhere else. Once consumed, Sara's nutrients expanded to fill any suggestion of a waist while leaving her B-cup chest exactly the same size.

Her tea finished, Sara got up, stacked the dirty plates, and took them to the kitchen. She found a disappointing old cloth and sadly wiped the bench.

'What about the shearing shed,' suggested Dad.

Sara paused and glanced over. With his elbow on the table, Dad had leant towards Ryan. 'Can't break anything down there.'

'Yeah?' said Ryan. 'Bit dirty, but I could clean it up.'

Dad grinned in the way that reminded Sara of a lizard about to eat a bird's egg. She carefully put the plug in the sink and turned on the hot tap.

Dad shrugged. 'You could, Ryan.'

'Don't s'pose I'll be paid for cleaning it up?'

Dad threw back his head and laughed. 'You want a free venue, mate, you gotta expect some work.' He brushed some crumbs into a pile on the tablecloth then pushed his chair back and stood up.

Ryan stood and stuck his hand out towards Dad. 'Alright then. You've got a deal.'

They shook over the table.

Dad inhaled in a satisfied way and, with his free hand, adjusted his balls. 'I'll get a keg for you.' He leant close to Ryan, one hand on his shoulder. 'Got plenty of women coming?' He tapped the side of his nose.

Sara shot a quick glance at Ryan, but his face was inscrutable. She turned off the tap.

With her hand full of teacups, Anne shoved Sara over and began to wash the dishes. Sara picked up a tea towel.

'A few, I guess.' Ryan cleared his throat. Sara thought she could feel the discomfort coming off Ryan in a wave. But if he felt it, he didn't do anything. Dad slapped him on the back.

'That's the way, mate!'

With Dad's hand square on Ryan's back, they both walked out through the laundry.

Sara touched Anne's arm. 'Reckon we'll be able to sneak down?' she whispered.

'Don't be ridiculous. You're fifteen.'

'Nearly sixteen!'

Anne glanced at the place the men had disappeared, smiling a little.

Sara gasped. 'You're going, aren't you?'

Anne shrugged, placed a plate neatly behind the last, bubbles sliding slowly down. 'Could be some hot guys.' She pointed a sudsy finger at Sara. 'Don't you say a word.'

Sara huffed, hung up the tea towel and dumped herself in front of her untouched scone at the dining table. She began to eat and then put it down and took the plate to the sink. If she wanted to look good, she needed to stop stuffing food into her mouth. 'I'm going too.' She tipped the scone into the bucket of chicken's scraps.

Anne laughed.

That afternoon, as the pine forests became thick with shadows, Ryan was still cleaning.

The shearing shed; a large, rectangular, corrugated iron structure, and sheep yards, were a few hundred metres down the lane from the main house. Behind them was a concrete tank, a metal trough used for footrot treatment, and a tiny holding shed for sick sheep. Nearby was the hayshed, and behind both buildings was a cluster of tall gum trees and the cattle yards.

By the time Sara walked down, a thin strip of cloud ribbed a pink-tinged sky as the sunset left gold on the gum leaves. The edge of it flecked her vision, which put a hole in everything she looked at.

Ryan emerged shirtless and sweating, strode over to a tap, and then washed his hands and face.

Sara poured tea from the thermos and gave him two

biscuits wrapped in a serviette.

'Thanks,' he said but didn't look away as he ate. Sara felt like Ryan was a big magnet, and she was full of metal filaments.

'Better get back,' Sara said as she jumped down from the railing. She walked uphill, aware of Ryan like a flame on her back.

## Chapter 12

### Friday – 21 days before Alec's death

According to the World Health Organisation, AIDS infections still hadn't reached their peak. News of severe bashings of gay men by gangs in Sydney was filtering through. The unexplained deaths of at least two young men, who'd plunged off cliffs, were argued by gay rights activists as hate crimes instead of suicides; the latter suggested by police. Sara wasn't sure what was rumour and what was fact. It seemed unbelievable and very far away.

In Pine Creek, Sara watched as Alec strode towards the forest like his spine was stiff. Almost a week had passed since she'd seen him hit by a rock. As he walked, he was kicking stones and slapping the tops of the grass.

Sara wondered why he was here again on a Friday. She checked back over her shoulder and scratched her arm, almost nervous because he'd turned up so soon. She stopped behind the red gum while Alec walked down the firebreak.

It was the soft part of the evening, and a pink glow

encircled the edge of the sky. She stepped on a twig, which reared snake-like, and scraped her ankle. She dealt with the scratch and then slapped a mosquito on her arm and wondered whose blood could be mixed up in the legs and thorax and rust coloured smear. Maybe someone with AIDS? Could the mosquito's proboscis give her the virus? Sara quickly wiped her arm on her jumper.

The zoom of a motorbike engine caught her attention. Sara squatted down and then watched as the flock of sheep bent away from Robbie's Honda as it whizzed across the paddock. Robbie stopped by the fence, kicked down the stand and then pulled off his helmet.

From the forest side, Alec walked over to the fence and put his hands on the top wire. Robbie jogged over, stopped in front of Alec and crossed his arms.

Alec gesticulated with his hands as he said something.

While Alec talked, Robbie's posture changed. He slowly unfolded his arms, pushed back his hair and looked back towards home.

Robbie nodded, said something and then leant on the wire not far from where Alec was. They seemed deep in conversation, but even when she strained her ears, Sara could only hear murmuring.

After a few minutes, Robbie got back on the motorbike, kicked it to life and then rode away, cutting a straight line between the gates to the house.

With his arms hanging at his sides, Alec watched Robbie disappear.

After a minute, Alec turned away and walked further along the firebreak. He glanced around and then began talking.

Sara noticed Alec followed a similar pattern to the

previous time she'd watched him. But this time he kept dropping his arms like they were too heavy. At one point, he dropped his head back and groaned. Then he lifted his arms, and after a pause, he began to sing. This was the moment Sara realised she'd been waiting for. She closed her eyes. But the melody was weighted as a saturated albatross, and plunged downwards.

Alec stopped. He covered his face with his hands, and his shoulders shuddered. Sara could hear him crying.

She sank down in shame and gnawed the skin at the edge of her thumbnail until it hurt. Maybe the man had really scared Alec, and his bravado afterwards had just been an act.

Eventually, Alec walked back along the firebreak towards the road.

Once she thought he was far enough ahead not to see her, Sara jogged across the paddock towards home. Then she noticed that Alec had stopped opposite his driveway and hadn't crossed the road.

A truck sped past, ruffling Alec's long hair and the flaps of his colourful coat. He didn't even look up.

Sara slowed and then stopped. She willed Alec to go home. A horrible thought twisted her stomach. Was Alec about to walk out in front of a car?

Alec turned around. Sara realised he was looking at their house. She looked for her brother, but she saw no movement.

*No.* Sara screwed up her hands.

If Alec took a step in the direction of her house, she would intercept. She knew she wouldn't leave until Alec was safe, like her presence somehow anchored him.

After a moment, Alec finally turned back and crossed the road.

## Chapter 13

### Friday – 21 days before Alec's death

When Sara got home, she didn't get a chance to ask Robbie about Alec. Despite being Friday, Dad sat at the head of the table, leaning forwards onto his elbows. Not showering, not dressed in his best jeans. Mum and Anne stood like extras waiting for the 'action' cue on a movie set: Mum in the kitchen; Anne on the edge of the dining area.

Anne scooped the air, and Sara followed her into Mum's loungeroom.

'Dad waffled on about some dickhead at the pub,' she said in a low voice. 'Probably why he came home so quickly on Saturday. Luckily, we didn't start anything.'

Sara grimaced.

The back door clicked. Anne and Sara peered around the doorway. Robbie, hair ruffled, appeared behind Dad. He had probably noticed the Hilux in the shed when he put his bike away. His eyes swept the scene. He finger-raked his fringe back, glanced towards Anne and Sara. Anne shook her head and lifted her palms.

Sara saw something in her brother's eyes as he leant against the doorframe and crossed his arms. He stared at the back of Dad's head, with the bitter expression of someone who'd swallowed something rotten.

'Hello, Robbie,' said Mum in a watery voice. She cleared her throat. 'We're all here now. Righto then, what should I cook for dinner?'

Sara closed her eyes, felt a lump expand inside her throat.

Dad stretched all the way back in his chair and spread his legs, unbending his knees so his socked feet slid under the table. He scratched his chest. 'Ah, steak and chips? Yeah, that's what I feel like.' He nodded, and the corner of his mouth lifted. 'And beer. It is Friday.'

Mum blanched. 'There's steak but no chips.' She shot a scared look at Anne, who just shrugged, wide-eyed.

Making the usual noises, Dad got up slowly and walked into the lounge. 'Feed the dogs, Robbie.' He picked up the remote control, squinted at the TV and thumbed a button. Bright cheering and colour burst from the set. Dad felt for the armrest of his chair and then planted his bottom. 'Chips, Ellen,' he said, voice deep with ridicule. 'Chopped potatoes, for Chrissakes. Buy some from the servo, if you're that useless.' He shook his head.

'Right, okay.' Mum did one of her little tremor nods while she got the dog food from the fridge and then handed it to Robbie. The back door slammed.

Dad looked over his shoulder and narrowed his eyes.

'I wish I'd known. I'd have been better prepared,' said Mum.

Dad gave her a look. 'I have to tell you I'm staying in? No wonder I go out.' He adjusted the front of his jeans, shook his head and stared at the television. 'Least you could do is smile, Ellen. You're so goddam sour-faced all the time.'

Later, when Sara heard the TV turn off, she waited until there were sounds of someone showering. She poked her head out, checked it was Dad who was in the bathroom and then started making toast.

Sara ate in her room. She had her Genesis', 'Land of Confusion' album playing quietly on her stereo. The stereo had a double-tape deck so she could record music straight from the radio onto a TDK tape.

Maybe she should make Ryan a mix tape. Jimmy Barnes and James Blundell were solid choices, but some American country singers would go well too. Maybe something heavy like ACDC, because she'd once heard the mess of electric guitar she recognised from 'Thunderstruck' coming from Ryan's open car window. She could add a ballad from Guns N' Roses to hint at her feelings for him.

On her desk was a maidenhair fern and string of pearls plant. She snapped off a few pearls and pushed the end back into the soil where it usually kept growing like nothing had happened.

When Sara walked out of her bedroom, plate in hand, all the lights were out.

The fridge door opened, and Robbie stood in the yellow light. He grabbed a carton of milk, filled a glass and then drank it in a few gulps. He put the glass in the sink. 'Hey.' He held the fridge door open, and the light stayed on.

Anne and Mum emerged too.

'Mum?' said Sara.

Mum shook her head. 'Don't know, love. He's out of sorts.'

Sara sighed. She knew they would all try to avoid Dad's

next explosion. Do more chores, be quiet and agreeable. She also knew it wouldn't work.

Anne grabbed some biscuits, sighed and walked out.

'Goodnight,' Mum whispered. She then backed away silently.

Sara checked that she and Robbie were alone. 'I went for a walk this arvo,' said Sara, reaching up for the Milo and then spooning it into a cup. 'I saw you near the boundary.'

Robbie shrugged and handed her the milk.

'Did you see anyone else over there? I'm sure I saw someone.' Sara poured milk into her cup.

Robbie let the fridge door close. 'No. Don't think so. G'night.' He walked out. After a moment, his door closed quietly.

*Chapter 14*

**Saturday – 20 days before Alec's death**

That week on the bus home from school, Sara had seen Anne pull a white denim cut-off top with front buttons from her bag. Sara imagined the buttons would be very easy for a boy to undo.

Sara had nothing to wear to Ryan's party but had snuck into her sister's bedroom when she was showering and found what she wanted. In Anne's bottom drawer was a soft light-pink sweater. She remembered Anne wearing it when she'd almost been sixteen, the same age Sara was now.

It had been mid-morning, and Dad had left early for a merino stud a couple of hours away. She knew that he intended to buy a new ram. Sara ran past the shearing shed and stopped to catch her breath. A light spot near the creek caught her eye. Anne's pink top looked like an accidental splodge on the sweeping landscape painting of the winding creek and gum trees, their downwards-shedding bark like dark lace stockings. Sara heard a tinkle of laughter and saw her sister with her head thrown back, skirt hem in her hands. She could see Anne's black knickers and the creamy tops of her thighs.

Deep laughter came from behind a patch of tussocks in front of Anne. The sound of a man's voice caught in the mist. Sara caught a glimpse of a blue shirt. She broke into a run before they saw her.

Sara ran and ran until she was sobbing for breath. She swiped at her nose and looked back; a hill behind her, so she couldn't see them anymore.

If she told Dad, he would flush blue shirt out like a fox from it's lair; the righteous farmer defending their honour with a pitchfork. Anne would be forced to return to the family, with her head bowed and eyes on the ground.

But Dad rewarded and then punished, sometimes the same person. Sometimes on the same day. It was as though he had no loyalty, or favourite, but himself. Sara knew it was no use.

Anne got to keep her secret.

The day of Ryan's eighteenth birthday arrived with a blue sky and cool breeze. The music from the shearing shed had bumped a regular beat into the cold Saturday evening as cars and utes drove past the house and down the lane. Earlier, Sara had watched people set up lights, speakers and a barbeque.

'My period is killing me,' Anne moaned. Her bedroom door was open and the light off but Sara bet Anne had her party clothes on underneath the blankets.

Mum hurried through the door with a hot water bottle.

Sara followed her in and stared at her sister.

'Thanks, Mum,' Anne said meekly, pulling the covers to

her chin.

Mum leant down and kissed Anne's forehead. Over Mum's shoulder, Sara shook her head at her sister. Anne narrowed her eyes like she was warning Sara to keep quiet.

'Where's Dad?' Sara asked, following Mum out.

'Killing some rats. They've been getting at the eggs again. But I think he's going out.'

Sara stuck her head out through the back door. She could see the dark shape of her father near the chook shed and heard the repeated thud and tin sound of something being belted with a shovel. Dad swore.

After dinner, Sara showered but waited until Dad was in the bathroom before she got dressed. In her room, she applied huge amounts of eyeliner, lip gloss, and hairspray.

After Dad had taken a six pack of beer from the fridge, Sara heard his ute start up and drive out.

'Goodnight,' Sara called and snuck through the kitchen. She paused in the laundry for a few minutes.

Sara slipped outside, closing the door quietly behind her. She walked past the dog cages. 'Good dogs,' she said in a low voice.

The working dogs, Rusty and Jack, each had a large cage which contained a wooden box stuffed with an old rug. They were not house pets but lithe canine athletes, ribs bumpy beneath their coats. When moving sheep and cattle, they awaited Dad's whistle, eyes scanning, ears pricked, before streaking off, guiding and steering, dropping down and then running again. They were fed in their cages at night, the gate secured so they couldn't find their own entertainment.

Sara paused at the top of the lane where the line of pine trees began. Downhill, fairy lights twinkled at the shearing shed entrance. Around the back, near the sheep yards, rainbow-coloured light globes bobbed a line of innocent merriment over a chattering stew of people and barbeque smoke.

'Jimmy! Jimmy! Jimmy!'

Through the night air came an electric guitar solo, long notes and sliding metal. Sara clutched the ends of her sleeves as her heart rate sped up. Jimmy Barnes' gravel voice belted out 'Driving Wheels'. Sara moved downhill, staying close to the trees as Jimmy's concert poured from the shed as though it was a corrugated iron sieve.

She skirted the edge of the activity, checking every corner for Dad just in case he'd waited, ready to ambush them.

There were people everywhere: girls with permed hair, wearing doc martens, and crop tops like Britney Spears. The boys wore Wrangler or Levi jeans, and blue, red, or brown button-down shirts with embroidery across the chest and shining leather boots, like American cowboys.

The game Twister had been set up in one of the yards, and sand scuffed as people wrapped around each other and fell over laughing.

Sara moved to the moonless side of the shed. She sensed movement nearby.

A shadow became a dense, tall figure. An unzipping and a sigh were followed by the sound of a heavy stream drilling the ground. Sara folded her arms tight and shivered.

Over by the little shed, someone flipped sausages on a barbeque.

Inside, 'Tucker's Daughter' started playing but got a boo.

'Jimmy! Jimmy! Jimmy!'

More electric keyboard, 'Working Class Man'. The shed vibrated with stomping boots and music.

Suddenly, Anne appeared wearing the white crop top. She'd teased up her hair.

Ryan emerged from the crowd. Sara held her breath as he loped over to Anne with both arms extended. Pulled her in. He said something, laughed, then kissed Anne quickly, but on the lips.

Sara's throat clenched like she'd swallowed a corkscrew grass seed, the tip driving into the flesh. She looked away. Hated Anne because it was so easy for her.

Sara was the only girl she knew of who didn't go to parties. Dad said his daughters wouldn't be found at gatherings that included boys and alcohol. If she or Anne asked to go anywhere, they'd had to list every person invited, yet he still threatened to come inside and check for himself.

Anne lied about staying at girlfriends' houses when she went to parties. Anne was a good liar. Sara didn't bother asking to go out anymore.

In front of Anne, Ryan swayed and teetered.

A chant came from the shed. 'Ryan! Ryaaaan!'

Anne laughed, flounced away from Ryan. Someone handed her a can of beer.

Ryan moved his hand along the wall all the way to the door where heads were poking out.

Numerous arms hauled him inside the shed.

Sara clenched her hands. Listened for what was going on inside.

Everywhere, voices were singing, 'Happy Birthday ... For he's a jolly good fellow.' There was clapping and laughter.

Sara looked down at the pale-pink youth of her jumper. She gazed upwards. Beyond the shed eaves was a wide black expanse of sky, stars dotted like sparks. She waited for a sign to tell her to go or stay. She watched laughing people stumble out of the shed. Couples folded themselves into the shadows.

Sara looked for Ryan. Her whole body craved his closeness. To be near enough to smell his cologne and feel the fabric of his shirt against her arm.

In Sara's year at school, not all the boys had filled out like Ryan, or these men. They were still caught somewhere between boy and man, some too tall for their bodies. Some were stocky boys with furred jaws they were too clueless to shave. When dropping them off to school, mothers still kissed some of them on the forehead as they ducked and shrugged free.

Behind Sara, with the silent audience of trees, anonymous male shapes shook their shoulders, hands to groin, unzipped and sighed relief. She felt dirty for being so close.

Ryan appeared near the barbeque, face lit in nauseous blue by a nearby light globe. The next globe was red, then green, then yellow. Rachel was grabbing at his wrist and speaking into his face. Ryan had his eyes closed, hands lifted, palms forward. Rachel planted her hands on her hips, as her mouth moved quickly. Ryan shook his head. With heavy shoulders, he turned and walked back up the ramp into the shed.

A girl took Rachel by the arm, but Rachel shook her off and strode away.

Sara saw a blonde guy walk up to Rachel and touch her shoulder. Sara recognised him as Ryan's friend Freddie, who was in the same rugby team and had been to the farm a couple of times. Freddie said something to Rachel and the two walked off, side by side.

Sara rubbed her arms and walked around the shed and then back up the lane. She noticed that Dad's ute was still out.

Inside the quiet house, the air was warm.

Everything was tidy. Anne and Robbie's doors were closed. Mum was probably reading. Sara was released, free for the night, yet there was nowhere and no one for her to go to. Not like Anne, welcomed in like an old friend. At least Anne knew what to do at a party. Had Sara stayed, she would've been too awkward to enjoy herself anyway. She'd rather have Ryan all to herself in a paddock while they caught and dealt with fly-struck sheep. Which they had done once in the rain.

Afterwards, both starving, stinking and quiet, she'd hopped on the back of the motorbike behind him as he sped back up the lane. She'd had one hand on the rack where the shears were secured, leaving the other to loop around his waist. Halfway home, she had rested her cheek on his upper back. He had patted her leg for a moment before gripping the handle again. For a few seconds, her sodden stinking clothes and the vile task they'd completed simply melted away.

After changing into her nightwear and dressing gown, Sara sat in the dark with the curtains open, socked feet on the windowsill. Starlight and a chunk of moon silvered her pot plants.

Beyond their property, between the dense black of the pine plantation and the sky, the treetops were the teeth of a saw. In the darkness, something moved. Sara sat up.

Between the trees and the Stynes' boundary, a pair of headlights came slowly towards the road, up and down like a vehicle encountering potholes. The lights paused at the highway, bent round in Sara's direction, crawled west then turned in and came through their front gate. After a minute, Sara heard the reversing whir of an engine and then nothing but distant music from the party. Not even the dogs barking.

Sara's skin prickled all the way down to her pyjama pants.

The laundry door clicked carefully.

Sara waited, face turned towards her door. The kitchen floor creaked and then the bathroom door clicked shut.

Suddenly cold, Sara got into bed still wearing her nightgown, hugged the blanket to her neck and shut her eyes.

Sleep wouldn't come. A creeping unease kept her awake until well after the music from the shearing shed had been turned off.

## Chapter 15

### Sunday – 19 days before Alec's death

Tooting horns had punctuated the morning as most of the partygoers, who'd slept in utes, or swags inside the shed, had all driven away with their arms waving from the windows.

Sara went to Anne's bedroom. The door was open. 'Anne, are you and Ryan together?'

Anne was putting folded clothes into her drawer. 'Nope. Not now.'

Sara swallowed hard. 'When?'

Anne cleared her throat and wandered to her window, elbows in her hands. Outside, a brown common myna swooped in and stabbed his yellow beak into the grass and then lifted off with a worm moustache, ends curled. 'About a year ago.'

'You mean, you've slept together?'

Anne swung round. 'No!' She got the fat-lip look she used when she thought something was stupid. 'God, Sara. As if I'd do that with him. He's always here.'

'So, it didn't last?'

'We kissed, end.' She sighed dramatically. 'I want someone different. Someone who shows me there's a whole world out there.' She gave her room a judgemental once over and then laughed suddenly. 'He told me to come down to the Workers' one night.' She shook her head.

'Ryan did?' Sara swallowed. 'Do you think he'll be hurt? He's a nice guy.'

'No!' Anne turned, scowling. 'I think he was joking. Jesus, you need to get out more.'

Sara watched Anne shove her drawer closed then gaze out the window as though she'd forgotten Sara was still there. But Sara didn't mind. She had the feeling of a weight lifted.

She locked herself in the bathroom. She plucked her brows into thin arches and put mascara and kohl on her eyes. She took off her jeans and knickers and began to pluck out hairs from the patch between her legs. Sucked air with the pain of it. She'd heard warnings about using a razor down there but found one anyway and finished the job. Left was a neat triangle. Sara scrunched mousse into her hair and teased up her fringe. She grabbed a big colourful jumper and then pulled on her ripped jeans – as close to Kim Wilde's look as she could manage.

Before Ryan reappeared from the Workers', where he and a couple of friends had gone to shower, Sara strode down the old highway and walked across to Alec's driveway. Fresh in her mind was Dad driving in the forest and then creeping in afterwards. She reasoned that he might've diverted there after the pub if he saw lights or dogs or wild pigs. Someone had found a patch of marijuana in there once. But how could he dictate what they did and who they could talk to while he did whatever he liked?

At Alec's gate Sara noticed a shiny chain looped around twice with a heavy lock securing the ends. From where she stood, she couldn't see if anyone was home because the garage door was closed. She wasn't sure if they were churchgoers, out early on Sundays, but she doubted it, knowing what she did about Alec. Sara walked back home, remembering the man who threw a stone at him. Maybe they'd decided to lock up more securely.

Ryan drove up to the main house with Toby in the passenger side and Freddie in the backseat. Ryan had brought these two once before. Toby also played in their rugby team. On his first visit, Toby – thickset and with longish blonde hair – had worn dark corduroy jeans, a white t-shirt, and runners. Country boys wore leather boots. But Sara had liked him right away. He had a gentle voice and didn't talk too much. Sara hadn't seen him at the party. If she had, she might've stayed.

As Ryan parked the Escort, Sara saw little white lights that looked like snowflakes. She sat down on the couch. For a week, she'd halved the amount she normally ate. She believed she had a better chance of getting a boyfriend, preferably Ryan, if she was slim.

Through the window, she saw Freddie slam the rear door of the car, rub his nose vigorously, nostril edges rosy. His mouth was moving, then came a fleeting smile as he laughed at something one of the others had said. He reminded Sara of an allergy-ridden kid she'd sat beside in primary school. The allergy kid tried too hard to become friends, which seemed to repel everyone. The teacher had told Sara the boy needed a friend who was kind, like her. Sara had wondered why kindness felt like punishment.

Freddie was long-necked and adrenaline skinny, and Sara didn't like when he came. She didn't know what Ryan saw in him and had, long ago, decided that Freddie had thieving eyes.

Sara watched as Ryan shook Dad's hand. Ryan was wearing a red and brown western shirt like Jimmy Barnes. His dark-blue jeans were fastened by the belt which had the big silver buckle. She felt a heavy drugged sensation, which went all the way down to her waist. Ryan yawned and leant languidly against the side of his car. Sara could have written a song, a long desperate one, on those few seconds of desire.

Her hand shook as she drank a glass of water.

Outside, Dad's face loosened into a grin. Freddie stood behind the other two boys, one of his legs jumping. He slapped an insect on his face and examined it while crushing it between thumb and forefinger.

Dad's hands were drawing lines in front of him. Sara knew several creek crossings needed to be cleaned up and then reinforced with rocks.

After Dad had driven away with the tractor, the boys in the car, and Ryan on a motorbike, Sara yelled out to Robbie and Anne. Anne, rubbing sleep from her eyes, drove Dad's Hilux to the hayshed and backed it up. The three of them threw hay bales into the tray and then drove east to a paddock with a mob of heifers who would soon be joined with the bull.

Beneath the cold clear sky, Sara cut the baling twine with her pocketknife, and then she and Robbie took turns shoving bale slices off the back. When a big clump hit the ground, Robbie jumped off, broke it up with his boot and then ran back and swung himself up behind the cab.

A cold wind picked up, and clouds gathered over hills to

the east. Sara and Robbie squinted hard, coughed on the swirling hay flecks and diesel fumes. Once the tray was empty, they retreated to the cab. The cattle frolicked alongside as Anne arced the ute around and headed for home.

It was lunch time when they arrived at the house. Sara hurriedly made sandwiches. Mum was outside weeding around the pear trees next to the chickens. A raspberry and coconut slice cooled on a wire rack on the bench.

Anne disappeared into her room. Robbie grabbed a muesli bar and then paused as though unsure of something, shook his head and then walked out the door. After a minute, his motorbike started, the sound of the engine soon distant.

After they'd kicked their boots off in the laundry, Ryan and Toby whooped when they saw Sara's pile of roast beef and salad sandwiches. They slid into chairs at the table. Sara hid her blush in the kitchen as she filled the kettle and lined up five mugs.

The laundry door slammed. Dad stopped in the doorway, boots still on, jangled the keys to his trail bike. 'Sara, shift the flock to Stirling's before the storm. We've got a damaged boundary fence down the back where the bull is. Take Rusty.' He looked over his shoulder. 'Where's your bloody brother?'

Sara raced over, reached for the keys. 'Probably riding around. I'll do it.'

Dad kept hold. 'Take that bloody jumper off. It'll scare the mob.'

'Yes, Dad.'

He let go of the keys.

From the table, Toby twisted around, eager-eyed. 'Can we help?'

'Yeah, get a move on,' said Dad.

After the door slammed, Toby looked from Sara to Ryan.

Ryan was stuffing a sandwich into his mouth as fast as he could.

'Is it serious, the fence?' Toby asked.

'Hell, yes, with the highway this close,' Ryan said, scratchy voiced and a little nasal. Sara wondered if he was hungover from the night before. Meat fell from his sandwich and he picked it up and held it while he spoke. 'A neighbour's beast got hit by a truck a while back, didn't it, Sara? He lost hundreds of dollars' worth of black angus steer and had to pay damages.'

Sara nodded then noticed how empty the table looked. 'Where's Freddie?'

Toby and Ryan exchanged a glance.

Ryan's cheek bulged, and he held a knuckle to his lips. 'He drove the tractor too close to some rocks and scraped the paint. Your dad told him to bugger off.'

Sara winced. 'Was he still drunk from last night?'

Ryan lifted his brow. 'Probably. Stunk like a brewery. I should've sent him home.'

'How are you guys feeling? Sounded like a good party.'

Ryan grinned, glanced at Toby and cleared his throat.

'Fine,' they said in unison.

Sara changed into a flannelette shirt and work jeans. In the laundry, she pulled on a duffle coat and did up the wooden buttons. She, Ryan and Toby headed out on two motorbikes, with Rusty running alongside.

Once in the paddock with the flock, Toby jumped off the back of Ryan's bike and jogged along behind them. Sara raced ahead and opened the gate.

Sara's heart lifted as the sheep moved towards the opening. She glanced over to see Ryan grin and wink. She reached down and scratched Rusty between the ears. 'Good girl.'

Ryan closed the gate and then rode over. 'I'll go help your dad,' he called over the noise of the engines. He nodded at Toby. 'You alright here with Sara?'

Toby gave the thumbs up.

Ryan grinned at Sara then flicked off the clutch and tore away uphill. Dirt spun out behind his rear wheel and left a dark rip in the grass.

Ryan turned left into the laneway, revved the engine, arms wide, like he was on a Harley Davidson motorcycle. He sped along, belly as concave as the bite out of an apple, shirt shuddering at his back. Sara watched with a heavy, hungry sensation.

'Ryan's pretty cool, hey?' Toby smiled.

'He's great. Been coming here since he was fifteen.' Sara's stomach growled.

'You like him?'

Sara twisted away. 'He and Anne were sort of together.'

'You can't help who you like,' said Toby. He frowned slightly and pointed across the fence to a lone sheep against a big blackberry bush. 'Is that one alright?'

'Nah, she'll be caught up in the vines.' Rusty was sitting, tongue lolling, ears pricked. The house was across the other side of the paddock. Sara pointed at the house. 'Home!'

Rusty stood up, looked up and back.

'Good girl, home!' Sara repeated.

Rusty sprang forwards and raced off in that direction.

Sara watched until Rusty had jumped the gate and disappeared behind the trees near the dog pens. She knew she could trust Rusty to stay near the house. She turned to Toby and then walked the bike round. 'We'll drop into the shearing shed and grab some hand shears. Jump on.'

Toby climbed on behind her.

After grabbing the shears, Sara cast a wary eye at the thickened cloud mass overhead. Threads of lightning shimmered across the surface.

Sara pulled the bike to a stop alongside the trapped ewe and cut the engine. The sheep's eyes were wide, fearful marbles. She bleated loudly; nostrils full of dirty mucus.

Toby slid off the bike and approached the sheep with both hands up. 'Steady. We're just going to help you out.' He knelt in front of her.

She struggled closer to the blackberry and her hind legs trembled as her flanks billowed.

Sara kicked the bike stand down. 'Sheep are used to being led,' she said and stood behind Toby. 'They won't come, no matter how nice you are.' She wished it were Ryan here with her. 'Hey, I'll show you how to use the shears. You cut while I hold her.' Sara undid the Occy strap from the back of the bike to release the shears. They looked like big black scissors, made from a length of flat metal bent in half, the open ends sharpened into triangular blades. Sara's hand looked small on the sprung part of the handle as she carefully slid the back blade across the front. She handed them to Toby.

'Like this?' said Toby. The tendon moved in his wide hand as he snipped the blades a few times, creating the same whetstone sound Ryan's pocketknife made when he sharpened it.

'Yep, that's right.' Sara turned for the sheep and then launched her body at it. Struggling to her feet, ewe in the crook of her arm, she got up and threw her leg over the ewe's neck. 'Okay, Toby? Now!' said Sara.

Toby blinked, arms at his sides.

Sara suddenly imagined herself: dirty, sweaty. Rough. She swallowed hard and looked away. No wonder Ryan liked Anne. Sara probably looked like the farm girl peasants from medieval movies. Flooded by sudden, desperate sadness, Sara rubbed her nose with the back of her wrist. 'Just do one at a time. And try not to go too deep.' She jerked her thumb back over her shoulder. 'Rain'll get in, wool gets soggy, maggots move in.'

'Right. Right. I need the practice. I'm studying to be a vet.' Toby came in close and examined the trapped vines. He clenched a handful of wool but let go quickly. Grimacing, he shook his hand.

Sara noticed his clean-shaven face, his very white shirt under his barely worn, blue check flannelette. His nice jeans and runners. 'The weather's coming in. We'd better hurry,' she said, looking away.

A strong breeze swept leaves along the ground around them.

In a nearby row of pines, parrots shrieked as they swooped in and out of the trees. A lone crow emitted a strangled caw as it battled the currents. The blades rasped as Toby worked. 'Good girl,' he said to the sheep.

Wind hissed high in the trees. Beside her, Sara noticed lines in the dirt; tiny rabbit highways led underneath the blackberry bushes, the crown of thorns protection for their warren. Small black droppings scattered like ball bearings.

'Okay, done.' Toby got up.

'Really?' Sara discovered the sheep was free. 'Good job. Let's get her onto the motorbike before this rain starts.'

'You mean carry her?' said Toby with his brow raised. He glanced at the bike.

Sara nodded. 'Yeah. Put her across your lap behind me.

There's a little shed next to the yards where we keep the sickies.'

The skin around Toby's eyes gathered. 'Geez, I'd hate to drop her.'

'Can you ride?' asked Sara.

The sky crackled and pounded like an earthquake.

Toby ducked. 'Only once,' he said, voice raised. His eyes flickered skyward. 'Ryan once showed me when we were waiting for your dad.'

'It's only a few hundred metres,' said Sara. 'You ride. I'll hold the sheep.' She noticed the clouds had become pewter coloured.

Sheep balanced across her lap, Sara waited as Toby climbed carefully on in front of her. 'Easy on the clutch,' she warned.

The motorbike revved, jerked forwards and cut out. The sheep bleated. Sara made herself exhale calmly.

'Sorry.' Toby restarted the bike, held in the clutch, released it slowly, lifted his feet, and they were off.

They deposited the ewe into the sick shed, checked the bucket had water in it and then left some hay.

Sara sheltered behind Toby as big raindrops slapped her face and they sped the last hundred metres uphill.

Slowing near the machinery shed, Toby steered the bike around the corner.

Dad was standing next to the Hilux, an oily rag in one hand, a sparkplug in the other. His eyes followed Toby as he rode the bike in, cut the engine and kicked down the stand. Eyes on them, Dad lifted the spark plug and blew into the top.

A sudden flash seared white veins into the underside of a malicious purple cloud. Around Sara, the air felt thick and toxic.

Grinning and pulling up his collar, Toby jogged out. 'See you at dinner!' He broke into a run towards the Workers'. Dad's eyes followed him.

Sara steered the bike out from where Toby had parked, and then backed it in. When she looked up, she was alone.

Once inside the house, Sara pulled off her boots and left them by the laundry wall.

Dad was standing beneath the dining room light. The angle created dark moons below his eyes. 'There you are,' he said.

## Chapter 16

### Sunday – 19 days before Alec's death

Sara's spine stiffened, one vertebra at a time. Lightning flashed through the window. 'We freed a sheep from a blackberry bush and then put her in the sick shed,' she said.

A loud boom of thunder shook the glass in the window.

Dad's eyes were fixed on her face, his chest puffed. He wiped his hands across each other, and his biceps flexed.

Sara sensed intentional silence. Nothing moved. The TV screen was blank. On the stovetop, a pot steamed softly. Mum's knee made a crack-pop as she knelt in front of the pot-bellied stove. She winced in an apologetic expression as she undid the door quietly and fed in a piece of wood.

Robbie and Anne would stay behind their closed doors. Sara knew they'd be grateful not to be Dad's target. The three of them had once tried to join and defend each other against Dad, but it had backfired. He'd yelled until they were all silent and cowed.

'When did I say it was okay for that boy to ride my

motorbike?' said Dad in a low voice.

Rain tapped against the window and Sara saw something move. A bat flew across the sky.

'He said he'd ridden once before, and I was worried he'd drop the sheep, so I let him. It was only for a minute.' Sara panicked for air the same way she did in the pool when she raced freestyle. She usually ended up with a bellyful of chlorinated water.

'*You* let him?' Dad said with an edge so sharp it could slice a hair lengthways.

Sara swallowed. 'Yeah, I—'

'You mean yes!'

Sara noticed a white dot of spittle on her dad's lower lip and blue bulges in his neck.

'Yes. I let him.' Sara suddenly couldn't swallow, and the smell of the lamb roast threatened to make her gag. Hands behind her back, she stood straight as possible, pushing the fingers of one hand back and forth through the fingers of the other.

Dad tilted his head. 'So, you're saying you had the right and the authority to allow someone to be in complete control of my two thousand dollars' worth of farm vehicle without the knowledge or experience to operate it?' He scanned around as though he had an audience. Then he zeroed in on her. 'What gives you the right to hand out my belongings to everyone?' His brow lifted.

Sara got a metallic taste in her mouth. She checked the clock. Six pm. Dad's short explosions were forty-five minutes. 'We needed to get the sheep out of the rain.'

'Don't you be a bloody smartarse!' Dad stabbed the air with a finger. Sara felt the jabs in her stomach. 'You're as rude and untrustworthy as your mother!'

In the kitchen, Mum shook frozen peas out of a plastic bag into a saucepan. *Shake. Shake. Shake.* Her eyes stayed low.

'I'm sorry, Dad. I should have asked first.'

Dad's eyelids snapped. Brief uncertainty crossed his face. 'Damn right you should've, you privileged little upstart! I've worked my guts out! I won't have my daughter hand over my hard-earned stuff to some city kid!' His wet lips trembled. 'Don't for a second think I can't see through you.'

Sara's brain began to cloud. She knew this path, this aperture down into the darkness. Knew how deep Dad could drag her before he was done.

Dad's lip curled. 'I've always watched you, Sara. Because you're *sneaky. Selfish. Greedy.*'

Stab. Stab. Stab.

Sara knew this was her fault. As she stood there, the solution presented itself with aching simplicity. She should've made Toby hold the damn sheep. She felt a sudden thick hatred for the stupid sheep, and frustration at Toby – old enough and strong enough to carry the ewe, but too bloody scared! Sara grappled for words to shorten the lecture, but Dad had clicked onto familiar tracks and was headed downhill, gaining momentum.

'I see you flutter your eyes at these city boys. But let me tell you, girl, they'll take what's on offer because it's easy! They're not interested in *you.* Ha!' He laughed, a short mean grunt. 'No decent man wants a woman who's been screwing around.'

'Len,' Mum said, her voice sounding exhausted.

Sara felt a small flare of hope, but it was quickly smothered by the slump in her mum's shoulders.

'It's true, Ellen, for Chrissakes, and I won't sugar-coat it! She's got no idea how the world works, but I do! You do too, don't you, Ellen?'

Mum frowned softly. 'Mm.'

'Men know women like that, Sara. Decent men choose *quality* and leave the rest to the crap. You know what I mean by crap, don't you, Sara?' With his hand, he started stabbing the air again. 'The jobless, the gamblers, drunks, and wife-beaters!'

She felt every word like a blade through her skin.

'Do you want a bloke who beats the shit out of you!' he shouted. His head trembled, face crimson. 'Do you? Do you!' He tipped forwards onto his toes.

Sara wanted to hold her hands up as the noise punched into the sides of her head, her chest and her belly. She kept them firmly behind her back but let her eyes slide away from his to lessen the glare.

'You look at me!' Dad bellowed and tilted his chin up. 'Do you, Sara? Answer me!'

Sara flinched, could hardly breathe. She forced out a word. 'No.' *Agree. The shortest way out.*

'No, what? You disrespectful little shithead!'

Stab, stab, twist. Sara's hands went to her belly as if to soothe the cuts and bruises Dad inflicted. *It's not me. I wouldn't do those things. Why do you hate me so much? Why can't you trust me? Mum, help me. Please? I can bear it, Mum. Please make it stop.*

Sara looked for backup, but Mum's lips were tight.

'Sorry. No, I don't, Dad.' Her muscles were clenched so hard she could barely move. Her stubborn anger swelled like molten lava. It filled her body, flooded her veins and pulsed in her arteries. It was almost suffocating to hide it, to stay silent and calm. *Breathe, breathe.*

'She hasn't got a choice! She's lowered herself, made her bed, and she'll bloody lay in it!' As his voice lowered, Dad's nose skin gathered like a dog showing its side teeth. 'I can see you, Sara. I know who you are.'

Sara became keenly aware of herself. Her skin, her breasts, the secret part between her legs where she'd shaped the hair. She was a fox held in the glare of a spotlight. Her desires for Ryan were written on her face like graffiti – dirty, cheap and degrading. She was desperate to cross her arms and hide herself.

The corner of Dad's mouth pulled up as though she was transparent.

Sara dropped her eyes to the floor.

It wasn't fair. Why did she respond to Ryan's little smile, the gentle rock of his hips, the way she craved his weight pressed against her body? Why couldn't she be someone who was good?

'Women think they can do what they like! Women's libbers and their birth control pills that turn them into whores!' Dad bellowed.

*Breathe, breathe. It doesn't hurt. It's not true.*

Wearing oven gloves, Mum opened the stove, pulled out the sizzling roast and placed it on a wooden board.

Sara concentrated. She began to drift, through the air, through the dark, hundreds of kilometres away.

*The large, empty wooden house has verandas on all sides with stripey recliner chairs. Wisteria heavy with purple blossom is musical with bees. Bunches of seedless grapes droop down among the blossoms. Passionfruit vines curl around the poles, trellis and along the rafters, the indigo-coloured fruit large and sweet. Surrounding the house is a garden with flowers and vegetables and fruit trees, and there are all sorts of native animals and birds. There is a waterhole for swimming, where it is always warm. There is a bathtub outside, and the sky is chock-full of stars at night like hundreds and thousands on a Freckle lolly.*

'... they've brought it on themselves!' Dad shouted. He paused, chest moving up and down. 'Sara, what did I just say?'

Sara swallowed. Her brain swam unwillingly back, glad of the piece she'd left listening to Dad. 'They've brought it on themselves,' she said tonelessly. *Breathe, breathe.*

Sara watched her dad's face for the change. The point where his paranoia and rage intersected, and his reasoning flipped into strange territory. Then he would look at Sara or Mum or Anne and see conspirators, liars and strangers. Sara could hear her dad working himself closer to the intersection.

'Damn right they have!'

There it was, just as she had expected. His hard-cold face, the vicious shine in his staring eyes, which could see the evil of all women.

Sara knew the rest of Dad's speech. All you bloody women are the same. Sara was the enemy, a conniving woman like the rest of them. Like her, they all made him furious. He would call her cunning, surreptitious, premeditated. Ridicule her stupidity, her vanity and naivety. Sara knew if she cried, he would tell her she was manipulating, weak and pathetic, like all women are. She disgusted him. They all did.

*You don't hurt me, Len Hamilton. I will leave you. We will all leave you.*

Sara began to chant in her head to anchor herself as the madness rained down, licking at her grip on reality, trying to draw her into its black core. *The skull bone's connected to the backbone.*

Dad's words punched out reasons for Sara's flaws. Not just because she was female but because she had Italian blood, and Italians were useless.

*The back bone's connected to the hip bone.*

Then it was Mum's fault. Dad yelled that Mum had ruined them, made them insufferable, flawed, argumentative. She'd been too soft.

*The hip bone's connected to the leg bone.*

Her dad's voice had become a loud pulse.

Sara's mind blurred as she tried to escape his senseless ranting but words cut through the fog like a blind bayonet. 'You! Right! Dare!'

She wanted to remind him she was only four feet away.

*The leg bone's connected to the ankle bone.*

'You see!' Dad shouted.

Sara wished she was her younger child-self, who had unquestioningly believed she deserved the punishment. Thought her confusion was her inability to understand, not Dad's inability to make sense. 'Yes, Dad.' Her head pulsed. Her belly sucked in on itself, and her ears rang. She risked a quick look at the microwave clock. Seven fifteen.

'Len?' Mum said quietly. 'The boys are coming shortly. Perhaps Sara should tidy herself up.'

Dad glanced around at the doorway to the laundry, straightened his belt and cleared his throat.

*Ryan.* A small lifeline. Sara stayed quite still, careful not to show any emotion or impatience. *Anything.* Weakness, pain, joy. *Nothing.*

'Got it, Sara? No showing off to these boys.' Dad sounded hoarse, the sting gone from his words.

'Yes, Dad.' Magic words. She would say it again, and again. It was the only escape from the anger and the noise.

A knock sounded behind them.

'Hi? Just us.' Ryan and Toby stuck their heads in one after the other like a double act. Sara thought their smiles were forced.

'Come on in, fellahs.' Dad laughed in a big 'Ho Ho' – as genuine as a Santa with a white nylon beard.

Sara raced to the bathroom and quickly got beneath the water. Once dry and dressed, she paused at the door and grabbed the towel rail with both hands. Eyes screwed shut, Sara bit her tongue and squeezed harder and harder. She tasted blood as the towel rail came loose. When she opened her eyes, the rail was disconnected from the wall, its weight in her hands. Breathing steadily, Sara bent down and carefully placed it on the floor, her palms red with early bruises.

## Chapter 17

**Sunday – 19 days before Alec's death**

Dinner went without incident. The rules were followed, his lordship's discontent avoided at all costs.

Outside, the rain eased to a light patter, and occasional wind gusts drove droplets at the window.

After washing the dishes, Sara walked through Robbie's room and climbed out the window, closing it behind her. His bedroom faced the steps to the back veranda, whereas hers faced the garden and had a two-metre drop.

Grass squelched beneath her bare feet. She took several deep breaths. Over by the front gate, Ryan and Toby were talking quietly as they let themselves through and climbed into Ryan's car. The interior light snapped an image of their heads: one dark, one light. Headlights strobed the darkness, and then red taillights moved away.

Toby had told them earlier he'd be catching the train home after dinner to get his assessments done. Ryan was staying so that he could help Dad with some cattle work in the morning.

Sara walked through the dark garden, ran her hand across the spiky holly leaves and shook water from the hydrangea blooms.

Above her, the bedroom windows were large, dark squares divided into nine by wooden strips where sometimes she played imaginary naughts and crosses. She squatted down, wrapped her arms around her legs and closed her eyes.

No one could know that Sara just stood there when Dad shouted. How she held everything inside where it burnt like fire, but she didn't fight back.

She cried; her fire turned to water as quiet, heavy drops of rain fell on her head.

At school when the teacher asked a question, even when she knew the answer, Sara never raised her hand. The teachers usually didn't ask her anything directly. They probably saw something in her face and skipped the void, the nothing of Sara Hamilton. She felt invisible, but at least invisible was safe.

She wiped her eyes and nose on the back of her wrist. She thought about Alec and his coat. Remembered how he'd flapped it like a matador after he'd been hit by a rock. How he practised his singing and lines out there in the forest. How brave he must be.

The darkness dripped, and the water trickled in unseen streams. From a way off, a dog barked. Inside the house, Dad was shouting again.

Sara walked around the garden until she was damp and cold. The rain had stopped but lightning shivered across the horizon. Thunder drummed close and then drew away. Close then far, a tide going out.

Sara climbed back into the warmth of Robbie's room and then wrestled her arm out of a damp sleeve as she walked into her own room in the dark.

'Sara?'

Sara jumped, hand to chest. 'Robbie?' she whispered.

'Where were you?'

'Went outside for a bit.' Sara closed her door and slipped her jumper off. She hung it over the back of a chair.

'Dad would go nuts.'

'Dad always goes nuts.'

Sara heard a staggered sniffle. She went to the sound, wrapped her arms around and squeezed Robbie's warm solidness into her chest. 'What happened?'

'Dad made me fix a towel rail that came off the wall,' he said, and hiccupped. 'You're wet.'

'Sorry!' Reality rushed back after the quiet of the garden. 'Shit, that was me. Are you alright?'

'I knew it would be you. I said it was me. You've had enough today.'

'I'm sorry, Robbie.' She released him. 'Thank you.'

'It's okay. God, I'm so dumb!' Robbie sniffled and swallowed. 'I kept dropping the tools and I didn't know which tool was which. I can't think when he shouts.'

'I know! Fucking bloody bastard!' Sara whispered angrily.

Robbie's breath stuttered. 'It doesn't matter. Nothing matters.'

'Don't let him get to you.' Sara squeezed his arm.

Robbie sighed. 'He makes me feel like I'm dying.'

'Don't you ever fucking say that!' she cried.

'I'm sorry,' said Robbie.

'It's not you. Shh. Sit on the bed for a bit.'

Robbie sat down. Sara felt around for her pyjamas, found

the messy lump beneath her pillow and began to get changed.

Robbie sighed and turned to face the window. 'I don't want to die,' he whispered. 'I'm not going to kill myself. He just makes me *feel* like I'm dying. Me. He takes up the whole house. I can't be myself. I can't breathe. Yet he's such a fucking hypocrite.'

Sara pulled her long-sleeved pyjamas on. 'What do you mean?'

Robbie's silence thickened the dark.

Sara turned to face her brother, remembering the way he'd been looking at Dad lately.

Robbie stood up.

Sara grabbed his hand. 'Tell me,' she said, as steadily as she could. 'Has something happened? Do you know why he's grumpy and keeps coming home early?'

Robbie swallowed. 'Sort of. I can't say.'

'Why?'

'People ... will get hurt. Just don't worry. It'll get sorted.'

'What will? Shit, Robbie!' She thought quickly as she felt him pull away. 'I know you've talked to that kid Alec, from next door. I saw you the other day. And I saw how upset he looked afterwards.'

Slowly, Robbie sat down, leant forwards, elbows on his thighs. 'Yeah. I guess we're friends.'

'Okay. I know what people are saying about him, but I don't care. What's he like?'

'He's cool.'

Sara bit her lip. 'I saw someone chuck a rock at him. By the highway.'

Robbie straightened. 'Who?'

'No idea. He mucked around afterwards. So, I knew he was

okay.'

Robbie rubbed his face. 'He's brave, I'll give him that. And he cares about people, you know?'

'I got the feeling the other day that he wanted to come over or something,' said Sara. 'He just stood near his driveway, looking at our house.'

Robbie gave a low, incredulous laugh that wasn't a laugh. He chopped the air with his hand. 'No way! Absolutely, no fucking way.'

'I know. That's what I thought,' said Sara. She chose her words carefully. 'So, why is Dad a hypocrite?'

Robbie cleared his throat. Slowly, he got up. 'I don't even know why I'm surprised,' he said as he moved towards the door. 'I'll sort it. Don't worry.' He walked out. Sara heard his door click shut.

Shivering, Sara climbed into bed.

Despite the warmth, bed wasn't the usual comfort. In the dark, Sara imagined the track across the dam wall to the Workers' House. Thunder rumbled as though it came up from the bottom of the ocean. Sara envisioned Ryan's window ajar, curtain flapping in the wind.

## Chapter 18

**Sunday night – 19 days before Alec's death**

Sara opened Robbie's bedroom door slowly and closed it behind her. In his bed, Robbie sighed and turned over. When his breathing sounded deep and regular, Sara crept past the bed to the window, lifted it up and climbed out.

Across the paddock, the dam wall was slippery. Rain pattered cold drops along her arms, and grass whipped her legs as she ran with her hands shading her face.

She stopped outside the Workers' House. The windows were dark. Ryan's Escort was parked in the little shed.

Sara opened the door and stood in the entryway. She blindly wobbled on one leg and then the other as she pulled off her shoes. The rain intensified – loud, louder – became static through the open door.

'Hello?' Ryan's voice sounded like he was up the other end of the house.

Sara froze. 'Hi! Just me.' It was real suddenly. Alone and at night, she was with Ryan.

Outside, the water poured from the roof and slapped into puddles.

'God, did you walk—'

A sharp explosion of thunder cut him off as it clapped above the house and reverberated around.

'Jesus! Sorry, I'm—' His voice was lost in the pound of the thunderstorm. 'I'll get dressed!'

'No, no, stay there. I'll come in!' Sara closed the back door, pulled her jumper off, shook her legs out of the wet denim and felt around for the dryer. She fed her clothes in and turned it on. She patted along until she found a towel. Pulled it around her. It smelled of Ryan.

Wearing only a damp t-shirt and underwear, she stood wrapped and shaking. No neat words arrived to describe the driving force that had delivered her — no thermos or biscuits or excuses.

She imagined Ryan listening from the bed, his naked body stretched out beneath the covers. The darkness before her eyes filled with Michelangelo's *The Creation of Adam*, which she'd admired from her art teacher's book collection.

'Come in and get warm!'

A clap of thunder drove Sara up the step into the kitchen. She felt too much heat in herself to return to the cold sadness in her bedroom. She stopped in front of the wide black expanse of the loungeroom window.

Across the paddock was her house. The big tree leant forwards, so the building was a wombat with its head in a burrow. Jagged silver sliced the sky. Trees swung wildly, ravers in strobe lights.

'Get in here, you must be freezing!' Ryan's voice came from the doorway to her right. 'Ah.'

Neither of them moved.

'Want me to stoke up the fire up so you can get warm?' he suggested gently.

The fireplace glowed soft rose.

'No.'

'Sara.' It almost sounded like a question, but the rest didn't come.

'Were you expecting Anne?'

After a pause, he said no, which Sara didn't quite believe. Her teeth began to chatter. 'I just ... I just—'

He walked over. 'C'mere.' He pulled her into his chest.

She shivered against him.

'You're freezing. Here.' Ryan's tall frame loomed. His arms were suddenly around her. Sara was caught inside the towel as Ryan scooped behind her back and knees and carried her into the dark. In his bedroom, he leant down and rolled her onto the bed.

Sara found the opening of the covers and wriggled in.

'I only just got out of the shower,' said Ryan. 'Is that the dryer going?' He bent and pulled something up his legs. Sara realised he'd been naked.

The drumming rain settled into a steady noise. 'Yeah. I was soaked. When did Toby leave?'

'What?'

Rain thundered against the roof like hooves on concrete.

'Toby?'

'Train...Sydney.'

The bed rocked with the weight of him. Warm arms encircled, pulled her in tight. Hot skin. He was only wearing boxer shorts. 'Are you alright? I heard your dad shouting.'

'Yeah.'

He paused then kissed her forehead. 'Your hair is wet.' He released her, moved around, and gently tousled her hair with the towel. He threw it off to the side.

'So's my shirt.'

'It'll dry.'

Sara could hear the smile in his words. She tucked her hands between them. 'Thank you. For not throwing me out.'

'I'd never throw you out.'

The storm clattered and drummed as heavy streams of water poured off the roof hard enough to gouge pools in the lawn.

Her teeth chattered. 'My hands ...'

'Here.' He reached around and pulled her close.

She curled into him.

He gave a satisfied noise and settled into the bed. 'That's it.' He kissed her temple, and then her cheek. He covered her backside with one hand and urged her closer. One of her knees slipped between his.

She felt his breath on her lips.

She leant forwards, felt him ease out of reach.

'Sara?'

'Please, Ryan.'

She heard him swallow.

'Your dad would kill me.'

'Can you just ... hold me?'

'Yes. Of course. God.' He kissed her temple and held her tight. 'What has he done to you?'

More thunder rumbled outside.

Ryan rubbed her back and upper arms.

After a moment, Sara felt him come closer, so close it felt like they were breathing together. Then Ryan's full, firm lips were against her mouth for a couple of seconds. A soft kiss. He eased back.

She reached for his face and felt the contour of his cheek,

the dimple and then down the side of his throat next to the bump of his Adam's apple.

'Why was Len shouting?'

She felt his cheek move as he spoke. Her jaw trembled. 'I let Toby ride the motorbike.'

'Shit.' His arms squeezed her and then relaxed. 'House was almost vibrating. We weren't sure if we should interrupt.'

'Glad you didn't.'

'You all looked like you'd been whipped.' Ryan stroked his hand down her back. 'Doesn't get physical, does it?'

'N-no.' Sara thought she could hear her neck creak. 'Let's not talk about it.' She touched the edge of his jaw, found his mouth. Initiated a kiss.

He hesitated. 'Sara,' he said solemnly, 'you're not even sixteen.'

'I will be soon.' After a moment, she kissed him again. This time, he kissed her back.

His sigh sounded like he might be considering doing more. She swept her hand back and forth across his chest. He took her hand and kissed the back. After a moment, she reached down between them where the air was warm. Gently, she brushed below his belly button where she liked to be touched. He murmured appreciatively and didn't move away.

Sara felt the elastic of his underwear beneath her fingertips.

Ryan gasped and held her gently by the upper arms. 'Sara.'

'I want it to be you.'

His hands loosened slightly. 'Jesus.'

The rain slapped against the window. After a moment, Sara felt a firm, warm part of Ryan against her thigh. Even blind and through boxer shorts, she knew what it was. 'It's okay,' she said. She reached up and gently kissed his neck. 'But I've never...' Sara started.

'I know. I'm here every fortnight. Are you even allowed to date?' He rolled away, onto his back, and put one hand along his forehead, shading his eyes.

'Apparently, we have to wait until we're married. Anne gets around him, but I'm not a good liar. Ryan, I want to choose.' Sara clenched her jaw, wishing she sounded more confident. She could hear her fragility on the surface, an insect balanced on water.

Ryan exhaled, reached over and cupped the side of her head. 'I'd feel like I was taking advantage of you.'

'Only if you didn't care about me.'

He stroked her cheek gently with the back of his fingers. 'I do care about you.'

'Ryan, I've never had feelings for anyone else.'

He hummed in an unconvincing way.

'What?' said Sara.

'You haven't had many options.'

'I don't like the guys at school. I like you,' she said, emphasising the last word.

'I tried not to see you that way. You were just a girl when I first came here.'

Sara prised at the confusion she heard in his tone. 'But?' she said.

Ryan sighed, which sounded like the start of a long story, but if it was, he kept it to himself. Finally, he spoke. 'You're lovely.' He rolled to face her and sighed in a way that sounded slightly defeated. 'And you make me laugh.'

'Me too.' She knew she had to ask. 'Do you still like Anne? She told me you invited her down here.'

'I was joking.' He paused. 'Anne's not someone who'll let you get close. She's, I don't know, messing around until she can start her life. It was never serious.'

'She's waiting until she can leave home,' said Sara. 'I think we all are. I'm counting the days.'

Ryan pushed hair back from her neck. 'You know, I don't need to come down every fortnight, but I wanted to take the pressure off your family by getting your dad out. He's happy down in the paddock. Chats away.'

'Not with us.'

Ryan squeezed her hand. 'I'm sorry. You don't deserve it.'

In the quiet, she listened to her heartbeat and the rain thrumming rhythmically. 'I could stay like this for days,' said Sara.

'You'd get hungry.'

They both chuckled.

'I climbed out through the window,' she said.

'I can imagine that.' Ryan lifted his head. 'I think the dryer has finished with your clothes.'

He leant over her, and they began kissing again until he was urging her mouth open.

She felt the tip of his tongue brush against hers. A tingling sensation went from Sara's neck to her feet. Her heart pounded. 'Does it hurt?' she whispered.

Ryan drew back a little. 'The first time, apparently. But not for long.'

'You haven't been with ... a virgin?'

'No.' He lay back on his pillow, hands beneath his head. 'I'm still not sure, Sara. That could've been a goodbye kiss.'

Sara stayed on her side against him, worried she'd say the wrong thing. 'Tell me about your first time.' She heard his head turn on the pillow.

'I was fifteen. She was nineteen. I was tall for my age.'

'Did she know how old you were?'

'I told her.' He stroked her arm with one finger. 'It was a good thing. She showed me what to do.'

'Let's not talk about that.'

He eased closer, found her jaw and held her still while he kissed her. 'Okay.' He paused an inch from her face, like he was waiting for her. 'Are you going?'

'No.' Sara was scared by his stillness. Ryan was used to girls who knew what they wanted. She thought about leaving, then remembered how she'd felt before she came. 'I want this, Ryan, so much, but I don't know what to do.' The confession felt the same as a wild run down a steep hill.

'It's okay.' Ryan kissed her slowly then drew his lips across her cheek to her ear. 'Let's just relax. We don't have to go all the way.'

'I'll just take this off.' Sara sat up and pulled her t-shirt off and dropped it beside the bed.

Ryan propped on one elbow then hugged her again. His chest felt hot against her breasts, which had cooled in the wet shirt. 'You feel beautiful,' said Ryan.

'Thankyou.' Sara closed her eyes, aware of the precipice she stood on. 'You don't have to touch me, do you?'

'Sorry?'

Sara cringed. 'I'm not sure if I'm nice, down there.' She felt him ease back.

The wind sucked against the trees, and the house creaked.

Ryan cleared his throat. 'When it happens, touching helps,' he whispered gently. 'You need to be ready. Especially the first time.'

Something which sounded like a tree nut dropped onto the roof and then rolled off.

Ryan nuzzled into the space between Sara's face and neck then, slowly, he kissed all the way down over her collarbones to her breasts. 'Touching yourself is completely natural.'

'I don't do that.' She felt him pause.

'What do you do when you feel tense or want something sexy?' He pulled the covers up over his head and ran his hands down her sides.

'I drink a lot of water.'

Ryan kissed her right nipple.

Sara gasped.

Ryan pulled back the cover. 'Water? How does that help?'

Sara grabbed the covers and pulled them up, submerging Ryan's head. 'I was worried about spontaneous combustion.'

'Is that when someone explodes?' Ryan started chuckling, and it built until the bed was shaking.

Sara joined in laughing. 'I saw a documentary on it!' she said, trying to get herself under control.

Ryan's head moved lower, and he laughed into her belly. Sara writhed sideways, away from his hot mouth. 'Ryan, stop it!' Giggles kept bubbling up. 'An old man exploded and ... and his chair burnt.' Now, it just sounded ridiculous. Sara wiped her eyes.

Outside, the rain had stopped, and the wet leaves released a tinkling of droplets.

Ryan's head popped out from the cover, chin on the flat part between her ribs. 'I think you're going to like it.' Ryan's voice had become deep and secret. 'But if we're doing this, you need to trust me and ... I'm going to touch you.' He paused as though he was waiting for her response. Then he moved onto his back and slid his boxers down his legs. He came close again and pulled the covers all around them.

'Okay,' Sara whispered. 'Would you like me to go down on you?' She remembered the line about the ice-cream in the book. Something she'd never practised, but an ice-cream was an ice-cream, and who hadn't had one of those?

'Really?'

'I think I'll be quite good at that.'

Ryan chuckled. 'Maybe. Let's see how we go.'

Sara found the touching wasn't too bad, but it tickled. She kept twitching and knew it wasn't the right response. She was supposed to be writhing in pleasure, raptures ... moaning even.

Ryan moved away then stretched up and hugged his arms around her. His hands spread out to cover her whole back. Sara's face fell into the angle between his chin and shoulder where she could feel the smooth warm skin of his neck. She loved his beautiful hands on her, but she felt the moment had cooled. She hadn't reacted the right way. There was something wrong with her.

Sara half sat up. Ryan loosened his arms.

She reached down and found his readiness with her hand. Ryan drew a short, quick breath. Sara moved down the bed. It was nothing like an ice-cream. For a start, it was covered in silky smooth, taut skin, and the tip was salty. She had to adjust a little bit so she could breathe and move simultaneously. Curled around his abdomen, she could hear the background patter of rain again, and Ryan's stomach gurgling.

Sara was encouraged by Ryan's deep breaths and soft intermittent moans, sounds she suspected she should have made.

'Stop! Stop!' Ryan gently pushed her and then lay back onto the bed, a hand over his eyes. She noticed he was holding the blanket against his groin. He exhaled carefully.

'What?' Sara wiped her mouth.

'Jesus!'

Sara waited, propped on her elbow. 'Oh.' She grinned.

'Here.' Ryan shifted, encircled her waist and then lifted her over on top of him. He pulled the blanket up to cover them. She lay her cheek on his shoulder as he put his hands back under his head. 'Just give me a sec.'

As the heat of his skin seeped into her, she felt tension ease away.

Ryan's arms came down from his head. He grasped her by the ribcage and brought their bodies level. Her weight settled over him; upper body and breasts spread across his chest, hip bones slightly above and outside Ryan's like two compatible halves. He squeezed her hips and pulled her tight against him.

'Gosh, you feel so good,' he said, then he moaned and laughed at himself.

'You do too. You're so much warmer than me.' She stretched upwards so her mouth was beside his ear. 'I'm ready if you want to,' she whispered.

Ryan went still. 'You're sure?' His lower abdomen tightened as he lifted his head.

'I ran through a damn storm to get here.'

They kissed gently. Sara felt Ryan's muscles soften as though his world was open for her to fall into.

Where he was hard, she was soft, the length of him neat between her closed thighs. She wriggled down. Her body loosened beautifully, and warmth spread across her skin, infusing her belly and causing the craving that usually instigated water guzzling. But this time, she knew they'd settle it.

Ryan pulled apart from her for a moment and wrestled with himself.

Sara realised he was applying a condom. He lifted her back on top and guided her hips further forwards and then held her by the waist. She felt a tight searing pressure like sunburn, and then everything became wet and free. Sara didn't think she could move. She lay with her face on Ryan's chest, her heart pounding. She still felt whole, even though he was inside her. He was breathing steadily.

While the rain diminished and the wind sighed, Ryan withdrew slowly and moved Sara to the side. He rolled her onto her back and balanced above her on his elbows. Then he opened her legs with his knees. 'Are you okay?' he said.

'Yes.'

Ryan pulled her knees up around his waist as he lowered his body and pushed inside. Sara had a moment of confusion. The goal had been achieved, and she was still tender. Then she realised that Ryan had not achieved his own goal.

It was easier the second time. The line of a Divinyls' song about a 'fine line' sprang into her head as a delicious sensation ran across her belly where pleasure and pain crossed over. Sara became aware that the bed was squeaking and realised that at least some of what she'd read was true.

Ryan groaned. It wasn't a sound Sara had ever heard from a person, more like a cow being branded. It was guttural and desperate, like Ryan had made a noble sacrifice and may be injured. But she knew it must have been pleasurable. She felt the glow of being the person who had delivered a wonderful gift.

Ryan put the condom beside the bed. He pulled her over, so they were facing one another.

Sara's arm flopped across his hip, loose and relaxed.

'It's okay,' he whispered as he touched her face and kissed her softly. 'I'll make sure you enjoy this.'

Again confused, Sara realised this was a project which was not yet complete.

After a moment, Ryan rustled around again, applied another condom and positioned himself over her. Sara tried not to think about why he had so many condoms. She assumed guys were all carrying copious supplies. Wasn't that what they'd been told to do?

Hands over her breasts, Sara suddenly understood trust.

She became aware of Ryan, his body, his warmth, his strength; all the experiences that had brought him to this moment. She touched the bumps of his ribs down his sides, the soft hair that curled at the back of his neck, the muscles that moved in his shoulders as he held his weight.

As Ryan pressed his chest closer, Sara marvelled at his completeness, his perfection, his instinctive movements. She'd worried unnecessarily about this moment.

Ryan's fingertips brushed her thighs. A delicate pain made her breathe slowly in then out as he guided himself inside. The rain pattered and drummed. Lightning probed the edges of the blind, like soft lasers.

Sara didn't know how many times Ryan was going to keep applying condoms. She had never thought about how much a man needed before he was finished. She suddenly felt lost, as though she'd switched on a foreign movie without subtitles or a run time.

Maybe she should be keeping a record. She thought for a moment. They'd already had sex three times.

Ryan grew more urgent and slipped his hand beneath her buttocks so he could reach parts of her he was intent to go. Again, he moaned, but more quietly, and then immediately afterwards, he made a sound of disappointment. 'Sorry.' He rolled onto his back.

Baffled, Sara curled onto her side. 'Are you alright?' she asked.

'Yep. Just a minute.'

Outside, the wind had picked up. Sara felt a little of the rain's coolness seep into the room, unsurprising with the age of the house, which could be forgiven a few leaks.

Ryan moved. It sounded like he was working on something, which Sara soon understood when he rolled over her again. This time she winced.

He stilled and then came forwards on his elbows. He gently held her head as he kissed her with such tenderness, it had an analgesic affect. It began again.

'Here.'

Something touched Sara's lip. She opened her mouth and felt his finger on her tongue.

'Good.' He pressed his lips against hers as he lifted his hips and reached down between them. He brushed a part of her more sensitive than the rest, a part which had deep anchors inside and clenched deliciously.

An overwhelming sensation started from her core, spread outwards and stimulated an internal chain of tightening that drew everything in.

Sara grabbed Ryan's waist and held him against her.

Ryan responded with his full weight, but Sara sensed she could take a heavier weight with more vigour. She moaned softly as her belly cramped.

Around the edges of the blind, lightning pulsed in tentative flashes.

They lay breathing together, Sara's skin stuck to Ryan. As his weight lifted, she felt light enough to rise to the ceiling.

Lazily, she pulled up the covers.

Ryan dealt with the final condom and sank down close to her. 'Okay?' he asked against her ear, his cheek hot and damp.

Sara felt slightly guilty that she'd made him work so hard. 'Yeah,' she whispered.

He pulled her upper body across his, and then his arms flopped down onto the bed.

Eyes closed and with her head on his chest, Sara could feel the beat of Ryan's heart.

## Chapter 19

### Monday – 18 days before Alec's death

Ryan's Escort pulled up in front of the house, a splash spurting from a puddle beneath the left front wheel. Ryan emerged from the car, ran his hand back through his hair, his lips funnelled like he was whistling. In the front room, Sara stood up with a simultaneous feeling – both weightless and full, as if she'd won a prize and would be happy forever.

In the early hours of the morning, Sara had roused, her cheek near Ryan's collarbone. She'd kissed him, and he'd mumbled and rolled over. She'd made a quick return through Robbie's window and into her bedroom without disturbing her brother.

When her alarm went off, she'd hurriedly dressed in her school uniform.

Ryan pulled opened the front door, bounced in and stopped like he'd hit a wall. 'Hi, Sara.'

She understood what it meant to be held by a gaze. Ryan's eyes reflected their secret night.

Wearing pyjamas, Anne wandered into the kitchen and stood close to Mum. 'Hi,' she said, not looking at anyone. 'Dad out?'

Mum made a sound in the affirmative.

Anne yawned and dropped two slices of bread into the toaster.

Ryan swallowed; an awareness passed over his face. He looked from Anne to Sara. 'Ah, Len's already out?' He glanced back at Sara and walked into the kitchen.

Anne frowned. 'Looks that way. It is Monday, Ryan.'

'I've finished exams. Got the week off.'

Anne shrugged and wandered towards the bathroom. The door clicked.

'This toast is warm if you're hungry,' said Mum. 'We've got bacon and eggs too, when Len comes in.'

'You're a legend,' said Ryan.

Sara was aware of some tenderness inside her body as she shifted her weight.

Ryan took a slice of toast. He threw back his head to feed the whole thing into his mouth. 'Starving,' he said through the bread. He picked up another slice and looked back over his shoulder, grinning.

Sara tried to hold back the smile, but gave in.

'Do you know which paddock he's in?' said Ryan. He kept looking at Sara while he spoke, their secret pulsing between them.

'Hm?' Mum never seemed to have a direct answer. Even if she knew what it was.

Ryan turned and gently touched Mum's shoulder.

Sara melted.

He finished his mouthful and brushed his hands together. He walked towards Sara. She felt him like a big jet flying in –

the quiet roar of his body, and the heat of his energy. She perched on the edge of the couch.

He sat on the armrest behind her, and his hand came down and wrapped gently around her wrist. His skin felt warm and beautiful. As Sara's heart pulsed, the tenderness inside throbbed. 'How are you?' Ryan said gently.

'Good.' Sara hoped her face would convey how much the night had meant to her.

A cough alerted Sara that Anne was back in the kitchen.

Ryan sprang to his feet.

'Kids on the bus were saying our neighbours might get kicked out,' said Anne.

Sara cleared her throat. 'Really, why?'

Anne sighed in a way that indicated she was stating facts rather than her concern. 'Lillian keeps complaining about the power going out. Then said she'd been locked in. Said that someone chained up her front gate for twenty-four hours. They reckon she's just trying to avoid paying rent.' Anne rubbed her nose with the heel of her hand. 'I heard she's been cleaning people's houses.'

Sara remembered the chain she'd seen on their gate. 'Isn't she a bookkeeper?' she said. 'Maybe they're struggling.'

Anne shrugged. 'Shouldn't have moved here, if she can't handle it.'

Sara knew Lillian's mother was in an aged-care home in Milton. 'That's mean, Anne.'

Ryan caught her eye and smiled. Her horizon filled with him.

'It's weird she hasn't got a bloke.' Anne buttered her toast, put it on a plate and licked her fingers. 'If she went out, she could take her pick.' She glanced up.

Ryan looked at the floor.

Anne's eyes narrowed, then widened. Her cheek moved as though she'd clenched her teeth. 'Ryan,' she said, 'everything okay?'

Ryan nodded and frowned. 'Sure.' His brow went up as he bit his lips together. He stared at the door for a moment and then surged towards it. 'I'd better get going.'

Anne double blinked. Her eyes followed Ryan out. After the door had closed, she strode over to Sara and leant close. 'What the hell's going on?' she said in an angry whisper.

Mum rattled around the drawers, pulling out cutlery and plates.

'None of your business,' said Sara.

Anne grabbed her wrist. 'Not Ryan!' She squeezed hard.

'Don't!' Sara yanked her hand away.

'Don't be selfish! What if Dad finds out?' Anne sounded a bit desperate.

'Leave me alone.'

Sara folded her arms as she stared at the carpet.

Anne sighed hard and walked off. The bedroom door slammed.

Sara got up and leant two handed on the windowsill. A motorbike kicked to life, engine sudden and then gradually distant. Outside, the garden was dull and damp, the sky cold grey. Movement caught Sara's eye from the kitchen. Mum was staring intently at two cups. Sara walked over. 'Mum?'

Slight frown on her face, Mum was looking from a squat mug patterned with blue irises, to a tall yellow cup. She picked one up, looked over at the dining table, then put it down. She picked up the other.

Sara rubbed her eyes. 'What are you doing?'

'Hm?' Mum's eyebrows went up, and on came her slight, automatic smile as though tripped by an internal sensor.

Sara touched her arm. 'He likes both.'

Mum's eyes focused, and then her face fell. Mum had two levels, the auto smiling and the real one. This was the real one. The one Sara had heard quietly sobbing. 'I know. It's silly. Silly me.'

'What is? That you keep trying to get it right? I think he does it on purpose.' Sara heard and hated herself. She wondered how she could be so bold, to say it out loud, to mess with the order of things.

Mum frowned hard. 'Hm?'

'Dad changes his mind, so you always get it wrong.'

Rapidly, Mum put down the cup and cradled her elbows.

Scared to break the fragile thing that kept Mum in one piece, Sara opened her arms.

Mum was crying before Sara had pulled her into her chest. She hardened herself so Mum had something to hold on to.

After a minute, Mum drew back, wiped her face with her hands and tidied her clothes.

Sara's heart clenched. 'Mum, it's okay if you leave.'

It sat there between them like a suspended rock.

Sara couldn't believe she'd said it.

Mum shook her head hard and fast, turned away and then filled the kettle with water, set it over the hob and lit it. She turned on the tap and squirted detergent into the sink.

Sara bit her lip. 'I have an idea.'

'Hm?'

'Let's put out both cups and let him decide.'

'What do you mean?' In the dishwater, Mum's hands stilled.

'He waits to see which cup you give him and then says it's wrong because it's got too many flowers or it's too blue, or not big enough, even if it was perfect yesterday. So, put both out. See what happens.'

Mum wiped her hands on a dish towel and nodded. 'Right,' she said, closing her eyes for a moment. 'Right.'

Sara watched her mum put out three cups then shrug and grimace at Sara like she was a little girl.

The sound of the ute bleached Mum's expression. Her hands shook as she lit the flame beneath a frying pan. Moving as though to avoid breakage, she added eggs and then bacon to the pan.

'It'll be okay,' said Sara. She leaned in the doorway.

Dad walked in. 'Where's Robbie?' he said gruffly.

Sara withdrew slightly.

'Hm?' Mum replied, hovering near the dining table.

'Probably still in bed.' Dad cleared his throat noisily and sat at the table. The three mugs were in a line in his place. His head turned one way and then the other. 'Why are all the cups out, Ellen?'

Mum paused. 'So that you can choose which one you want.'

'Don't be bloody ridiculous.' He flapped his hand at the cups.

Mum reached to take one.

Dad's brow rose.

Mum retracted her hand.

He struck his lap with both fists. 'For God's sake, woman! They're cups!'

Mum stared at him.

'Well?'

'Don't—' Mum's shoulders lifted and then sank.

'Don't what?'

Sara shrank further back, guilty she'd encouraged her mum to rock the boat.

'Len ...' Mum's tone was even. 'I don't like it when you call me *woman.*'

Sara couldn't hear anything. She peered in.

Dad had closed his eyes and pulled his lips back from his teeth. 'My deepest and most sincere apologies, Ellen. Am I going to get my breakfast, or do I have to wait until Christmas?'

Mum turned for the kitchen and Sara saw her eyes had softened and glazed over. Slowly, she walked to the stovetop. 'I'll get breakfast,' she said quietly, 'but Ellen isn't my proper name either.'

Sara pressed her hand over her mouth, wrapped the other arm around her ribs and held on hard. She listened, cheek to doorframe as the minutes ticked by. She heard the tea being poured, cutlery scraping a plate, a throat cleared. Robbie yawning and scraping a chair as he pulled it out. Ryan joining them. More bacon and eggs bubbled in the frying pan.

'Late night, Robbie?' Dad said in a tone that put Sara on alert.

'Ah, no,' Robbie replied as though he hadn't noticed. 'Just tired.'

Dad commented on something, and Mum replied.

Talk rolled along.

Sara realised that Mum had held her ground, possibly for the first time. She walked out and sat across the table from Ryan as she listened for the bus. Dad kept casting looks at Robbie, which Sara couldn't read.

Anne walked out with her bag on her back. 'C'mon, you two. Bus is nearly here.'

Robbie groaned and jumped up from the table.

Sara smirked at Ryan as she slung her bag onto her

shoulder and headed out the door. With Dad there, she understood when he didn't return her smile.

## Chapter 20

### Monday – 18 days before Alec's death

Ryan's car was still at the Workers', but he wasn't there after the bus dropped Sara home. Sara changed out of her uniform and then killed time by refurbishing the hens' nests with fresh straw. The blood from Dad's week-old rat massacre was still splattered on the water tank next to the coop. Sara heard Ryan's car leaving just as she reached the house. She hurried inside, and then she heard Anne's bedroom door click.

Sara knocked and let herself in.

Anne gave her a resentful look from where she sat in the middle of the bed with her legs crossed.

'Has Ryan gone home?' Sara asked.

'M-hm.'

A lump grew in Sara's throat. 'What the hell did you say to him, Anne?' Her fingers dug into her hips.

Anne shook her head. 'He had to get back.' She gave Sara a look. 'I asked him if anything was going on.'

'What did he say?' Sara got closer.

'He told me it was none of my business. Which means there is.' She looked up at Sara. 'So don't be an idiot, Sara. We all have to live here.'

'You said you didn't like him.'

'It's not that ... jeez.' Anne squeezed her eyes shut for a moment. 'It's Dad.'

Sara swallowed.

Anne held up one hand. 'Look, I don't really want to know. As long as it doesn't happen again.'

Sara chewed the inside of her lip. She looked outside, half-expecting to see the Escort.

'He said he'd call later.' Anne rolled onto her stomach and pulled a textbook closer. 'I need to study.'

Sara couldn't do anything except walk down and check that Ryan really had left. She went for a run, arcing back towards the Workers' several times in case he showed up again. But his belongings were gone, and the place was locked. Sara didn't want to clean up until she was sure, as though starting the clean had the power to influence his return. She unlocked the house once the sky had darkened. Inside, she checked the bed, crawling in on her knees, but Ryan had stripped off the sheets. Sara found them in the washing machine. They were damp when she pulled them out and fed them into the dryer. As the heat came out and the sheets flopped around in circles, she leant back against the machine and wondered if her blood had been on them.

Ryan phoned after dinner. Sara ran into the kitchen, but Anne was already there. Sara bounced on her toes.

Anne held up her hand in front of Sara, made small, agreeable noises and then sighed. 'She's right here.'

Sara grabbed the phone.

Anne dropped her gaze and patted Sara's back.

Sara shook her off. 'Ryan?'

'Sara, I'm sorry. Last night should never have happened. It's my fault. I'm really sorry. I'm not going to come down for a bit.'

His voice, though deep and sweet and familiar, was saying all the wrong things.

'Please don't do this, Ryan,' Sara pleaded, voice stuck to the back of her throat.

'I'm really sorry,' said Ryan thickly. 'I don't know what I was thinking. I never want to hurt you or your family.'

'How long?' Sara almost choked on her words. 'Till you come back?'

'A while.' He sighed. 'I'm sorry.'

Sara listened to his goodbye and put down the phone, tears streaming down her face.

Hours became days. Food burnt Sara's belly. She cried on and off and listened to loud music to stifle the sobs. She became angry about crying.

She once got hayfever for a month when the pines' thick yellow pollen coated everything, including the inside of her eyelids. Without pollen to blame, she still watered and sniffled as though toxic piles of it were sweeping across the hardest, cruellest earth.

She wondered how anyone had survived heartbreak, how they continued to walk through the agony and not lay down and die.

Robbie told them he'd sold his motorbike and explained that he was saving for a car. Dad seemed unworried and commented it had been a bloody waste of petrol anyway.

When Sara went running, she glanced across at the

Stynes' front gate. She could see no chain. She'd heard nothing more about their possible eviction. She turned right and ran further into the property, thoughts of Lillian or Alec's troubles disappearing beneath her own waves of pain.

## Chapter 21

### Saturday – 13 days before Alec's death

Dad was eating breakfast at the table in stony silence. He'd stayed in again the previous night.

Sara heard a car come up the drive. She raced to the window.

Instead of the blue Escort, a sporty yellow Torana with a black hood scoop and rear spoiler was parked at the garden gate. Its engine rumbled quietly. Sara slumped. It would be one of Anne's friends. The Torana was the same type which had been driven to victory multiple times during a local touring car race on nearby Mount Tumulus. Dad liked to watch the race every year on TV rather than at the track, because the annual racing crowds descended on Parkwood like drunk seagulls.

The car was parked so the passenger-side door was right next to the gate.

Sara walked out into the kitchen just as Dad, sitting alone in his dining chair, stretched up and peered through the window.

Anne rushed from her bedroom, a cardigan in one hand, shoes in the other.

Dad stood slowly, knuckles on the table. 'Who the hell's that?' He looked Anne over.

'A friend.' Anne bent down to pull her Doc Martens on. She straightened and threaded her arms into a bright-yellow cardigan.

Dad's chin pulled in like a rooster swallowing something too big. 'Where the hell do you think you're going?'

'Town. Mum said it was okay.'

Dad's head swivelled. 'Ellen! Come out here.' Despite Mum's stand, he still hadn't called her by her real name.

Mum rushed in, stopped, and clasped her hands. 'Yes, Len?' Her eyes swept around, saw Anne and then looked towards the window as an engine revved.

The compact muscle car hovered like a sleek metal pod of masculinity.

Mum's cheeks paled, and her lips moved like she was praying. 'She just said she was going with friends. She's finished her homework.'

Anne had stilled and was staring at Dad with an unusually intense gaze.

A car horn beeped, an unmistakable, unmissable demand.

Sara, Robbie, Mum and Anne all exchanged glances as though to confirm what they'd heard. Sara peered out. The driver had a man's profile, his head touching the roof. She imagined a blind, stupid, neanderthal oaf. He hadn't got out, sought the man of the house, kowtowed, or even offered to shake Dad's hand.

Instead, he had demanded Len Hamilton's daughter, loudly, unapologetically into his metal cave with a big, bone-jarring hoot. Sara thought he couldn't possibly have been local. Or sane.

Dad's chest lifted, the back of his neck stiffened, and he walked slowly outside.

Sara crowded at the open front door with Mum, Anne and Robbie.

Dad swelled as he swaggered down the path. When he got to the Torana, he grabbed the passenger window frame and stuck his head in the car. Sara imagined Dad pulling himself inside, headbutting, and then driving his boot into the guy.

Dad withdrew his head and threw an arm towards the front gate. 'Get out! I'll get the gun if you show your face again!'

Sara backed into the house.

The car revved, and then accelerated down the driveway.

A huge Len Hamilton explosion followed. A bad one. Three-hour shouting match: Dad, Anne, Dad, Anne. Anne had her hands balled into fists at her sides. Dad slapped her hard on the face and Anne stopped answering back. The loud, sharp sound of palm to skin was a full stop. Dad had been pushed too far. He was the ruler of his kingdom. They'd been warned.

Silence followed briefly, and then Dad started yelling again.

From her bedroom, Sara prayed Anne would say, 'yes, Dad' because Dad never stopped until they did.

Anne didn't say it.

Dad kept shouting. An hour of noise became two hours.

Sara, Mum and Robbie began to move around the house, ducking their heads as they passed Dad and Anne. Sara was hungry and put bread into the toaster. Robbie joined her.

'Are you really saving for a car?' Sara whispered.

Robbie looked sideways at her and then shrugged. 'Sorted that thing I told you about.' He cast a quick glance at Dad. Sara elbowed him, hoping he'd tell her what was going on.

Robbie seemed to understand and shook his head. 'Doesn't matter,' he said, and then smiled tightly as he walked away.

Near the dining table, Dad shouted new rules in his yar-yar voice. Sara could see Anne wasn't listening, even though she stood right there in front of him. Since the slap, Anne had closed lips and looking-away eyes that slid over things. Initially angry with Anne, Sara began to feel sympathetic.

The morning became midday. Dad had to release Anne on bail despite not hearing the magic 'yes, Dad'. He had begun looking around like he wanted Mum. He was probably hungry.

## Chapter 22

### In the second last week before Alec's death

In the following days, Dad looked hard and accusing as his eyes tracked Anne whenever she moved around the house. He crashed around in the morning and complained that he hadn't slept a wink. At the dinner table, he choked on his food.

When they got home from school, Dad started yelling before Anne was fully through the door. He hollered that she'd dumped her bag in a way that showed temper and insolence. His arguments went from explaining to Anne that her innocence needed to be preserved ... to his certainty she was already a whore.

Anne's gaze floated, glazed and passive. Sara was fascinated by the slight upturn of her sister's mouth and her peaceful, unmarkable dignity. She realised that at some point during all the yelling, Anne had completely stopped speaking.

At one stage, Dad resorted to religion.

Anne's eyes followed a bird outside the window.

Sara became irritated by the incessant noise and wished Anne would do something to bring it to an end.

After school, Sara and Robbie quickly changed into outdoor clothes, ate and left the house as soon as possible. While Robbie strode off with sketchpad and pencils in his hand, Sara wandered around, doing chores and filling the wheelbarrow with firewood. When she'd run out of things to do, she sat at Dad's wooden tool bench and picked at the splinters. Her yearning for Ryan was as bad as a throbbing tooth abscess. She wondered what it would be like to have a tooth pulled out using pliers, as if they lived in the old days. Sara found Dad's needle-nosed pliers. They lay beside a long-handled tool with metal cutters that were in the shape of a fish beak.

*Bolt cutters*, she thought as she remembered Robbie being unable to name the tools while Dad shouted at him. She lifted the cutters two handed, surprised by the weight. She opened and closed the end by levering the handles. A shiny mark on the blade indicated recent use. Sara noted Dad's heavy metal chain on the end of the bench. It was used to fashion gate closers, or to extend the tow rope if needed for a bogged vehicle. Sara pulled the end of the chain closer. A piece came away from the main pile with a clunk. A lock was attached to the end. It was large and solid. Sara swallowed. She was sure she'd seen it before. It looked exactly like the one she'd seen on the Stynes' gate.

Sara felt her muscles pull tight across her chest. She might have been the only other person to have seen it. Why was it here in Dad's shed?

'Sara!' Mum's voice came from the house. 'Dinner!' Sara replaced the chain so it looked undisturbed. She hurried out, filled with the sudden need to be away from it.

Sara sat quietly in her room and reasoned Dad had always kept hardware like chains and locks. She knew she was letting herself off the hook, but also she knew she didn't have the power to change anything. Her voice wasn't as loud as Dad's, and she had no right to make things worse for the family. Anne had done that already.

All week, Dad had imposed tighter restrictions, which included timed showers and a ban on phone use and outings. With her lifted cheeks and glowing, secret eyes, any connection Anne once had to Dad seemed severed. Like a chain with bolt cutters.

One night, Dad had ordered Anne to be locked in her room without food. Anne locked the door herself.

Dad eventually gave up on her and confronted Mum. He yelled that Anne's behaviour was her fault.

Mum stood there with wide rabbit eyes and rounded shoulders. She cast looks at Anne and swallowed as if there were hot coals in her throat. The fingers of her right hand rolled her wedding band round and round her ring finger.

Each year, Sara felt she'd watched her mum shrink slowly. As Dad announced everyone guilty until proven innocent, Mum drew closer to the ground. Sara thought that if a hole opened up, Mum would gratefully disappear into it. After being yelled at for hours, Mum looked as though dignity, vertebrae and fear were all that kept her upright. Watching the contactless battering of her mum, Sara felt like a butterfly staked to a display board, unable to turn away or intervene.

She often hugged Mum afterwards, but it was just sweeping glass after it had been broken.

Sara also hated the fact that, unlike them, Mum's torment didn't end at bedtime. Dad whispered anger late into the night, and then came the heavy breathing. *Marital bliss.* Sara's feelings for her mum swung between desperate frustration to aching love. Sara hoped whatever glue held Mum together would be strong enough to last until she could make her escape.

That week, Anne didn't speak or go out, except to school. At night, she sat at the dinner table in front of an untouched plate of food, eyes on the opposite wall. Robbie glared until Dad noticed him, and then his eyes slid away as if Dad was unclean.

One night, after everyone had gone to bed, Sara got up to the bathroom and saw Anne with a pile of toast on a plate. They stared at each other, two foxes crossing paths in the dark. Anne glided into her bedroom and closed the door.

## Chapter 23

### Saturday – One week before Alec's death

In a house prickly with triggers, Sara felt a shift and unnatural stillness that reminded her of a previous wintry night in which clouds had thickened and cast a strange, greenish light. A massive thunderclap had come next. The ensuing storm had felled numerous drought-stunted trees that blocked tracks and roads, their muddied roots in undignified surrender.

Sara waited for the thunderclap, almost willed it in, so it could be over with.

Dad went out to the pub that Friday night but came home early again. Sara was glad they'd been too weary and jumpy to have one of their special nights.

Sara looked for Alec but didn't see him arrive and knew it would be at least another week before she could talk to him. She hoped that the Stynes wouldn't be evicted from their house. If nothing else, she would miss Alec's colourful jacket.

Now Saturday evening, Sara was helping Mum in the

kitchen. Robbie had picked up the phone and stretched the cord as long as it would go, and he was just outside the room.

'Yeah, hi, it's me,' Sara heard him say in a low voice. 'I just wanted to say good luck.'

Dad walked in wearing work gear, put his hands on his hips and yelled at the TV about the scourge on society and morality, seemingly rejuvenated after a full day of slashing saffron thistles with the tractor.

Robbie placed the phone down in its usual location and turned to walk out of the room.

'Who was that?' Dad called out.

Robbie slowed. 'Just a friend.' He turned and looked at Dad.

There was something different about Robbie's face, a new set to his jaw and darkness in his eyes. Sara caught her brother's eye. He dipped his head, turned and left the room.

Dad narrowed his eyes at Robbie's back, then strode off to the bathroom. Sounds of the shower came through the wall.

Sara turned down the flame as she watched the tight bubbles form beneath the water in a saucepan on the stovetop. At the cutting board, she exchanged a tense look with Mum and then sliced up some beans and carrots that Mum had put there.

In the last few weeks, the news had stated the number of people contracting AIDS was rising steadily, and infections were yet to reach a peak. A treatment called AZT was discussed on talkback radio and current affairs programs.

Safe-sex messages and info ads were played between TV shows. The ads advised that anyone could catch AIDS: women, children, haemophiliacs. During a debate at school, a boy announced that if he was smashed up in a car accident, he'd rather die than have a blood transfusion. Someone blew a dozen condoms up like balloons and left them on the wet grass of the school oval. Sara vowed never to use a public toilet when she heard that AIDS could be contracted from the seat.

Like black nets, Dad often threw out opinions which justified gay bashing. He said it was what civilized society had been forced to do. Citizens had every right to keep the place clean. To weed out the evil. Sara knew from talk at school that he wasn't the only one who felt that way.

Dad emerged from the shower in clean jeans and a jumper, hair combed, small water droplets sliding down the nape of his neck.

Robbie had sat down in front of the TV.

Dad walked into the lounge. 'What's on?'

'Current affairs.'

Dad grunted, took the remote control and sat in his chair. 'Ellen, beer.' He frowned at the screen as Mum placed a beer in his hand. His voice dropped low. 'Is this about the bloody homos?'

'It's about a treatment for AIDS,' said Robbie.

Dad sucked a big breath. 'Bloody poofters! Should be locked away, rounded up and killed off!' His ensuing diatribe included the usual: beat the poofters; they were all paedos, dirty, disgusting ... blah blah blah.

It was the strangest thing, Robbie staying there, hands tucked beneath his legs.

Then he spoke quietly. 'No one deserves AIDS.'

Mum froze.

Dad seemed unable to exhale, his mouth open. The pause was as grotesque as the seconds between a pulled grenade pin and the explosion. 'What did you say?' Dad's face was blotchy. His body had a stiff, dangerous look.

Robbie's jaw moved inside his cheek, but his face remained angled towards the screen.

Dad jumped to his feet and started yelling. He marched over to Robbie and hauled him up by the collar.

Robbie first cowered away, and then suddenly, he was on his feet and overbalanced.

Dad shook him, which straightened him up. 'You come outside! Show me you're not one of those disgusting poofters! So help me, I'll knock your bloody head off!'

Robbie's arms, down by his sides, swayed heavy and wooden.

Sara's blood caught fire. 'Leave Robbie alone! He's not gay!' The words came out so fast, she grabbed the bench to steady herself.

Slowly, Dad's head turned – blue eyes hard as flint. Every second of time crystallised. 'Keep out of it, girl,' he said in his low, dangerous voice. '*My* son will not speak to me like that!' He dragged Robbie along and then marched him out through the laundry.

The door slammed.

Mum walked as if over glass, stood opposite the laundry door, a cloth in her hands.

Anne emerged from her room and stood beside Mum.

Sara heard Dad's shouting as it became staggered. With each pause, another sound. An *oof* sound.

Mum dropped the cloth.

After a few minutes, Robbie came in, blood oozing from both nostrils.

Mum lurched forwards. Robbie swatted, face turned away, walked into his room and slammed the door.

Mum's eyes followed Dad as he walked past her and

grabbed a six pack of beer from the fridge and walked back out. After the door smacked shut, an engine flared, and tyres spun on dirt as the ute headed down the lane into the property.

Sara shivered, suddenly cold, as if the house had slipped inside a cloud.

No one moved.

Anne suddenly took a long breath, exhaled carefully and then knocked quietly on Robbie's door. 'Just me,' she said.

Mum stepped forwards, but Anne shook her head, let herself through the door and closed it behind her.

Sara imagined Dad on a hill swigging beer as he scanned his kingdom, convincing himself he was justified. His family, like disciples, must agree with him.

Mum floated into the kitchen; a space traveller who'd let go of the mothership. She looked around at the new planet, her hands fluttered like they were remembering patterns they should follow, but then they settled at her sides. After a moment, she walked out.

Sara felt as if the world had dropped away. She knew Mum couldn't bind them anymore. The violence had broken something irreparably.

Finally, Sara went to her room and crawled into bed. She heard the scrape of a chair in the kitchen, which must've been Anne. The first aid box was kept in a cupboard over the stove. Sara was glad her sister knew what to do.

On Sunday morning, everyone emerged from their rooms like scared rabbits sniffing the air for danger. Robbie, stonily silent, had indigo smudges below both eyes and a black crust lining his nostrils. Anne and Mum were red-eyed. Mum didn't make happy, pretend conversation or smile her way over the wounds. For once, Sara wished she would.

At dinner, Robbie sat behind his untouched plate. Dad, at the head of the table as always, chomped into his braised lamb chops. Sara hated the crack and crunch of gristle, the way Dad turned the bones in his greasy fingers and his lips pulled back off his teeth.

Outside the window, beyond the silent pine, bruised sky turned to black.

No one spoke.

Mum offered everyone plates automatically. As Sara watched, she thought of a living cadaver.

That night, when Dad finished, they all got up. The evening routine emerged as though it was choreographed. They scraped their plates into the chook bucket, fed the dogs and washed the dishes.

A day passed. Then another.

Despite the terrible thing that had happened, nothing more was said.

## Chapter 24

### Wednesday – Two days before Alec's death

Sara returned from collecting the chicken eggs and closed the laundry door behind her. Toe to heel, she pulled off her boots.

'I know, but I can't wait—' Anne said, a whine in her voice.

Sara paused, one boot half-off.

'You don't know what it's like.' Sara heard Anne sniffle.

It had been three days since Dad had done the unthinkable. Robbie's bruises had developed a deep-purplish hue.

There seemed no guidelines about what should follow.

Sara hovered, shoulder to doorframe. *Maybe Anne knows what to do.*

After a pause, Anne's breath shuddered. 'Yes, I'll work it out once I'm out of here.'

*Out of here?* Sara knew Anne had friends who had moved away from home, but she wouldn't go. Would she?

'I know. Yep, that's the best. Seven, to be safe.' Hope had returned to Anne's tone. 'Hang on. Quiet.'

Sara held her breath.

'I think someone's here. Better go, bye.'

The phone holder clicked.

Sara went to the outside door, opened and closed it loudly, and then shuffled her boots against the wall. She walked in.

Anne was coming towards her, eyes down, nose shiny and red.

Sara held the bucket of chicken eggs against her belly. 'Anne, are you okay?'

Anne nodded, walked around Sara to her room. 'Yep.'

'Anne?'

Anne stopped.

Sara floundered for the right words. 'Um, have you applied for university?'

'Still haven't decided.' Anne half-turned towards Sara, seemed to change her mind, and walked into her room.

'Don't leave us,' said Sara.

Anne held the door partway open. She turned and peered through the gap, her face younger and more fragile than Sara could remember. 'Sara.' She took a long breath. 'We'll all leave sometime. I'm nearly through school.'

A big lump in Sara's chest worked its way up to her throat. 'But …' She stopped because she knew it was silly to argue. Anne had been going for a while, long before she stopped speaking to their dad. 'Nothing.' Sara shook her head to release her sister.

Anne gazed at her a moment longer, withdrew and closed the door. But not before Sara saw apology in her eyes.

Sara got her stereo, Mum's sewing scissors and a picture of Madonna she'd cut out of a magazine. She took them to the bathroom and plugged in the stereo. She sticky taped the picture to the mirror and shut the door. With ACDC's

'Thunderstruck' playing on high volume, Sara examined Madonna's short platinum-blond hair. Apparently Madonna meant to imitate Marylin Monroe's style from the movie *Seven Year Itch*. Sara could imagine how much better her life would be if she looked like Madonna. All she needed was a drastic haircut and some good peroxide. The change might help stop her thinking, and shift the desperate ache that was more than just about Ryan. She wished she was someone else.

With Mum's scissors, Sara began to snip faster and faster, so she didn't lose the courage. Every snip felt shocking, and the more she cut, the more she looked like a prisoner of war from pictures she'd seen.

'Shit, Sara!'

Sara jumped.

Anne stood at the open door, still holding the handle. Anne's eyes were wide, other hand over her mouth. Her gaze travelled down to the floor.

Sara's hair lay in an arc around her feet.

Anne turned off the stereo and then approached slowly, as if to a crime scene. 'What did you do?' She reached out and touched the ends of Sara's chopped hair.

'I needed a change.' Sara could feel her hands shaking, her breaths short and fast.

Outside the window came the sharp whine of Dad's circular saw – loud then low, loud then low.

'God, I hate this place!' Sara yelled. She grabbed another wad of her hair and lifted the scissors.

'No!' Anne grabbed Sara's wrist and lowered her arm like the scissors were a weapon. 'Stop it. You're making a terrible mess. Why didn't you at least ask me to help ... or go to the hairdressers?' She pointed at the picture stuck to the glass.

'Madonna has a special cut, not a freaking hacksaw job. Probably cost a hundred dollars.'

Sara ripped the picture off the mirror, scrunched it up and tossed it onto the floor.

Anne watched as the picture partly opened up. She reached over and touched Sara gently. 'It's for the best.'

'What the fuck are you talking about?' Sara said roughly, throwing her arm up.

'I'm sorry. I know how much you liked Ryan,' said Anne.

Sara turned away and supported herself on the sink. 'It's not just that,' she said through her teeth. 'It's fucking everything. Just go away.'

Anne didn't leave. When she did go, she returned with a brush and shovel. She knelt and began to sweep up the hair.

'Leave it,' said Sara.

Anne kept brushing until it was all gone.

At dinner, Dad was yelling a new tune. Mum had done the grocery shopping that afternoon. 'I hate bloody Vic Bitter!' he shouted. 'Tastes like camel's piss!'

Sara wondered how Dad knew the precise taste of camel urine, considering he'd almost certainly never drunk it.

'They were all out of Fosters, Len,' Mum said soothingly.

Later, Sara got out a pen and writing pad and sat at her desk. Her hand was shaking. She couldn't remember when she'd last eaten. She wrote *Alec* on the front of the envelope and again at the top of a piece of note paper. She explained that her family were not bad people, but their dad was very strict, and it was better if he didn't come to the house.

Sara stopped and winced when she thought of Robbie's face. She didn't want to say what Dad had done. If he knew the truth, Alec might not want anything to do with her.

*I'd like to talk. I think you're very talented, and I'm sorry I've never spoken to you.*

*It would be great to be friends. Can we meet up? Maybe halfway between my house and yours. I know you come on weekends. I'll keep an eye out for you. If you get this letter and don't want to, I'll understand. Just don't come to our house.*

Sara stared at the white beneath the writing. She signed her name.

## Chapter 25

**Friday – Alec's last day**

The light was falling when Sara walked out to the old highway with Alec's note in her pocket. At school, the other girls had talked about their weekend sport, parties, part-time jobs, and boyfriends. Friday chatter was lighter and happier than other weekdays, and Sara listened to them, enviously.

She saw Alec's colourful coat, about a hundred metres ahead. The edges flapped as he jogged towards the forest.

Sara looked around. She was alone. Cold wind buffeted against her. If Alec wanted to beat the weather and the dark, he'd have to hurry. She patted her pocket and felt happy for the first time in weeks. She imagined catching Alec's attention as he made his way back. How they would be friends right away. He'd notice her hair. Mum had tidied it up so it looked a bit better. Maybe, she'd tell him about Ryan. He would be a good person to tell all her secrets. And, given the chance, she would keep all his.

Ahead of her, Alec moved fast, glancing right towards their property. She wondered if Robbie had told him he'd sold his motorbike. It must be Robbie whom Alec was looking for.

Sara stopped as Alec reached the edge of the forest, turned a sharp right and disappeared into the trees.

That afternoon, Robbie had looked pale as they'd walked up the driveway together. He said he'd explained his bruised face by lying about an accident with a cricket ball. Since they'd arrived home, he hadn't come out of his room.

Sara huddled deeper into her coat and shivered. The sky was the same solid grey it went before sleet, which meant freezing winds sharpened raindrops into tiny daggers. Sleet drove people indoors and animals into huddles to protect their faces.

A low rumbling came from the west, but the storm was still a way off. Wind whipped up and pushed the grass sideways. On a low branch nearby, three robins perched wing to wing, a trio of ruffle-feathered balls.

Sara, opposite Alec's drive, checked both ways and then ran across. The wind chilled her scalp as she put her note into his letterbox. Her heart pounded with the adrenaline of her trespass. She turned. Alec was still out of sight. She hurried back home.

Up at the machinery shed, Dad's ute was parked, ghostlike in the usual spot. Dusk had become evening.

Sara entered the house, puffing and fizzy with rebellion. As she stood in the laundry, a sound caught her attention. She stayed very still. She could make out groaning and urgent talk that came from the back of the house.

She removed her shoes and ran through Anne's open door.

Anne looked up from where she sat on the edge of her bed.

She was pale with dark smudges beneath her eyes. 'Robbie's really, really sick,' she said.

Sara noticed Anne's school bag bulging with clothes, the zip undone.

'Where are you going?' Sara asked.

Anne shook her head.

Sara rushed out of the room and towards the groaning and retching. Yeasty, sour and rotten smells hit her. She clamped her hand over her mouth and nose.

The outer door from the back patio slammed.

Dad filled the doorway. He was wearing dirty work jeans and an old, collared shirt rolled up above his elbows. His face was red. 'For God's sake, stop it! The bloody toilet's blocked!'

Through the bathroom door was Mum, sleeves rolled up, wet flannel in her hand. She moved a towel with her feet. Over the toilet bowl, Robbie's bare torso was draped like a flayed slave. There was an old bruise below his ribs. The back of his underpants was wet, and his jeans were in a pile next to him.

'He can't, Len.' Tendons stood out down the side of Mum's neck. 'He must have gastro. Or food poisoning.'

'Get him out of here!' Dad exploded. Mum flinched. 'Take him to the goddam hospital!' His big arm swung up. 'I'll have to open the sewerage tank to fix this mess!'

Dad shoved the back door wide open and strode out. It slammed behind him.

Blank-faced, Anne appeared behind Sara. 'I'll drive,' she said.

Sara and Mum helped Robbie to the car, where he crawled into the backseat. Mum put a bucket in the leg space and handed Sara a towel. Sara spread it over the seat, and Robbie lay his head on it. Sara pinched her nostrils together.

Anne started the car and drove to the edge of the road, indicator ticking gently. Dark skies sprayed rain onto the windshield. Anne checked the highway for cars for a long time. There were no streetlights this far from town. Sara was sure she saw Anne staring at the Workers' House. Finally, she accelerated towards Parkwood. Robbie heaved and grabbed the bucket, but nothing slopped into the bottom. He groaned, spat and lay his head down on the towel.

Slashes of rain swept through the beams of their headlights. Anne scowled, lips tight, body pulled towards the steering wheel. Mum gripped the seat next to her thigh, and the handle over the window. She glanced back at Robbie several times.

Parkwood Emergency Department was lit in storm-defying fluorescent.

Anne pulled the car up behind an ambulance near a set of double glass doors. Mum jumped out of the car and went in.

When she returned, she was accompanied by a nurse wearing a white smock and navy pants. Behind them came a small man wearing a blue uniform buttoned tight over his belly. He held onto the side of a stretcher bed on wheels, which was turning on an angle and rolling down the ramp.

The staff assisted Robbie out of the car and onto the bed. Once they were all inside, a nurse closed a curtain.

Sara stood on the outside with Anne.

'I'll show you the waiting room,' said a smaller, older nurse wearing glasses, which fish-bowled her eyes and reminded Sara of the alien in the movie *E.T.*

Sara and Anne were led to a small room with dark-green carpet, a table with magazines on it, and a small TV. They sat down on grey plastic chairs.

Outside the window, trees swayed, their leaves whipping.

A row of hedges convulsed.

A man in an overcoat holding a purple handbag shouted silently up at the sky, strips of grey hair stuck to his face like old bandaids.

A small, black-haired woman wearing a tracksuit, a headscarf and red lipstick came in, straightened the magazines on the table and wiped a blue rag along the windowsill. Sara noticed a small gold ring in her nostril. 'Storms stir up the crazies,' she said, indicating the man outside. 'They head for the lights, like moths.' She walked over and switched the TV channel, her large dark, kohl-lined eyes reflecting the glare as several upcoming shows were advertised: cooking, travel, something about the Queen. Sara thought she looked young to be a cleaner, and very beautiful, but noticed a shiny gold ring on her left ring finger. Her name badge said Mina.

Anne covered her eyes and tucked her legs beneath her bottom on the seat.

The news commenced. Seven pm. The opening trumpet piece was a drop of normality in the close yellow light.

Sara looked through the window for the man with the handbag. The sidewalk was empty. Her stomach growled.

A current affairs program filled another half-hour.

Mina came back in and switched channels. The movie *Footloose* started. She winked. 'One of my favourites.'

Sara realised the mole she'd seen beside Mina's lip was drawn on. 'Excuse me,' she said. 'Do you know where we can get some food?'

Mina nodded and quickly disappeared. She returned with biscuits in little plastic packets. She handed them to Sara. 'Don't tell anyone else,' she whispered.

Sara thanked her and offered two packets to Anne, but her

sister shook her head.

Mina pointed to a white door across the hall. 'You can get tea and coffee in there.'

'Great.' Sara got up and made two cups of tea. She carried them into the waiting room and handed one to Anne. Anne's face softened slightly as she accepted the cup. Together, they ate all the biscuits.

Kevin Bacon was on the TV screen in skin-tight jeans that showed the lump on one side of his crotch. Every dance song was incongruent with the fluorescent lights and the plastic squeak of the chairs and the sound of a child crying. Passing headlights caught and fractured rain drops on the window, creating tiny fairy lights. It reminded Sara of the shearing shed on the night of Ryan's eighteenth.

Sara wondered if her hair would've grown out by the time Ryan came back. She ran her hand over her head. After Mum had fixed the worst of it, Sara thought she looked like Kim Wilde or a tomboy. It didn't look too bad when she parted it to the side and tied one of Anne's scarves around her head.

She settled back and tried to watch the movie.

Next to her, Anne had finished her tea and put her cup on the table. She alternated between watching the movie, leafing through a coverless magazine, and pacing like a watchman.

Outside, the rain had stopped, but the wind gusts shook water off the leaves every now and again.

Sara thought about when she'd seen Alec earlier. Maybe he and Robbie had set up a meeting. She imagined Robbie going under a bright light, a scalpel cutting the white skin of his belly. The mauve bruise near his ribs. Sara decided that tomorrow she would go and knock on Alec's door. Cross the great divide, introduce herself and then tell him about

Robbie's operation. He must have found her letter by now.

When the movie was finished Mum came in, her skirt very creased. 'Robbie's gone into the operating room,' she said. 'I finally got your father.'

Once Robbie was settled on a ward, they were advised to return in the morning. Sara walked out into the icy night with Mum and Anne. Cold pushed down her collar and up her coat sleeves.

This time, Mum drove, while Anne slumped against the front passenger door, with her knees drawn up.

Sara woke suddenly when the car shuddered over the cattle grate at their front gate.

In the dark house, Sara heard her dad snoring.

## Chapter 26

**Saturday – June 1989**

The run down to the Workers' House, after Dad had told them they weren't allowed to help search for Alec, felt like the longest Sara could remember. From where she stood behind the gate, Sara's eyes were automatically drawn to the yellow vests. Most of them were in one place now, around the channel by the highway. The rest of the crowd stood at a respectful distance.

Minutes after she'd disappeared, Lillian was being helped to her feet. Sara could still feel the chill which Lillian's agonised cries had sent deep into her bones. The word 'found' had given Sara stupid hope for a few seconds. Because found was no longer lost. But the word was said so solemnly that Sara knew there would be no quick relief or celebration.

There'd been a flurry and then a stillness.

Alec was confirmed dead, his body found over a metre deep at the bottom of the channel. Sara couldn't possibly imagine how he'd ended up in there. She saw a flash of purple in the crowd and flinched reflexively, remembering Alec's coat as he ran, when she saw him yesterday.

Not far from where Sara watched, people stood close to each other with their shock and tragedy expressions, which softened and drew them closer, as if they'd been pummelled by a meat tenderizer.

Sara felt sick. She heard the sirens coming from a long way off and sensed their safe sounds converge with the yellow vests, like heroes coming to the rescue. She knew there would be no rescue. The reality Alec was dead repeatedly grabbed her attention if she was distracted, even for a second.

The group near the road became organised. The sirens turned off. Police, an ambulance and a fire truck emerged with lights flashing and wove through the crowd, which slowed the traffic. One by one, the vehicles' lights turned off.

Dazed, Sara watched people move orange cones and police direct traffic and tie black and yellow tape to things. Trucks groaned as they slowed and joined the queue.

Sara couldn't see anything but the back of people's coats near the channel. Lillian's red scarf had emerged briefly and then disappeared again.

Cold sun probed blankets of cloud. Everyone had fog in front of their mouths, even when they weren't talking. The top of Sara's ears tingled, and she pulled her beanie down. She put her hands over her cheeks and stamped her feet to fight the unsteadiness in her legs.

She began to hear people talking as they moved around with more purpose, though Sara was unsure what purpose, as they didn't seem to be doing anything. The word 'body' kept being added to Alec, like a surname. Sara wanted to get on the other side of the gate and shake someone. Tell them about Alec Stynes. He could sing, he was talented and brave. He wasn't 'Alec's body'. How could they so cruelly rename the boy in the colourful coat when yesterday he had been living and running and full of life?

By the time a stretcher was lowered into the channel inside a wall of blue canvas, Sara had heard bits of news like ash drifting from the sky, staining where it fell so it couldn't be washed off.

Alec's body had been found face down in a few inches of water. He was wearing a t-shirt, jeans and socks. He'd probably been killed in a car accident: a hit and run. There was other stuff Sara didn't want to hear, about his arms and legs being at the wrong angles, head misshapen like his skull was a broken eggshell, his fingernails purple. She hated everyone who repeated the Chinese whispers, and she wanted to scream, 'SHUT UP!' It wasn't fair when Alec was unable to defend himself, couldn't jump a gate or shake his coat like a matador.

Police in blue plastic coveralls slipped down beside the road. One held a camera up as if they didn't want it to get wet.

Eventually, a long bag on a stretcher was pushed into the back of an ambulance. The crowd collectively looked at their feet and shuffled into each other while the ambulance made a sombre path through.

Once the ambulance had left, Sara thought she'd choke on the frigid air. She jumped the gate to the old highway and sprinted back to her house.

Dirt crunched beneath her boots as Sara walked in.

Mum was in the kitchen. Her face showed that the news had already reached this far. 'I got a phone call. About Alec. Where have you been?'

'Alec's dead!' Sara clutched a handful of her jacket while she tried to undo the zip.

Mum closed her eyes.

Sara walked into her mum's chest. Mum overbalanced slightly and then wrapped Sara in a tight hug. Mum's mouth was near Sara's ear, and the kiss was loud, but Sara was grateful for it. Alec would never hear such a thing, and his mum could never do it.

'Oh God.' Mum breathed. 'That poor woman.'

'They're saying he got hit by a car.' Sara's voice had gone up high.

Mum hugged her tighter, and then she pulled off Sara's beanie and stroked the back of her head.

Over the next few hours, the piece of channel where Alec had been found became a big Petri dish. Sara didn't like people stomping all over it. At home, she couldn't think of anything but the incident, so she returned to her earlier vantage point with a blanket, thermos of hot tea and some food. She wasn't the only one. People offered each other steaming cups while police took samples, shone strong lights, crouched with their heads together. She imagined the hole being scraped raw behind the blue plastic. She desperately wanted to fill Alec's piece of channel with colourful flowers, so it seemed less naked and vulnerable.

By the time the crowds had thinned, and the cars drove away, it was dark. Sara couldn't imagine Alec as a pale, frozen body in a morgue. She hoped they put a blanket over him or at least dressed him in warm clothes.

That night, after calling out, "dinnertime" to Dad, who was in the shed cleaning the Hilux, Sara joined the rest of the family as they watched the news. Police gave the details of the place and approximate time of the alleged hit-and-run, and then Alec's dad, Peter, made an appeal.

He read from a sheet of paper.

*'Alec went for a walk to a nearby forest then returned and ate dinner with his mother. She believes he left the house at around ten pm after saying goodnight. He was hit as he crossed the highway.'*

Sara saw a woman who looked like Lillian behind Peter, but her face was on such a down-facing angle, she couldn't be sure.

*'Alec didn't have enemies and was a talented, friendly kid. He performed the lead role of Joseph in* Joseph and the Amazing Technicolor Dreamcoat *last weekend. His distinctive patchwork coat is missing, as is one of his shoes. Please, if you are the driver of the vehicle that hit Alec, or were in the vicinity between ten and midnight, or have seen these items, I urge you to come forwards. Thank you.'* He looked directly into the camera and seemed bewildered. The screen changed.

A number was shown. Then three photographs.

Sara's breath caught. In the first one, Alec was wearing his coloured coat. He was on stage, head tilted back, arm lifted towards the ceiling. It seemed that the whole morning had been a mistake, because there was Alec just as she remembered him. But then Alec's school photograph was shown like all the missing and murdered children always were. Next was a picture of Alec's shoes, clearly taken from a bigger shot that had been cropped and enlarged so that it was slightly out of focus.

That night, Dad sat at the head of the table, eating his steak.

Robbie was still in hospital because the doctor had told Mum he was in too much pain to be discharged.

Sara's belly gnawed, empty even after she'd eaten. 'Can I

have seconds, Mum?'

Dad glanced up, forked a big piece of potato into his mouth and chewed silently.

Anne pushed food around her plate. 'What if he stood on the road on purpose? Or wanted to leave home?'

Mum glanced at Dad before she said in a low voice, 'Apparently, Lillian said that Alec left his bag behind. Remember he was found without his jacket? She's sure he would've been wearing that.'

Suddenly, Sara remembered her letter. Her hands tingled. A cold thought slipped into the edge of her mind. Maybe Alec had got her letter. Maybe he'd decided to leave his house because of it.

'Can I have yours?' Sara asked Anne. 'If you're not going to eat it?'

Anne shrugged and lifted her arm to allow Sara to pull the plate away. Sara's hands shook as she cut potato in smaller and smaller pieces, but none seemed small enough to fit down her throat. She placed the cutlery neatly on the edge of the plate.

'It was a special jacket,' said Mum. 'His multicoloured dreamcoat from his school play. Apparently, he wore it all the time.'

'Not at the dinner table.' Dad's eyes were on his meal, his usual fire gone. Even though the room was barely warm enough to stop Sara shivering, there was a single drop of sweat silvered on Dad's temple.

Sara stared outside at the shape of the giant tree. Mum was right. It did lean towards the house. It felt even closer when it was dark. She felt uneasy and was grateful that Dad had stopped them talking about Alec.

## Chapter 27

**A few days later**

Over the next few days, the police visited twice.

One of the officers who came was a red-faced man with a rash on his neck. He had grey eyes and white crusts in his mouth corners and his badge said DC Michael Thoroughgood. He invited them to call him Michael.

The other officer was a young woman who said very little.

'We've been asked to assist local police to help determine what happened on Friday night,' said Michael. 'Our investigative team have examined the scene for evidence. Unless anything suspicious is found, the case will be handled by Traffic Division. We're just asking locals a few questions. We want to know if anyone saw anything. Alec's time of death was between ten pm and midnight.' He flinched a smile. 'No one is in trouble.'

Sara sat at the dining table with the police officers. Dad sat directly across from her. He'd done the same with Anne because they were under eighteen and needed an adult present. Anne said she'd never seen Alec and wasn't at home the night he died. Mum said something similar but expressed her devastation for Lillian. Mum's normal look, which clung to her as firmly as stockings, was nervous and guilty, so Sara was glad when she finished and went outside.

'Sara,' said Michael. 'Did you see Alec Stynes at any time the Friday afternoon or evening he died?'

Sara nodded. 'It was still light. He was going for a jog between our boundary and the highway heading towards the city.'

'Sydney? So, east?'

'Yes. It was his usual route. Then he'd turn right down the firebreak of our boundary near the forest there.' She indicated the direction. 'I used to walk that way sometimes. I saw him practising for a play once.' She tucked her hands under her legs.

'Was he alone?'

Sara noticed that every few minutes, Michael put his finger inside his collar and tugged. The other officer had sat at the far end of the table, big blue eyes taking everything in. Sara wondered if she was a trainee. 'Yes. He was always alone.' She remembered Robbie that time by the fence, but she glanced at her dad and knew it was best not to mention it.

Michael looked up from his notepad. 'Did you see him return home?'

Sara shook her head. 'I thought he'd better hurry though. The storm was coming in.'

'Did you see him again that night?'

'No. My brother was sick, and we took him straight to the hospital in Parkwood. We got home after midnight and went to bed. We didn't know anything was wrong until we got up and Lillian ... Mrs Stynes came to our door and told us he was missing.' Sara cleared her throat. 'Then I saw them searching and ...' She shrugged to finish with the inevitable.

'Sara, can you tell me anything else about your neighbour, Alec Stynes?' he said.

'My daughter never met the kid,' said Dad.

Michael looked at Dad and gave him a nod. He returned his attention to Sara, his mouth corner twitching into a bland smile.

'I never met him,' Sara said, annoyed at how quiet her voice was.

Dad crossed his arms and sat back in his chair.

'But I heard him singing once,' she said with her eyes down.

It was the least she could do for Alec. He couldn't sing or talk anymore. She glanced up. Dad's frozen stare was locked on her face.

'How long ago was that?' Michael said, pen busy on his small notebook. His eyebrows lifted, and his pen stilled.

Sara shook her head. 'Weeks ago.'

Michael nodded and then frowned at his teacup, which he hadn't touched. 'Sara, Alec's mother made some complaints of harassment recently—'

'That's got nothing to do with us,' said Dad, jaw clenched.

Michael nodded slowly and glanced at Dad. Though he was a bit scared looking, Sara got the impression he could deal with people like Dad.

Sara bit her lower lip and willed Michael to ask a simpler question so she could just answer yes or no.

Michael got a puzzled look on his face. 'Did you ever see anything at your neighbour's that seemed strange?'

'Yes,' Sara answered quickly. She felt she'd wedged her foot into a closing door.

Dad breathed out and tilted his head. Sara wondered if they'd asked him the same questions. When they'd spoken to him, he insisted they speak outside so he could show them the sewer. He had explained the sewerage system and described what existed in sewerage tanks aside from shit, specifically the dangerous microbes. Sara wasn't surprised when the officer took a few steps away and suggested they go inside. They didn't take Dad up on his offer to show his boots, gloves and the equipment he'd used to unblock the toilet.

Sara knew they had nothing to worry about, because her whole family had alibis. 'I did see a lock on their gate once,' Sara offered.

'Jesus, Sara,' said Dad with a warning smile. 'How would you know that when you're not allowed to go over there?'

Sara's tongue tingled. The officer wouldn't be here for long, and she'd be left to deal with Dad. 'I saw it from across the road,' she said. 'When I went for a walk.'

Dad gave a dismissive wave, leant forwards and used a tone as if Sara might be simple. 'Most people chain their gates, honey. Who knows what you saw across the road at that distance …' He frowned and pinched his chin. 'What would it be, Sara? From our side to the top of the Stynes' driveway? Fifty metres?' He looked genuinely puzzled, but Sara wasn't fooled.

She nodded.

Michael looked from Sara to Dad, face professionally neutral. His neck, however, had reddened. He tugged at his collar.

Dad's smile disappeared as he turned towards the detective. 'Are you done yet, Michael?' he said, like they were friends. 'Farm won't run itself, unfortunately.'

'One more thing,' said Sara, her last word almost inaudible. 'I saw a man pull off the highway and throw a stone at Alec a few weeks ago.'

Michael's eyes lit up. 'Can you give me an exact date or time, Sara?'

Sara noticed Dad didn't look angry now. Instead, the skin beneath his eyes gathered the way it did when he was trying to figure something out, such as whether he'd moved the sheep on a Wednesday or Thursday. He leant his elbow on the table and rested his jaw against his fist.

'What kind of vehicle?' asked Dad.

Michael glanced Dad's way.

Sara felt encouraged that they were suddenly all walking the same path. 'A Holden one-tonner. With an antenna,' she said. 'I'd have to check my diary for the exact date.' She looked at Dad, and he gave a nod. She then got up and speed-walked to her room with the sensation she knew something important. She opened her school diary and counted back a few Fridays, remembering she'd been surprised Alec had come that day, and that she had been mulling over a maths test which she now found clearly written.

When she walked back out, both men had an elbow on the table. Michael was nodding at something Dad had said. Dad crossed his arms, watching Sara as she sat down. His mouth briefly pulled into a small smile, which to Sara looked genuine.

'Three weeks ago,' she said, placing the diary on the table in front of her.

Michael's eyes flickered over to it. 'Do you remember what the man looked like?'

Sara had the fleeting sensation she was on stage with

cameras beaming her image around the country. 'I only saw him from the back, but he was tall and strong-looking. I thought he might be going out because his shirt and jeans were neat. He also slipped when he tried to run, so he probably wasn't wearing work boots.' Sara felt a swell of pride that she'd remembered such a detail.

'Age?'

Sara shrugged and then thought about Ryan's friends, their man bodies combined with youth, which set them apart from the older men. 'Maybe twenty. Old enough for the pub.'

Michael cleaned his mouth corner with his tongue. 'And did he climb out of the passenger or driver's side of the car?'

Sara realised what it meant and became nervous. Two people not one. 'Passenger,' she said clearly.

Michael nodded. 'Did you see the driver?'

Sara shook her head. 'Didn't even look,' she said. 'I was worried the man was going to catch Alec, but then he slipped, and Alec raced uphill like a jackrabbit and jumped the gate.'

Michael smiled slightly. 'Excellent, thanks, Sara. So, can you tell me what happened when the man threw the stone?'

'How close were you?' queried Dad; without any menace, Sara thought.

Sara looked from Dad to the officer. Michael indicated she answer Dad. 'I was on the old highway, not quite at the Workers' House. A hundred and fifty metres?'

Both men nodded. Dad's bottom lip jutted. Michael wrote something.

Sara moistened her lips before she spoke again. 'Alec flinched hard. It reminded me of a movie when someone got shot in the back. That's why I knew he'd been hit.'

Michael noted this. 'Then what happened?'

'The man got back in, and the tyres spun on the gravel before they sped off.'

'Happen to remember a number plate?'

Sara shook her head.

'Had you seen this ute before?'

'Lots of the same around here, you'll find,' said Dad, sounding cooperative.

Sara nodded that she agreed and felt the rare comfort of Dad's approval.

Michael chewed his inner lip and gave a long nod. 'No worries. We can check it out. It all helps build a picture. Gives us something to prompt people's memories.' He tucked the notebook into his top chest pocket beside two pens. There was a dark patch along the lower seam where ink had soaked through. 'Do you own a ute, Mr Hamilton?'

'Course I do. Toyota Hilux. You can check it out whenever you have the right paperwork.' He hitched up the front of his pants.

The officer thanked them and handed Dad a card with a number they should ring if they remembered anything else.

Dad shook Michael's hand and then stood beside Sara with his hand on her shoulder as they watched the police car pull away. 'That's that,' he said.

Later, Mum asked Sara to go and let Dad know it was dinnertime. She found him in the machinery shed next to the Hilux again. The passenger-side door was open, Dad bending in, one elbow on the seat. Sara walked carefully, heel to toe, to get a closer look before Dad heard her. Most of his body blocked what he was doing, but she could see he was pressing a plastic fertilizer bag down into the foot space. Dad always kept one there to save the car from muddy boots or a wet dog if the weather was bad.

'Dad, dinner's ready.'

Dad stilled, hand on the lower rim of the doorframe. He brushed it with his hand and picked out a leaf wedged between the rubber and the lining. 'Goodo,' he said. He turned around, arms empty.

Sara felt like she'd been expecting him to be holding something. 'See you down there,' she said.

Sara headed for the house. Then she remembered the last time she had called him down for dinner, Dad had been cradling four or five beer cans in one hand. By their haphazard angles and open tops, it was clear they were empty. She'd heard the tinny jangle of cans being dropped into the rubbish, and remembered thinking that Dad must've been able to handle beer that tasted of camel's piss, after all.

After dinner, Sara found DC Michael Thoroughgood's card in the bin. It had been ripped in half.

## Chapter 28

**A few weeks later**

When Robbie got home from hospital, he went straight to bed. 'Leave me alone,' he said and turned over to face the wall. 'Close the door.'

He stayed like that for the next few days, huddled sick, small, and pinched-looking. Gradually, the bruising around his eyes faded.

More information came out about Alec. He'd been hit by a powerful vehicle, probably with a bull bar, sustained life-threatening injuries from the impact, and then drowned in the channel.

Robbie refused food. Mum returned him to the doctor. When they got home, he slammed his bedroom door. A few minutes later, they heard the sound of something breaking.

Sara followed Anne and Mum into Robbie's room. They stopped and stared like three soldiers after an IED had exploded. There were clothes everywhere, and a broken chair. Fragments of athletics trophies were on the floor.

Chips of paint off the wall. Robbie lay on the bed crying and hiccupping.

Mum reached out for him.

Robbie flinched. 'Go away!' He brought his knees up to his chest, wrapped them in his arms and buried his face.

A picture of the ute Sara had described was shown to her by an officer she hadn't met, and then it appeared on the news. Described as a 'sighting of possible interest, in regard to the hit-and-run death of Alec Stynes', Sara wondered why there was no mention of her name. Later, when she heard the kids talking on the bus, the reason became clear.

'Bloody troublemaker,' she heard them say. 'Bet they made up the ute thing to get attention.'

Local utes which fit the description were checked by police, but nothing came of it.

Sara noticed initially, there were a few cars going in and out of Lillian's drive several times a day, a sight which grew less common as the days passed. Sara heard the CWA ladies and some other local people, had been leaving meals for her.

In the afternoons, before it got dark, Sara walked up and down the edge of the road, several kilometres in both directions, scanning for the autumn colours of Alec's coat against the winter green. She checked culverts, the channel, in trees, and poked around in the grass beside the verge. She found waterlogged rubbish, old Coke bottles and faded plastic toys entwined in long grass, but no jacket.

The days following Alec's death became weeks. No one offered any information. Locals agreed the weather had been foul, and the hour late for an outing. Sara heard a rumour that the driver may have been a truckie who had hit Alec without realising what he'd done. They said that Alec had probably jumped out and committed suicide. Then they talked about how people threw themselves in front of trains all the time, which wasn't fair for the train drivers, or the police tasked with scraping up what was left. To Sara it seemed like everyone had decided on what had happened, and then filed Alec's death away.

Anne attended her formal dance.

The school bus arrived every day.

Sara and Anne went to school.

After the first week passed, Robbie, sluggish and dull-eyed, got dressed in his school uniform, went to school and then came home. He sat at the table with them and picked at his food as if it was wet cardboard.

One night, Sara walked into his room and sat on the bed beside him. He looked sideways and frowned. 'Hey, sis? What's goin' on?' He'd developed an odd way of speaking, since he'd been hanging out with a different group who'd included him after he'd arrived at school with two black eyes. Sara knew they had a reputation for stealing, smoking and truancy.

'Robbie, can you tell me now what Dad was lying about? It's just that I—'

'Jesus, Sara.' Robbie covered his eyes with his hand, the other hand tucked tight beneath his armpit. 'It doesn't matter anymore. It's over. Done. Finished, for fuck's sake.'

'I just think Dad's been... quiet. Since the hit and run.'

Robbie got up and went to the window. He thumped the side of his fist against the wall in a dull repetitive thud.

Sara chewed the inside of her lip. Maybe Robbie was always going to change like this. Maybe his youthful softness was something he had to grow out of. 'He seems strange, that's all I was going to say,' said Sara.

Robbie's thumping stopped for a few seconds before it continued. 'He was shovelling shit that night, remember. My shit.' He added sarcastically, 'Hilux doesn't have a bull bar.'

Sara was surprised that Robbie had considered this. She stood up. Perhaps Robbie was right. The police hadn't found anything to indicate Alec's death was suspicious. Maybe she should just accept it and stop trying shift her guilt by stirring things up.

Once Robbie was back at school, Mum stopped wringing her hands. She began cooking cakes, slices and biscuits again, which made the surface of their life seem more normal.

Sara was surprised how quickly the story about Alec faded away. Once the ute was shown and nothing came up, the police said the investigation was 'ongoing' and it disappeared from the news. The topic dwindled from locals' conversations too. Alec became 'that kid that got killed in the hit-and-run'. It seemed to Sara that it was easier to accept Alec's solo journey on a cold winter's night as an unsolved mystery, because he'd never belonged to Pine Creek.

One evening at the dinner table, Sara saw Anne look around at them like she had woken in the wrong house and didn't recognise anyone. Her gaze stopped on Sara. She blinked, paused, and then kept eating her meal.

After dinner, Sara knocked on her door.

'Come in.'

Sara let herself through the door and rested back against

it. The packed bag Sara had seen beneath Anne's bed once before, was open, Anne's clothes splayed all over the doona. There was a suitcase standing against the wardrobe, one Sara had seen in Mum's room.

'Where are you going?' Sara asked. A raw feeling grew into a big hole inside her.

'I'm doing my exams at another school in the city. I've applied for universities down there. My marks are good, so I should get in to the one I want.' Anne chewed her lower lip. 'I have a place to stay until uni starts.'

'Can I come?'

Anne pulled a pile of clothes towards her and began to stack them into the bag. 'Someone needs to stay. For Mum and Robbie.'

'That's not fair!'

Anne stopped for a moment. 'Don't cry, Sara. It ... it's crazy here.' Her chin quivered as she continued packing. 'Mum knows. She told Dad, but he didn't comment.' Anne looked over. 'That's not even normal, is it? He hasn't yelled. He seems to have forgotten I'm the whore of the district. I mean, nothing around here has been normal for weeks.'

'That's because Alec got killed. And because Dad hit Robbie. What do you expect? You can't leave!' said Sara.

Anne gave her a heavy look, sighed, and continued packing. 'I'll die if I stay here.' Anne's bag was full. She leant onto the top of the clothes while she closed the zipper. She went down onto her elbow, but still the zipper didn't budge. She sighed and removed one item. It was the pale-pink jumper Sara had stolen for Ryan's party. After frowning at it for a moment, she held it out to Sara. 'You can have this, if you like.'

Sara swallowed hard. She accepted the jumper. 'When are

you going?' she asked, tucking it beneath her arm.

'This weekend.'

'What about Robbie?'

Anne bunched her mouth. 'Robbie needs time. He'll be okay, but it's been rough for him. You know how soft he is.' She sat on the edge of the bed. 'He told me he'd met Alec. Before he got killed. Then he clammed up and wouldn't say anything else.' She shrugged. 'I can't help him right now. I just have to go.'

Sara could see Anne really meant it. 'I'm not giving you a goodbye present,' she said.

Anne smiled a little and then walked over and hugged Sara. 'You're about the only one I'm not worried about.'

Tears ran down Sara's face as she held onto her sister.

Anne kissed her hair, something only their mum did. 'Sara, keep annoying Dad. It's too quiet around here.'

## Chapter 29

**A few months later**

Anne left home on a Saturday morning while Dad was out working. Robbie had said a quick goodbye and then disappeared on Dad's motorbike. Mum drove Anne to the train station in Coltan. Sara went along, just to spend another forty-five minutes thinking of them as a family of five, not four. She regretted it as the train pulled away, and the rawness gaped before her when the train disappeared, leaving the tracks empty.

That night, Dad turned up the volume of the TV during a rugby match. Mum shut herself inside Anne's bedroom. When Sara knocked, Mum didn't answer, but Sara could hear her sniffling. She decided to leave her alone.

Sara became so hungry she made toast and eggs for herself and then made some for Dad and Robbie. Both said thank you. Robbie ate in his room. He had stubble on his upper lip and cheeks and Sara noticed he kept twitching. Dad ate while sitting on the couch. A first, as far as Sara could remember.

Later, Sara heard Dad pleading with Mum not to leave him. Mum had finally come out of Anne's room and gone to her own. Dad even used her real name.

'Hm,' Sara heard Mum murmur flatly.

Over the next few weeks, the school kept ringing about Robbie. His absences clocked up, even though he caught the bus with Sara each day. He didn't attend exams. He smelt of cigarettes and wore dirty clothes. He grew thinner till his cheeks sucked inwards. He was due to turn seventeen two weeks after Anne turned eighteen.

Mum phoned Anne at dinnertime the day of her birthday. Sara had been waiting to speak to Anne all day. It was as though the phone call was a sunbeam that could shine through a chink in the curtains for a few minutes.

Dad sat in front of the blank TV with the light off and a beer in his hand. The silence throbbed around him. There had been more beer bottles and cans in the bins than usual, even on weeknights. Sara had noticed a fullness to the front of Dad's shirt that hadn't been there a few weeks before.

'Are you happy?' asked Sara, once Mum had handed her the phone.

'Yes, I am.' Anne then listed happy occasions: a party, a university orientation, a trip to see flowers.

There was a bright force to Anne's voice Sara had never heard before. It emphasised the cold, shadowy feel of the house.

'I miss you all, of course, but ... I'm happy. Are you okay?'

'You know,' said Sara.

Anne paused. 'Has Ryan been back?'

'No.' Sara sighed. 'It's so depressing around here.'

'How's Robbie?'

'I'll get him in a sec.'

'But how is he?' Anne insisted.

Sara bit her inner cheek and hoped the truth might bring Anne back. 'I think he's been hanging around with the rough kids. He's smoking and wagging school.'

'Poor Robbie,' Anne murmured. 'Okay. I'll talk to him.'

Robbie wasn't on the phone long before hitching up his jeans and returning to his room.

With the call finished, Sara felt the brief sunbeam disappear.

Mum suggested an electrician apprenticeship might suit Robbie better than school. When she filled out forms at the breakfast table, Dad held the newspaper in front of his face.

A few weeks later, Robbie went missing for two days.

Mum found him and brought him home.

Days later, he disappeared again, but it took Mum longer to find him. When she did, he was sleeping beneath a bridge with two homeless people. She took him to the hospital.

Sara felt like she didn't know her brother anymore.

After he was brought home, Dad didn't yell at Robbie. He told him to go away and stay away.

Robbie left during the night. Only a few clothes and his backpack were gone, plus all the cash from the money tin Mum kept in the kitchen.

Sara found Mum with the empty tin in her hands. 'Shh,' she said. 'At least he has money.'

Mum quickly got her purse and shoved notes and coins in, closed and returned it to the shelf.

'Where do you think he is?' said Sara.

Mum's eyes softened. 'He told me about a boarding house

for homeless kids. There are other boys his age there. He didn't want me to know where it was.' She gasped and slapped a hand over her mouth. Her face collapsed, and shoulders heaved. She turned away.

'Mum?' Sara hugged her from behind.

Mum held Sara's hand tight against her stomach. 'Have I been such a bad mother?' she whispered in short gasps.

'No. No!' said Sara, screwing her eyes shut.

Mum's body shuddered. 'So why must you kids leave?'

'It's not you, Mum. It's Dad.'

Mum turned her face. Sara could see the ridge of her cheekbone and the wet caught in her eyelashes. 'Are you going to leave too?' Mum's breath shuddered.

Sara bit her inner cheek. 'Not until I'm sixteen.'

Mum gripped Sara's hand so tight she winced. After a moment, Mum extracted herself from the hug. She straightened her clothes, wiped her face with her sleeve and lifted her chest. 'Right. Well, we'd better get some things together for you.' She shuddered a breath and appeared to refocus. 'Now, you'll need a plate and some pots and a fry pan.' Mum went over to the cupboards, got down onto her knees and then opened the doors below the sink. 'You can have whatever you need.'

Sara knew Anne hadn't taken any of Mum's cookware and felt guilty for the special treatment.

'Will you be alright, Mum?' she said.

Mum stayed in front of the open cupboard. 'Yes.' She sounded a bit lighter. 'But I need you to look after something for me.'

Sara knew right away what it was. She cast a quick glance around. 'The jewellery box?'

Mum nodded.

'But, Mum, it's your special thing. When would I give it back to you?'

Mum was still for a few moments. 'When it's my turn to leave.'

Sara turned sixteen. She was grateful Mum didn't try to fuss or have a party. She did make a cake though. A big chocolate cake with cherries and chocolate swirls on the top, which could feed a dozen people. Sara forced a slice down, to make Mum happy. Dad wasn't around. Every day he went out early and came in late.

'I got something for you,' said Mum with a secret smile after the two of them had shared the cake. Sara's stomach hurt.

Mum returned with a small parcel wrapped in pink tissue paper. Inside was a pink bra and matching underwear with lace around the edges.

'They're beautiful, Mum!'

The door slammed.

Dad walked in, eyes on the present in Sara's hands. His face closed over and turned red. 'What the hell are you doing, Ellen?' he yelled.

Sara jumped. She hadn't heard him yell in ages.

He marched right in wearing his boots. He leant over Sara. 'You want to end up like your sister? You want to end up on the streets?' His arm hammered the air with each point, so close, Sara could feel the wind move near her face.

*Anne isn't on the streets. Anne's happy.*

Sara wondered if Dad was going to hit her like he had Robbie. A calm came over her. She stared at her parents as if they were a long way off. Saw Dad's bloated, scarlet face, and Mum standing behind him with her eyes down.

She felt completely alone.

*Chapter 30*

**Four months later**

Sara's decision to go to a boarding house for country students was accepted with a bout of tears from Mum and no comment from Dad. Anne had finished her exams and was staying with friends north of Sydney until university started. It was close to where Sara would be living. Mum said she was pleased her girls would be together.

It was a Monday morning when Sara walked out of the house and down the front path, her backpack over one shoulder. Her other arm was attached to a big suitcase, which clunked along behind her. She hadn't intended to look back, but at the last moment, she did. Mum stood framed by the cave made by the tree and dark doorway. The tree looked ready to crush the house if it leant any further, or at least devour the front room, its spiky branches knocking down the television and the turntable. She waved and Mum waved back.

Sara struggled across the cattle grate with her bag. A big

green bus with a yellow stripe slowed and pulled off the highway. The door sucked open, and the driver, wearing a white shirt and navy pants, jumped clear. He took Sara's big suitcase down along the side of the bus, lifted a door and shoved it in. A truck passed, and the bus shifted slightly with the force of it. Only one passenger looked up, then went back to his magazine.

At the door, Sara put her foot on the bottom step. Emanating through the creaks and smells were other leavings, other arrivals, and other journeys. Sara had stopped counting the days between home and freedom. She looked up at the fresh blue sky and felt the world open before her as she grabbed the handrail above the stairs and pulled herself inside.

# Part Two

## Chapter 31

**Autumn 1999**

Sara remembered the year she turned fifteen, there had been rainbow flags in Sydney and protesters holding placards that said: *AIDS: understand and educate.* Watching the news, her dad had bellowed at the television.

Today, a decade later, a small gathering was celebrating Gay Pride week across the road from where Sara worked. They held flowers and rainbow flags. A car beeped. In return, the group waved, smiled and danced.

Inside the Blue Mountains Family Counselling Centre, with the coat of arms – emu and kangaroo – at the entrance, Sara remembered she had a client.

'I will never forget her eyes.'

Sara slowly returned from her thoughts. Her seventy-year-old client, Daryl, had lost his wife ten years before. Bereavement. A malady that kept the appointment book full, the waiting room a steady procession of sad-eyed people with scarves around their necks and coats keeping out the Blue Mountains' chill.

The shared consulting room had brown carpet and furniture, and pictures of nondescript flowers. Beige venetian blinds were fitted to the windows.

Daryl looked up, watery-eyed. 'Her eyes spoke before her mouth did.' His smile trembled.

The window of the room faced native bush. Sara glanced out at the freedom – the clusters of leaves moving with birdlife, the crawling, flying, cocooning insects, the sleeping bulk of a koala high in a gum tree.

Sara knew she'd landed a good job. She had nice colleagues who smiled and said hello to her in the staff room as they filled their cups with cheap coffee, then walked out before a real conversation began.

'The way her eyeballs moved beneath the thin skin of her eyelids like she was searching for something in her sleep.' Daryl fluttered his eyes. 'I write poetry.'

'That's nice. I mean, expressing your feelings,' said Sara, with a twist of impatience. She stared out the window. Silently she recited the five stages of grief: denial, anger, bargaining, depression, and acceptance. She couldn't decide whether Daryl had settled yet on depression. She'd crack a bottle of champagne when they swam to the shores of acceptance. Sara cleared her throat, faced Daryl and forced a smile. 'You were saying, ah ... you watched her?'

Daryl's eyelids snapped twice. 'Well, not like *that*. You know, lovingly.' His face melted and creased.

Sara dropped her eyes as she handed him the box of tissues. She would have to try harder, reach deep down for her empathy. Daryl's wife had been, and still was, the love of his life. Sara smiled gently as she watched him wipe his cheeks. *Real tears. Poor man.*

Daryl blew his nose loudly into a tissue. 'Have you ever been in love?'

Sara shifted in her chair. She hated when they did this.

'A long time ago,' she said.

Sara remembered love. When she was fifteen, the grief of losing it had felt catastrophic. The world had no right to keep turning, to let the sun come up and the hours click past when all she'd wanted was him. *Ryan.* Occasionally, she thought she saw him; pushing a trolley through the carpark, or sitting in the driver's seat of a four-wheel drive in the lane beside her, elbow on the windowsill. She still imagined kissing him, remembered how his lips felt warm, soft and a little fuller than hers.

Sometimes as she walked the footpath listening to headphones, she found her head on an angle as if they were about to kiss. When she received the wedding invitation for *Ryan & Rachel*, she binned it. She stopped Mum from describing how flattering the bride's dress had been, considering Rachel had been seven months pregnant.

Instead, Sara imagined Ryan single and waiting for her to call. Maybe he was in the army or working on a remote island where he couldn't access a phone? Thunder still excited her. She loved listening to the rain as she tried to sleep. She once took sick leave when the weather was bad and gave herself a treat; imagined their night together. Four times, she remembered. She used the whole day and relived it all.

Daryl frowned. 'Are you alright?'

Caught off guard, Sara quickly smiled. 'Of course. Now, where were we? You were admiring the memory of your wife's eyes.'

For three years, Daryl had been on the end of her client list on alternate Friday afternoons, which meant she was last to leave the office. *Great start to the weekend.*

Once Daryl left, Sara binned the tissues, sighed and took the bin out of the room. She strode back in and checked her handbag. Inside was a new bottle of pills. She paused, checked she was alone and read the label: *Sara Hamilton. Lorazepam 1 mg. Take 1–2 as prescribed.*

She walked into the bathroom, slung the handbag strap over a tap and then regarded herself critically in the mirror. Weary bloodshot eyes stared back. Tucking professionally bobbed and blonde hair in behind her ears, Sara again regretted the two hundred dollars it had cost. Self-indulgence. Waste.

Sara had peroxided her hair ever since she'd left home. She approved of the contrast between the blonde and her dark eyebrows because she thought it highlighted her green eyes. She also felt it made her appear dissimilar to either of her parents.

Bent over the basin, she washed her face and then pulled a paper towel out, patted her face dry and rolled her hands in it.

A year ago, her GP had listened intently when Sara had finally told him about her episodes. Then he'd written a script for medication to treat depressed people and said for best results, it should be combined with psychology. Sara heard blah-blah and took the script. She'd only just managed to fill it before it went out of date. She had then changed to a new GP, who was quite handsome. No need to talk about the episodes at all.

Sara sighed hard, dropped the pills back into her bag and

returned to the counselling room. She did a quick scan of the room, which on Monday morning would be someone else's. She started at ten am on Mondays, which gave her headache pills time to work.

She rounded the desk where the computer hummed quietly. She tapped a button and the screen lit up.

New email. Message from Laura Dennison, ABC Investigative Reporter.

Sara frowned, opened the message.

*Hello Sara,*

*We're in the research phase for a new program on cold cases, which is due to go to air next year.*

*We would like to include the Alec Stynes case.*

*Alec's mother has agreed to participate, along with others involved in the original investigation. We realise you were only fifteen at the time; however, because you lived next door, we'd love to speak to you.*

*Laura Dennison.*

*ABC Investigative Reporting Team.*

Sara breathed rapidly and shut down the computer. She grabbed the bottle of pills from her handbag and dry-swallowed one, paused, grabbed a second and threw it at the back of her throat. She gagged, reached for the nearest glass of water and gulped it down, hoping it hadn't been used by the client with the cough. She switched off the lights as she exited the building and then strode to her car.

Sara's hands trembled while she slid the key into the ignition.

*Breathe slowly in, and slowly out.*

*Boom boom!*

Too late. Adrenaline coursed through her body. Why did

Miss Dennison have to ruin her day? It had been a good day. Bearable.

Sara's knuckles grew white as she focused hard on the blue bitumen and white centre line. Her arms and legs shook and sweat misted her face before trickling down her cheeks.

Sara pulled into a numbered parking bay of a set of units in the leafy centre of the Blue Mountains. She intentionally drew her focus back to her five senses: sight, sound, smell, touch and taste. Sara turned off the ignition, closed her eyes and rested her head back.

*Blue Mountains haze; dark, dense green; eucalypt and wattle. Rainbow lorikeets shrill squarks. Smell of a piney fragrance tree, which swings from the rear-view mirror. The tight carpet feel of the car seat covers beneath my clammy hands. Bitter metallic taste of water and pills on the back of my tongue.*

After a few minutes, the shaking stopped, and eventually her heart rate slowed. She opened her eyes.

Sara's unit was one of nine. They were stacked three up, and three back, and the exterior was blue. Next to hers was an identical block. Sara liked that they were uniform and visually pleasing. There were neat gardens at the front of the ground-floor units. The second and third floors had a balcony, and most had potted plants on them.

She wiped her face with a tissue from the console and then opened the door and swung her legs out. Solid ground. She rolled her shoulders twice, collected her handbag, then headed for the stairs that led to the third floor. From the garden of a ground-floor unit, an elderly couple's small, brown and white terrier yapped. A neighbouring dog, a messy grey mongrel with an underbite, joined in.

'Quiet, Chewbacca!' Sara said to the grey one and rubbed her temple with two fingers. She climbed the steps, hand on the rail. Inside her unit, she locked the front door and slid down to the floor.

## Chapter 32

*Slam! Alec is flying. Not like a bird, soaring or floating, but with propulsion. A rock fired from a cannon. Arcing downwards, the long side of an isosceles triangle. Falling, heavier and faster. T-shirt and jeans, long skinny arms and legs. Wooden puppet. Broken.*

*The silt is disturbed by weak breaths in the puddle beneath Alec's face. Twigs and leaves stick to his bare neck, the cold of the water reaching through the cotton threads of his t-shirt. Smell of decay in the dead leaves, metallic taste of water, sound of silence.*

*Across the paddock, there's another face, familiar and sweet.*

*Robbie is watching, tears dripping off his jaw. He is cold and pale from a burst appendix. There are track marks on the inside of his arms from the drugs he injects. He fades away.*

*Down in the dark wet, Alec is suddenly gone.*

*Sara panics as she looks for him.*

*His voice sings on the breeze. He sings about the light dimming. And the dream...*

Sara gasped and woke as if breaking through a watery surface. She blinked in the harsh morning light as she remembered the song Alec had been singing all those years ago.

She knew the song now. It was 'Any Dream Will Do', from *Joseph and the Amazing Technicoloured Dreamcoat*. She'd watched the musical once and listened for it. When it came on, tears had streamed down her face.

Sara checked everything was in it's place: dresser, walk-in robe, chair with clothes folded neatly so she could wear them on Monday. 'Ohhhh, man.' She sat up slowly and put her legs over the side. Her head swooned and throbbed. She outwaited the dizzy spell, rubbed her sore temples and held her hand flat in front of her. It was shaking.

She remembered a piece of the previous afternoon. The desperate need to sleep after the tablets. She'd managed a shower and two glasses of shiraz. Rice crackers may have been dinner. Or maybe that was the night before.

An empty glass with the dark red drop at the bottom stood in the kitchen sink. She washed and then upended it in the dishrack and flicked on the kettle. She turned on the computer before she walked out through the sliding glass door onto her veranda, hugging herself against the cold, shoulders shaking, skin covered in goose flesh.

The leaves of the tall maple and conifer trees dappled the azure sky. The nutty smell of bird poop, the pines and the earthiness of the undergrowth forced Sara to swallow and concentrate on not throwing up.

Not fond of heights, Sara had surprised herself with her choice of apartment, but it was more private up here. She was fine if she didn't look down.

Being the third floor, leafy boughs allowed colourful rosellas within arm's reach. Sara grabbed her jar of birdseed and refilled a bowl she kept on the balcony. She swept husks off the railing. Two rainbow lorikeets weaved through the leaves and stepped onto the rail, heads tilted. Their wings fluttered as they bounced towards the seed. Colour moved within the trees, and more lorikeets emerged.

Sara backed away.

On her computer was a new email from Pene, her best friend. They'd studied counselling together, but their similarities ended there. A success, Pene was married and trying for a baby. She had a good job in Sydney.

*Are you going for a holiday this weekend? I can book for you if you don't have time.*

*Pene, Xx.*

Sara ran a hand across her eyes. The beauty of computers – clean, anonymous, efficient. If she didn't have to leave her house, she wouldn't. Counselling was enough to keep her involved with the outside world.

Sara read Pene's previous three messages, all very similar, and Sara's answer to only one of them.

*Too busy! x*

Sara leant her chin on her hand and stared out the window.

After a moment, she began to type …

*The ABC wants to feature Alec's hit-and-run on a cold case program. They asked me to be involved.*

Sara waited.

A new email popped up.

*Oh, my gosh! Are you going to do it?*

\*\*\*

Sara took a long breath and began to type.

*I'm terrified.*

Sara jumped and winced as the phone rang from the kitchen bench. She stared at the phone. It stopped ringing.

Another email came in.

*Answer the phone!*

Sara made herself a cup of black tea and took it with her when she sat back in front of the computer. There was a new email.

*What have you got to lose? You didn't know him, did you?*

Sara swallowed and licked her lips. Her fingers hovered over the keyboard until both hands were shaking. She typed a reply quickly and then hit send.

Next to the kitchen, Sara checked a whiteboard. On it was a list that she hadn't needed to change for a long time.

*Walk*
   *Breakfast*
   *Work*
   *Morning tea*
   *Work*
   *Lunch*
   *Rest*
   *Work*

*Exercise*
*Dinner*
*Shower and bed*

She bit her lip, opened the kitchen drawer and then checked her notebook.

*Apple +50 calories*
  *Toast and vegemite +100 calories*
  *muesli bar +200 calories*
  *black tea/coffee +0 calories*
  *Ham and salad sandwich +500 calories*
  *Cake +500 calories*
  *Sausages and vegetables +500 calories*
  *Run -300 calories*

Sara grabbed an apple from the fruit bowl, put a slice of bread into the toaster and then ticked breakfast on the whiteboard with a black marker.

The phone rang. Something flinched internally when she saw the number. 'Yes, Mum?'

'Honey, I'm going away for a few days ... and there's no one to look in on your father.'

'Oh, Mum.' Sara covered her eyes with one hand and leant on the bench. A fortnight had passed since her father had suffered a stroke. He was in a rehabilitation centre called 'Blooms'.

'You don't have to stay long or even visit much. Or do his washing. Just be around for any emergencies.'

'Mum, you left him. Why are you doing his washing?'

When they'd separated, Sara hadn't felt the immediate relief she expected. Instead, a sadness had soaked her. About the years lost, pointless pain and the damage done.

'He still can't speak. No barked orders, ridicule or insults.'

Yet Sara felt his anchor ropes remained, their hooked ends firmly wedged into Mum's new life. Since Dad's stroke, she'd returned to being his dutiful wife.

'Sara, you haven't been back.'

Sara turned and watched the parrots as they fluttered around the seed on the balcony.

Mum sighed. 'Let's not do this now. Your father is a sick man.'

Sara swallowed, closed her eyes, opened a little of herself to the dark place where her past lived. 'Do they think he'll learn to walk and speak again?'

'They're not too sure. The occupational therapist and physio are with him every day.'

'Right,' Sara said quietly before sighing out her resignation. 'I want to help you. I just don't know if I can see Dad. I guess ... I could try and come to the farm.'

'Okay, honey,' Mum said quietly. She paused. 'It's empty, of course, but Rusty is still there. She'd love company.'

'What?' Sara put a hand to her sore forehead and looked around for her headache pills. 'Has she been alone since Dad's stroke?'

'Yes, Sara. There's no room at my flat, and I don't think she'd come anyway. She's probably waiting for Len. Don't worry, I go out every day to walk and feed her.'

'My God, poor Rusty.' Sara found a silver strip of pills and popped two out with one hand. She filled a glass of water. 'You could've stayed with her. It's not like Dad's there to bother you.'

'You know I can't stay there. I don't even go inside.' Mum made a sound like she'd shivered. 'Gosh, it took me so long to leave.'

Sara threw the pills into her mouth and drank all the water. Since leaving on that big bus ten years ago, she hadn't returned home. Apart from meeting Mum in the Blue Mountains for lunch a few times, she rarely saw her.

'Please, darling.' Mum sounded exhausted. 'It's been hard. The separation, then moving house, then your father's stroke. I need a break.'

Sara swallowed. 'What's happening with the farm? Dad was selling, wasn't he?'

'Yes, well, maybe. No rush. Let's see how he recovers, hm? There's nothing to worry about. The sheep have been whittled down to a few ewes, and the cattle have all been sold. He was almost ready to list it when he had the stroke.'

'Do I really have to stay there?'

There was a weighty silence.

'No. I wouldn't force any of you to stay, but if you do, it won't cost you anything.'

*Not true. It would definitely cost me.* 'Okay.'

'You'll stay?'

'Yes.'

'Thank you, darling. I'm going down south to see my brother, Bruno, for a few days. We'll celebrate a belated birthday together.'

'It's still weird to think of you as a twin, Mum. But I'm so happy for you.'

'He's looking forward to meeting you. Here, I'll read out his mobile and home phone numbers. Do you have a pen?'

'Sure, go ahead.' Sara listened and then wrote the numbers down.

'Oh, when you get here, please go to the local pub,' said Mum. 'It was someone from there who found your father after he'd had the stroke. Just pass on our thanks.'

'Okay.' Sara chewed her inner lip. 'Mum? Would it be so bad if Dad never spoke again?'

Mum was quiet for a few seconds. 'Safe trip, Sara.'

## Chapter 33

As Sara munched through her apple, she re-read Laura Dennison's email and wondered if her ill-timed letter really had enticed Alec outside on that wintry night. Even if it had, it didn't explain why he chose the late hour, had been completely unprepared, and got hit crossing a road he was so familiar with.

The obvious assumption that had solidified over time was that Alec had committed suicide.

Sara pulled her cooled toast out of the toaster and scraped vegemite on. She chewed through her hard breakfast. Imagined driving past the section of channel where Alec died, and up the Hamilton driveway to the old house. She took a big gulp of tea. A wave of nausea rolled through her body as she coughed, and her eyes watered. She wiped her eyes and leant against the bench.

Her body began shaking, and she felt her pulse quicken. She got down onto the floor and lay down on her back. Fingertips to temples, she lifted her shoulders up and down. 'One, two, three ...'

A few minutes later, the shaking stopped. Sara's forehead and hairline were soaked. She sank back against the cold floor, arms and legs out. She licked sweat off her upper lip. Maybe the ABC program and a return to the farm would help her move forwards. *Maybe cows would fly.*

Pene, the success, would say to give it a try. That she deserved some happiness.

Sara walked outside. She clenched the railing, took a few good lungsful of air. Crisp and fresh, it always felt cleansing. She stilled as she heard soft music.

Mr Taylor, a retired schoolteacher, listened to Classical.

Next to his unit lived a young man who'd recently entertained a female visitor. The sounds that came from his apartment had changed from rock'n'roll to Celine Dion and Kylie Minogue. Today, it was quiet. They were probably visiting the giant, rocky Three Sisters, which rose from the forest like craggy mountains. Maybe they'd share coffee and cake at the Cliff's Edge Motel overlooking the rainforest, canyons and tall trees of the Blue Mountains National Park. If they were, she envied them. It was ten minutes away, but she'd never been.

On Sara's last birthday, she'd turned twenty-five, and told colleagues she'd planned a trip to Bali. Instead, though, she'd holed up in her apartment for three days with a cask of red wine and a bottle of vodka. At some point, in a dark place, she'd considered ending her life, but had decided not to. Which meant she'd chosen to live.

Shakily, and with a great sigh, Sara walked inside her apartment, locked the door, pulled the blind and went to pack her bag.

Sara left a message, saying she needed a week off for family reasons, on the work answer machine. They'd probably wonder what family. She'd never spoken about them. She may as well have been an orphan dropped by a stork when she started work there.

As she walked out to the car, she glanced at her mobile phone. A message from Pene.

*What do you mean, there's something you never told me?*

## Chapter 34

Sara hated the drive west into the Central Tablelands. She had only travelled part-way a few times and that was to access running trails. Must-haves safely packed, she drove along the winding, hilly Great Western Highway. She ticked things off in her head: exercise clothes, calorie counter, pillow, emergency contact number (Pene), computer, three bottles of shiraz, the only fresh food she had – apples, tomatoes, bread and eggs – a carton of long-life milk, and several freezer meals. In her cup holder was a travel mug full of black coffee.

Sara checked the rear-view mirror several times and listened to the engine of her Volvo for an off note. She then pulled over to the edge of the road and checked the tyres. She was bodily buffeted by a passing truck as she climbed back inside the car. She slipped an Enya CD into the slot and turned the volume to low. Alternating sips of coffee and water, she checked her teeth for stains in the mirror. Counted four on the in breath, four on the out breath.

When she reached the section of road where the highway

had been sliced into the mountainside, the crag still bearing the scars, Sara held her breath. The thick metal guard between the road and the sharp drop into the trees was dented and coloured with paint from cars.

Descending into gentler curves, the road became bordered by fields and big trees. Leaves met overhead, the canopy creating shaded tunnels.

As she drove, Sara imagined the busy shearing shed, her mum with the scones, her dad setting up the empty wool bags. She suddenly missed the inclusion that shearing had once brought. 'All hands on deck,' Mum would say as she baked the entire day before.

Sara had loved the warmth and hum of shearing time; the sheep, thick with fleece, mustered into the wooden yards by lithe sheepdogs. The shearers walking around in old blue singlets and patched pants, thick-chested with hands grown big from gripping the handpiece. Bow-legged, bent-backed, they pulled moccasins onto their feet and reversed through swing doors, and then reappeared dragging a sheep by its upper half. With the sheep's head behind an elbow, they pushed the spiked comb into the woolly topknot, which landed softly on the floor.

Bent double all day, the men pushed the clippers back and forth. The shaft above each shearer spun as the fleece peeled off in big sweeps. The roustabout's broom kept busy separating the dirty crutchings from the clean wool. Dad ready to hug the fleece, lift and cast it onto the table, clean side up, before Sara and Anne's fingers nibbled the skirtings. Sara and Anne were always separated from the men by the skirting table and the line Dad made in a hard-heeled walk across the wood floor between them.

Flocks of sheep grazed in the fields bordering the road. Sara remembered the pristine white of the gangly Merinos in the sun after they'd been shorn.

Finally, Sara passed through the blue smoke of Coltan, steep descending roads that twisted inside valleys, and then the countryside which opened out on the flats. She passed the sign that said *Pine Creek*, the painted letters peeling.

Sara's ears popped as she crested a hill and braked a little on the downslope. Thick, sullen cloud spread in a blanket over the town and leached the colours from the land like a sepia print. She glanced sideways at the channel where Alec's body had been located on that bitter, strange morning ten years ago.

She indicated left when she saw the large white letterbox fixed to a post. Above it, the weathered sign: *Hamilton's*.

She stopped at the gate, climbed out to undo the chain, and let the gate swing open. Pausing, she took a deep breath and smelt the familiar pine, eucalypt and livestock as she turned to gaze across the paddocks.

Long green grass with pink-tipped seed heads furred the ground. Beyond were rolling green hills, clusters of native trees and granite rocks, brownish, egg-shaped dams, ringlock fences, and gates she'd opened dozens of times. She could imagine, on the hillside opposite, Dad's Hilux bumping across a bare paddock, the Hereford cattle frolicking alongside in anticipation of feed.

Down to her left, embraced by overgrown grass and pear trees, was the Workers' House. If she closed her eyes, she could still see Ryan swagger out to his car, raise his hand in a wave and then smile. She smiled back, opened her eyes and glanced around. 'Idiot,' she said.

Sara drove her car across the cattle grate. Its corrugations shuddered through her body.

At the end of the curving driveway, lined with pines, the

Hamilton homestead emerged.

Beside the fenced garden, Sara turned off the engine and heard a dog barking. The windows of the main house appeared huge, the curtains half-drawn, like dead eyes.

There was too much sky. Something was missing.

Sara gasped. In the middle of the lawn was a massive tree stump that appeared to have been cut recently. The huge pine was gone. Around the stump were piles of sawdust. Sara realised she'd never seen the windows from this angle. It looked like a different house.

Sara climbed slowly from the car into the tangy scent of the cut tree and then walked briskly up to the back gate.

Next to the house yard, the empty dog pens had grass growing through the open gates.

Rusty stood in the back garden with her ears pricked. A bit rounded, no ribs visible, the black and tan Kelpie was now thirteen years old.

'Hi!' Sara grinned and whistled as she walked through the gate.

Propelled by her tail, Rusty jogged over, circled Sara's legs and snuffled her jeans.

'Hey, girl!' Sara got down onto her knees and held out her arms. Rusty nuzzled into her waist. Sara rubbed her neck. 'Poor bugger. Did you get left behind?'

Rusty dropped her hips then flopped onto her side.

Sara scratched her belly. 'There you go, old girl. Sorry you had no one here.'

Across the sloped, grassy yard, the chicken coop was empty, the vegetable garden overgrown. A rusted-out wheelbarrow sat at the edge. Along the back wall of the house, outside the laundry, was a row of canned dog food.

Sara lifted the doormat and found the key.

Inside was the same washing machine and clothes basket Sara remembered. The basket was full. Along the side wall, a smudged brown line marked the absent row of work footwear where now, only two pairs of boots remained.

Once she'd gone out and got her bags, Sara shuffled sideways through the laundry, dirt crunching beneath her runners. She lifted her foot backwards, scowled at the sole, and leant on the wall to pull her shoes off.

Sara peered inside. To the left of the doorway, most of the furniture was still in the same place: Dad's big seat, a couch and TV. The dining table was bare and sprinkled with crumbs. Perhaps Dad had given up after Mum moved out. Stopped washing his clothes or wiping the bench. On the walls, pale rectangles indicated absent pictures. In the kitchen, old vegetable wallpaper peeled at the corners. Everything glowed with bare light from the front windows.

'Hello?'

The lounge, where Mum had once read her forbidden books next to the fire, seemed hunkered in darkness. Sara yanked the curtain back from the window.

She poked her head into her old room, dumped her bag on the stripped mattress and opened the curtains. A puff of dust made her sneeze. She shivered in the cold and then tested the light switch. Nothing happened. She went and found light globes in the laundry cupboards, next to washing powder, boot polish and toilet cleaner.

In the pantry were a few cans of beans, ham, and fruit salad, an almost empty box of onions and potatoes and a carton of beer. Sara dragged a chair into her room and replaced the light bulb. She then closed most of the other rooms. Her parents' bed was the only one that was roughly made up and looked lived in. Anne's old bed sagged beneath several boxes. Robbie's room had become a storage space with boxes and bric-a-brac. Sara wondered how long it had taken Mum to strip the beds after they'd all left.

According to Anne, Robbie had never been back. Anne stayed one night with a toddler, but Dad's bad mood had forced her to move into town and shorten her visit. When Anne visited again, with two children and husband Rob in tow, she booked accommodation in town. Rob had never liked Dad and didn't pretend to. A couple of years had passed since then.

Sara got a doona from the linen cupboard, made up her bed and added her own pillow. She grabbed the blackened kettle off the stovetop and turned on a tap. Some yellowy water came out and disturbed a dead fly. She waited for it to run clear.

The kettle had almost boiled itself dry by the time Sara remembered. It hissed when she refilled it.

Sara noted a mouldy loaf of bread on the bench. She checked the fridge. There was a carton of milk, a green-coloured steak, plenty of beer and a takeaway container half full of something unidentifiable. The milk was three weeks past its use-by date. Sara poured the sour-smelling lumps down the drain and flushed the sink with water. The bin had no liner, so she slipped a plastic shopping bag into it before throwing in the carton, steak, takeaway and bread.

Hot cup of black tea in hand, Sara swept an arc in the dust and crumbs on the surface of the dining table and sat down.

These days Anne lived with her family almost six hours away in a small coastal town. Sara didn't call regularly, and neither did Anne. Instead, they each sent a Christmas card every year with news of deaths or dramas about people they both knew.

A few years before, Anne mentioned Robbie had been involved with a guy charged with break, enter and theft and might have to face charges too. Sara had shrunk at the thought of her gentle brother in prison. She told Anne she couldn't deal with those kinds of updates.

Sara knew it was possible Robbie could have contracted AIDS from sharing needles. She couldn't bear the thought of him dying a sore-covered skeleton in an AIDS ward. Or a prison. Anne went silent, then said, 'Fine.'

Sara checked her phone. One unanswered call: Pene. She shook her head, got up and set up her stereo. The hiss of electricity was loud in the silence, but the little red lights were reassuring. She turned on, 'I'm Free' by The Soup Dragons.

Sara fidgeted. The music bounced hard from the empty walls. She turned it off, raced out to the car and retrieved her bags and then the box of food. She washed a wine glass from the kitchen cupboard and filled it from one of her bottles of shiraz, took a long drink and winced.

Sara had had boyfriends after she left home. With her eyes closed, they were all Ryan. She felt for Ryan's chest, his hair, his lips. But they'd all felt wrong. She hadn't dated in a year. Or was it two?

Sara emptied the rest of the wine down her throat, refilled the glass and placed it on the bench. 'I'm free!' she sang to the roof and the walls. The shadows eased back as music filled the space and her veins ran with the delicious, hot feel of alcohol.

## Chapter 35

After a second glass of wine, Sara went to her room. As she shucked off her jeans and shirt, she calculated calories from the day's food and alcohol. Twenty minutes of moderate running up a hilly course. No harm done.

As Sara noted her nude form in the full-length mirror, she turned sideways, patted her firm, flat stomach and judged the muscular legs she'd earnt from running.

She dressed in a t-shirt and leggings and then pulled on joggers.

From her bag she found an elastic band and tied her hair into a small ponytail. She pulled headphones over her ears and walked outside. Alanis Morrisette's *Jagged Little Pill*, was still in her discman. She increased the volume, welcoming Alanis' anger.

Rusty wagged.

'Stay. I'll be back soon.'

Sara headed up towards the machinery shed and the top of the lane, which then sloped down in a straight line through the middle of the property.

At the back of the shed, something caught her eye. Beyond her dad's white Hilux, which, Sara noted, had been updated to a younger model and parked front-in, was a shovel. Next to it was a mound of dirt.

Sara pulled down her headphones and walked in.

Over the years, the gravelled floor had been hard-packed by vehicles, machinery, stacks of fertilizer bags, and drums of oil, drench, insecticide, and herbicide. It was all gone now, but right near the back wall was a hole about half a foot deep and twice as wide. Spread out either side were ripples in the dirt like shark gills.

Perhaps Dad had been digging when he'd had the stroke. Sara had heard he was found in the ute by the ambulance officers.

Sara replaced her headphones. As she walked, the sun warmed her back. At the top of the lane, two red and purple darts – crimson rosellas – sprang from a pine tree. They became specks against the raw blue sky. On the ground, they'd left gnawed pine nuts.

In the side paddock, rabbit tunnels dimpled a green mound next to a scatter of blue-grey granite. Sara had seen weakened mounds collapse beneath heavy rain, the dirt washing into the creek and darkening the water. But today, in the afternoon sun, the land looked beautiful.

On the flats, bronzewing pigeons and sulphur-crested cockatoos gorged and fluttered in the silver, brome, and barley grasses. Sara remembered being with Ryan on a motorbike, speeding towards a similar flock, laughing as the wave of grey and white splashed the sky, and the birds squawking indignantly.

On the opposite hillside near a group of trees, shadow-coloured mounds became eastern grey kangaroos. They lifted their heads and then bounded downhill.

Sara began to jog as she passed Stirling's paddock.

A year or two ago, Mum told her Dad was having blood pressure trouble and would soon be unable to run the farm.

No offers had been made to Sara or, as Anne later told her, to her or Robbie either. Instead, Dad had whinged to Mum that the farm had to be sold because his useless bloody kids had pissed off every which way instead of showing their loyalty, courage, and grit.

Mum said she didn't hear the end of it.

Sara couldn't imagine herself living in the place where the sandstone walls had witnessed years of Mum's soft sobbing.

Mum's phone calls were often months apart, but each time, they pulled Sara into a place she still worked hard to escape. While Mum explained the day-to-day and told her what Dad was carrying on about, and then mentioned any Pine Creek news, Sara thought: *just leave, just leave, just leave.* She was equally glad and guilty at the end of each call.

Six months before Dad's stroke, Mum told Sara she had packed her belongings into the car and left her wedding ring on the kitchen table. Sara was so shocked, she couldn't speak.

'Hello? Hello? These cordless phones!' Mum had said, clearly assuming a technical issue.

Reportedly, Dad had sent Mum out through the door with a last barb, 'Enjoy being a dried-up, divorced nobody.' Not that there'd been an official divorce.

Now Mum was washing Dad's laundry again.

Sara shook her head of the thoughts which often led to the comfort of red wine. As she jogged, Sara felt the lift she was accustomed to, fullness in her lungs, a trickle of warm sweat between her breasts. This was real; this was good.

Near some granite rocks above a creek crossing, Sara saw

a dozen unshorn ewes. They froze mid-chew and goggled, yellow-eyed, then bumped into each other as they moved away. Sara slowed to a stop.

A wooded area close by reminded Sara of where Dad had chain-sawed logs into foot lengths. Robbie, Anne and Mum would then stack them into the back of the ute to stock the woodshed for the indoor fires.

Sara moved forwards, climbing the hill that led to the centre of the property; a killer that created more burn through the backs of her legs than the gym treadmill on a ten-percent incline. She reached the top and paused for a moment before jogging back to the house.

Sara opened a can of dog food, emptied half into a clean bowl and put it outside, returning the can to the fridge. Beneath the garden tap was a bucket of water. Sara washed it out and then refilled it. She gave Rusty a good pat and headed inside.

Sara went through her supplies. She pulled out a frozen dinner and took it into the kitchen. The microwave had a warped look, and the door was missing. Sara noted melted plastic around the edges and black scorch marks inside the machine. She could imagine Dad swearing as it emitted smoke.

Sara checked the freezer and found a tray of steak, two freezer meals like her own, and an open bag of potato chips.

Her stomach gurgled, acidic with hunger and red wine. She craved proper food, prepared in the right size with the calories written on the back. The picture on the box in her hand was of sliced meat, peas, carrots, and mashed potato. When she opened it, she found a rectangular, multi-coloured ice block.

She placed it in a bowl and grabbed her car keys.

The Milton pub was a short drive east along the highway and down a winding country road that became gravel about halfway. She passed pine and eucalypt forests, grazing sheep and cattle, looping creeks with trees lining the edges, big letterboxes at the end of driveways.

When she pulled into the small carpark, it was empty. Sara felt a wave of fondness for the pub. For a brief time, pub nights had been their one respite from Dad. The only time Mum really smiled.

Inside, behind the bar, numerous, multi-coloured spirit bottles were backlit by lights. The bar, made of natural looking wood grain, was lacquered and spread with beer-branded bar towels. Three brass beer taps shone beneath a fine layer of condensation.

Sara looked around. It was empty but for chairs, a pool table and a jukebox. She tried to imagine farmers with frothy beers and the laughter growing steadily louder as the night progressed. Talk of weather and stock prices turning into jokes and lighter topics. A man came out from a back room and stood behind the bar with a cloth in his hand. He smiled, offered his hand and introduced himself as the owner-manager, Garry.

Sara introduced herself. Garry leant on his side of the bar, frowning slightly as Sara explained why she was there. His frown turned to puzzlement and then confidence as he explained he'd worked there for fifteen years and had heard of her father. He was friendly and talked and talked.

After ten minutes, Sara walked out, head shaking. As she drove back to the farm, she drummed her fingers on the steering wheel. She felt something; a slight discomfort which happened when things didn't line up. She liked lines, as well as lists and ticks against each task once they were complete.

In the empty house, she located a pan and left her meal to simmer as she wiped the benches. She put the other meals in the fridge with her carton of long-life milk. On the bench she placed the eggs, bread, apples and tomatoes.

To the pasty-looking meal, Sara added a lot of salt and then sat down in front of the old TV. The back cover of the remote was gone, battery space empty. She got up and clicked it on manually.

The seven o'clock news came on, but Sara's eyes strayed to the glass front door. She could see a sky full of stars instead of the huge pine that had been a blackout between the Hamiltons and the rest of the world.

Sara remembered when she'd seen Dad driving out of the pine forest the night of Ryan's party. When they thought he was at the pub. The same pub she'd just left.

Garry, the owner, had just told her he'd been a junior back before Alec Stynes was killed. He was nice and open, friendly, as Sara expected the owner-manager of a small country pub would be.

Garry was certain that Len Hamilton never came to the pub on Fridays, or any other nights.

## Chapter 36

Rusty barked. Then came her low warning growl.

Hairs stood up along Sara's arms. She put her food aside, switched off the TV and padded into the laundry. Hand to wall, she pulled on her joggers.

Suddenly aware of the kilometres of darkness that separated her from the nearest houses, she felt very alone. She had an old dog, no idea where Dad kept the gun, if he still kept one, and there was no one within cooee.

An explosion of barks came from the machinery shed.

Sara hurried out. 'Rusty?' She realised she should have closed the gate, but usually the old dog stayed around the house. Maybe she'd cornered a feral cat in there.

A crackling in nearby undergrowth emitted a scramble and then a thud. A kangaroo bounded along the side paddock and then disappeared.

'C'mon, girl. It was just a roo.' Relieved, Sara reached the shed and felt inside the wall for the light switch. *Click*. Nothing. Inside stayed black as creosote.

From the darkness came scuffling and then a yelp. Rusty

ran past her. Sara felt a sudden strike across her back. She fell onto her hands and knees, gasping.

Something clattered to the ground. Running footsteps drew away.

Against the sky, Sara saw a lean, sprinting figure vault, hand to rail, over the front fence.

Next to her, Rusty panted, muscles trembling. Sara slipped her hand around the dog's collar. Drops of saliva slid down Sara's wrist. She struggled onto her side. 'Stay here. Good girl.' Her teeth began to chatter. Carefully, she got to her feet then sucked air as a sharp pain grabbed her side.

Rusty stood up, yelped and quickly sat down.

'You hurt, girl? Slowly, slowly.'

Tail between her legs, head down, the old dog limped towards the house.

'Come on, let's get you to the vet.' Sara checked around for movement before she followed Rusty.

Once back at the house, she clicked on the porch light and retrieved her car keys and phone. At the car, she helped Rusty onto the backseat.

## Chapter 37

From the farm, Burt Street Veterinary Hospital, Parkwood, was a twenty-five-minute drive. Sara pulled up in front of the small building between two elm trees. A lone streetlight transferred the angled shapes of the leaves onto her car bonnet.

Sara winced as she climbed out. She opened the passenger side door. 'C'mon, girl.'

Rusty uncurled, hobbled out of the car and limped into the vet's reception area.

The receptionist, a young, thick-waisted brunette wearing lots of blue eyeshadow, worked gum in her jaw. 'Closed at six. Emergencies only,' she said.

Sara glanced at the wall clock. It was after eight. 'My dog got hit by a ninja with a plank of wood. It might be serious.'

'You're lucky. Vet's still in. It was a busy night.' The receptionist leant down to the side of the desk. She made kissing noises and clicked her fingers.

Rusty wagged her tail and limped over.

'Poor baby.'

Sara held back the urge to tell her Rusty had been a fine sheepdog and was able to move a flock by herself.

The receptionist sat up, lifted the phone to her ear and stabbed a button. She spoke in a resigned monotone. 'Yep, I know. But you got a beat-up guard dog.' Her eyes did a lift and scan as though Sara was a grocery item. 'And human,' she added.

Sara scratched Rusty's head. The old dog's brown eyes were surrounded by grey hairs, which made her look half-brushtail possum, half dog. Sara swallowed hard. 'Good girl.'

The receptionist tapped her keyboard as she asked for Sara's address, and Rusty's breed and age. 'Doctor Tee will see ya now.'

The door to the right opened, and a dark-blonde man in a white coat tipped himself onto a comical angle. 'Hey, there! Where's the brave soldier?' His grin disappeared. 'Sara?' Toby wore a dirty white coat, moleskin pants and a checked flannelette shirt. The whole outfit needed a wash.

'Hey Toby,' said Sara, with a surge of relief. She hadn't been expecting this when she saw her first familiar face. 'Last time I looked, you were in the newspaper social pages.' She was careful not to breath too deeply, which hurt. 'With a stunning lady at a charity event.'

'Oh, yes.' Toby straightened and pocketed his hands. 'We went down to Sydney for a fundraiser. Médecins Sans Frontières.'

'She's a saint? Nice work.' Sara made a point of looking down at Toby's feet. She smiled when she recognised the famous riding boots brand and the creases of wear across the top. 'They RMs?'

Toby rested one boot on its heel. 'The one and only.'

"Bout time.' Sara smirked.

'I've been here three years now.' Toby held out his hand and shook hers. 'Enough about me. How are you?'

'Could be better.' Sara indicated the dog. 'Rusty got whacked.'

Toby's brow lifted. His knees clicked as he crouched. 'Hey, hey.' Toby gently ran his hand over Rusty from front to back and then checked each limb.

Tail tucked between her back legs, Rusty trembled.

'Someone hit her when she baled them up in the machinery shed.'

Toby glanced up. 'You're living here?'

'No, I only arrived today. I'm helping Mum. Dad had a stroke a few weeks ago.'

Toby frowned. 'Oh, sorry to hear that.' He stood. 'Rusty will need an x-ray, but it's not available until tomorrow. She can stay here overnight with our vet nurse.'

Sara started to bend down but straightened fast.

'What is it, Sara? Here.' Toby guided her to a seat.

Sara took a moment to catch her breath. 'I got hit too. My ribs.'

'Hey.' Toby used a low voice like he had with Rusty. Sara remembered him sounding the same when he spoke to a sheep tangled in a blackberry bush. 'Easy, easy. You need to get checked out at the hospital and then report it to police.'

Sara shook her head. 'Nothing to see. It'll be a bruise. I'll drop into the police station tomorrow.'

Toby pointed to the phone. 'Just give them a call from here. Please.'

Sara sighed, got to her feet slowly, and then accepted the phone from the receptionist.

After a minute, she put the phone down. 'They want me to

do the report in the morning. Someone is checking the place tonight, and they'll put word out about it. It'll be fine.'

Toby sighed. 'Okay, that's good. But let us drive you home.'

The receptionist's chair scraped back. 'You got that dog, remember?'

'Ah,' said Toby, and he rubbed his blonde-stubbled chin.

'Toby has a heart of gold and a backyard full of holes,' explained the young woman. She pulled a cardigan off the back of her chair and pushed her arms into the sleeves. 'Owners or rangers bring 'em in, and if no one claims 'em, he hasn't the heart to put a single one down. Kennels are full, so he adopts the lot.' She grinned. Bag slung over her shoulder, she walked past. 'Nighty, night. I'll take this girl out back.' She seduced Rusty with the kissing-clicking combo, and the two disappeared through a set of swing doors.

Toby scratched his head. 'I've got a dog who bit his owner on the arm because he got beat with a stick. He was only protecting himself.' He looked at his watch.

'I'll be fine. I can still drive,' said Sara.

Toby shook his head. 'Look, you're not driving all the way to the farm after an assault. You don't even have a guard dog.' He dipped his head. 'Please?'

'But I haven't—'

Toby held up his hand. 'Follow me.' He led them out into a small gravel courtyard. He pointed at a chunky Land Rover ute as it drove over. 'Here's our ride, jump in.'

Jumping wasn't an option. Sara held on to the rail beside the door, put one foot on the step and gently hauled herself into the passenger seat. She exhaled and rested back.

A grey-haired woman looked over.

'Hello?' said Sara.

'This is Dawn,' said Toby. 'Right, I'll go and get the dog.' He jogged back into the building.

'Oh.' Sara struggled for conversation as she and Dawn sat side by side. 'Are you and Toby related?'

'Nope.' Dawn faced ahead, hands on the steering wheel.

Sara noticed Dawn's seat was all the way forwards, and there was a cushion beneath her bottom. 'Doesn't Toby have a car?'

'This is it. He lost his licence.'

'Oh, right. You drive him around?'

'Yep.'

Sara carefully twisted around and then opened her window.

Toby came out of the back of the building with a white and brown dalmatian dancing on the end of a lead. They stopped behind the ute. Toby dropped the back of the tray edge, clicked and whistled. The dog jumped up. Toby secured the lead and then walked around to the passenger-side window. 'What should we call him?'

'We?' Sara looked over at Dawn.

Dawn continued to stare through the windscreen.

'He looks like a Barney,' said Sara.

Toby tapped the windowsill. 'Barney he is. I'll ride on the back.'

'Where are we going?' said Sara.

Dawn turned the volume up on the radio. John Williamson was singing 'True Blue'.

'My place!' Toby called. The cab rocked as he hauled himself up the side ladder. He sat down beside Barney, with his hand on the dog's neck.

Once on the open road, Sara's hair flapped in the breeze from the window. Behind them, Barney's ears did the same.

A black CB radio crackled as it picked up a signal. Someone laughed and said something inaudible through the static. Sara smiled at the familiar sound. Probably truckies out on the highway.

## Chapter 38

Dawn pulled into a driveway overgrown with gum and flame trees. The house was brick and tile with matching ones either side. Immediately, Barney began to bark. Answering barks came from the darkness. Sara felt the vehicle bounce.

The Land Rover's headlights lit the back of a corrugated iron shed, where dusty spiderwebs laced the corners. When the lights were turned off, Sara was momentarily blinded, which left her with an impression of Toby's bull bar. Recognition stirred, though she couldn't place it. She rubbed her temple gently.

Toby opened her door.

'Thanks.' Sara climbed out carefully. 'You have a house here?'

'I'm renting. Always loved this area. Good memories.'

Dawn got out and slammed the door. 'Night!' She marched down the driveway, turned at the bottom and approached the neighbouring house.

'Thanks!' Toby called and then turned to Sara. 'Got two dogs out the back.' He indicated a side gate and spoke in that direction. 'Quiet, you two! Settle down. Easy.'

'How'd you lose your licence?'

Toby dropped the side of the tray, and Barney jumped off, lead flying. Toby caught it mid-air. 'Speeding.'

Barney wriggled like a brown and white fish on the end of a line.

Toby wrestled the lead. 'Settle. Sit!'

Barney sat.

Sara swung the side of the tray up and pushed the pin through the metal peg to secure it, the familiar task still in her hands. 'Really? Must've been bad to lose your licence.'

'Three times. I'm nine months into a year's suspension. Just wait a tick while I pop him into a pen out back. He can stay there until they get used to each other. Barney, good boy.' He clicked his fingers and walked into the darkness.

Sara waited. Aside from the dogs, the frogs were making a racket too. So much for the quiet of the countryside.

Toby re-emerged alone and pointed towards the front of the house. They brushed past hydrangea bushes as he guided Sara up two steps.

'Welcome to my humble home.' He ushered her into darkness inside the front door and closed it behind them. Sara could feel his arm against her shoulder, smell the soap she'd noticed from the vet practice and the burnt lemony tang of an armpit after a long day.

Toby cleared his throat. The light came on. 'S'cuse me.'

A small, narrow hallway led to a kitchen.

Sara noticed the way Toby wouldn't look at her. 'I don't think I should stay with you.'

Toby, walking ahead, waved a hand. 'I have a spare room. It's comfy, I promise. You can't go to the farm, the way you are.'

The kitchen was an unfussy, narrow room that contained a small square table, two chairs and a little U-shaped bench. There were green tiles with onions, turnips, and something purple on them, and big knobbly water taps. Unwashed dishes filled the sink, and a used coffee cup sat on the table. The two seats reminded Sara of the doctor.

She sat down. 'Is your girlfriend away?'

'Di is in Nepal.' Toby dropped two slices of bread into the toaster and grabbed a can of baked beans off the shelf. He held it up, but Sara shook her head.

'When is she back?'

Toby shrugged, then put his head in the pantry. 'She calls when she wants to be collected from the airport.'

Sara rubbed her forehead and closed her eyes.

'Any other injuries aside from the rib?' said Toby. 'Did you hit your head or lose consciousness?'

'No, I'm just tired.' Sara felt a wave of fondness for her neat house in the mountains. The way she could close the door and the world stayed on the other side. Her knee stung. There was dirt all over her leggings and up her arms. Sara held out one leg then the other, did the same with each arm, tested her neck by looking left and then right. She leant forwards, head in hands. 'I can't believe what's happened in the last few hours.'

Toby poured beans into a saucepan. 'I'll get you some of my clothes, and you can hog the shower while I take care of the dogs. Okay?'

'Sorry to bust in on your life. I'm usually so organised.'

Toby laughed. 'I'm happy to help.'

In the shower, Sara stood beneath the drumming hot water until her muscles released. Her grazes stung. After a while, the water ran cold.

As she came out of the bathroom, a warm cloud behind her, Sara could hear Toby whistling. She was wearing a clean pair of his trackpants and a blue-checked flannelette shirt, cuffs covering her hands.

Toby smiled. 'That's better.'

'Sorry, but I used all the hot water.'

He winced good naturedly. 'You need it more than me.' He ladled stuff out of a can into three bowls.

'What will you do with Barney? I suppose you wouldn't be able to keep them all.'

His face pulled down. 'Find him a new home. Should be easy. He's not antisocial and walks well on a lead. The owner should be charged. We've removed a dog from him before.' He looked up. 'Hey, you might be able to help me out.'

Sara held up her hands. 'I can't cope with another dog right now. One night with poor Rusty and look at us.'

Toby put a hand on his hip. 'No, I mean, take some cute pictures of the dog. You know, the ones that make people goo-gah? Dog on a fluffy blanket. Dog having chin stroked. Dog with a little scarf.'

'People really go for that?'

Toby grinned. 'It's amazing what a little glamour shoot can do.'

'Okay, sure.'

Toby grabbed three dishes and walked outside. 'Come and get it!' The dogs were completely focused on Toby and the bowls; the two of them standing on their hind legs, their eyes following his hands.

The article that included Toby and his girlfriend had been about an art sale to raise funds for her work in disaster-affected areas such as the Philippines. The photo showed Toby wearing a suit and bow tie. Sara knew he would've had to force himself into a suit, given that he was made to wear one at school because it was the school uniform. He'd once confided to her he'd never wear another unless he was at a wedding or a funeral.

She wondered if he'd worn one to Ryan's wedding.

From outside came Toby's laughter; the full-bodied, gulping kind. Sara walked over to the window and wiped a tear off her cheek. Here with Toby, she knew it was real. Ryan had married Rachel and they'd had a son.

She gazed at the scrabble of man and dogs outside. A red setter cross stood over Toby, lapping his face, while a short brown dachshund rolled on its back nearby.

Sara smiled.

## Chapter 39

A rooster crowed, and a disjointed bird opera of pink and grey galahs, crows, magpies, finches and wrens rose into a crescendo. The sound reminded Sara of waking on the farm.

She opened her eyes.

The small room had flowery curtains, too much furniture jammed in with boxes on top, and the walls were painted mauve. Despite the clutter Sara had slept well. Still groggy, she tried to move. 'Oh, my God!' She breathed through the pain and then got up slowly, gently pulled on a cardigan that she found in a box by the bed and hobbled out to the kitchen. 'Coffee. Please.'

Toby looked over from the sink, hands buried in bubbles. 'How's the ribs this morning? And don't lie. Bruising is always worse the next day.' Tea towel slung over one shoulder, he dried his hands and cracked a flame beneath a kettle. Sara could hear the hum of a washing machine.

'You said it.' Sara exhaled loudly as she lowered herself onto a chair.

Toby frowned. 'You heading into the police station

shortly? I'm happy to come with you.'

'Yeah, I guess.'

Toby sniffed. 'Why do you smell like mothballs?'

Sara indicated the mauve cardigan. 'I borrowed it.'

'Keep it. Previous resident left some stuff ... they're not coming back.' He winced. 'They died.' Toby spooned coffee into two mugs. 'Last night, did you happen to get a good look at who hit you?'

Sara shook her head. 'Nope. It was dark, and they were dressed like a ninja.'

Toby's lip corner twitched. 'A ninja?'

'Head to toe in tight black clothes. Maybe even wearing a balaclava. I can't say what sort of hair or skin colour they had. They were definitely lean and athletic. Probably a hurdler going by the way they glided over the fence. Didn't even pause.'

'Knew what they were doing.'

Sara frowned as she remembered. 'It was like ... they knew where they were *going*.'

'Could've scoped the place out beforehand.'

'True.'

Toby crossed his arms over his chest. 'Glad it wasn't worse. Hey, I'll get you some toast, and coffee. You just take it easy.' He dropped bread into a toaster.

Sara yawned into both hands. 'Sure. Oh, bugger. This means I can't do sit ups, doesn't it?'

Toby gave her a quizzical look.

Sara got up, winced, one hand gripping the edge of the table. 'Don't you have to get to work? I can drop into the station myself. My car is still at the vet's.'

'No, it's Sunday. Someone else is on call now. After we see the cops, I'll come out to the farm with you.'

'Thank you, but—'

He held up his hand. 'Let's work together.'

Sara let out a tight breath and nodded.

'Good. Now eat up while I sort these puppies before they dig their way to China.'

Sara looked out. The sky was flecked with cloud, and though bright, it was cold. As the receptionist had mentioned, the lawn resembled a mole warren.

'Those two aren't house-trained.' Toby pointed. 'That little guy … the dachshund? Lifts his leg on everything. I've got a good set-up out there for them, but I'm gone all day. It's too long for dogs to be left alone.'

Sara nodded and remembered poor Rusty had been alone on the farm for two weeks.

After breakfast, Dawn dropped Toby and Sara off at the practice. The x-ray showed Rusty had no broken bones. Toby diagnosed heavy bruising around the hip. Rusty limped stiffly but wagged her tail and put her nose up.

'Good girl.' Sara ruffled her fur.

They drove to the police station in Sara's car, with Rusty on the backseat.

Once she'd reported the assault, and agreed to call if anything else happened, Sara walked outside with Toby. 'I'm glad it was all quiet when they checked out there,' she said. Her phone rang. 'Yes?'

'Oh, hi. Have I got Sara Hamilton? This is Laura Dennison from the ABC.'

'How did you get my number?' Sara walked away from her car and mimed drinking from a cup. With a little smile, Toby pointed to a café a few doors down with a brown awning and picture of a steaming cup. *Thank goodness for fellow caffeine addicts.* She gave a thumbs up and mouthed, '*black.*'

'We called your mother. I hope you don't mind. My colleague reported on Alec Styne's death back when it happened.'

With her shoe, Sara lined up the decorative rocks at the front of the police station. Someone had messed with them and not bothered to fit them back into their grooves. She rubbed her temple with two fingers where the soft throb of a headache brewed. 'I saw the email.'

Sara listened while Laura told her they wanted to set up a good backstory for the program before they added details from the police.

'Are you happy to be interviewed?'

Sara watched a Holden ute park beside her car. She had a sudden flash of memory. The ute had the same metal tray as the one she'd seen pull up beside Alec before the passenger threw a rock at him. She remembered the picture shown on the TV, and a small stirring of recognition swam close and then out of reach like a fish in cloudy water. Sara saw Toby was over near her car with a paper coffee cup in each hand. 'My dog is injured, and I'm with the vet. I have to go.'

'Sara, this could help Alec's parents find closure.'

*Just breathe ...* 'Okay.'

## Chapter 40

By the time Sara and Toby drove towards the farm it was mid-morning.

'Nice coffee, thanks.' Sara took a long swig through the tiny hole in the plastic lid and placed it in the cup holder. She reached for her water bottle, then felt how light it was. Slight irritation rippled over her. She looked across at Toby in the passenger seat. He was wearing clean jeans and a red flannelette shirt. 'What brought you back this way?' she said.

Toby pulled his eyes away from the side mirror. Elbow on the windowsill, he smiled faintly. 'I always loved coming out here when I was at uni. Country air has this sweetness.'

'That's animal dung.'

Toby laughed. 'Maybe you've overdosed on it.' He opened his hands as he spoke. 'But there's this release you feel once the suburbs drop off. It's like you don't know how wired you are until you can get outside. For me, it felt like a reset. Cleared my head.'

The road out was lined with pencil poplars covered in tiny yellow leaves. In a few weeks, the branches would be bare.

'Did you see much of Ryan after the last time you visited our place?'

'Not really. He was caught up getting married, being a new dad, earning money.' He looked over. 'I heard you all left home after that boy got killed. What happened?'

Sara took a long breath, mentally picking out the bits she used for this type of question. 'Too much tension at home. I finished school and then got a job, and eventually got into counselling. At one stage, I went a bit off the rails, but I pulled it together. Didn't want to end up like Robbie.'

'How is Robbie?'

Sara shook her head. 'Managed to avoid jail a couple of years back. Anne keeps track. I find it too depressing.'

Toby sighed. 'Hm ... that's sad. He was a nice guy. I see your mum sometimes. She told me that Anne is a busy mum down south and you work in the Blue Mountains.'

Sara rubbed her eye. 'My family hardly talk.'

'Why not?'

She looked over at him. 'It's hard to explain. I guess it just brings everything back.'

'Stuff from home, or the hit-and-run?'

'Both. Mostly home.'

Toby touched her forearm.

Sara automatically tightened. Sympathy had a way of undoing the knots which held her together. She stared ahead at the road. 'No use talking about it.'

Toby shook his head slightly. 'I never understood why your father got so angry. I only heard him going off once, but Ryan said he was often like that.'

'Ryan eased the pressure off us by working with Dad.' A painful lump filled her throat.

'You three were so quiet. And your mum is a darling. It

might be good to reconnect with your brother and sister.'

Sara straightened in the seat. 'One day.'

Bordered by farm boundaries, the road hummed beneath them. The blue sky was patterned by cloud tufts, which barely cast a shadow. Sunshine was succeeding in brightening the farmland. Red, wallaby, and spear grasses waved softly in a breeze, and cows lifted their heads, lower jaws working.

Sara noticed the paddocks looked better than she remembered, despite the drought in 1996–97. But from one property to the next, the land quality differed. Some were better managed, with a good understorey of fallen logs, fenced-off dry sclerophyll forest: eucalypts, waratahs, banksias, wattles, pea flowers and tea-trees. She saw a barricaded creek edge, which kept away destructive hooves; Dad had done this on their farm. Here though, there were some bare hillsides, and in one paddock, erosion carved out sides of the slope, which created great cracks along the flat. Some ravines had slid inwards, probably due to rabbit infestation. Sara recognised salt-resistant plants along scalded areas, the salinity assured once the land had been robbed of its deep-rooted trees.

One thing her father did well was farming. After each drought, he culled the stock and protected the water sources. Rested the paddocks between seeding. When it finally happened, the Hamilton property would sell easily.

Sara moved to accommodate her sore rib. 'It's ten years since Alec died. An ABC reporter just called me. They want to feature his death on a cold case program.'

Toby's eyebrows went up. 'Really?' He looked thoughtful. 'Can you imagine if you were the driver … and the program came on? All along, he feels like he's gotten away with it, and then it's right on the screen in front of him. Maybe he'll feel guilty enough to confess this time.'

Sara felt a hot painful rush and sucked in a staggered breath as her eyes filled.

'What, Sara?' Toby touched the back of her hand. 'Are you alright?'

Sara swallowed, tried to speak, had to clear her throat. She retrieved her hand and then wiped her nose with her wrist as tears dribbled down her cheeks. 'I left Alec a letter that afternoon, asking to meet. I never told anyone, and it seems crazy, because it was so late and terrible weather, but I think he might've tried to come over.'

## Chapter 41

Sara could see Toby trying to hide his surprise with a frown. 'What time were you supposed to meet?'

Sara shook her head. 'We didn't make a time. I just said I hoped we could be friends. I distinctly told him *not* to come to the house.'

Toby winced in a puzzled way. 'It would be really strange for him to head out in the middle of a storm if you hadn't even arranged a time. And, on the off chance he did decide to go see you, someone else hit him.'

'Alec's mum said she didn't know why he went out.' Sara glanced at Toby. 'Shortly before he was killed I saw him speak to Robbie at the boundary. He was clearly upset. Afterwards, Robbie was out of sorts. What if it was him Alec wanted to see?'

Toby nodded and then rocked his head sideways, like he was weighing things up. 'Maybe he wanted to run away ... or end his life. He wouldn't be the first.'

'I don't know, Toby. I never really bought that.'

Toby looked out the side window, quiet for a moment.

'Rumour was he was gay.'

Sara nodded, opened her mouth, but Toby held up his hand and she stopped.

'He was probably living a private hell. Everyone hated gay men. People wanted to kill them, blamed them for AIDS. Don't you remember?' Toby's hand closed into a fist on his lap.

'Of course, I remember.' Sara noticed Toby's fingers go white, and she went on cautiously. 'There was just so much bullshit around. Hard to tell what was real.'

Toby snorted, shook his head and looked away. Sara gave him plenty of time, but he didn't take it.

'Toby?' she said.

Toby's eyes narrowed and then he pointed through the windscreen. 'There's your turn off.' His voice lightened, and he smirked. 'Been so long, you forgot.'

Sara slowed and turned right. The tyres crunched into the dirt and then they rumbled over the cattle grid.

Toby stretched and yawned. 'How long are you here for?'

Sara sensed Toby had changed the subject too quickly. She decided not to pursue it. 'A week.' She cast Toby a quick look. 'How do you manage without a driver's licence?'

Toby sighed. 'I can't drive out to farms, so I don't treat livestock now; it's annoying. Just cats, dogs, budgies, and rabbits at the clinic. That'll teach me to speed.'

'Three times?'

'I may have been a fair few clicks over the limit. I get a heavy foot during emergencies. We need a proper animal ambulance.'

'I didn't know this place was so well policed.'

Toby pulled his chin in. 'A certain Constable Frederick Murray has got it in for me.' His mouth twisted wryly.

'What did you do? Steal his girlfriend?'

Toby gave her a look. 'You don't remember Freddie?'

'Freddie? Ryan's mate? He's a cop now?'

'A-huh. One with a long memory.'

'God, I couldn't think of anyone worse! You think he has a grudge because Dad chucked him off the farm that time?'

Toby took a deep breath. 'Ah, he's got lots of grudges. You know his father gave him a really hard time? Freddie came to training with a black eye more than once. During games, he was a mean player, you know, dirty. Stuck the boot in if he could. Always getting penalties.'

'Geez.' Sara pulled in beside the house yard and glanced around. 'Toby, you're welcome to stay. Heaps of empty rooms.' The idea was suddenly very appealing.

'Dawn will be here shortly. I just wanted to check there were no ninjas around.'

'Thanks. I appreciate it,' Sara said, trying not to sound disappointed.

## Chapter 42

Toby walked towards the machinery shed. As he passed a tree, he grabbed a handful of bark and crumbled it onto the ground.

Sara joined him.

'This where it happened?' he asked.

'Yes.' Sara pointed into the shed and then noticed a length of wood on the ground. She nudged it with her foot. 'Pretty sure this is what I got hit with.'

Toby picked up the wood, frowned as he turned it over. It was hand-thickness, about a metre long. 'Wonder what they were after.' He looked around. His eyes settled on the Hilux for a moment and then he threw the wood off to the side and brushed his hands together. 'It's weird it all being so empty. Are your parents going to sell?' He walked inside the shed. Sara followed.

'Dad had planned to, but Mum isn't sure. She's not interested in farming; Dad cured us all of that. Before he had the stroke, he'd destocked, and got it ready. That's why it's quiet.'

'How bad was the stroke?'

'Pretty bad. He's silent and struggles to walk. Mum says the rehab looks and sounds like an old people's home. At least therapy is right there, but ... God, I dread to see him like that.'

'You haven't seen him?'

'No. Not for years. Don't really speak.'

Toby squeezed her shoulder. 'Anything I can do?'

'I have to visit him sometime, if you're free.'

'Sure.'

Sara almost turned for the house and then noticed something. At the back of the shed was the shovel, but the dirt pile now looked flat. She walked over. 'That's strange.' She held her side as she squatted. 'There was a hole here yesterday. Someone's filled it in.' Sara grabbed the shovel. 'Let's see what's down there.'

'No. Please don't,' Toby held out his hand. 'I'll do the digging.'

Sara handed it over. 'Careful.'

Toby scooped out all the loose dirt. He got to the bottom. There was nothing there.

He made a face. 'Want me to fill it back in?'

'Yeah. But why would someone go to the effort of filling an empty hole?'

They examined the rest of the shed floor. Nothing else appeared to have been disturbed.

'Sara, do you think it's safe to stay here?'

'I'll be fine. Check out my vicious guard dog.'

Looking back over her shoulder, Rusty stood facing the house gate.

Sara grinned. 'Sorry, girl. Keen to get home, eh?'

Rusty wagged.

Toby jogged over and held the gate open. 'How 'bout I take a look around?'

Sara showed her palms. 'Go for it.'

After ten minutes, Toby joined Sara inside. He scooped a small plastic bottle from his shirt pocket. 'Here's some anti-inflammatory meds, if Rusty needs them. Make sure she's comfortable enough to walk around the yard, at least.' He dropped the bottle into Sara's hand.

Rusty barked when Toby's ute came up the drive.

Sara followed Toby outside. Dawn lifted one finger off the steering wheel while her eyes stayed off to the right like she was examining the empty paddock.

Toby opened the door and hoisted his bum onto the passenger seat. 'Call me if you have any more trouble.'

Sara waved and watched the vehicle leave. She then turned a circle. It was a different scene for her as to what it would be for Toby. He probably saw rolling green hills, freedom and beauty. Unlike her, he'd always been able to leave. Return to the comfort of the city suburbs after a taste of country, tell some stories, wash off the hard-earned sweat.

Sara's view was clouded by memories, which led straight to the tight knots she'd worked so hard to secure. Already, she could feel them loosening.

## Chapter 43

Sara grabbed the Workers' House keys and walked the familiar track across the paddock. Her eyes scanned for reptilian movement. Tiger snakes were common, and she'd seen more than one red-bellied black snake on the farm. Both had a bite that could kill a dog. She tripped in a dry mud hole the shape of a cow's hoof.

The little house had dark-orange rust patches on the roof, grass swamping the small yard, and an empty carport. The track between the gate and the house had disappeared.

The door creaked open readily. Cold and mildew wafted into Sara's face as though the building had finally exhaled. Mum had told her after they all left, Ryan had never been back. Dad still had contractors stay there from time to time, but not since Mum moved out. Mum didn't think he'd know how to clean the place anyway.

Sara left her boots in the entrance by the tiny bathroom. It was the same: crammed with a square, water-stained bath, a plastic curtain, and a sink with a small mirror. A water heater took up one corner, and exposed metal pipes were attached to the back wall. Stuck to the pipe by one leg was the thin shell of a huntsman spider. It rocked with the draft of her presence.

Sara stood in front of the mirror, lifted her shirt and checked her ribs. Developing on her side was a blue-red bruise the width of her hand. Sara pulled her shirt down and glanced around. She'd never showered here. After her night with Ryan, she'd slipped silently back home with her chest full of gold.

She ran her hand along the empty towel rail. She remembered undressing and then joining Ryan in bed as if she'd been delivered by the storm.

In the pokey rectangular kitchen, laminated yellow benchtops were crusted with something white and seasoned with mouse droppings. The cupboards gaped, hinges broken.

The small fridge was ajar. Dry green-black mould coloured the rubber seals.

Sara walked through the house and checked the bedrooms. Each had rusted springform bases, naked, stripey mattresses, and pillows. In the loungeroom, the blackened red-brick fireplace contained white ash.

The furniture was ripped, sagging, and hunkered into old brown carpet. Everything looked as dead and empty as the spider in the bathroom.

Though Sara felt a strong urge to leave, she paused at the window.

A hundred metres down the road was the edge of the old highway where Alec used to cross over.

She remembered checking down here with Anne after Lillian had told them he was missing. Arguing with Anne because the electricity had been left on, and Sara knew it wasn't her fault. She'd been certain, because after Ryan left, she remembered staying until the dryer was finished so she could switch everything off at the mains. Of course she'd left the damn fridge ajar! She knew how a closed fridge went rotten if the power wasn't on. Anne had stared into the fireplace, silent at first, before angrily telling Sara to hurry up because she was tired and needed to go back to bed. A silly sister fight. The whole time, Alec had been dead, his body awaiting discovery only a short distance away.

After locking the Workers' House, Sara strode back the way she'd come, rubbing heat into her upper arms with her palms. The bent grass spoke of her recent passage. There was no ill will in the house paddock. It was a relief, a hyphen to the smaller house where some freedoms had happened. Where once, briefly, she'd felt loved.

## Chapter 44

Sara walked up to the woodshed. It was only midday, but she craved the company of a crackling fire the same way she craved hot chocolate in winter. Chopped wood was stacked down one side of the corrugated iron wall, and only a few layers deep. She'd never seen it this low. The ground was littered with knife-sized pieces of kindling. Sara noticed something at the back. Glancing out behind her, she walked in and saw a lumpy area of freshly disturbed soil, squashed down with a zig-zag pattern on top.

With a shard of wood Sara dug until she hit firmer ground. Nothing. She brushed it over and stomped it flat.

She wondered if Dad had hidden something of value and someone knew he was sick and had come looking.

She imagined him bending over a shovel, glancing around, burying a package. She remembered Friday nights ... when they thought he was at the pub.

What was he doing while the rest of the family enjoyed his absence? A memory brushed close but disappeared before Sara could see it properly like a fox moving through fog.

Something about Dad. Pub nights. Something that didn't quite fit. Then it was gone.

Sara sighed and collected some pieces of wood. Balancing them in one arm, she looked around as she entered the house. She locked the door behind her and then walked through to Mum's lounge and put her armload into the empty box. Then she opened the small door of the pot-bellied stove, wrapped some paper around a handful of kindling and shoved it in. Fine white ash clung to the back of her fingers. She remembered another fire. Down at the Workers' House, the night she'd been with Ryan. Left to burn to fine ash. A memory resurfaced. Something about the fireplace. Sara shook herself. This place was giving her the creeps.

Sara added chunks of firewood, and then found matches. Her mobile phone rang. She pulled it from her pocket and flipped it open.

'Hello?'

'Hi, I'm Jason, Nurse Unit Manager from Blooms. Sorry to bother you. It's about your father.'

Sara resented Jason's sudden voice, which had wrenched the reality of her father's illness right into the room. She breathed calmly and visualised the Workers' House fireplace. Her memory shifted and offered daylight. It was early and cold – the Workers' House on the morning Alec had gone missing.

'Oh, okay. You usually call Mum, don't you?' Sara steered her brain away from sterile rehab images. In her memory she looked over Anne's shoulder as she stared into the fireplace. Sara remembered seeing charred wood and coals.

'We were told to get in touch with you while she's away, Sara. You were the next contact?' Jason sounded unsure.

The coals in the hearth had been black and wet-looking.

'Sara?'

'Ah, Sorry. Go on.' The question hung in the air, even though Jason had simply waited in silence. *He's your father. Don't you care? Why haven't you been in?*

'Is this a bad time? I really do need to chat.'

'Sure, sure. Sorry. How can I help?' said Sara. The progress of her thoughts rolled steadily on by themselves. The only decent fire, which would leave wet coals and unburnt wood, was a doused one.

'It's a legal matter, unfortunately. A family member, a cousin, I think he said, has been in. He wanted your dad to sign some papers.'

'What cousin, sorry? Papers?' Sara tried to focus.

'I'm unsure, but they're legal documents, and your father is unable to make any decisions at present.'

Sara scratched something off the cast-iron stove with her fingernail. 'Dad is an only child. We're not close to Mum's family, because Dad doesn't like them. They wouldn't visit.'

'Um, our visitors log says Ryan Finch.'

'Ryan?' The internal jolt stole her breath. 'He's here? When? Um, I mean, he's not related.' Sara got up to her feet. The hot, shaky feel of adrenaline flickered through her. 'I'll be there as soon as I can.'

'It's okay – he left,' Jason said quickly. 'We asked him to come back tomorrow at two pm.'

'Two?' Sara breathed fast, paced back and forth, ran her fingers through her hair. 'Where is he? Staying, I mean. He lives south of Sydney. I didn't know he was here.' She started counting her in and out breaths, to slow the onset of the little stars she sometimes saw when she got worked up.

'Ah,' said Jason, sounding uncertain. 'I'm sorry, I don't have any of that information. He didn't leave a phone number. Look, there's no need to come in today. Your father is exhausted. He's still recovering.' Jason sounded like he was back in control. 'Please. Come at two pm tomorrow.'

Sara thanked him and said goodbye.

She stood with both hands on her cheeks. When she was calm enough, she dialled Mum.

Years ago, Mum had redirected Ryan and Rachel's wedding invitation to Sara. Maybe she still had his contact details.

Mum's phone rang out.

There was a chance Dad and Ryan had made an agreement in the event Dad got sick or died. Maybe he had left everything to Ryan in his Will.

Not from generosity, but to punish her family.

## Chapter 45

Sara pocketed her phone and paced the length of the house. She walked outside and did a lap of the garden. Rusty watched from her bed on the patio, ears pricked.

Inside again, Sara got busy. She swept the floors and then found cleaning spray and cloths. She dusted and wiped, cleaned toilets, and then scrubbed the bathroom. Her thoughts looped backwards, further and further, and she felt the undoing of the knots she'd so carefully tied.

She opened the basket in the laundry, pulled Dad's clothes out and then shoved them into the washing machine.

Sara would be surprised if Dad had actually learnt how to operate it. Women's work. Demeaning for the mighty Len Hamilton. Sara slammed the lid and wound the dial to wash.

She thought once that Dad must view women like spiders: crouching, waiting to trap, deceive and damage men. Remove men's rightful power, eat them up, crush them, suck their blood. That's why women had to be subdued and controlled.

She remembered they'd all been forced to watch Dad tell

Mum she was useless, flawed and defective. It was agony to see her face crumple, her shoulders slump, the light fade from her eyes – their Mum, whom they loved, who tried so hard but still got chastised every day. And Robbie – punished because he had a heart that couldn't hate.

Outside, Sara beat a mat against the wall until she was sweaty and covered in grit.

At night, almost every night, Sara had heard her mum's heavy breathing. *Marital bliss.*

She slammed the mat at the wall a few more times, yanked open the door, replaced the mat, tears snaking down her face. Rubbed one eye with her knuckle. She felt the knot untie, and then the memories began to climb out.

Sara sank down onto her knees, palms on the tiled floor. She slapped one of her hands down repeatedly until it stung.

Sara remembered when, aged twelve, Robbie had put his arm around Mum's shoulders after Dad unleashed a bellyful of nastiness at her. Something hadn't gone right for him down in the paddock. As usual, Dad had made it Mum's fault. Robbie was sent to the woodshed to chop wood, which he did until his hands were blistered and bleeding. Sara remembered the night Dad had beaten Robbie; the awful sound of her brother being punched. She remembered Dad slapping Anne's face, and the shouting, shouting, shouting!

She remembered everything.

Her tears poured. Sara craved Anne and Robbie between her arms, their chests tightly pressed together, like they did sometimes when they were younger. She crouched, forehead to thighs, ached for Mum as tears and snot ran onto Toby's trackpants.

*Breathe, just breathe.*

After a while, she was calmer, colder. She got up and

staggered down to her room, climbed into bed and curled up.

Sometime later, Sara woke dull and heavy with memories. The sun was low when, wineglass in hand, eyes puffy, Sara wandered through the doorway of Anne's old bedroom.

With a finger, she traced dust along the windowsill. She remembered the silence after Anne and Robbie had left. The thick, suffocating sadness, and then her anger at being abandoned by them.

Sara balanced the wineglass on a bare edge of the table, moved a box from the bed onto the floor and sat down. Through the window were the burnt-orange leaves of an ornamental pear, and the spiky, burgundy-coloured Japanese maple.

On Anne's study table was Mum's sewing machine. Mum had said that her flat was too small for all her belongings. It was also located around the corner from Blooms, but she left all of Dad's care to the nurses. She told Sara she was no longer at Dad's beck and call, just picked up his dirty clothes. They *were* still married.

Sara pushed a photo album aside and picked up a book. It looked like one of her mum's old romance novels. She stood and wandered out, flicking through the pages, then turned it over and read the back cover.

Sara looked up at the unfettered window. The light pouring in. This had been the book Dad had caught her reading the day Mum got burnt rescuing her heirloom. The windswept lady and a man in uniform on the front cover. Love and fantasy, courting and sex. Ice-cream.

*Ryan.*

## Chapter 46

Sara woke, hauled herself out of bed and into the bathroom, where she washed her face and drank thirstily from the tap. She'd slept well, considering it was only her first night in the house, but she remembered sleep had been helped by a decent amount of wine. She held her hand out and watched it shake, then she sighed and dug through her toiletry bag for headache tablets. She gulped two and then got dressed in fresh leggings and runners.

Outside, the morning was cool, clear and still. She locked the door behind her and looked around, a habit since her assault. Her jog was slow, but still hurt her ribs.

Wincing, holding her side, Sara instead speed-walked. A flat area in the grass beside the track made a good squat and lunge pad. As she worked out, good cramps bit into her muscles. She climbed onto her hands and knees carefully and did push-ups. Usually, she did them on her toes, but that made her ribs hurt too.

A sudden belly pain caused Sara to lurch forwards. She vomited on the grass. Panting, eyes and nose watery, she shivered and spat.

Walking back towards the house, Sara passed the shearing shed. One edge of the corrugated iron corner was dog-eared upwards.

Mum had told her the sheep were the first to go. Too much work for Dad on his own. He'd sold all but a handful and focused on the cattle to keep the farm viable. Their red heeler, Jack, was hit on his way across the road just a couple of years ago. He must've been on the return journey, because the neighbour's dog, Dolly, had a litter of beautiful red heeler puppies two months later. Dad was left with Rusty to help with stock work.

Buffed shiny by lanolin, the old wooden sheep railings still bore tuffs of wool. Small strips of grass grew underneath. A sharp smell lingered from the hoof-churned soil – years of ammonia from dung and urine.

Sara remembered the empty trucks when they rattled down the lane, the dust brewing out behind double sets of tyres. The grind and *beep-beep* as one reversed up to the shed so the truck gates and shed ramp aligned.

She remembered how the tentative sheep shuffled to the edge, their noses outstretched. She could almost hear the whistle and bark, the clapping at their heels – 'Hey-hey! Get up!' One by one the flock would leap from the shed to the truck, and clatter through the cages, filling the top and then the lower deck, all the way to the back of the cab.

Even now several lengths of black polystyrene pipe remained in a pile beside the yards. They'd poked the pipe through side slats to crowd the sheep tighter and prevent them falling down, which usually meant injuries or death by trampling. Finally, when the truck was full, there'd be a metallic slam as the bolt slid home. The dogs would be panting as the load was counted. Then the truck lumbered slowly uphill, saleyard bound, money on the way.

Back at the house, Sara made black coffee, took a sip and winced.

While she'd been exercising, Sara had made a decision. She would go and see Lillian Stynes. Today. Confess about the letter. Lean the telling towards innocence and curiosity. She'd only been a year older than Alec when she wrote it. Besides, it would be revealed when she was interviewed, anyway.

Sara cringed as she imagined a journalist quizzing her.

*'You sent a letter asking the victim to meet you hours before he was killed?'*

She owed Alec something. He'd just been a boy; a talented boy, and she'd waited too long to reach out. She hadn't been driving the car that killed Alec but felt part of the journey which resulted in him being hit by one.

Worrying, her lower lip between thumb and finger, Sara looked through the window towards Lillian's. Mum said she'd never moved away. Her gaze crossed to the Workers' House, and she revisited her thoughts of last night, before she wrote herself off on a bottle and a half of wine. She was certain a fire had been doused down there the night of the hit and run.

Sara recalled the morning Alec went missing. She and Anne had rushed in, both trying to be first. Neither had removed their boots, because the entrance was already muddy with footprints. Sara had been the one to mop after Ryan had left, and she'd done it properly, lovingly. She had remembered to turn the power off, but they'd found it was left on.

Separately, these things could be written off as mistakes or a faulty memory, but together they meant someone may have been down there the night Alec died.

Sara dialled Mum again. This time she picked up. 'Mum, remember when Alec was killed? The Workers' House had been empty for weeks, right?'

'What? Oh, yes. Gosh, its early.' Mum's voice was soft and scratchy. 'Let me get a gown on.' Sounds of rustling. Mum yawned and cleared her throat. 'I'm just putting the kettle on.'

Sara heard the water run. 'When Anne and I went down there, the entrance was muddy, and a fire had been put out. The electricity had also been left on.'

Silence.

Sara went on. 'Anne was quick to switch off the electricity and get out.'

'Anne's good at tidying up.'

'Anne ...' Sara swallowed as she remembered Anne's impatience. She'd had a packed bag beneath her bed that night. Ready to go. They'd been stuck at the hospital for hours, and Sara remembered Anne had paced and sulked for most of them. 'Alec was killed that night. We probably shouldn't have touched anything, and we should have told the police.'

'Don't be silly. Alec was hit by a car out on the road.'

'But when I cleaned the house after Ryan left, no one else was going to stay there and I'm sure I didn't leave it like that.'

'It's easy to forget little things. Especially after what happened.'

Sara took a slow breath. 'Mum, maybe someone went in there the night Alec died. There's no security. It could've been where Alec was headed.'

'Sara? I really don't know if we should be talking about this.'

'Alec's mum mentioned Robbie.' Sara persisted.

'Robbie was in hospital.'

'I know, I know, it's okay, Mum. I'm just thinking things through.' Sara took a deep breath and heard her mum do the same. 'Let's say that Alec wanted to meet up with Robbie. I did see them chat once on the boundary.'

'Robbie was kind to strangers.'

'They didn't look like ...' Sara closed her eyes for a moment. 'Anne told me they'd been friends. Robbie went weird after Alec died, remember?'

'Well, it was such a shock. I don't think we should speculate, Sara.'

'Mum, the ABC's cold case program is doing Alec's case? They're arranging interviews now. You can bet they'll ask questions like this.'

Mum's voice became secretive and clearer, like she'd gotten closer to the mouthpiece. 'Sara, the police had a good look around. Questioned everyone. Don't you say anything about this to the ABC. We'll be crucified. I feel wobbly. I think I should sit down.'

Sara could hear a definite shake in Mum's voice. 'I'm sorry. Are you okay?'

'Mm.'

Sara waited. 'How's it going with your brother?'

'It's lovely. You need to meet Bruno.'

'I will, Mum.'

'Sara?'

Sara felt a little hardening against the sound at the back of Mum's voice. 'Yes, Mum?'

'I'm going dancing next week. I've joined a group who

meet at the Parkwood Community Centre.'

Sara exhaled. 'That's great.'

'It is?'

'Of course, it is. Dancing makes you happy.'

The silence was long. Her mum then said quietly, 'I still feel guilty about so many things. Not just letting you kids down, but when I do something Len doesn't like.'

'Dad doesn't like *anything*. I don't know anyone that hates so many things. Except dogs. At least he was good with the dogs.' Sara rubbed her eye. 'No one has the right to take away your happiness like he did.'

A sniffle came down the line. Sara closed her eyes as her throat tightened – her mum's pain was an arrow to a deep part of her heart. 'Oh, Mum. You can do what you want now.'

'Can I?' Asked like a little girl's question.

Sara fought the heavy tug of her throat, blinked back tears. 'You don't have to ask anyone, Mum. You can dance on the roof in your knickers, if you want!' Sara wiped her face with her hand. 'It's *your life.*'

'I'd better have that cuppa.' Mum chuckled in a sad way. 'You get on now. I'll be fine.'

'I love you, Mum.'

A pause. 'I love you too.'

Sara wanted to tell her more. About the holes, the assault, about Ryan turning up with papers, but she knew it would be too much. 'Mum, you said that it was a friend from the pub who found Dad after his stroke?'

'That's right. Haven't you been and thanked them yet? Your father could have been stranded for days.'

*Maybe a simple miscommunication*, Sara thought. 'Ah, okay.' She looked out and saw so much light from the dining room window. 'Was it you who had the big pine cut down?'

'Yes, it was.'

'Amazing difference. It's like there's more oxygen.'

'You have no idea how good that felt.'

Sara smiled. 'I think I do. Take care, Mum.'

As she replaced the phone, Sara paused. Despite Mum's resistance to the idea, the fact remained. The Workers' House, the closest building to Alec's house, had been used the night Alec died.

Who would do that? Her best guess: someone with something to hide.

Someone who knew something about Alec's death.

## Chapter 47

Sara took the same path in reverse that Lillian would have taken the morning Alec went missing. Her heart must have been pounding, as she'd considered increasingly awful possibilities.

Still on the Hamilton side of the highway, Sara drew level with the Stynes' driveway. She kept walking.

Hands jammed into the pockets of her tracksuit top, she stopped at the edge of the channel. She looked down along its length until it disappeared with the natural curve of the highway. After all this time, she couldn't be sure exactly where Alec's body had been found. She peered in. It was boggy at the bottom, and a few insects hovered around weeds growing on the sides.

After the police tape was removed and all the vehicles had left, people had occasionally come to look. They were often kids, prodding with a stick in the wrong place. The bouquets of flowers that had been left by passers-by, indicating the site, were soon spread by the weather. A small white cross that someone had planted there disappeared too.

*Nothing stays still*, Sara thought as a breeze ruffled her hair. The scarring left by the activity of that forty-eight hours soon faded. Rain washed things away. A few days after the police left, even the channel, scraped of non-existent evidence, was again just a conduit for excess water.

Sara walked about twenty metres and squatted. Her eyes snagged on a brown reed the shape of a shoelace, and then on purple clover leaves. She realised she was still looking for Alec's missing shoe and coat.

Sara had heard that in the months following Alec's death, his mum had gone to big truck company depots in Sydney and Melbourne. She put up posters – with pictures of Alec wearing his patchwork jacket, a school portrait, and his shoes – on electrical poles and outside shops. She visited the local council member's office dozens of times. Sara heard he eventually gave his secretary a code word and stayed quiet behind his door when Lillian visited.

Sara eyed the driveway from where she was. She'd walked about thirty metres past it. She remembered the ute she'd seen, which produced a man who'd thrown a rock at Alec. That afternoon had she been standing where she was now, she would have seen their faces.

She remembered DC Thoroughgood and wondered where he'd ended up ... *probably not regional*. Even then, she'd been disappointed in him. He wasn't local, which meant a lot in Pine Creek. So why had he even come? Nothing was publicised about the intimidation Lillian had complained of. It felt as if they had been very quick to decide that suicide or an accident had claimed Alec's life.

Sara headed for Lillian's driveway with the sinking feeling that she had nothing to give. She still felt bad about being relieved her letter had never turned up.

Before she lost the courage, she strode across the slick blue skin of the resurfaced road. At the bottom of the driveway, she realised she was standing where Alec had been when the mystery ute stopped. The driveway turned a 180-degree angle and sloped upwards, running parallel with the highway, to the Stynes' front gate.

A silver car sped past.

Sara re-tucked her hair after the whoosh of air. The shadow of a memory came and then disappeared like the car.

At the gate, Sara scanned for the two alpacas and few sheep that used to be there. She'd never been close to an alpaca but was wary of their long necks and huge teeth. Across the vacant paddock, empty seed heads quivered atop fine yellow stalks. Thick bracken fern populated the back third of the property.

Lillian's small house was dark brick with a dull red roof. Along the front wall were scratchy overgrown lavender bushes and a scatter of calendula plants with buds on them. On the left side, the garage was open, and Sara could see the old red Suzuki.

Sara's knocks on the front door sounded intrusive. As soon as she paused, she could hear distant traffic. Wind sighed against the house.

Sara waited. She knocked again but felt relief when she heard nothing from inside.

Sara glanced up. A shiny black spider crouched inside a web underneath the guttering. There was a slight whistle as the wind moved around the eaves. She wondered which window Alec had climbed out of the night he died, and where Lillian had been as her son headed for the highway. Sara remembered how Lillian had stated that she hadn't seen him leave and had no idea where he'd intended to go.

Sara glanced about and then walked to the back of the house. She passed a rusted-out forty-gallon drum and some old wooden boxes. Along the back wall were three large windows.

Behind the glass of the first one was the back of a closed curtain. The next revealed a queen-sized bed with the covers peeled: corner to the middle, like the start of a paper aeroplane.

On the lived-in side of the room was a side drawer, a chair with clothes on it, a book, a lamp, and a teacup.

Sara headed for the last window. Mirrored was the day: cloud, blue sky and gum trees. She cupped her eyes against the glass. Inside was a single bed, a desk and chair, a colourful poster on the wall. Boy colours. Alec's room. Then she saw coloured squares. Her heart staggered a beat. As she looked closely, she made out a patchwork jacket.

Sara stepped backwards, tripped, and crashed down hard.

## Chapter 48

Lying on her back, Sara couldn't draw breath. Throat constricted; her ribs squeezed. She sucked at the air like a gaped-mouth fish. Warm tears ran into her ears.

Overhead, a cup hovered between her and the blue and then slowly tipped. Water hit her eyeballs. Sara struggled, fought and coughed. Something was gently pressed against her mouth and crackled as she breathed.

'Breathe slowly, slowly.' A woman's soft voice came down a long tunnel.

Sara scrabbled at the thing over her mouth, but it was only paper.

'It's just a bag,' said the voice. 'I think you're hyperventilating. Can you breathe slower? It's okay. It's okay.'

Sara held the bag. She wanted to get up and run away, but all her energy was focused on oxygen, on opening her throat to the wide blue sky.

'Is that better?' said the voice.

Sara took the bag away from her mouth and wiped her

top lip with the back of her hand. She twisted around awkwardly.

'Are you alright?' Looking down was Lillian, Alec's mum. Her large blue eyes and delicate skin were more lined than Sara remembered, her hair flecked with grey and grown into a soft bob. Lillian was about mid-fifties. She wore plain blue jeans and a large pink jumper with frayed sleeves. She shuffled back a foot, and her cheeks lifted in a friendly expression. She was still very beautiful.

Sara pushed herself up, so they were eye level. 'I saw ...' She swallowed. 'Alec's jacket.'

'Ah.' Lillian closed her eyes for a moment. She started to push herself up from the ground, brushed her backside and then her hands. 'You're one of the Hamilton girls, aren't you?'

'Sara.'

Lillian nodded and flinched a smile. 'Thought so. You look like your mother. How about you come inside?'

On the bench in the small kitchen, Lillian placed two cups and then added a teabag and teaspoon of sugar into each. She clicked a lever on the back of a plastic kettle. In the room beside them, a four-seater table took up most of the space. Next to it, the lounge was just big enough for a couch and TV in front of a fireplace. Everything was spotless.

As Sara wiped her face with a tissue, she was aware of Lillian glancing over. When Sara turned, Lillian looked away.

Seated at the dining table, Sara took a drink from a glass of water Lillian had given her. 'I don't take sugar,' she said.

Lillian hesitated. 'It might help after your panic attack.' She smoothed her jumper down over her hips, lower lip caught in her teeth.

'I don't have panic attacks. I just winded myself.'

Lillian watched Sara for a moment, unfolding and then refolding her frayed cuffs. She picked up one cup, tipped the sugar into the sink and replaced the teabag.

Sara combed her hair back with her fingers.

Lillian poured the boiling water and then added milk to both cups. She opened a container, put biscuits on a plate, and then carried them to the table. They were plain ones with crusted sugar on the top.

'How's your father?' she asked.

Sara's mouth watered. She remembered she'd only had black coffee for breakfast. 'Dad can't walk or speak properly yet. I don't eat biscuits, sorry.'

Lillian inhaled and nodded. She sat down silently and tucked her hair behind her ear. She looked over, her lips pressed together and, Sara thought, a wariness in her blue gaze. 'What brings you here?'

Sara cleared her throat, took a sip of tea and placed it down. 'I came to see you, but then you didn't answer.' She stopped because the rest was both obvious and embarrassing. 'Sorry.'

Lillian nodded and smiled gently. 'That's okay. The coat you saw is a replica. Alec's has never been found, and neither has his second shoe.' She looked at the table as she stroked the edge of her cheek with her thumb.

'May I ask what the jacket is for?'

'The cold case program on the ABC.' Lillian bit her lip and looked away. 'It will be hard, but it might lead to something.'

'I've been asked to participate. I said I would,' said Sara.

'Thank you.'

'Lillian, I came here to talk about something.'

Lillian took a deep breath and nodded as if she was

steeling herself.

Sara forced herself on. 'This has been bothering me for years. I'm really sorry.'

Lillian's brow went up, her eyes wide and attentive.

'I left something for Alec. It was just after I saw him on the Friday afternoon, before... he died.' Sara swallowed hard. 'I left a letter.'

Lillian blinked a couple of times. 'Oh, right. Yes. I found it at the bottom of the letterbox beneath some other mail. I didn't check for days after Alec died. I have no idea where it is now.'

'Are you saying you found it unopened?'

Lillian nodded sadly, lips pressed. 'Alec didn't really have friends here. Apart from the occasional chat to Robbie, he was a bit of a lone ranger.' She smiled warmly and leant forwards onto her elbows. 'Robbie's a lovely young man. And it was comforting to find your letter, Sara.'

Sara's ears rang. 'I've ... oh, my God.' She slumped against the backrest. 'For ten years, I thought my letter made Alec go out that night.' The emotion came thick and fast and took her by surprise. Sara pressed her face into the bowl of her hands and cried.

'Oh, you poor thing.' Sara heard Lillian's chair scrape back. She then felt the warm circling of a hand behind her shoulder, as a heavy, dark feeling eased out.

The sound of tissues being ripped from a box preceded Lillian pressing them into Sara's hand.

Sara wiped her face and blew her nose. 'It's selfish to be relieved, I know. It must've been unbearable for you.'

Lillian leant back against the kitchen bench. 'The pain is ... indescribable.' She squinted softly. 'I thought it was my fault too. Why did Alec climb out through his window? Why didn't I hear him go? I know people were asking the same things.' She took a deep breath and exhaled for a long time. 'I always seemed to let Alec down, no matter how hard I tried.' She sat back down on the edge of her seat, side on to Sara.

'I'm sure that's not true,' said Sara.

Lillian's eyes filled with tears. 'I'm afraid it is,' she said quietly. She got up, pulled out a tissue and then wiped her eyes.

'We didn't feel like we knew you well enough to come over,' said Sara.

Lillian gave her a sideways look, and the wariness seemed to come back.

'Your mother sent a sympathy card,' she said tightly before giving a clearly forced smile.

Sara nodded, glad her mum had done something.

Lillian looked towards the window. 'Did you ever see Alec's dreamcoat?' she asked quietly. 'Beautiful. It was just a brown leather jacket, but he and I sewed coloured squares on until it resembled the one from *Joseph*.' Her face smoothed. 'He had it on when I collected him from the train the day he died. I checked, but it wasn't in his room when he went missing.'

'I saw him wearing it that last afternoon,' said Sara. She didn't know what else to say to offer comfort. 'I heard him sing once too.'

Lillian's face lit up. 'You should have seen him on stage.' She held her hands prayerlike against her chest. 'He was... magnificent. The crowd cheered so loudly at the end that he put his hands over his ears as a joke.' She laughed softly but it petered out and gradually, her face fell.

Sara felt like she was watching the air leave someone who'd been punctured.

'His father only agreed to Alec going to the specialist Arts

College if he won a scholarship. But he missed out. Alec's dad had two more kids by then, so I decided to pay tuition. That's why I moved here, because I was close to my mum, and the rent was low.' Lillian twisted her face away, clearly struggling with her emotions.

Sara grappled with how to continue. 'What do you think happened to Alec's other shoe?' She looked over at the door then felt a rush of guilt because she just wanted to leave.

Lillian, seemingly calmer, spoke to her hands. 'Police said the shoe I found, probably came off on impact. They were too big. Alec got them second-hand, and wore them everywhere, like the jacket.' She smiled softly, and then a frown gathered in the pale skin of her forehead. 'But the police noticed the sock on his right foot was muddy. It's the right shoe that's never been found.'

'The channel was muddy, wasn't it?'

Lillian nodded and spoke quietly, but in a controlled way. 'The autopsy showed that there were fresh stone bruises on Alec's right foot. Because we don't bruise after death, it's likely Alec lost his shoe before he died, and then ran some way without it.' Lillian gave Sara a look as if assessing her response.

'Do you think he couldn't find it in the dark?'

Lillian shook her head. 'I don't think he would have kept going in one shoe if he was simply meeting someone. I think he was in a hurry.'

'What did the police make of it?'

'They said it didn't rule out suicide.' Lillian shrugged, a hopelessness to the gesture. 'I looked everywhere for that shoe.' After a moment, she gave Sara a steady look. 'It wasn't suicide. Alec was really happy before he died.'

Sara nodded, unwilling to disagree with a grieving

mother. She decided to change direction. 'I heard that you made complaints of harassment.'

Lillian nodded. 'The power kept going off but they had the electrician come and check our connection and he told me not to use all my appliances at once.' She chewed her inner lip, eyes on the table as though remembering.

'I did see a chain locked onto your gate once.'

Lillian's face became sharply focused. 'You saw it?' she said.

Sara nodded, felt her pulse quicken uncomfortably. 'I was the one who saw a ute pull up with the man who threw a stone at Alec a few weeks before the hit-and-run, too.'

Lillian's frown and head shake told Sara this was the first time she'd heard this.

'I saw the whole thing from the back, and it was just a few seconds, so it wasn't very helpful. Sorry.'

Lillian turned fully, so she was facing Sara. 'Alec never said anything about that.' She put her finger on her lips and was quiet for a short time. 'I was told someone saw a ute near our driveway, but the description was vague. It just sounded like it had pulled over.'

'I'm sorry I didn't see more,' Sara admitted lamely. She regretted mentioning the event.

Lillian sighed and gazed downward.

Sara realised she'd been waiting for a break in the conversation. After a second, she pushed her chair back. 'I should go, Lillian. Thanks for the tea.'

Lillian didn't get up, eyes glazed in a faraway expression. 'I felt like no one wanted us here.'

Sara paused. 'Did you ever want to move away?'

'My mother was in care in Milton until she passed away last year.'

'I'm sorry to hear that,' said Sara.

'But I've put off leaving,' Lillian admitted. She got up and smoothed her jumper over her hips again. 'It probably sounds strange, but I feel like there's still something here. Something to do with Alec.'

Sara felt a small shiver.

'Alec's grave is in Sydney. I visit on the anniversary. There are always fresh flowers. I'm not sure who leaves them, but I'm glad they do.'

Sara leant down and took the two cups in one hand and the biscuit plate in the other. Lillian waved for her to put them down. Sara complied.

'I knew about Alec.' Lillian gave Sara a steady look. 'I once asked jokingly if he was going to start dating. Then he just came out with it. Said he was attracted to the boys, not the girls.' She gave a tiny shrug. 'I didn't care. He was my boy, my beautiful son. But I was scared for him.'

'I can understand that,' said Sara. 'Thanks again for the tea.' She started walking down the small hallway towards the front door. 'You've never met anyone else, Lillian?' She reached the door and felt an uncomfortable silence. She turned instinctively.

Lillian stood at the other end of the hall, one hand on her hip, lower lip caught hard in her teeth.

Sara got a strange feeling. 'Sorry, that was probably a bit personal.'

Lillian; eyes unblinking, nodded.

'Sorry.' Sara opened the front door and moved out into the sunshine.

Lillian came down and held the door. Sara could tell she was attempting to smile, though she wasn't meeting Sara's eyes. 'Thanks for coming,' she said.

Sara backed away with a friendly wave then felt a flinch of surprise.

Below Lillian's bottom lip was a bite mark where it had been caught in her teeth.

## Chapter 49

Before Sara ran back across the road from Lillian's driveway, she looked over and realised she still couldn't be sure of the exact location Alec had been found. True, she'd never seen it from this angle, but it was still frustrating how easily something so significant could disappear. She checked over her shoulder, unsettled about her chat with Lillian.

When Sara arrived home to a wagging welcome from Rusty, she felt some tightness ease from her shoulders. 'Thank goodness for dogs, Rusty.' She opened the gate and patted Rusty's head. Rusty whined and then barked. 'How about a walk?' asked Sara.

Rusty froze like the word had flicked an internal switch.

'Come on then!' Sara chuckled as she secured the gate and then rolled her shoulders to loosen the feeling of discomfort.

As they walked past the back of the garden, there was movement to her left.

Inside the dog cages was a moving white and brown ...

*Dog?* Sara stopped. 'Barney?'

Rusty jogged over to the cage, and the dogs sniffed noses

through the wire. Rusty then looked over her shoulder with her tail wagging as if asking whether she could keep him.

Next to the pen was a big yellow bag of dog food, and tied to the fence was an envelope. Sara tore it open.

*It's me, Barney! I'm so excited to be here!*

*Please feed and walk me every day.*

*Think of me as your 'guard dog in waiting'.*

*I can jump high, but the house yard should be okay – the vet checked it for you.*

*Please don't throw me a stick, because I get confused.*

*My last owner hit me with a stick, and I bit his arm.*

*Love, Barney and Toby*

*P.S. No one was here, so I put him in the pen for safety. Thanks so much!*

There was a lead hooked onto the wire of the fence. Sara unclipped it and cautiously opened the gate. 'Hello, Barney. Are we going to be friends?'

Barney sat on his bottom, his tail a windscreen wiper pushing leaves to the sides of the cage.

Sara clipped the lead onto his collar. 'Good boy. Good boy.' Gently, she patted the side of his head.

Barney sat and stood half a dozen times like he was desperate to behave but too excited. He didn't look like a dog who'd bite her arm. Rusty licked his ear.

'Huh. Best buddies, already?'

Together they walked down the lane, Rusty a little angular and limping.

Barney didn't pull on the lead but repeatedly looked up as though awaiting instructions.

When they returned, Sara let Barney into the house yard and then watched as he bounded around, then propped in front of Rusty with his butt up.

Rusty turned her face away and then walked over and sat down on her bed.

'Leave Rusty alone,' Sara said. 'She has war wounds.'

Barney barked and leapt away with his mouth wide open like a toddler enjoying a new playground.

Noting the time, Sara rushed inside and turned on the shower. Once dressed in the best she had – jeans and a soft cream jumper – she grabbed her makeup purse. Hands shaking, she poked herself in the eye with the mascara. She then took a deep breath and gently wiped her eye with a tissue. Next, she blow-dried her hair, rolling the ends under with her fingers like the hairdresser had done.

As she stuffed toast into her mouth, she saw her half-full bottle of red wine. It was all she had left. Sara wagged her finger at it. 'Bad idea.' She went to her handbag and found the bottle of Lorazepam. As she wrestled with the childproof lid, she imagined walking into the rehab and seeing her father in a wheelchair. She popped a pill to the back of her mouth and winced as she swallowed.

Lid in one hand, open bottle in the other, Sara imagined Ryan with his small, half-smile. She grabbed another pill, opened her mouth and froze, the small tablet nestled in her palm. Remembering the last time she'd taken two, she funnelled it back into the bottle and dropped it into her bag.

The dogs started barking. Toby's ute emerged and then a door slammed and it drove away. Sara could hear him talking to the dogs.

'Knock, knock.' When Toby had suggested they drive to the two o'clock appointment together, Sara had accepted gratefully. He walked into the kitchen with two bulging plastic bags and opened the fridge. 'You're pale. Have you eaten?' He piled food onto the fridge shelves.

'Thanks. Yes, I had toast.'

'Are you nervous?'

'Yeah. Don't try to distract me.' She lifted her index finger. 'Barney?'

Toby grinned. 'I bring gifts. Hey, you look happier today.' He checked his watch.

Sara grabbed her keys and they headed for the car.

'I suppose, yeah, I am. I went next door. Alec's mum Lillian found my note unopened in the letterbox. He never got it.'

Toby patted her back. 'There you go. It had nothing to do with you.'

Sara climbed in to the driver's seat.

'Lillian was a bit odd. Not that I've met or counselled parents who've experienced what she's been through. But she did tell me something interesting. Alec was only wearing one shoe when he died. They found one, remember, but the other hasn't turned up? His sock, which matched the missing shoe, was muddy, and his foot had fresh stone bruises.'

'Shit, really?' Toby did up his seat belt and frowned. 'That doesn't fit with him walking down to the road and standing in front of a car.'

'That's what she thinks too, and I can definitely see her point.' Sara turned the key and rolled down the driveway. 'The thing that always bothered me was the missing jacket and shoe. I can understand how the hit and run could've been a total accident and the driver either freaked out or didn't know, but why did those two items go missing?' She stopped at the edge of the highway, waited for a car to pass, and then accelerated.

'Do you think the driver picked them up?'

Sara shook her head. 'They'd left a body. Why would anyone like that stop and risk being seen?'

'Evidence?'

Sara nodded slowly. 'Now I'm back, I keep thinking about the ute that pulled up near Alec that day. What if someone ran him down on purpose?' She noted that Toby checked the side mirror for about the third time. 'You did that the other day,' she said.

'What?'

'Kept checking behind us. Either you don't trust my driving, or you think we're being followed.'

Toby chewed his inner lip. 'Habit.' His eyes turned to a herd of black and white Holstein cattle. Sara thought the scene with the cows, standing under a rich-blue sky against the green hillside, could've been a tourist brochure.

She knew things often looked different from the outside. Probably the reason travellers were convinced to visit all sorts of godforsaken places locals wouldn't go. 'Because you were caught for speeding?' Sara said.

Toby rolled his shoulders. 'Freddie keeps an eye on me.'

'Toby, has something happened between you and Freddie?'

Toby yawned, but it was one of those fake ones. 'Not exactly.' He gave her a look and sighed hard. 'Sara, I'm gay.' He smiled tightly, 'He'd like to catch me doing something to prove it.'

When Sara realised her mouth was open, she closed it. 'You're dating Di, though.' She was momentarily disappointed in herself. 'Sorry, I didn't realise.' She touched Toby's arm. 'Thanks for trusting me.'

Toby nodded and looked out the window. 'You can't be

gay out here. You may as well shoot yourself.'

'Oh, Toby.'

A muscle twitched in his jaw. 'Di and I have an arrangement. She has a pushy Greek-catholic family that want her to settle down and have kids. The last thing Di wants. She loves her job and needs detoxing from the tragedy of her work, but after a few days, she's itching for action. She goes to Sydney to catch up with everyone and squeeze donations out of rich people, then she leaves again, and everyone's happy.'

'What if you met someone else?' said Sara. The new idea jangled inside her. Toby with a boyfriend instead of a girlfriend.

Toby pressed his lips together for a moment. 'Around here a quirky lesbian might stand half a chance, but not a gay man. I don't want to sneak around.' He looked at her. 'Tell me you didn't just get a weird feeling. I saw it in your face.'

Sara winced and gave a tiny, tight smile. 'It's just new. Please forgive me.'

They shared a smile.

Toby's face clouded. 'If you're gay, there're no rules. Freddie cornered me outside a bar after he saw me chatting to a soft drink rep. Said he could sniff out faggots.'

Sara's stomach twisted. An unpleasant image of a gang closing in on Toby flashed through her mind. 'That's harassment. Report him.'

Toby smiled wryly. 'To whom? His mates in the force? That would be worse.'

'He's a shrimp, Toby.'

'Nuh-uh.' Toby shook his head. 'Guys like Freddie don't fight fair. He'd have mates. In Sydney, some cops were into gay bashing.'

'Jesus.' Sara saw the sign to Blooms and then indicated. She blew air out through her lips.

Toby touched her hand. 'You okay?'

Sara shook her head and shrugged. 'I have no idea.'

'I'm right here.'

## Chapter 50

The steady blue sky was scored by the dispersing vapour trail of an aeroplane. Elm trees, which lined both sides of the road, had begun to turn yellow. Soon, just as they had when she was a teen, the deciduous golden ash, liquidambar, and oaks would light the streets and parks in gold.

Sara frowned at another sign they'd passed to go into Blooms' carpark. She understood why it was familiar. She'd sent cards to Mum but hadn't visited. Mum did live very close to Blooms. At least if she'd relegated herself to being Dad's slave again, she only had a quick walk to do it.

After Toby and Sara had signed in at reception, Jason greeted them and shook both their hands. He looked to be in his late thirties and had short, fine, white-blonde hair and eyelashes. Sara had imagined him older. He pointed to an open door. 'My office. Can we have a chat?'

Sara cast her eyes around. 'Is Ryan here yet?'

Jason shook his head as he led them into a small office.

Sara and Toby sat on the two chairs on one side of a neat desk.

'How are you?' Jason asked.

'Fine.' Sara's foot jumped. 'How's Dad?' She hoped the pill would kick in soon, and momentarily, she regretted not taking the second one.

'Our physio and therapist work with him every day, but it's a long process.'

Sara looked at Toby. She tried not to visualise her dad's face slack on one side. She glanced over her shoulder, knee jumping. Toby put his hand there. 'Do you know what papers Ryan had?'

'No. Ryan said it was something your father had asked for,' Jason replied.

'It would be void anyway, wouldn't it? Because of Len's condition?' said Toby. He squeezed Sara's leg – *focus, stay calm*, his movement seemed to say – and then took his hand away.

Jason nodded; his eyes flickered to Toby's hand as it left Sara's knee. 'Yes. Ryan seemed fine when I suggested we all talk about it.' Jason checked his watch and then addressed Sara. 'Are you happy for him to visit?'

'Yes. Ryan's a good guy.' Sara ran her hand back through her hair.

Palms to thighs, Jason looked ready to get up. 'Len Hamilton, room seventeen. Just a moment, though ... he was being showered. I'll check if he's back in his room.' He picked up the phone, waited, shook his head, and then put the phone down. 'Sorry, we're running late because a resident passed away this morning. Would you mind waiting in the seats by the entrance? I'll let you know when your father is back.'

Blooms was part rehab, part nursing home. Sara couldn't tell which part was which.

Sitting on chairs inside the glass entrance doors near the reception desk, Sara leant towards Toby. 'I remembered something about the morning Alec was found.'

Toby's eyes scanned as he turned towards her.

'Anne and I went down to the Workers' House. It looked as though someone had been there recently, even though it hadn't been used for three weeks.'

'Did you notice any lights over there that night?'

'No. Remember we went into town because Robbie needed surgery? We got home after midnight. Everything was dark, and Dad was snoring.'

'Yeah, I remember about Robbie.'

'Before we left, Dad was cranky as hell because he had to fix the sewerage. I was relieved to go to the hospital because Dad was feral when he was doing a job like that.'

An old lady with a walking frame shuffled by in blue satin slippers. Sara and Toby both said 'good afternoon' the way you speak to the elderly, then resumed talking while the lady was manoeuvring the frame through a doorway.

'Dad told police he saw and heard nothing because he was busy with the plumbing and then had a few beers.'

'Your father doesn't miss much.' Toby pinched his lower lip, eyes on the floor. 'What about Anne?'

'She was weird when we were down at the Workers' House that morning. Keen to turn off the power and get out. I saw a bag of clothes beneath her bed the night before and overheard her making plans on the phone. Dad had been giving her a really hard time. She was ready to go, but that night she was stuck with us at the hospital.'

A couple, aged somewhere in their fifties, walked past and stood in front of the double glass doors. The lady turned to look over her shoulder.

'Just opening now,' said a voice from behind reception.

The doors opened and the couple headed outside.

'Ryan was keen on Anne at one point. What happened there?' said Toby.

'Nothing. A kiss.' Sara crossed her arms.

'I was surprised when I heard he was marrying Rachel,' said Toby. 'By the look on his face at the wedding, he was too.'

Sara closed her eyes.

Toby touched her elbow. 'Hey?'

Sara chewed the inside of her lip and looked at her feet. 'Can I tell you something?'

Toby nodded quickly. 'Of course.'

'Remember that afternoon when you and I saved the sheep?'

'Yes. A proud moment for this budding stockman.' Toby grinned.

'After you left that night. Ryan was ... alone. At the Workers.' Sara rubbed her throat.

Toby's eyebrows went up, and his mouth opened. 'Are you saying he wasn't alone the whole time?'

Sara nodded and smiled slightly.

Toby smirked. 'Good on you,' he said.

'But he decided it was too risky ... because of Dad.'

Toby's face softened. 'That would've hurt.'

'Like you wouldn't believe.'

'Oh God,' said Toby. 'Then he's with Rachel and getting married.'

Sara looked at the floor.

Toby squeezed her wrist. 'If it's any consolation, I heard he was blind drunk when Rachel made her move and caused...' He motioned in front of his stomach like he was imitating a big belly.

Sara remembered her mother describing the expectant

bride. 'No, not really.' She shook her head as though still finding it all hard to believe. 'Drunk or not, they were together. But I guess it wasn't his idea that I visited when I did.'

Jason walked over to them with his hands folded together. 'Okay, ready!'

Sara and Toby followed him down a long, pale-green corridor.

A bulky, white-haired woman stood in the middle. She was wearing a lemon-yellow skirt and top, had one arm in a sling and a white plaster on her forearm. She watched them come, mouth slightly open, as if she thought it was her they'd come to see.

'Afternoon, Vera,' said Jason.

'Hello, dear,' Vera responded.

The patients' rooms were on the right. On the other side of the corridor were labelled doors: *Treatment Room; Dirty Utility; Showers.*

Sara could smell urine and hear the squeak of shoes on polished lino. She could also see the rooms each contained various handmade rugs, a variety of bedspreads, and had a television and pictures on the walls. The windows faced gardens and reflected bright colours of azaleas, irises, clematis, and pansies. In the centre of the garden was an archway thickly covered with pale-yellow banksia roses.

'I'll keep an ear out for Ryan. Will I let him come straight down?' Jason's near-invisible eyebrows were up.

'Sure.' Sara took a deep breath and felt butterflies pinging round her insides.

Jason gave a little bow. 'Call if you need my assistance.' He turned smartly and walked back down the corridor. 'Hello, Mr Redman. Hello, Mavis. Nice day, Terry.'

Toby watched him go and then took Sara's hand.

'Oh boy,' said Sara, exhaling slowly. She lowered her voice. 'This is really hard.'

Toby nodded, pressed her hand. 'Let's do it together.'

They stopped at the doorway of room seventeen. Sara hoped they'd find it empty – the suprising news that Dad was working down the back paddock, and this had been a mistake.

Instead, she found a man slumped in a wheelchair which angled towards the window. His dark hair, side-parted, was flecked with a lot of grey, and he had a blanket draped across his knees. A sling supported his right arm. On his feet were slippers.

Toby cleared his throat. 'Knock, knock.'

The old man's head turned shakily. Sara recognised the steely blue eyes of her dad.

Wide-eyed Dad began to rock back and forth, and then he gesticulated with his free arm, as if he was sending the dog around a flock of sheep. One of his lip corners sagged as he made small, childlike sounds.

Mum had warned Sara, but it still hit her in the chest. She gripped the door frame; her stomach twisted like a wet towel.

Toby saw Sara's face and then walked into the room ahead of her. 'Hello, Mr Hamilton.' He stepped around the furniture and squatted in front of the wheelchair. He took Dad's left hand out of the air and shook it gently. 'Toby.'

Apparently settled, Dad stared at Toby, and then closed his mouth.

Sara couldn't move or speak, throat raw like boiling water had blistered the inside.

'Nice day out there. Twenty degrees,' said Toby.

Despite her dad's silence, Sara felt the familiar grip of distrust. Was Dad mutely collecting evidence of their neglect, and would one day bellow it into their faces?

A round woman in navy pants and a white smock breezed in, smiled, her lips shiny with pink lipstick. 'You beat me!' she said cheerfully. She threw a rolled-up newspaper on the bed. 'Hi there. I'm Judy.' She bent over Dad and wiped his face with a wet washer.

He shut his eyes, face screwed up like a prune. There was something yellow on his collar. Mum had said Dad could only have special goo to eat now because he couldn't swallow and risked choking.

'I was just about to move your father into a comfy chair so we could read the paper.' Judy put her hands on Dad's knees. 'But we'll play musical chairs after your visitors leave, okay?' She looked over at Sara and winked. 'We like to read the main headlines. Don't we, Len?' Judy stepped back, grabbed the newspaper baton and tore off the plastic wrap.

Dad's eyes followed Judy. Beneath his ruddy, prickly cheeks, his jaw worked.

Sara could imagine what he was thinking. Judy was too confident and cheerful, her voice too loud for a woman in a lowly job, pants too tight, bottom too big. However, Sara thought he looked quite calm.

Toby went to stand up. 'Sorry.'

'No, no, you stay there.' Judy patted Toby's knee.

Sara looked at Toby. A metre away sat Dad, who'd previously shouted and snarled at the TV if there was anything on about gay men. She walked over to Toby and threw her arms around his wide shoulders, kissing him on the temple.

Off balance, Toby held onto Sara's arms. 'Whoa! What've I

done?'

'Thank you,' said Sara. Noticing Dad so close, she took a backwards step and clenched her hands.

Over the next ten minutes, Sara felt her heart rate slow down a bit as Judy read out the news. But she couldn't concentrate. She checked the door again and again, and then she felt guilty for doing so.

Sara noticed Dad's chin sinking down, his eyelids closing.

'Hello!' The doorway filled with Ryan.

Sara caught her breath.

He was a little thicker across the chest, with shorter hair, and he was wearing smart black pants, a white shirt, and shiny black shoes. But he was the same: blue-eyed, cowboy-Elvis.

'Hello.' Sara's butterflies had frozen and made it hard to exhale.

Ryan's face fell. Then he smiled like he was putting things back together. He licked his lips. 'The gang is back.' He walked over and held out a hand towards Toby. 'Haven't seen your ugly mug in years!' Muscles worked in his forearm as they shook hands. He then turned to Sara and opened his arms. There was the embrace she'd craved, but offered by a friend, not a lover.

They hugged. A quick chest to chest. There was a slight pause when they were supposed to part, like each thought the other would go first.

'You look great,' Ryan said near her ear. He withdrew and forced a laugh before he indicated the doorway.

A dark-haired woman stood there. She wore slick black clothes, professional looking make-up and big silver earrings.

Sara's heart sank.

'Rachel, you already know,' said Ryan.

Sara thought Rachel looked like a glamorous athlete ready for TV cameras. She was wearing high-heeled black pumps and gave Sara a tight smile before looking away.

On her shoulder was a large handbag. Her small hands gripped the strap. A boy drew in beside her, and Rachel put her arm around his back.

'And this is my son, Dereck,' said Ryan with warmth in his voice.

Sara could see Ryan's blue eyes in Dereck. She knew she should say congratulations, or sorry I couldn't make the wedding ... something.

'What brings you back down here?' said Toby.

Ryan cleared his throat. 'Some paperwork.'

Toby shot Sara a glance. 'Yes, we heard about that. What sort?'

A tired sounding bell began in the corridor.

'I'd better get that.' Judy excused herself.

There were seven people in the tiny room, and everyone was forced to shuffle around each other in the awkward way of strangers. Rachel sighed impatiently as she was forced to back out of the room for a moment. She quickly reclaimed her place once Judy was gone.

Ryan pocketed his hands. 'Enduring Power of Guardianship.' He looked over at Dad, whose head lolled slightly.

'But Mum can do that,' said Sara.

Ryan's eyes held her like they always had. She felt her fibres drawn towards him. 'Yes, I know,' he said gently. 'Your dad asked me to do it when your mum moved out. When he had the stroke, I felt guilty I'd left it too long. Still, I shouldn't have tried to force it. Sorry.' Ryan sighed, walked over and squeezed Dad's shoulder. 'Hey, Len.'

Dad looked up, winced with his lips pulled back. His eyes didn't show recognition.

Sara could feel Ryan's pause.

Ryan turned back, opened his palms. 'We should get out of your way. But let's catch up, Sara. Rach, Dereck, and I were going to stay in town for a couple of days.'

'Stay at the Workers' House,' Sara said, then flushed. The image of Ryan in the Workers, sprawled on the double bed, toes sticking up from the bottom of the covers flashed through her mind.

Rachel, shining silent and tense near the doorway, sniffed and looked at her feet.

Sara's image evaporated. 'It's pretty run down. You don't have to stay.'

'Thanks, but we'll—' Rachel started.

'Sure.' Ryan nodded and looked from Rachel to Sara. 'I don't mind. It would be great to see the place.'

Dereck brightened. 'Are we going to the farm, Daddy? I'd like to chase the sheep, just like you used to.'

'Dereck!' Rachel said tersely. 'We're not here to work.' She tried to smile, which wasn't quite achieved because her face was pulled so tight. 'We're on holiday.'

Ryan gave Rachel a look and then smiled gently at his son. 'Muster,' he corrected.

Sara took a deep breath and let it out slowly. Ryan knew how to run the farm, and even though it was now destocked, there were things to do. 'If you want to look around, Ryan, see if anything needs doing? That would be good.'

Ryan's eyes brightened. 'I'd love to. I've missed it.' Something passed across his eyes. He glanced at Rachel.

Rachel's mouth twisted as she chewed her inner lip. Her hold on Dereck tightened, and the boy grimaced and wriggled out of her embrace.

'Great. I'll leave the key down there,' said Sara.

After quiet goodbyes, since Len's eyes were closed, they all filed out.

Sara walked over. Her dad was slumped, apparently asleep. He'd never looked so harmless. She reached into the space between them. Dad sucked in a long breath. Sara flinched. Dad exhaled. His eyes didn't open. Sara pocketed her hands and left the room. She only just made the front doors, which had been opened for the other four. Sara turned to say thanks to the receptionist, but the lady was twisted around in her chair, fingers poking the photocopier buttons.

Once they'd walked outside, Toby and Ryan stood close together, talking. Rachel wandered over to the banksia roses on the arch and fiddled with the flowers. She dropped the petals in her fingers and then picked at another bloom.

Sara said her goodbyes and backed away. She noticed Ryan's eyes followed her even as he spoke to Toby. She waved, turned and walked to her car. Two cars down, Dawn waited in Toby's ute, an elbow on the open windowsill, eyes closed. When Sara saw Toby's vehicle, she realised what had been niggling for her attention.

She walked quickly back to the men. 'Hey, Toby, why is your antenna mounted on the bull bar?'

Toby's chin pulled in. 'I had the bull bar and CB radio installed after I bought it. That's just how it came.'

'The antenna's too big for the car,' said Ryan.

Sara tried to focus on his words not his lips as he explained.

'A small one can be stuck on the side of the windscreen, but a big one would be too unstable.'

Sara clearly recalled the big antenna in front of Alec's face that day. Now she understood why the ute on the news had looked wrong, even though she'd only seen it from the back. It was too streamlined. No big antenna and no bull bar on which to mount it.

'The ute had a bull bar,' said Sara, with excitement.

Strangely, this had the opposite effect on Ryan. His face fell and he glanced to the right, at Rachel.

Sara noticed Rachel approaching.

'What's wrong?' she said, eyebrows raised at Ryan. She looked at Sara and pulled a quick social expression, which looked a bit off.

Ryan cleared his throat. 'We were just discussing cars.'

Rachel looked a little relieved, but not much.

Sara felt the air crackle with tension. She glanced at Toby. His shrug was almost invisible, but then he held her eyes and gave a slight nod. Sara hoped Toby's look meant he'd tell her more later. 'Dawn's here,' she said.

Toby eyebrows went up. 'Already? Okay.'

'I'd better go,' Sara said, backing away.

She was on the road headed for the farm when she realised the significance. Police had said that Alec was probably hit by a vehicle with a bull bar because of his injuries. People had assumed it was a truck and the driver mustn't have seen Alec. But what if the driver had seen him and it wasn't an accident at all?

Sara remembered the feeling she'd had when she saw the man hurl a rock at Alec. That they could have really hurt him and had probably intended to.

She released a breath she didn't realise she'd been holding. If Alec's death was intentional, it explained why no one had ever claimed responsibility. A heavy sensation settled across her shoulders.

Sara may have seen the vehicle responsible for killing Alec.

## Chapter 51

At the farm, Sara heard barking as soon as she got out of the car. She paused, listening, then walked up to the yards. 'No way.'

Inside one of the cages were two new dogs: the dachshund from Toby's backyard, and a small grey terrier. The dachshund produced some polite *yak-yak* barks. The terrier emitted a volley of auditory bullets.

Sara covered her ears. 'No! Stop it.'

Both dogs stilled, ears pointed.

The terrier's face was all hair, no eyes.

'You've got to be kidding, Toby!' Sara glanced around and rubbed her forehead. A letter was tied to the cage. Sara groaned and ripped it off.

*Hello!*

*We are 'pee-on-furniture dachshund' and 'friendly little silky terrier-cross' (feel free to rename us).*

*We have already been fed and are so excited to be with you.*

*P.S. Got new dogs and no room left. You've already met one of these little champions. You're a sport, Sara!*

*P.P.S. I feel happy knowing you are surrounded by canine warriors!*

'Great, just great.' Sara rolled her eyes. There was a big red bag of dry dog biscuits by the gate and three cans of dog food. It had to have been Dawn. *A Dawn raid.* No wonder Toby had been suprised she'd been waiting for him.

Sara sighed hard and then remembered how Toby had left Barney in a holding pen so the dogs could get used to each other before they met. This gave her time to sort out her head, and her stomach.

'Later,' promised Sara. She strode down to the house, washed her hands in the laundry and drank from the tap. She could feel something nagging at her about the morning. When she'd been to see Lillian.

She pulled off her shoes and made a cup of tea. She remembered how they had watched the appeal by Alec's parents after his death, and then discovered later through a comment from his drama teacher, that although Alec was friendly and talented, he had also been bullied. This added to the suicide theory and had made sense to Sara at the time because she'd seen him crying. Yet today Lillian had seemed quite certain that her son was happy before he died.

Sara found Lillian's number and dialled from the house phone. 'Hello, Lillian, it's Sara,' she said gently. 'I hope I didn't upset you this morning.'

There was a slight pause. 'I'm fine, Sara. What can I do for you?'

'Um, actually ... I worked something out about the ute I saw. I haven't said anything yet, but I believe it did have a bull bar.'

A pause. 'Have you told the police?'

Sara winced. She could imagine the police officer's underwhelmed expression in reaction to her unconfirmed, decade-old memory. 'Not yet, but I will.'

Another pause. 'There was something else?'

Sara chewed her lip, less sure about her suspicions with Alec's mother on the phone. 'I was just thinking about you telling me that Alec was happy before he died.'

'Yes, he was.'

Sara thought Lillian sounded sure.

'But the police were still certain he took his own life?' Sara twisted her fingers through the telephone cord and waited.

'When he hugged me good night for the last time, he gave me this tight squeeze like he was excited. He told me he was in love.'

Sara blinked. *Love?* She tried to imagine Alec climbing out the window and running towards the road, losing his shoe, almost oblivious to his surroundings, even the weather. *Full of love. It still didn't quite work. Unless ...* 'Lillian, did Alec say who he was in love with?'

'No,' Lillian added with a tired-sounding sigh. 'He said it was no one I knew. He went to school in Sydney, and I wasn't all that familiar with his friends, even before I moved. I lived a long way away, so he was often at his dad's to avoid the long train rides.'

Sara bit her lip. 'You're sure it wasn't someone here?'

'No. But he didn't say anything else.'

Sara swallowed as she remembered her brother meeting Alec at the boundary. But it had not looked romantic to Sara at all. Instead, it appeared Alec had been telling Robbie something which worried her brother and made him seem angrier with Dad than he'd ever been before.

Sara shook her head, confused where the trails seemed to

lead and then didn't. 'It's really nice that he was happy,' said Sara, realising that this made it even less likely Alec had taken his own life.

Lillian seemed to read her thoughts. 'It wasn't suicide, Sara.'

## Chapter 52

'Call me, Anne! I need Robbie's number.' Anne's answer machine had taken her message.

Sara's stomach growled. She felt Mum's presence in the kitchen as she peeled and chopped vegetables, washed two pots and half-filled them with water. She remembered Mum moving efficiently around the small space night after night. Except on Fridays for a brief time.

Sara recalled what Garry had told her. Dad hadn't been to the pub. Was the time Sara noticed him as he drove out of the forest just one of many? Had he sat in his car alone? She knew he didn't get along with many people, but was he really that isolated? A vague memory stirred again as she thought about Fridays, but she couldn't grasp it.

Sara remembered how her mother used to dance, and knew she would again because she'd joined a group. The thought made her smile.

Sara watched naked white potato chunks dance a slow ballet in the pot and then turned the burner down to low. She lay a piece of crumbed chicken breast into a preheated frypan and stood back as it hissed and popped.

Toby had given her all the basics, as though he knew exactly what she'd need. Sara had also found a box of chocolates on the top shelf of the fridge, and it was, as yet, unopened. Seeing the chocolates made her happy in a way she couldn't describe. It occurred to her then what a good husband Toby would make. She paused as the idea settled in her. She just wanted him to be happy.

Sara sipped on her glass of red, the heat in her throat like a warm, comforting blanket that had opened and spread around. Sara knew some blackcurrant flavours and red wine tannins would help smooth her out. Not to mention the 14% alcohol. It was the last bottle though, and – she'd promised herself – her last drink for a while.

After eating, Sara found an old bedspread in the linen cupboard, folded it into quarters and lay it outside the back door. The light had dimmed. The glow of sunset behind the trees to the west. Sara realised something was missing. She listened. Gone were the murmurs of sheep and cattle as they configured themselves in preparation for the night.

She switched on the outside light and then walked up to the dog pens. She cautiously opened the gate. The two new dogs squirmed, wagged and bunny-hopped, eager to follow Sara into the back garden. The dachshund greeted the two larger dogs, butt-sniffing, circling and wagging. When the other dogs crowded in on the small terrier, she cowered behind Sara and then lay down on her back. Suddenly she sprang to her feet, growling.

'Okay, you'd better come with me.' Sara opened the laundry door, and the terrier slipped inside. 'That was fast.' Sara smiled.

Outside, the other three dogs danced around, and then the

dachshund trotted over to the house wall, lifted his leg and urinated.

'You're called Lifter,' said Sara.

Lifter joined the two larger dogs as they rollicked, rolled and ran – Rusty still moving a little stiffly. Lifter danced around outside of them, commenting with his *yak-yak* bark without getting involved.

Sara watched them for a few minutes and then went inside and made a cup of tea. She watched the terrier as it walked around sniffing everything.

When Sara sat down on the couch, the dog jumped up beside her. 'Not on the furniture!'

Still on the couch, the terrier ducked its head and rolled over, tail wagging between her back legs like a white flag. Sara shook her head. 'I'm not patting you. Stop it.'

The terrier rolled onto her belly, front paws out and then lay her chin down. There was something likeable about the hairy little face.

'Fine,' Sara said quietly. 'But you'll need a wash.'

She put her empty teacup aside, got up and filled the laundry sink with warm water. The little dog followed Sara into the bathroom when Sara fetched her shampoo. In the laundry, she placed a towel on the bench. The dog waited near her feet. Sara lifted her up in two hands, surprised how light she was.

The water plastered hair against the dog's tiny frame. 'Are you sure you're not a cat?' queried Sara.

The dog turned her head away.

'Hey, it's not so bad. The water is warm. This is my special shampoo. See how nice it bubbles in your wiry ... dirty ... smelly coat.'

In the tub, the water was tea stained.

Sara rubbed her nose in the crook of her elbow. 'Where've you been?'

The little dog sat back on its haunches and lifted both front feet. Her tiny paws quivered. The water had parted the hair on her face and revealed liquid-brown eyes. With her small pink tongue, she licked a droplet off her lips. Sara thought she looked sad.

'Gosh,' Sara put her fingers beneath the paws, 'where'd you learn to do that?' She felt a surge of something inside her. Like she didn't want to fail her little friend.

Sara wrapped the dog in a towel and then used a hair dryer to dry and fluff her coat. A shade lighter and much smoother, the terrier began to wag her tail. 'Right, I'm naming you Nellie, after Dame Nellie Melba, because of your high-pitched bark.'

Nellie trotted along behind and then watched from the doorway while Sara showered. When Sara stuck her head out to see where Nellie had gone, she noticed a grey ball beside her pillow.

'My bed?'

Nellie's tail patted up and down.

'Well, I suppose I did name you after a dame.'

Sara got under the covers, grateful not to be alone with thoughts about bull bars, lost shoes, and Alec's secret love. 'Goodnight, Nellie.'

## Chapter 53

When she woke, Sara checked her watch. Then checked it again. She couldn't remember the last time she'd slept for eight hours.

Nellie stretched and yawned, her tiny mouth wide.

'Hello.' Sara didn't get the usual feeling of empty stillness. And that little pink tongue was very cute.

Nellie jumped off the bed, trotted through the house and waited at the laundry door. Sara let her out and watched as she squatted delicately by the fence, a tiny back paw lifted as though she dreaded getting it wet.

In the kitchen, Sara put the kettle on. She heard a whine. She opened the door, and the little dog jogged back inside. 'At your service, Nellie.'

Outside, Barney and Rusty were sleeping together on Rusty's bed, and Lifter was curled into a ball on the bedspread. All three got up slowly and stretched, yoga-like, hips high. Each jogged off for a wee, a sniff and greeted each other with a wag. On the grass, Sara noted several piles she would have to clean up.

Once she'd drunk her coffee, Sara put a lead on Barney and called Rusty. Lifter squeaked as they left.

'Hush, you're next.'

When she returned, Sara got Nellie and Lifter. The two trotted along, leads taut, shoulder to shoulder, heads and tails up. They sniffed the places the two bigger dogs had been, conferring nose to nose. Sara followed them down to the shearing shed, and then back up to the house.

As she approached, Dawn drove the ute in, and Toby slid from the passenger side. 'Morning!'

Sara released Lifter and Nellie into the house yard.

'Hello, puppies!' Toby patted them over the top of the fence.

The dogs squeaked and bounced.

Sara opened the laundry door, and Nellie disappeared inside.

Toby jumped the fence and hugged Sara. 'I see you're all getting along.'

'Like I get a choice,' Sara said mildly, in case he took them all away again.

Toby laughed. 'I'll help you feed them.'

In the kitchen, he dished out food into several cereal bowls. Sara left one in the laundry for Nellie.

Toby came in. 'This one's special, isn't she. Bit of a lady.' He got down onto one knee. Nellie ran up his thigh and licked his nostrils. Eyes squeezed tight, Toby laughed. He put her on the floor and got back up. 'How are you today?'

'I actually slept. Hey, Toby, Lillian told me something really interesting yesterday. The night he died, Alec confided to her that he was in love.'

Toby nodded slowly. 'Really? Okay, so then he jumps out the window late at night.' His eyebrows went up. 'What teen hasn't done something crazy because they were in love?' He smiled in a way that suggested their recent conversation about Ryan.

'True.' She smiled a little. 'Lillian told the police he was happy, but they still seemed pretty sure he took his own life.'

Toby winced as though uncertain. 'Saying he's happy is different to saying he was in love. That's a powerful bunch of chemicals, Sara, and very potent when you're young.' Toby crossed his arms. 'It shines a whole different light. Could've been why he went out.'

'Alec said the person he loved wasn't anyone Lillian knew. She thinks it was someone from his school in Sydney.'

Toby shrugged. 'What if it wasn't? Kid was probably used to keeping secrets. How close was he to Robbie? Maybe he told him something.'

'I saw them speaking at the boundary once, but I was too far away to hear. I wasn't exactly spying. I wanted to say hello to Alec. No one seemed to hang around with him.' Sara looked out the window at the soft, yellow-orange colours of the maple, a dull shine on the wet leaves. Tiny brown-headed honeyeaters chirped and snapped insects from the air. 'But the day I saw him, he was upset. Robbie seemed bothered by what Alec was saying. He was quiet and grumpy later. It certainly didn't look romantic, if that's what you're thinking.'

'I always felt bad for Alec.' Toby gave Sara a look she now understood. 'Any progress with your ninja or the disappearing hole?'

Sara shook her head. 'Holes. I didn't tell you, but I found another one at the back of the woodshed, which had been filled in too.' She showed her palms.

'Someone must think there's something buried around

here. Did you tell the police?'

Sara shook her head, put her elbows on the bench and supported her chin. 'I forgot. There's one more thing, Toby.'

Toby came over and mimicked her pose. 'Go on.'

'For maybe four or five months, Dad had a weekly Friday night out at the local pub, and the occasional Saturday. It's called Garry's now. We loved Fridays because we were free to do stuff Dad didn't allow. Mum used to put on her music and dance. It made her so happy.'

Toby sighed. 'I admire your family. Sorry, but Len was awful.'

Sara chewed her lip. 'Mum wanted me to thank the person who found Dad after his stroke. She was told it was someone from Garry's who'd called the ambulance. But when I went to the pub, Garry said my dad had never been, and he's worked there for fifteen years.'

Toby tilted his head. 'So, where'd he go? To a different pub?'

'Maybe. He used to dress like he was going out. I saw him in the forest once.' Sara pointed in that direction. 'Down there along the highway.'

Toby twisted around for a moment. When he turned back, he looked thoughtful. 'Any chance your dad could've been caught up in something?'

'He ... was different a few weeks before the hit-and-run. One Friday, he came home early and nearly caught us partying. Then he almost stopped going out. He was bad-tempered and preoccupied.'

'Maybe he got on the wrong side of someone. Was your family in financial trouble?'

'Mum and Dad didn't talk about money in front of us. I remember him complaining about feed prices during the drought, though. He had to kill a flock of sheep because we didn't have the money to feed them.'

Toby closed his eyes for a second. 'I knew about that, but it still makes my stomach churn.'

Sara pinched her lip. 'What if Alec knew something about what Dad was up to? The time I saw Dad in the forest, it wasn't far from the Stynes' house.' Sara frowned as she thought back. 'Maybe that's what Alec was talking to Robbie about when I saw them. Robbie did say once that Dad was a hypocrite, but he wouldn't tell me why.'

Nellie's toenails clicked on the hard floor as she trotted over and stood in front of Sara.

'So maybe he'd been meeting someone and was involved in something illegal.'

Sara shrugged and went to the phone. 'I'll ask Mum if she knew anything.' She rolled her eyes to indicate she doubted it.

As Sara dialled, Toby stood in front of her and watched, hip against the bench in a relaxed pose except that his toe kept tapping the floor.

Nellie was standing between them, eyes on Sara.

'Yes?' said Mum.

'I need to ask you something.'

'Go ahead,' Mum said.

'Are ... are you okay? You sound like you used to when I called home and Dad was there listening.'

Mum sighed. 'I haven't slept since you talked about that ABC program.'

Sara bit her lip. 'Mum, we need to talk about Dad. Do you know if we were in some kind of financial trouble back when everything got bad?' There was a pause.

'Not that I know of.'

Something about Mum's tone put Sara on alert. It was too flat. Just like she used to sound when she responded with a 'Hm,' instead of answering. 'You know, Mum, I did go to Garry's to thank them. But Garry said that Dad never went there.'

'What do you mean?' Again, the lifeless tone. Like it held no surprise for her. Or she was too tired to respond, which, Sara decided, was more likely.

'He lied about going to the pub on Friday nights. Garry was sure.'

'Well, where ...' Mum was quiet for a long time. Long enough for Sara to remember a comment Mum had made the night they were stuck in the hospital for hours. Mum had called Dad repeatedly from the hospital payphone. *I finally got your father.*

'Do you remember when we were at the hospital with Robbie, and you couldn't get hold of Dad until late?' Sara could hear breathing. 'Mum?'

'Yes,' Mum said carefully. 'I think I should come back home. I'm not sleeping well. Bruno and I can leave in the morning. He'll have his mobile if you need anything. We'll talk later.' The phone clicked in Sara's ear.

The kettle began to whistle, grew louder until it shrilled.

'I think Mum does know something,' said Sara.

## Chapter 54

After the call, Toby made Sara sit at the table. He put a hot drink in her hands, refilled the kettle and lit the burner. He carried Nellie to the couch and put her down, but she promptly jumped off and ran back. She sat on her bottom beside Sara, with her eyes fixed upwards.

'The night Alec died, when we were with Robbie in hospital, the eight-thirty movie was almost over when Mum said she finally got Dad. It must have been well after ten thirty pm.' She was staring at Toby. 'I didn't even realise the significance at the time.'

'Do you think he went out?'

'He said he was in all night.' She reached down and patted Nellie's head. The silky softness gave her a little relief from the direction of her thoughts. 'I'm worried he was caught up in something. He obviously lied to us about Fridays, but lying to the police is a whole different thing.' She took a gulp of her hot tea, hoping to absorb its warmth. 'What if he did see something?'

'Ah, Sara,' Toby indicated the kitchen window. 'Ryan's

here.'

Sara looked out.

A big blue four-wheel drive attached to a massive white and gold caravan pulled up alongside the Workers' House. A small person spilled out the back door of the car. Then the adults climbed out, and Sara saw Ryan interlock his fingers and stretch his arms above his head.

Sara noted the way Ryan's waist thinned and lengthened, and his head went back as he yawned. 'Mum's avoiding something. She sounded really cagey.'

Toby shook his head and rubbed Sara's arms. 'Have a chat when she gets here. Aren't you glad you have all your guard dogs around in case anything happens? In fact, there's what ... four dog pens up there? I have another little Jack Russell-cross, and a—'

'No, Toby.'

'I was joking.'

Sara pinched her chin. 'I'm really worried, Toby.'

'One thing at a time.' Toby sighed. 'I have to go, though. Maybe you should talk to Ryan.'

'Did he say anything after I left Blooms?'

'No. They left soon after.'

'I haven't spoken to him in years. What I'd really like to do is stay here with Nellie and have some wine.' Sara looked around and remembered her earlier pledge to stop drinking. *Damn.*

'You should probably know Ryan and Rachel separated recently. He just told me.'

Sara took a moment to register and then frowned. 'So why are they both here in a caravan?'

'They decided to come down as a family.' Toby shrugged. 'Could be because of Dereck. Ryan told me they would have separated sooner, if not for him. He said Rachel will sleep in the van while he's in the house. She really wanted to stay in town.' Toby's face lit up. 'I just had a great idea. I'll sort Rachel and Dereck with some accommodation in town, and that will give you and Ryan some space to talk.'

Sara closed her eyes.

Toby squeezed her hand. 'Okay?'

'Okay,' said Sara, appreciating his unwavering support.

## Chapter 55

At dusk, the car and van drove away from the Workers' House. Toby called to tell Sara that Rachel and Dereck were staying in Parkwood. Rachel had jumped at the chance, explaining there were too many mice and spiders at the farm. Sara could have disagreed. About the mice anyway. The feral cats tended to keep them under control.

Sara had spent the afternoon cleaning up the backyard and pulling weeds while the dogs explored.

Before she left, Sara calculated how long the round trip to a bottle shop in Milton would be. She dismissed the idea, mainly because she was so distracted, and it was almost dark. Maybe the extra miles were a higher power helping her stick to her plan of not drinking. She gave the sky a dark look.

From the Worker's House chimney, there was smoke threading up into the twilight sky.

When she got down there, the door was open.

'Knock, knock,' Sara called. She took a deep breath and walked in.

'Hi.' Ryan wore navy tracksuit pants and a white t-shirt.

He smiled wearily, pushed one hand back over his short hair. Sara was sure he'd become more handsome with age.

'Do you need anything?' she asked.

Ryan shook his head and then indicated the lounge. 'Come sit down.' He'd covered the couch with a blanket. A fire crackled in the hearth.

She glanced around. Maybe it was the dark, but it looked a lot better than it had earlier. 'You make this place seem warm.'

A ghost of a smile crossed Ryan's face. He sat down. Facing the fire, he leant forwards, elbows on his knees. 'How are you, Sara?'

Sara sat beside him. 'It was hard to come back, but it's nice to see you. And Toby,' she said.

Ryan gazed into the flames, hands softly together in front of his knees. 'Anne and your parents came to the wedding,' he said.

'Sorry. I couldn't make it.'

'I missed you.'

'I was at a new school.'

'No, I mean, I missed working with you.' Ryan shook his head gently. 'I wouldn't have gone to the wedding either. Except that I was the groom.'

Sara gave him a long look. 'Toby said it hasn't worked out.'

Ryan shrugged. 'It was never easy. But our hearts were in the right place. Dereck needed two parents.' He began to rub his hands slowly back and forth against each other. 'I caught up with Anne at the reception.'

'Nice to see her, I guess.' Sara bit her inner lip.

Ryan semi-shrugged but stayed caught in it, shoulders stiff. 'Anne once asked me to help her leave home.'

Sara remembered Anne's packed bag. And the phone call she overheard. Something clicked into place. 'Was Anne planning to leave the night Robbie got sick?'

Ryan paused before he nodded. 'She didn't turn up.'

'Turn up where?' Sara noted her voice had taken on an odd tone, as if a boiled sweet was stuck in her throat. Half her attention waited for the answer, the other half searched for any other possible place Ryan meant than here.

Ryan exhaled and let his head drop all the way back. After a few moments, he lifted his head back up and stared ahead without blinking.

Sara's throat pulsed, her nerves tingling. 'Did you wait for Anne here, Ryan?' She remembered the electricity left on, the dirty entryway, the doused fire.

Ryan gave her a heavy look, his mouth pulled down. Then he nodded and kept rubbing his hands together.

'Ryan?' she almost whispered.

Ryan looked at her, took her hand and slid his fingers through hers.

Sara swallowed, her hand limp in his. 'Were you here when Alec was killed?'

Ryan exhaled like air leaving a tyre. He almost said something but stopped. He looked towards the window. 'Sara, you wouldn't understand.'

'Talk to me.' Her throat felt parched. 'This is serious, Ryan. What did you see?' Sara's pulse took over her whole body. She began to shake.

'I didn't see anything.' He covered his eyes with his free hand.

'Oh, thank god!' Sara dropped her head forwards and breathed again. It explained why the Workers' had looked lived in that morning.

Ryan stayed still and quiet beside her, which set off prickles all over Sara's skin. She squeezed his hand. 'Ryan, for God's sake, what is it?'

Ryan sucked a staggered breath and screwed his eyes shut. He took his hand back and then fisted both against his mouth. 'I'm sorry,' he whispered like it took great effort to get the words out. 'I'm not … I'm not the man you used to know.'

Sara waited, and her heart calmed a little, though not from relief, from numbness. 'Please tell me what happened, Ryan. I'm scared. Did you *hear* something?'

Ryan swallowed and then slowly shook his head from side to side.

'No? Or you can't say?' Sara touched his arm.

He closed his eyes.

Sara realised that what he said was true. Ryan didn't seem the same; he wasn't sure of himself or quick to smile like he used to be. 'Are you alright?' she said gently.

'I'm exhausted,' said Ryan quietly. 'Being here with Rachel sucks the life out of me.'

After a moment, Sara stood up. 'We should talk tomorrow. There's … a lot going on.'

Ryan blinked, eyes glassy. 'Yeah.'

From the fireplace something popped.

Ryan went forwards onto his knees and tended to it with a metal poker. 'Night, Sara.'

Sara chewed her inner lip. 'Night.'

Outside, Sara looked around until she found the thin arc of moon. Beneath the slight, brave glow, she walked heavily back to the house. Ryan had been the one in the Workers' House the night Alec died. Something had happened, and it had changed him.

She didn't dare imagine.

## Chapter 56

Sara tossed and turned with half-awake dreams that featured Dad in the forest and then Ryan. Ryan had been here the night of the hit-and-run. But his car had no bull bar. He hadn't seen anything. But maybe he knew something. He was loyal. Was he protecting Dad? Sara rolled over and found herself praying. *Please, don't let Ryan be involved.*

Morning came heavily – a relief.

Nellie was down the end of the bed. Sara felt her little look of reproach. Sara got up, yawned, washed her face and quickly dressed in her running clothes.

A white layer hovered over the dam on her left, misting the top of the grasses. Rushes and reeds bordered the edges. As the sun warmed, shiny blue-black moorhens would duck and feed near last season's browned weed nests. In spring, there'd be speckled, grey-white eggs hidden inside. The sheep had spread out and were grazing on the green flats. Birdsong pierced the cold air. The forest was quiet.

Arm held tight against the tender rib, Sara jogged carefully, her warm breath fogging the air. She remembered that sometimes when it was cold, she and Robbie used to grab a twig and suck on it like a cigarette, blow out slowly and pretend they were smoking.

On her right was a paddock that undulated down to a small dam. It was called Cornwall Paddock because it looked like a piece of England. It was too small to be used for much except when the rams were separated from the flock. It had also been a cemetery. Fifty slaughtered sheep had been buried there. During the drought, plummeted prices and steep feed costs had made them financially worthless. Better the bullet than starvation. With his bulldozer, a man Dad knew had dug the giant hole next to some granite boulders.

While it happened, Mum had taken Sara, Anne and Robbie to the library and then out the other side of town to a wildflower walk. Mum had stayed in the car. When they'd returned, she had watery eyes and a red nose. She smiled, like she always did, and asked about their walk, and they'd talked about happier times.

When Sara was young, it had been Mum's job to create light chatter after bad things happened. As Sara got older, it irritated her. It felt as if Mum wanted to pretend everything was okay. Even now, Sara wondered if Mum was hiding something for the same reason.

On the way back up the lane, Sara could see smoke coming from the Workers' House chimney. She imagined Ryan stoking the fire, wearing his flannelette shirt and leather boots.

She saw movement on the far hillside. A black-clothed jogger moved across the Central Paddock, keeping to the narrow sheep tracks. She got a sensation like a cold breeze up her back. She realised it was just Ryan and the wrong shape to be the ninja. She wished she didn't have to consider such a thing. She watched him disappear behind a coppice of eucalypts before she turned for the house.

Sara was greeted by a barking, wagging, yowling mass of joy. Her burden lifted a little. 'Alright, alright! It's your turn!'

Sara had just walked the dogs and returned them to the garden when Ryan jogged up. All four started barking. Even Nellie from inside the house. 'Quiet!' said Sara, as she watched Ryan approach.

He nodded to Sara and then turned his attention to the dogs. 'Hey, hey now. You're okay. I'm not going to hurt you.' He squatted down outside the fence and offered the back of his hand. Sweat shone at his temples and along his upper lip. He was clean shaven and smelled good. He wiped the back of his forearm across his forehead.

Rusty wagged and licked Ryan's hand through the wire. Barney slid in by Rusty's shoulder and did the same. Lifter stood with his nose up, eyes fixed like he'd had an electric shock.

'Why does that one look so stunned?' said Ryan, indicating the dachshund.

Sara smiled, glad of something to talk about. 'I think it's his default expression. He doesn't have much of a range.'

Ryan looked around. 'There's so many.'

'Toby.'

He nodded. 'There, see,' he said as he let he dogs lap his fingers and then his palm. Once they withdrew, he stood up. His gaze swung beneath Sara's.

'Do you need a car? Dad's ute is still here.' Sara indicated the shed.

Ryan looked back over his shoulder. 'Latest model,' he noted.

'Yeah. I haven't started it or anything. But feel free.'

Ryan was still looking over his shoulder. 'Who's been

driving it?'

Sara shook her head. 'No one.'

'He doesn't park that way.' He smiled slightly. 'Thanks, I'll come and grab it if I need to.'

Sara looked for something in Ryan's face, something to tell her how the last decade had changed him.

Ryan shifted as though aware of her scrutiny and looked at his shoes. 'So, how about dinner tonight? All four of us?'

'Sure. I'll ask Toby. He's back this afternoon. You can come up here.'

Ryan nodded. 'Will do. It'll just be Rachel and I. Dereck is staying with friends in town. We'll talk.' He gave her a long look, nodded, and then walked away. After a few steps, he rolled into a jog.

Sara glanced up towards the ute. Ryan was right. Dad had never parked nose-in.

As she walked down to the house, she finally grasped what had been eluding her. She walked to the pantry, stared at the beer she'd found on her arrival, and felt stupid for a moment. When Dad went out, he always took beer. Who would take beer to the pub? Not only that. Why hadn't any of them noticed?

## Chapter 57

Sara called Toby. 'I spoke to Ryan last night. I knew someone had been in the Workers' House the night Alec died. It was Ryan.' She placed a frypan over a burner.

'God; why didn't he say something?'

'He said he didn't see anything. Apparently, Anne had arranged a lift with him so she could leave secretly, but she got caught up with Robbie. I think Ryan knows something, though. He's not himself.'

'I agree,' said Toby. 'The other day, I got the impression he was a bit wired.'

Sara sighed. 'They're coming for dinner. He wants to talk. Can you come early? Say four o'clock?

'No worries,' said Toby.

Sara fried an egg and dropped a slice of bread into the toaster, too hungry to care about counting the calories.

She fried a second egg and made a cup of coffee. Nellie followed her to the table and sat beside her feet, tail springing side to side. Sara leant sideways and patted her head. 'You're actually very sweet.'

Nellie licked her lips.

'Nellie,' Sara tried to sound stern. 'This is mine. Yours is in the laundry. Chicken and vegetable casserole, remember?'

Nellie whined, sat back on her haunches and lifted her front feet.

Sara shook her head and ignored her. 'Don't beg.' In her peripheral vision, Nellie quivered and whined. When Sara got to the final square of egg and toast she looked down. Nellie was flat on her stomach, face between her paws. 'You don't need words, Nellie.'

The little dog closed her eyes.

'Really? Fine. C'mon.'

Nellie sat up rapidly, ears sharp.

Sara bit her lips.

In the laundry, Sara put her breakfast plate with the final square of egg and toast she'd saved down on the floor. 'I can't believe I'm doing this.'

In Nellie's bowl, a light-pink, pea-studded blob taken from a can the previous evening remained untouched.

Nellie walked over cautiously and nibbled at the egg. Sara retreated to the doorway. Nellie gulped the egg and toast. Her little pink tongue cleaned her lip corners. She gave Sara a direct stare, looked at the bare plate and then back at Sara.

Sara went to the kitchen and fried another egg, buttered a slice of toast, cut it into pieces and placed it in the laundry. 'Don't tell anyone,' she said.

Nellie wagged tentatively and then ate the lot. She burped.

Sara put the rejected pink blob outside the door.

Barney galloped over and gulped it in one go.

While Sara watched the other dogs through the door, Nellie sat down next to her leg. Sara stroked the top of her head with one finger. She couldn't look down. 'Don't look at me like that. You'll find a good home one day.'

When Sara dialled Anne's number, she got the machine. 'It's me, again.' She sighed. 'We all really need to talk.'

Earlier, Sara had yearned for the convenience of home when she had been forced to make a fifty-minute round trip to a shop that sold her a lamb roast for twice the price she was accustomed to.

When she was almost back at the farm, she saw a figure beside the road. He was standing with a foot either side of the channel, looking down. As she got closer, she saw it was a tall man in jeans, wearing a grey sweatshirt.

Sara had eased her foot off the accelerator and glanced across to the Stynes' driveway to assess if he stood somewhere near the place where Alec was found. She could see the embankment, which had borne the scuff marks searchers had pointed out. She remembered the man in the yellow vest walking across from there to the channel, then calling out.

Sara's pulse jolted, and she pressed down on the accelerator.

As though he'd heard the car coming, he turned.

*Ryan.*

Sara was sure he was standing right where Alec's body had been.

## Chapter 58

By three pm, the lamb leg was in the oven with chunks of potato, pumpkin and onion. It would be ready too early, Sara knew, but she'd needed to keep busy. At least her hands had stopped shaking.

Sara rinsed her fingers, dried them using an old tea towel and went outside to stand in the backyard. Absently, she patted the soft heads that bumped beneath her hands. It made sense that Ryan would go down the road to have a look. But it was still unsettling to see him staring into the channel.

He said he hadn't seen anything, but both he and Dad had been in unexpected places that night and hadn't been forthcoming about it. Would Ryan hide something for Dad?

Sara shook her head, went inside and picked up the phone.

This time, Mum answered on Bruno's mobile. Mum sighed. 'We're halfway to Parkwood. Just stopped for petrol. And we're looking for a pharmacy.'

'Okay. I rang because I wanted to ask you if Dad ever buried anything. Maybe something valuable?'

'Honestly, Sara. I don't think so. What is it?'

'Oh, nothing,' she said, surprised by Mum's impatient tone. 'I just found a couple of holes around the place. Don't worry about it. Will you be staying here? I can make up a bed for you?' She looked out the window and wondered where Ryan was.

'No, darling, that's okay. I'll go to my unit with Bruno.' Mum's voice sounded as if she was rallying. 'I told your father I'd never sleep there again as long as I lived. The last argument we had was about the big pine tree, and some stinging nettles. *Tch*. I just got sick of being yelled at like I was a child. Don't marry someone who doesn't respect you.'

'Okay, Mum.'

'Least I got my way with the giant in the front yard. I watched the tree lopper take it down piece by piece. Mind you, that wasn't until after Len had his stroke.'

Sara looked at the sky. It was as though a huge, dark presence had simply vanished. 'Good work ...' she said. 'Hang on, did you seriously argue about stinging nettles? Isn't that patch long gone? I didn't see any when I was weeding.'

'No, not the patch beside the veggie garden. There's another crop behind the shed. I was just trying to be helpful, but he went off. It was the last straw.'

'Which shed?'

'Hm? Oh, the machinery shed.'

Sara tapped a finger on the counter. 'Okay, I need to go. I'm making dinner.'

She put down the phone and ran straight out through the back door.

## Chapter 59

Sara reached the machinery shed, passed her dad's ute, and grabbed the shovel. As she walked around to the back, she thought about the whole family with their private battles ten years ago and even now. How they drew their own separate lines, which over time had intersected briefly, then barely at all.

The crop of stinging nettles sprouted out of a leafy compost mat punctured by small yellow toadstools.

Sara scanned the ground like she'd dropped a diamond. She walked across, testing for softness, but it all crunched and sank equally. She squatted down, found a long stick and poked the ground in several places. Hairy nettle leaves stung the back of her hand.

She stood up, grabbed the shovel and began to dig. She flinched a few times as her bruises made themselves known, but soon she'd scraped the top layer back, and a pile of nettles were heaped like miniature trees.

Sara levered up chunks of dirt full of wiry roots and kept going until she was surrounded by a warren of holes.

In the past, Dad had to bury the occasional carcass to deter the dogs or to hide the smell if it was too close to the house. Usually foxes, crows, and wedge-tailed eagles cleaned up any dead or dying creatures on the farm. Then she remembered Dad's dog Jack, and she shivered. She hoped she wasn't about to unearth his bones.

Sara wiped the back of her hand across her forehead. Her earlier, burning certainty that Dad was up to something had died down to a smoulder. She looked around at the mess and then thought about the big tree Mum had had cut down. She could imagine Dad fighting about that tree out of principle. But stinging nettles?

Sara remembered Dad's voice begging Mum not to leave. She visualised the full laundry basket and unclean house. Would Dad really run the risk of having to care for himself over a few stinging nettles?

Sara took a deep breath, selected the hole in the middle of the others and kept digging.

Almost immediately, the shovel squished into something that had more give than the dirt. Sara squatted down, grabbed a stick and prodded at it.

After a bit more digging, she discovered a mass the size of a large basketball inside opaque plastic. Sara scratched the edge carefully with her stick and then leant closer. She could see threads. Weft and weave, dark and light. She scraped the dirt away and then found a small hole. When she poked the stick through, she found black stuff that reminded her of rotting hide stretched across a cow skeleton. *Leather?*

Amid the wet, smoky smell of compost and dirt, Sara peered closely at the bag. She saw a big tortoiseshell button. She sat back on her heels and gathered it all in her mind. *Fabric. Leather. Button.*

Lillian's words came to her.

'... just a brown leather jacket, but he and I sewed coloured squares on.'

'Nonononono!' Sara stumbled back; she was full of sudden heat, her pulse pounding. She sucked breaths so fast she saw stars.

She leant against the shed and got her breathing under control and began her calming, awareness mantra. 'I can smell the dirt, see the nettles, feel the sweat in my hair.' Her voice faltered. She blew out slowly and stepped closer to her find. 'I can hear the ringing in my ears, and taste ...' Sara swallowed and looked around.

The air was cool, and the sun was low but bright, casting long shadows.

*They'll be here soon.*

Sara grabbed a longer stick. Carefully, like she would a snake, she lifted the edge of the fabric through the hole in the plastic. Out popped a sleeve and cuff.

She'd almost convinced herself it wasn't, but it was.

Alec's dreamcoat.

## Chapter 60

The dogs started barking. A car pulled up on the other side of the shed. The engine stopped, and two doors opened and then closed.

'Sara?' Ryan called.

'Up behind the shed!'

Ryan rounded the corner and then stopped dead. His mouth opened.

Rachel appeared. 'What?' She bumped into Ryan, and then put her hand over her mouth. 'Fuck.'

Ryan lifted his hand. 'Sara, don't touch that.'

Wide-eyed, Rachel stared at Sara. 'Hand it over!'

Ryan closed his eyes for a moment. 'She means just leave it there.'

The two exchanged a glance, and Rachel scowled.

'Do you know what this is?' said Sara. 'Is it Alec's jacket?'

Ryan walked over and squatted to get a closer look. Then he stood slowly and walked back to Rachel. 'I think so.'

'How did it get here?' Sara persisted, her throat dry.

Ryan's shoulders lifted with a deep breath. 'A few weeks

ago, your dad told me it was buried at the back of the shed.'

'How did my dad get it?' Blackness edged in. *Fridays. Dad lying about where he was.*

Rachel grabbed Ryan's wrist.

Ryan shook his head at her. 'It's time, Rachel.'

'What about Dereck?' Rachel's eyes filled with tears.

'Are you saying it was my dad who ran Alec down?' asked Sara. She looked from one to the other. She remembered Dad's hatred, his nose snarled like a dog's. 'Ryan!'

Ryan held up his hands. 'No! It wasn't him, Sara.'

Sara took a good breath. 'Who then?'

Four dogs began to bark.

A car got closer and braked. A door slammed.

Ryan glanced towards the house and scowled. 'What's he doing here?'

Rachel flexed her hands, bounced on her heels. 'He called. I told him we were out here.'

'Who is it?' said Sara.

They heard a voice call out. 'Hello! Anyone home?'

Sara concentrated. She knew that voice. 'Is that Freddie?'

Ryan nodded, mouth tight.

The barking went crazy: Rusty's woof; Nellie's sharp terrier bullets; the deep, salivary sound of Barney; and the short yak-yak of Lifter.

Freddie swore and then made barking sounds.

The barking intensified, vicious and wet, like a dog fight.

Freddie laughed.

Rachel stirred, eyes everywhere. 'Up here!' Her eyes focused deep into Sara like she was pinning her. 'Behind the shed!'

Sara's mind whirred as she positioned herself over the hole.

Restless, adrenaline-filled Freddie. Rachel, Ryan. Dad.

Freddie came around the corner. He was wearing black jeans and a green, long-sleeved shirt. His head was a shiny dome, his body compact and muscular.

Ryan narrowed his eyes.

Freddie put his hands on his hips. 'What's going on here?' Eyebrows raised, he had the superior look of a captain who'd caught them misbehaving.

Rachel spoke quickly, her hand busy explaining. 'Sara dug up that kid's jacket. Remember the hit-and-run? Her dad buried it here.' She pointed at Sara's feet.

Freddie's eyes zipped over to the hole. His lips parted, and he ran a hand over his skull. 'Right, I see.' He licked his lips, eyes glued on the find. Sara noticed his skin had gone a sickly colour.

It had been ten years since Alec was killed. Sara wondered why Freddie had understood Rachel's brief explanation so quickly.

'Can you bag it up, Freddie?' Rachel asked, which disturbed Freddie's trance. She nodded, eyebrows up, silently communicating something.

Freddie blinked, and then his brow pulled down. 'Absolutely!' His voice then deepened as he said, 'Well done, Sara.' He nodded at the other two.

Ryan, face like a thundercloud, shook his head. The muscle in his jaw twitched.

Freddie ignored him and looked around. 'Stay there. I'll sort it out.' He walked briskly back the way he'd come.

Something was off with Rachel and Freddie. Sara thought that if Freddie got the jacket, it might disappear. She glanced at Ryan. His face was turned in the direction Freddie had disappeared. She wondered if she could trust him.

The barking became stuttered, like the dogs were listening. Sara wondered how they'd react if she screamed.

Freddie returned with an empty fertilizer bag, a thick plastic one – similar to the one Alec's jacket was in. The same type that her dad once kept on the floor of his ute. A flicker of recognition came to Sara. A memory turned uncomfortably within her. Dad pressing a new one onto the floor of the Hilux. She was distracted by the sound of more barking and another car.

A door slammed, and a car reversed.

The dogs yowled and squeaked.

Sara could hear Toby laugh over the excitement. 'Barney, down!'

In front of her, Freddie held out his hand. 'Sara. I'll get it,' he said evenly.

'No.'

Freddie's jaw muscle twitched. 'I'm a cop, Sara,' he said through his teeth.

Sara braced, expecting to be tackled.

'C'mon! I'm doing you and your father a favour.'

'What?' queried Ryan, wide-eyed.

'Sara?' Toby's voice came up from the house yard.

Freddie's smile fell off. He silenced everyone with his hand and took a step towards the hole.

Sara lifted the stick.

Freddie smirked.

'Don't touch her,' said Ryan.

Freddie lunged and grabbed the stick.

Sara's shoulder wrenched, and she fell forwards onto her knees and quickly rolled sideways off the hole.

From the ground, she saw Rachel hip and shoulder Ryan. Unprepared, he staggered sideways, and came down hard on one knee. Grimacing, he gripped his leg. Sara scrabbled on the ground as she tried to get up.

'Rachel!' called Freddie.

Rachel quickly balanced and turned around. A second later, she crashed down onto Sara, knee into her hip.

Sara cried out in pain.

'Hurry!' panted Rachel.

Sara, cheek in the dirt, hair in her eyes, heard the shovel nearby. 'Toby! Up here!' she called.

The barking started again. Sara thought quickly. She had fed the dogs for two days. Was it long enough for them to see her as part of the pack? 'Toby! Let the dogs out!'

Ryan staggered up to his feet and wobbled, face red, veins standing out along his neck. 'Freddie, Rachel, stop! You're making it worse!'

With a stick, Freddie scooped the mass of plastic with the hanging sleeve into the fertilizer bag. His face was contorted. Ryan took a step towards him and grimaced. Freddie grabbed the shovel off the ground and held it towards Ryan. 'Stay back!' he commanded.

Sara screamed. The dogs yowled and barked.

As though he realised what Sara intended, Ryan whistled.

Sara managed to inhale and whistled too.

Rachel shoved Sara's face into the dirt with the heel of her hand. But Sara didn't mind.

She knew, to a dog, it would look like an attack.

Sara heard a snarl. Rusty lurched at Rachel.

Rachel screamed and fell off Sara, with Rusty's mouth clamped on her wrist.

Spitting dirt out of her mouth, Sara wriggled backwards until she came up against the shed. 'Good girl, Rusty!' Sara wiped her lips with her sleeve.

Near Sara's feet, Barney faced Freddie, barking ferociously. Freddie turned, brandishing a stick.

Barney launched at Freddie and snapped onto his wrist. Yelling, Freddie fell and then scrambled backwards. Dirt spilled into the hole as dog and man wrestled.

Sara crawled forwards. Rachel shook free and grabbed Sara's leg. Rusty growled and snapped onto Rachel's wrist again. She screamed and slapped at the dog with her free hand. Sara caterpillar-crawled away. Rusty released Rachel and stayed on guard, growling and quivering. Rachel remained in a crouch, with her arms in front of her face.

Toby jogged around the corner with Nellie close behind.

Nellie barked so hard it looked like her head had come loose.

Barney, teeth fastened to Freddie's forearm, had propped onto his haunches.

Freddie slapped at the dog's face until Barney let go. Freddie fell onto his back and lay scabbed against the earth. Barney jumped and stood over him, snarling into his face.

Lifter walked around the corner. With no change of expression, he clambered over a pile of dirt and sniffed Freddie. He lined up his body, cocked his leg, and pissed on Freddie, who swatted and swore.

'Good dog,' said Toby. 'Rusty, Barney, come!'

Barney trotted over with his tail down. Toby gave him a vigorous pat. 'Good boy.'

Barney wagged cautiously. Lifter wandered away and peed on the back of the shed.

## Chapter 61

'Let Sara up or I'll release them,' said Toby. He had Rusty and Barney by their collars.

Rachel held up her hand, wincing and protecting her injured wrist.

Freddie cowered near the shed, cradling a bloodied arm.

Shaking, Sara made a messy approach to the fertilizer bag and lifted it clear of the hole.

'Are you alright, Sara?' Ryan limped over. His eyes flicked to the right. Rachel scrambled on all fours like a monkey, then ran towards the front fence.

Rusty surged against Toby's grip. 'No, Rusty! Stay!'

Rachel vaulted effortlessly over the fence.

'Ninja,' said Sara, a small piece falling into place.

'Ah.' Toby's eyes were drawn to the mess around the diggings. 'What happened, Sara?'

Freddie shifted.

'Don't move!' said Toby.

Barney snarled and pulled against his collar.

Freddie held up his hands and shook his head, wide-eyed.

Sara placed the bag down behind the dogs. 'I found Alec's coat. Dad buried it here.'

Toby's face changed. He gave Sara a long look. 'How did your dad get hold of it?'

'He just found it on the road,' Freddie said.

Barney barked.

Freddie's eyes bulged, and his face went pink. 'Put a goddam muzzle on that thing! I could have you charged! I'd have shot him already, if I'd had my weapon.'

Toby calmed Barney.

'I'm going to take this to the police personally,' said Ryan. 'Tell them everything.'

'Disloyal prick!' Freddie shouted. He got up awkwardly. His jaw moved inside his cheeks, face a dangerous red. 'Don't forget why we're here. You've got a kid now. Who's to say it wasn't you driving that night.' He glanced at Barney.

Ryan scowled. 'Don't threaten me, Freddie.'

Sara held up her hand. 'I want to hear everything, Ryan. But let's go to the police. We can talk in the car.'

Freddie looked from Sara to Toby. 'I'm an officer of the law, and I need this mongrel bite treated.' He held up his bloody arm, a jagged tear near his wrist.

Toby gave a nod. 'Go on then.'

Freddie spoke low as he walked past. 'Fag.'

Barney barked ferociously.

Freddie ran a few steps, looked back over his shoulder, dusted his hands together and then walked with a swagger.

'My hands are slipping!' Toby called.

Freddie spurted forwards into a run.

After Freddie had driven away, Sara and Toby returned the dogs to the house yard, fed them and checked they had water.

'Thanks for letting the dogs out,' said Sara, brushing dirt off her clothes and shaking it out of her hair.

'I saw Freddie's car and knew something was off,' said Toby.

Sara went inside, washed her face and then turned the oven off. The house smelled like a carvery. Her mouth watered. She locked the door and headed back outside.

Ryan limped over and stood beside his four-wheel drive. His shoulders were slumped and his hands were shoved inside his pockets. Sara caught his eye, pointed at her car. Ryan nodded and moved that way.

Sara handed Toby her keys. 'Can you drive? I'll sit in the back with Ryan. I don't think Freddie will pull you over tonight.'

With the bag containing Alec's jacket in the boot, all three climbed into Sara's car.

Toby looked back. 'Parkwood police? That's where he works.'

Sara exchanged a long look with Toby. 'Not tonight. Besides, even Freddie can't argue with what's in that bag.'

## Chapter 62

Once they were on the road to Parkwood, Sara asked the question that scared her the most.

'What did Dad do?'

Ryan ran his hand over his face. 'Tried to help me. He thought I was driving when Alec was hit.'

'But you weren't?'

'No. I told him I was. To protect Rachel.'

'Was Rachel driving?' said Sara, incredulously.

Ryan nodded. 'She was in Freddie's ute. He'd been drinking, so Rachel took the wheel. Apparently, Alec ran out suddenly.' He paused. 'I was inside the Workers' House when it happened, heard something but wasn't sure what it was. The ute had a bull bar and CB radio.'

Sara shook her head slowly in disbelief. She held up one hand. 'Okay. Before that, you were here to pick Anne up?'

Ryan nodded. 'I parked a way back on the old highway, so Len wouldn't see the car. Anne said he'd probably go out that night. I watched but the Hilux didn't leave until about nine pm. It was freezing. Got dark early. I left the house lights off, closed the curtains and lit the fire. About ten, I decided Anne wasn't coming so I packed up, ready to drive back home.'

Sara cast a look at Toby in the rear-view mirror. 'Dad went out at nine?' she said.

Ryan nodded. 'When I went outside to have a look, Freddie's ute pulled into the drive. He and Rachel got out, faces white as sheets. She ran over to the fence and vomited.'

In the front, Toby's head was tilted as though listening.

'Rachel was blubbering. She said she'd hit the kid from next door. She was repeating to herself, "He just ran out in front of me!" I asked where he was. They kept shaking their heads, so I started jogging out towards the highway. Freddie tackled me, punched me in the guts. He said it was too late. The kid was dead.'

'Alec didn't die straight away,' said Sara. 'He drowned.'

Ryan looked at her. 'I swear I didn't know that then. Freddie was dragging me with him, shouting in my face, saying it was my fault, that our lives would be a living hell. Then he just let go. He had his arm stuck out.'

Sara shifted in her seat and saw Toby's eyes in the mirror.

Ryan winced. 'Freddie started freaking out, saying something about AIDS.'

'What?'

Ryan closed his eyes. 'There was blood on Freddie's sleeve. That's when I knew it was real. They'd run down the boy Freddie called the little faggot in the poofy coat.'

'Ryan. Ryan? Was it really an accident?'

Ryan nodded quickly. 'Yes. Honestly. You should've seen them.'

'But they didn't try to help him?'

Ryan winced. 'Rachel said she reversed, and Freddie jumped out and ran up the road to check. When he got back in, he was pale and shaking. He told her that the kid was dead.'

'Freddie got blood on him but didn't know Alec was still alive?' Sara gave Ryan a look. 'Alec was in a ditch. Was Freddie covered in mud?'

Ryan shook his head and then he sagged. 'Rachel told me something recently. It was after Len called. She said that when Freddie ran back that night, she could see him hunched over something on the verge.' He showed his hands. 'But Alec was found in the channel.'

Sara got a shiver over her entire body. She hugged herself.

In the rear-view mirror, Toby's eyes were wide. 'Ryan, do you think Freddie rolled Alec into the ditch?' he said.

Ryan looked horrified; his face contorted. 'I honestly don't know!'

'Jesus.' Toby gripped the steering wheel straight-armed. 'That poor boy.'

Sara inhaled long and slow.

Ryan ran his hand back over his head. 'It started pouring with rain. We were arguing. Then Freddie pointed at Rachel. He said, "Rach, tell him." And Rachel explained that she was pregnant.' Ryan looked over.

Sara swallowed.

'I'm sorry, Sara. It was a few weeks before you and me. I'd had too much to drink.'

'I heard. It doesn't matter now.'

'It does matter. That night was one of the best ...'

'Don't.' Sara twisted her face towards the window. 'Tell me what happened next,' she said thickly.

'Rachel looked so small and scared. I forgot everything except for the tiny, innocent nugget inside her. I said I'd look after her and the baby.'

'Alec was dying!' Sara cried.

'I didn't know he had a chance, Sara!' Ryan sobbed, arms open, tears running down his face. 'I would have gone to him! I would have carried him to the car. Done fucking CPR on him. I've imagined driving to hospital ...' He choked and sobbed into both his hands, and his voice came out muffled. 'I'm sorry. I'm so sorry!'

Sara's jaw ached. She shifted in her seat and waited for him to calm down. 'What about Dad?' she said quietly.

Ryan used his shirt to wipe his face then slumped back against the seat, breath shuddering. 'He pulled in behind Freddie's car, from the highway, dressed like he'd been to the pub. He asked what we were doing in the goddam rain. Seemed a bit out of breath. Freddie panicked, stared at us. Rachel was in my arms, snivelling. Freddie told him that Rachel was pregnant with my baby. I realised what I had to do. I told Len I had been the one driving and I'd hit someone. Freddie butted in and told him it was the poof from across the road.'

'How did Dad react?'

'He just stared at me like he'd gone blank.' Ryan cleared his throat. 'Then he sort of woke up and looked around again like he was spooked. He asked, "You hit Alec?"'

Sara crossed her arms hard.

'He asked where Alec was. Freddie pointed towards the highway, bouncing around on his toes, and he told Len that he was dead in the ditch beside the road. Len turned his back to us and then after a minute asked if the kid was definitely dead. Freddie said he was. Real quietly, your dad said, "Don't touch anything."'

Sara wound down the window and sucked in the air. Tears pushed into the corners of her eyes and were dried by the wind. Her car swerved suddenly. Sara grabbed the windowsill. Ahead were taillights and a flash of red.

Toby checked her in the mirror and shook his head.

Sara held her head in her hands. 'How did Dad get Alec's jacket?' she said slowly.

Ryan cleared his throat. 'Len flinched. I could see why. Alec's coat was caught in the grille behind the bull bar of Freddie's ute.' Ryan took a deep breath. 'Len went over and pulled it out. Then he just looked at us. Said, "I'll bury it."'

'God,' Sara whispered, letting her hands fall.

'I said we had to tell the police, get an ambulance. Len stopped me. He said it was an accident. The kid was dead, and there was no fixing it. Told me I'd be jailbait if I confessed. Just said: "get married, get the hell out of there and never say a word". The last time I saw him, he was getting into the Hilux.'

Sara imagined her dad's silhouette, jacket hanging from his hand like a broken-necked rabbit.

## Chapter 63

'Okay, we're here.' Toby pulled up next to the Parkwood police station. He twisted around. 'I'll go in and make sure Constable Freddie hasn't turned up, and we can trust these guys.' He gave Ryan a steady look before he got out.

In the sudden quiet, Sara said, 'So, did you know where the jacket was buried?'

'Not exactly. Your dad called a few weeks ago about part ownership of the farm and the guardianship thing. I knew I couldn't work with him after what happened. Then he just went quiet and said, "That jacket is buried up the back of the shed." It all came back.' Ryan closed his eyes.

'Maybe he wanted you to confess. Why didn't you ever say anything?' said Sara.

Ryan looked at her with his mouth bunched. 'Freddie had told Rachel that she would be jailed if they found out she was the driver, then Len and I would get charged too. He said Dereck would end up in the system.'

Sara looked out the window. 'I can't believe Freddie became a cop.'

'He's a nasty bastard. He told me once that some police were into poofter bashing. You did see his ute that day, Sara. He laughed about it once, but said they were just mucking around, and Alec was fine.'

Sara took a moment to digest that. 'He hasn't changed. He harasses Toby. Threatens to do something if he can prove he's gay.' Sara felt Ryan turn towards her.

'Toby?'

Sara nodded and looked over.

'Toby's a good guy.' Ryan put his elbow on the windowsill and stared at the station. The lights from the building lit the concrete down the side, which joined the neat square of grass at the edge of the carpark. 'Each time there was a knock on the door, I expected to get dragged off to prison. Every anniversary of that night was a freaking nightmare.'

'Lillian said she found flowers on Alec's grave every year.'

Ryan nodded. Sara touched his arm, but he didn't turn. 'It was pathetic. Flowers.' He shook his head. 'Rachel and I were constantly trying to prove we were good people. We donated to all sorts of charities. We did all the parent jobs on weekends. I coached Dereck's sport teams, joined all the committees, travelled with the scouts. Rachel did volunteer work and baked for every disco, cake stall, and kids' birthday parties. It felt like a marathon with no end.'

Through the windscreen, Sara watched Toby emerge from the station.

'It was Rachel that dug the holes and whacked me, wasn't it?' Sara could feel more bruises developing.

'Yeah. After Len called, Rachel was desperate to get rid of that jacket. When we heard about Len's stroke, we decided to come down and look for it. Rachel went out to search around at the farm while I was in town with Dereck. I didn't know you were here. If we found it, I was going to go to the police. But we couldn't find it. I went to see Len, to ask him about it. We'd never talked about that night. I was shocked when I saw him. I didn't realise how sick he was.'

Toby opened the door. 'All good. Are you ready?'

Ryan unfolded his long legs and climbed out. As he drew level with Toby, he met his eyes, and then pulled his shoulders back. 'Toby, will you come in with me?'

Toby nodded. 'Sure. Nothing but the truth?'

Ryan nodded.

Toby squeezed his shoulder. 'Okay, mate.'

Sara's phone rang. 'Hi, Mum. I'll call you a bit later.'

'Everything alright?'

Sara closed her eyes. 'When will I see you? We need to talk. It's serious.'

'We're on the edge of town. What's wrong?'

Sara watched Toby and Ryan walk towards the station. She held up one finger for them to wait. Toby rested the bag containing Alec's jacket on the ground. They stopped just short of the door, which had a big 'No Smoking' sign in the middle. Sara cupped the mouthpiece and turned her back. 'Mum,' she said slowly and carefully. 'I found Alec Stynes' jacket. Dad buried it behind our machinery shed. Rachel, Ryan's wife, was the one who ran Alec down. It was an accident. I'm at the police station now.'

Mum wailed like a shot rabbit. 'Why would he do that! Oh God!' She kept repeating herself. In the background, Sara could hear a male voice. It must have been Bruno, her brother. Then Mum came on again. 'Rachel was the driver?' she said disbelievingly.

'Yes, Mum.'

'So, Len... hid it so she wouldn't get into trouble?'

'Sort of. For Ryan too. But Mum, he didn't even check to see if Alec was okay.' *Neither did Ryan.* But, she reasoned, Ryan was eighteen, scared, and had just found out he was going to be a father. 'Dad just left him there.'

'Sara? Sara?' Ryan called.

Sara turned towards the station.

'Is that Ryan?' Mum asked.

Sara kept walking, phone to ear. 'Hang on.'

Ryan was waving his hand and pointing at the fertilizer bag. When she reached them, both men were squatting down.

Sara covered the phone with her hand and leant closer. Through the opaque plastic, she saw criss-crossed string. A shoelace. The shoe was collapsed and dirty but Sara could still tell it was a match to the one Lillian had held out to them that morning.

'What is it, Sara?' said Mum, sounding strained. The question hung there as the white glow of the station lights gave the lawn a deep green hue.

Sara uncovered the mouthpiece. 'There's something else in the bag with Alec's jacket. I think it's his other shoe.'

She looked at Ryan. The confusion shown on his face answered her question.

He hadn't known about the shoe.

*Chapter 64*

The bag Sara had dug up was labelled and taken away by a policewoman wearing rubber gloves.

Sara, Toby and Ryan each spoke with the police and gave preliminary statements.

Sara was handed a cup of tea.

Interviews and a scene examination were scheduled for early the next morning. An officer was dispatched to secure the site.

Sara's stomach growled. Over two hours had passed since their arrival. She walked outside and breathed in the cool air.

The night sky was dark above the streetlights. Sara put her head back and looked at the stars. Toby joined her.

Ryan's phone rang. He lagged at the station door and then indicated Toby and Sara wait. After a minute, he closed the phone. 'Rachel's bringing herself in. She went and told Lillian first.' He gave Sara a long look. 'She's going to confess. And tell the police what she thinks Freddie did.'

Sara shivered and glanced around, half-expecting Freddie's bald head in the shadows.

Toby patted Sara's shoulder as though he knew what she was thinking. 'Don't worry, his arm looked nasty. They'll track him down.'

Sara pulled her phone from her pocket and turned the volume back on. Seven missed calls. It rang in her hand.

'Yes?'

'It's Jason from Blooms. I'm really sorry. I have some bad news.'

*Worse than my father burying a dead boy's belongings?*

Sara closed her eyes. 'Yes?'

'Are you close by?'

'Please, just tell me.'

'I'm sorry to do this over the phone, I really am. Sara, your father has passed away.'

Sara squinted. 'What? No, he ... he's had a stroke.' Images tumbled. Dad striding along with Alec's jacket. A sick, quiet man slumped in a chair.

'I'm so sorry. This must be a terrible shock,' Jason said gently. 'Unfortunately, Sara, a second stroke in your dad's case is not uncommon.'

'But I ...' Sara took a moment. Dad was dead. Gone. Would never be able to explain why he'd buried Alec's things. 'I'm coming.' Sara pressed the end button and then couldn't move. She felt a hand on her arm and found Toby's concerned face near hers. 'I have to go. It's Dad.' She stopped herself from telling him more. 'Just stay with Ryan.'

At Blooms, an old doctor in a brown suit and tie shook Sara's hand, patted her back and offered his condolences. He explained, eyebrows pulled into a sombre expression, Dad had been among the twenty five percent of people who survived a haemorrhagic stroke. He said a quarter of those survivors however, suffered a second stroke, like Dad had tonight, which was usually fatal.

Sara limply listened and numbly accepted. She noted the red threads of veins in the doctor's cheeks and the small patch of unshaven beard near his mouth. She felt as if she'd stepped into the scene of a play without knowing her lines.

Once the doctor had finished, Judy looped her arm through Sara's, and they walked to room seventeen together. The door was pulled almost closed, an inch of soft lighting around the edges.

Sara stared at the door. 'What am I supposed to do?'

Judy squeezed her hand.

'Your mother has just gone to the rest room,' she said. 'Would you like me to stay?'

Tightness high in her chest, Sara nodded and then pushed the door open. In the room was a bed and next to it, a cabinet with a vase of fresh flowers and a box of tissues on top. A side lamp cast a mellow glow.

On the pillow was Dad's lifeless face and dark hair.

Sara winced. 'Did he just die like this?' she whispered. 'In his sleep?'

'Yes. We put him to bed early. He seemed exhausted. We found him unconscious a couple of hours later. I'm so sorry.'

Sara turned to Judy, who stood there looking patient and gentle.

'We didn't really talk ...' said Sara.

Judy gave an understanding nod. 'Lots of family relationships are complex. Just use this opportunity for yourself. Take your time. For many people, this is an important part of the grieving process.'

Sara managed a watery smile. She remembered how kind Judy had been. She thought about how much care it took to feed, wash and clothe a helpless body, and the tightness in her chest eased a fraction. 'I'm okay now, thanks Judy. You've been wonderful.'

Judy backed out quietly.

Sara shifted closer to the bed. She waited for a rise in the covers over her dad's chest, a flicker behind his eyelids. She stared at his pale cheeks, the sunspots, the waxy skin that moulded across the bridge of his nose. He was as still as the furniture. Sara focused on the people who must have lifted him out of the Hilux and onto a stretcher after his stroke, and gently taken care of him. Pain ran along her jaw and throat.

The body in the bed was smaller than Dad. His flaccid arms lay on top of the covers by his sides. The sling from his arm was gone. His forearms were thick and tanned, and above his bicep there was a crusted drop of blood. Dad's wide fingers were slightly curled in towards the palm, nails rimmed by grease.

Sara took a deep breath and slowly picked up his hand. Still pliable, it was heavy and not yet cold.

In her memory, apart from when she was small, Sara hadn't held his hand.

She felt like an actor in a movie.

She had no prepared words and couldn't remember saying she loved him. She couldn't remember feeling it.

Sara took a deep breath. 'Dad?' Her voice shook as she tried to sort the clutter. She'd never imagined this moment. This harmless father.

Sara's tears fell, whether from pointlessness or sadness, she wasn't sure. She felt she hadn't known him or understood what he had wanted from her. She just remembered the angry blue eyes and the shouting. He hadn't got to know her either. What were they to each other but genetics and shared meals at the dinner table?

'Dad. I *need* to forgive you. One day, I hope I can.' She shuddered a breath and put her hand on her chest. 'For me.' Sara pulled tissues from a box by the bed and wiped her face. She breathed out for a long time. Her chest eased a little more.

'Anne and Robbie will be here soon.' Mum was standing at the door, her face drawn and blank.

'Are you alright?' Sara whispered.

Mum nodded and then slowly backed out. Sara worried she was in shock. It looked as though she hadn't cried, and she had a slowness to her movements like she was drugged.

Sara went over, embraced her. 'Where is your brother?'

'He dropped me here but had to go back to the hospital to sort out his medication. We lost it on the way.'

'Okay. Will you be alright at the flat?'

Mum nodded. 'Bruno will stay with me.'

A nurse pushing a trolley down the corridor stopped outside a door and fiddled with little plastic pill bottles. She knocked on an open door and entered.

Sara patted her mum's back. 'Mum, I feel like I'm ready to pass out. I just need to eat. Can I get you something?'

Mum shook her head. 'I'm alright, love.' She sat on a chair in the corridor outside the room and folded her hands around the handbag she'd put on her lap. 'I'll wait for Robbie and Anne to get here.'

Sara walked out to the carpark and leant against her car. Overhead, a panorama of sky glimmered with stars. Sara realised it was beautiful.

She climbed into the car and headed for the nearest fast-food restaurant. With the window down, the cold air made her feel more alert. The combination of hunger and exhaustion was doing a good job of making her twitchy.

Sara knew it made sense Dad had picked up Alec's shoe and jacket and buried them together. To protect Ryan. But tonight, when Ryan saw the shoe in the bag, he swore he hadn't seen it before.

At the drive-through, Sara ordered the largest burger on the menu, and a bottle of water. She was handed a paper bag, which she placed on the seat beside her. She pulled into a parking bay, found the burger and sank her mouth over as much of it as she could. Chewing, she slipped her free hand into the bag and found the water bottle. Her hand touched something else. A crinkly packet. Sara pulled it out. It was a toy in plastic wrapping. The kind that came with a child's meal. It must have been added mistakenly, or was already in the bag when they dropped the rest in.

The phone, on the seat beside her, rang. Sara quickly swallowed a big lump of food and gulped some water, spilling some down her front. It was Anne.

'Anne! Great to hear your voice,' said Sara. Anne took a moment to respond. Sara guessed she was probably surprised by her enthusiasm. As they quickly caught up, Sara wiped her wet shirt with a serviette.

'We're all meeting at Mum's flat. Robbie's here too.'

Sara clicked the indicator as she drove out onto the road and tried to imagine what Robbie might look like. But her thoughts were pulled back to the bag on the seat that contained the toy. She thought about the bag she'd dug out of the ground with the unexplained shoe.

As she pulled into a small driveway, Sara felt certainty, closely followed by fear. Rachel, Freddie and Ryan had seen Dad walk off with Alec's jacket. According to Ryan, there had been no shoe. But in the bag, there was.

Sara could only imagine one way that was possible.

Before he found the other three that night, Dad already had the shoe.

## Chapter 65

Sara and Robbie hugged for ages. Then they held each other back a little way.

'You look good, Robbie.' A silver chain glistened against his collarbones, and he wore a ring on his middle finger. His hair was long at the front, and coupled with Mum's features, he looked a little exotic. There were a few scars on Robbie's arms. Sara kept her eyes off the damage. Robbie was back. That was what mattered.

They were all together in Mum's tiny flat. The kitchen had everything you'd expect in a normal house in about a third of the space. The white tiles and paint made it feel airy. Mum flicked on her plastic kettle and opened a cupboard where cups sat in neat rows. Anne patted Mum's hands away and edged into the kitchen. Mum changed spots with her.

Anne's phone rang. 'Hi, honey. Yeah. We're back at Mum's now. What? Does he have a fever?' She paused, phone tucked between ear and shoulder, and then put teabags into the cups. 'Okay, so just give him the liquid painkiller. He likes that one.' Anne opened a drawer and put several spoons on the bench. 'Check the label and use the measuring cap it comes with.' Anne paused and then rolled her eyes. 'Your son is three years old,' she said pointedly. 'Remember the truck cake I made?' Another pause. 'Yep, that's it. And he's about fourteen kilos.'

Sara looked around, found herself in a photo on the wall wearing school uniform, with Anne and Robbie either side. Near the front door was a loose line of shoes. They'd all taken them off as they came in. The line reminded Sara of the empty row at the farm. But this row was less rigid and there were leaves spread around them.

She moved into the laundry. The small window overlooked a paved courtyard edged with azaleas.

'Here you go.' Mum came in and handed her a cup.

'It's nice here,' said Sara before taking a sip.

'Are you alright?' Mum had a deep crease between her eyebrows. 'It's a shocking business. Finding that bag.' She shivered then reached over and picked something out of Sara's hair.

'I do need a shower.' Sara had cleaned up a bit at the police station, but her skin itched beneath her clothes, and not just from the dirt. 'What were you going to speak to me about?'

Mum sighed. 'It doesn't matter now because of what's happened. But there was something I didn't say a long time ago, which I should have.'

Sara watched her mum's face carefully.

'Your father sounded ... odd when he answered the phone the night we were at the hospital.' Mum drew her hand across her eyes and took a long breath. 'In the morning, I found his good jeans in a bucket with his work clothes. There was mud on the cuffs and the knees. I just ...' She shrugged tightly. '... washed them like I always did.'

Sara bit the inside of her lip and tasted blood. She knew why Mum had never said anything. Mum kept the peace. 'I want to forgive Dad, but I can't yet,' said Sara. 'Not just for burying Alec's stuff, but because of how mean he was. What he did to Robbie.'

Mum closed her eyes for a moment and took a long breath. 'He thought Robbie was gay,' she said quietly.

'For God's sake,' said Sara.

Mum turned her face towards the window, the reflection from the outside light giving her a yellow glow. 'I didn't know he was capable of hurting Robbie, until that night.' A surge of tears welled, and Mum wiped them with a folded tissue she'd pulled from her sleeve. 'Len thought Alec and Robbie were together.'

Sara rubbed her temple with two fingers, hit by a sudden craving for shiraz. 'Alec? Why?'

Mum tucked the tissue back into her sleeve and ran her fingers back and forth across the washing machine controls. 'He saw them meeting at the boundary a couple of times. Then he heard Robbie climb back through his bedroom window the night after Ryan's party.' Mum brushed her fingers against her thumb.

Sara's mouth felt numb. 'That was me,' she whispered.

'You?' Mum frowned a little, and then the wrinkles eased. She blinked a couple of times. 'I'm not sure I want to know.' She took a sip of tea, her eyes distant through the window.

'Oh, my God, poor Robbie.' Sara looked over and felt a swell of love for her brother.

The small living room seemed full of Anne, Robbie and Bruno. They were all related. The room had a pulse, something binding that touched all of them. Sara couldn't remember the last time this had happened.

Anne walked over to a small couch, phone still squashed between her ear and shoulder, slight frown on her face as she dug through her bag, held up a card and read out a phone number. Sara watched her sister in amazement. It was like she was the central part of a merry-go-round with her family circling around her.

As midnight crept closer, Anne told Sara what Robbie still kept to himself. She said he had not contracted any diseases while using drugs and had avoided a jail sentence. In fact, Anne said, clearly proud of him, he'd been clean of drugs and alcohol for nearly two years. He was now an assistant nurse and lived in a flat with his girlfriend. Anne confided that when they were at Blooms, Robbie had held Dad's hand and said goodbye. Anne said she hadn't been able to do anything but stare.

Sara gave Anne a long hug. She knew that some of the deepest bruises were invisible.

## *Chapter 66*

Driving back to the farm the next morning, questions about Alec circulated through the mill of Sara's mind.

The previous night when everyone had finally stopped talking, they had slept at Mum's wherever there was space. Ryan had stayed at the Workers' House and checked in on Sara's pack of canine warriors.

Sara realised she was excited about seeing the dogs, and worried about Nellie.

A car passed, moving in the opposite direction. Sara watched as it grew smaller in the rear-view mirror. She remembered the ute and how, if it had been turned the other way, she would have had an entirely different view. She would have seen the bull bar, and who sat in the driver's seat.

She could have given the information to the police at the time ...

At least Freddie had finally turned himself in. Whether he was going to confess to pushing Alec into the channel or not, and whether he'd known Alec was alive when he'd touched him, was yet to be seen. Sara hoped that all these years later justice could still be done.

But something still nagged her. It was about Rachel not seeing Alec until the last second. Alec was in love, yet he had been running hard in one shoe when he was hit.

Sara flicked the indicator and then turned on the wipers when light drizzle speckled the windscreen. As she watched the rubber arms clear the glass, she pondered automatic responses. Routine things. Like Alec crossing the road.

*'He just ran out in front of me,'* Rachel had said.

Sara stopped thinking about where Alec had been running. Instead, she considered why? What was he running *away* from?

A cold shiver passed through her.

Maybe Alec had been running for his life.

## Chapter 67

A few days passed, the mornings cold again, and there were more leaves on the ground beneath the trees. Sara had got back into the habit of lighting a fire in the pot-bellied stove in the evening and putting a big chunk of wood on, and then moving the air control lever, to ensure there'd be live coals when she and Nellie woke.

Everyone had gone home, for the time between Dad's death and his funeral, but they were all coming to stay afterwards.

Sara kept thinking about the shoe in the bag.

If her dad did have it with him before he came across the other three that night, how had he got it?

It was unlikely he didn't already have it because he would've had to go back and search around in the dark after he'd got the jacket. For that, he would've needed to know Alec had lost the shoe, and where to look for it. He couldn't have gone later because Lillian or the searchers would probably have found it.

Sara dressed for her dad's funeral, in clothes borrowed

from Anne.

'Are you coming?' Anne, wearing a navy skirt and jacket, waited at the door. 'We're going to be late.'

At the cemetery, Mum stood shoulder to shoulder with her brother Bruno, a portly man who shared her green eyes. He had a wide, generous smile as he pulled a Winston Blue cigarette from the packet and tapped it on the lid before lighting up.

Before they went inside the chapel, Anne had elbowed Robbie as they stood by the rose garden. Sara saw who had caught their attention. Lillian wore a cream skirt and red coat and stood away from the group, with her hands folded. She was far enough away to appear she was there for another funeral or leaving flowers, except that her hands were empty, and she was alone. She nodded to Mum.

Sara noticed Mum frown slightly but return a composed little nod as she waited for Bruno to finish his cigarette. Then Lillian smiled warmly. Robbie walked directly over, and they embraced. Over Robbie's shoulder, Sara noticed Lillian had her eyes closed. Her hands, on Robbie's back, rubbed up and down. Then the two stood back a little way from each other talking, Lillian smiling and nodding. Anne caught Sara's eye, her eyebrows raised.

The group began moving towards the door of the chapel. Sara found her family, and they walked in together.

The congregation were told by someone in a suit, whom Sara had never seen before, that Len Hamilton had been a successful farmer and had a wonderful family. Sara looked to her left and her right, where Anne and Robbie were. Robbie gave her a wink.

Mum sat straight backed beside her brother, who had his

hand over hers. It must have been a great comfort for her to have him there. Sara noted how strong she appeared, blinking every now and again as if she was listening carefully. When Sara looked around, she couldn't see Lillian.

The service was short, a piece of music played on the organ and then the same man in the suit read something from the Bible.

Dad's coffin moved forwards on the tastefully concealed conveyor belt into the cremation furnace. The white bouquet trembled with the movement. Sara imagined the black part of the fire.

The pastor said something about ashes and the Lord.

Sara closed her eyes and let the thought, which had begun earlier, take shape.

Dad must have been near Alec the night he died. Close enough to grab the shoe when Alec lost it. Then he buried the shoe with the jacket, apparently, to protect Ryan.

Sara opened her eyes just as the curtains had dropped behind the wooden coffin. As the furnace hummed, Sara felt a presence in the quietness, like angels falling.

Dad could've been the reason Alec was running for his life.

So, Sara reasoned, when he buried Alec's jacket and shoe, Dad was protecting himself.

## Chapter 68

### Alec – Friday, June 1989

Alec felt something as soon as he opened his bedroom window, not a physical sensation but a change in the darkness. A tension. He told himself he'd just noticed the temperature difference from the warm house. It never got this cold in Sydney. This bitter. He could usually get by just wearing his dreamcoat.

There was a small break in the weather. The clouds had parted somewhere over the black mass of the pine plantation, allowing a slight moonglow through. He hated the pines. Never went in there. They were so silent and still, even if the wind was blowing outside.

Alec looked back at his closed door. It was almost time to meet Robbie. He could still hear music from the movie his mum was watching.

Performing *Joseph* the week before had been euphoric. He'd nailed his lines and songs, despite a slightly sore throat in the days leading up to opening night. The crowd had given him a standing ovation. People he didn't know, smiling and clapping, for *him*.

Behind the stage curtain, he'd bounced on his toes, whooped and high-fived one of the other actors. But he knew who he wanted to see. He swam through the dark and found Andy in the middle of swirling costumes and people and noise. Andy, with his curly brown hair, slim and graceful in his black tracksuit with 'Crew' on the back. He'd noticed him on the first day of school. Andreas. His slight accent, which, Alec discovered later, came from speaking German at home.

Alec was desperate to tell Robbie about how Andy had agreed to go out. On a date. He had said goodnight to his mum already, explained he was still tired from the weekend. He didn't like to lie, but she was a bit tense since the power kept going off and someone had chained the gate. He hadn't told her about the jerk who'd pegged a rock at him. No need to worry her.

Alec had known his dreamcoat was risky down here. He hadn't heard anything in little 'ole Pine Creek about him being a 'homo', but the fact that no one spoke to him or his mum was confirmation that they knew.

Alec shivered. Quietly, he climbed out through the window and lowered it down.

He headed towards the road.

He saw something move. Someone was near the pines!

It was Len Hamilton. *Fuck!* He'd arrived at the house earlier that evening, all smarmy.

Len moved. Alec took a few steps away. For a second, he wished he was back in Sydney. The cold here was mean, and there was no Andy, but Robbie was someone he trusted.

Len grunted. Alec wanted to say fuck off. But Len's silhouette reminded him of the school bully. Hairs stood up along the nape of his neck.

Alec glanced towards his bedroom window. Len was level with it. He knew if he tried to get back, Len might grab him. Alec was very aware of his mother inside, in her dressing gown and socks.

Alec kept walking backwards. Len followed, so Alec went faster. Len started to run. Alec turned, and one of his shoes came off. Instinct said leave it.

'Little faggot! Keep away from Robbie, or I'll break every bone in your body!'

Alec burst into a run. Behind him, he could hear fast footfalls. Alec felt rocks and lumps bite into the sole of his foot. He looked over at the Workers' House, and was sure he saw smoke waft from the chimney. If he could make it to the house, Robbie could help.

Len was pounding along behind, puffing.

Alec knew he could dart to the right down the driveway, but Len was on that side.

Alec was jolted by a pang of fear. Len might hurt him. More than spit balls, flicked rubber bands or being tripped in the school corridor.

Alec veered left, made a quick decision and headed for the embankment. He could hear Len's heavy steps.

'Little faggot!' Len growled.

Alec struggled across grassy, uneven ground and was suddenly at the drop. He steadied himself. Zaps of adrenaline burnt through him. He went over the top and down the other side. He stumbled, just managed to get his legs moving, and then he kept running.

*Fear can't win.*

He felt the bitumen slap against his foot.

*Andy.*

The thought of him was bright-yellow light that filled his chest and made him fly. He and Andy would start something. They'd dream up a different world. Blinding lights shone down Alec's left side. He didn't slow. He'd become pure energy, his mind filled with beauty and love, music ... and Andy.

## Chapter 69

Bruno came out to the farm after the funeral. Anne was due to drop him at the train station. He wrapped each of them in big hugs, which involved a memorable back pat. His big laugh punctuated conversation.

'Call me Uncle Bruno,' he insisted, standing back as Anne headed for her car. 'We're family. Visit anytime, you hear?' When he laughed, his big belly jumped.

'Take care, Bruno,' Mum said, her arms looped around his body. '*Please* stop smoking.'

Bruno rolled his eyes and grinned. 'Sure, tomorrow, darling.' He kissed her cheek, pressing right in like he was leaving an imprint.

'I'm serious!' Mum sandwiched his face between her hands. 'Have you taken your blood sugar?'

Bruno rolled his eyes. 'I've managed to stay alive all this time without your nagging. I'll check before I go, okay?' He bent, performed a rolling wave like a ringmaster before striding to the car. He leant into the passenger side, his belly hanging down, then he took out a small bag and unzipped the top. He fiddled with a little box, held it up for a minute and then got out a pen. He lifted his shirt and stabbed himself in the stomach. Sara realised it was an insulin pen, not a biro.

Next to Sara, Mum stared down at a weed she was nudging with her shoe.

'Does Uncle Bruno have diabetes?' Sara asked.

Mum nodded, lips pulled into a straight line. 'Be better if he didn't drink, smoke and eat so much.' Her mouth corner turned upwards. 'But Bruno is Bruno.'

'Is that what he lost on the drive up here? His insulin?'

Mum nodded. 'It was my fault. I was the one who got the script filled.' She cleared her throat. 'Silly me.'

Sara noted Mum was wearing the mauve cardigan from Toby's house. 'Nice cardi,' she said with a smile.

'I got cold.' Mum screwed up her nose. 'It smells like mothballs.'

'You can keep it.'

Mum shook her head. 'I just need my coat back. I had to lend it to someone.'

Long, thin rays of sun strobed between grey cloud as Anne's car drove down the driveway and hooted. Sara, Robbie and Mum waved until the car was out of sight. As the car came into view on the highway, it hooted once more, and everyone waved again. When Mum got into her car to return to her unit alone, Sara saw her wipe her eyes before she drove away.

As they washed the dishes, Robbie told Sara about Alec. 'We met one day and just talked about art.' He put a soapy plate in the dishrack, and Sara picked it up and wiped it. 'Then, a couple of weeks before he died, Alec got totally buzzed about this guy in his school play. He was working himself up to asking him out. We agreed to meet so he could tell me what happened. I decided it was worth celebrating, so I told him to come to the Workers' House at ten pm. It was usually safe by then.'

'Oh, Robbie.'

Robbie winced. 'That day I was so ill, I forgot the whole thing. When I found out Alec had died in a hit-and-run, I realised it was my fault.'

'No it wasn't.' Sara put her arm around his shoulder, and they leant into each other.

'I thought he was upset that time I saw you talking,' said Sara. 'What was that about?'

Robbie took a deep breath and shrugged. 'They had some problems.' Sara could see he wasn't going to tell her more.

'You know, the night he died, Alec told his mum he was in love,' Sara gave him a little smile. 'Must've gone well with the boy he liked.'

Robbie sighed and let his head roll back. 'I guess I should be glad.'

'I hear you have someone special in your life,' said Sara. 'Anne says she's sweet.' They exchanged a soft glance.

'Jenny. Yeah, she is.' Robbie put a cup in the dishrack with a sigh. 'She wants babies.'

'What do you want?'

'Whiskey in my coffee.' Robbie grinned and then shrugged. 'It was a deep hole I had to climb out of. I've just got my medication sorted. Not sure I'm ready to have a family yet.'

'Are you on antidepressants?'

Robbie nodded. 'And I talk to someone and sketch and get it all out one bit at a time.' He rolled his eyes but grinned, so Sara guessed that he didn't mind too much.

'You were always talented.'

'Dunno about that,' said Robbie. 'Sara, are you on anything?'

'I don't have depression.'

'You have something.'

Sara looked away. Robbie put his arm around her shoulder. 'It's okay.'

Sara cleared her throat and wiped a cup with the tea towel. 'Looked like you and Lillian were friendly when you saw each other at the funeral. Glad she likes one of us. She was a bit strange with me the other day.'

Robbie gave Sara a sideways glance. 'She's been through a lot.' He took back his arm, focused on the dishes, and a muscle twitched in his jaw.

Anne and Robbie stayed for a couple of days. Everyone made beds around the house. Ryan was still in the Workers' House.

Sara talked with Ryan and Anne until late as they sat outside near the stump of the pine tree. Sara could see stars for miles. There was just so much sky.

Not far from them, Robbie blew smoke over his head.

Mum came and went during the day, pausing to look at them before she left, a small smile on her lips.

Toby cornered Mum about some space for a dog rescue facility on the property. Ryan said he was keen to sell up in the city and manage the farm, should they need a manager. Dad hadn't changed his Will. The farm belonged to the family and the bank. Uncertainty and excitement simmered around the edges of conversation.

Before everyone left, they attended a memorial Lillian had organised for Alec. It was held at the local primary school.

Sara noticed that the replica dreamcoat was on a table with flowers, candles, and a picture of Alec on stage.

The ABC would not be including Alec's case in the program while it was part of an active investigation.

Sun glowed from behind a wall of trees, its light gentling the curves of the road and the jagged barbed wire at the top of the fence. Behind Sara in the big red gum trees, the birds were on the last song of their dusk concert. The earth vibrated gently beneath her feet as if it were full of insects and trapped energy.

Sara didn't need to count heads to see that most of Pine Creek had turned up. Among the crowd were non-locals wearing colourful clothes. Also present were three of the police officers from the station, one in uniform. Sara nodded and lifted her hand in a small wave of acknowledgement.

At the ceremony, Alec's father and a school friend spoke about Alec's life and quoted a poem. Two little girls, wearing dresses over stockings and boots, fondled the petals of some pink roses. A man came out of the group, crouched down and gently wrestled the girls' fingers from the petals. Then he put the smaller girl on his shoulder. She hid her face in his neck while the second girl traipsed along behind until they'd rejoined the group.

The man Sara witnessed throwing a stone at Alec had come forwards after Freddie had been questioned.

He said he'd travelled with Freddie to Parkwood because Freddie had met a girl at a rugby match there once. They'd driven all the way from Sydney, only for Freddie to be rejected, and were on the return journey when Freddie had seen Alec in the driveway. He'd encouraged his friend to, "give the little faggot a scare."

Sara looked around in the soft glow as the sun went down.

Some of the candles flickered out in a light breeze. Alec had briefly been part of this place. Maybe next time a strange-looking kid turned up, it would be different. Maybe there would be more than one person whom Alec could've shared good news with.

## Chapter 70

Sara returned to her flat among the eucalypts of the Blue Mountains with Nellie, who went wherever Sara went, even sleeping through car journeys on the backseat.

When Sara drove to the farm one weekend, the old *Hamilton's* sign was gone. The place felt different – horizon clear of thunderheads. Nellie got out, peed, sniffed noses with the other dogs and then waited at the door. Mum's car was parked outside.

Sara and Ryan had spoken on the phone many times. Sometimes, even Dereck took the phone. He told Sara what he liked about being a farmer. Apparently, to a ten-year-old boy, a few weeks on a farm made you a farmer. Ryan had enrolled him at the same local school Sara had attended with Robbie and Anne.

Toby wanted to call the farm 'Sunny Hills Canine Rescue' and start a centre ASAP. Mum said she'd think about it. She wanted to plant grapevines and have everyone over for music and dancing.

Sara made tea and walked out onto the front patio where

Mum was. She held one of two cups out.

Mum's head was tilted back as though looking for the big tree, and she straightened and took the offered cup. 'So much space, it's almost frightening.'

Nellie nudged the side of Sara's leg. Sara bent down and stroked beneath her chin.

Mum looked back at the sky. 'Do you know what sound the tree made after it was cut, Sara? While it was falling?'

Sara looked at the big stump. 'I think it would have been dramatic. Probably creaked and then whistled down and crashed with pollen and splinters flying everywhere.'

Mum frowned. 'No,' she said steadily. 'It was silent. Before it hit the ground, there was nothing.' She took a deep breath. 'But that's the scariest part, because you don't know where and when it will fall. When the next explosion will come.'

Sara squeezed her mum's hand then bent down and patted Nellie's head, which made the world seem less trembly. The dog closed her eyes. 'Mum, you don't have to worry about that anymore.'

Mum took a deep, shuddering breath. 'There's so much beauty, Sara,' she whispered. 'I feel like I couldn't see it with that monster in front of us.'

Sara hugged Mum and then went inside and got the bundle she'd remembered. She placed it in her mum's hands.

Mum's eyes widened. 'I'd almost forgotten,' she said. She unwrapped the old towel. The silver jewellery box sat in the centre. One leg was still blackened from the fire. Mum hadn't let Robbie polish it. She'd said she liked that it had survived, despite the damage. Mum closed her eyes and held it to her chest.

Sara kissed her. 'I love you, Mum.'

Inside the house, Toby, Dereck and Ryan were helping a

tradesman strip the walls, rip up the carpet and smash the tiles in the sunroom, kitchen and bathroom. It looked like a demolition site, necessitating a crunchy walk across the floor to switch the dusty kettle on and make tea. Amid the chaos, Sara had noticed Mum appear lost, like a girl who'd walked into the wrong room, but after a while, she crunched over the dirt like everyone else and drank tea with her backside against the bench.

Mum said she'd begun planning a housewarming. She said she might be able to live there if it felt like a different house. She wanted everyone to come, bring their families, their lovers. She said she wanted a house full of light where everyone could relax and be together.

The sound of the door made them both twist around.

Ryan gave Sara a knowing look as Lifter bounded out onto the patio. Lifter ran between Mum's legs, stopped, and looked up at her. She reached down and patted his head and floppy suede ear, and he licked her wrist as though the exchange was mutual.

'You have to keep him, Mum,' said Sara as the door slid closed.

Mum's face had relaxed. 'I don't think the decision is ours. I think they choose us.'

Which left Barney. But not for long.

Dawn had agreed to take Barney home.

Before he left, Sara held the dog's head and kissed his ear. 'You'll always be my hero, Barney.'

## Chapter 71

Sara was tasked with the collection of Dad's belongings from the rehab. As she walked through the carpark to Blooms' front doors, yellow-brown leaves stuck to her shoes. It was colder, and the leaves were darkening, thinner on the branches. In the garden, a man in blue overalls was raking leaves into piles, a wheelbarrow nearby.

After Sara wiped her shoes on the mat, the receptionist reminded her to sign in. She then directed Sara towards a storage room. The phone on the desk rang. Sara waved, indicating she was fine and then headed down the hall to a room full of stacked chairs and bags of clothes.

Sara turned the labels of the bags over: *Lennard Hamilton*.

A large lavender shape filled the doorway.

Sara jumped. 'Oh, Vera? You scared me.'

The old lady's palm felt cool and pillowy against Sara's forearm. 'What is it, dear? Are you lost?'

Sara realised that Vera may not remember her. She'd only been to Blooms twice. 'No. I'm picking up ... Len's things.'

Vera noticed the bag in Sara's hand. 'Oh, he passed, didn't

he, dear? I'm sorry. How is his wife coping?' Vera's watery blue eyes were curious.

'She's okay.'

Vera nodded. 'At least she saw him before he died. Those final words count when one is grieving.'

'How long till you go home?' Sara smiled politely and indicated Vera's plastered arm.

Vera blinked a few times, frowning at her plaster. 'Gosh, I'm a bit cloudy on that. Looks like I've done myself some damage.'

Sara smiled. She could feel the sticky warmth of Vera's loneliness. Then she had a thought. 'Mum came in *after* he died, Vera. We all came and said our goodbyes.'

Vera nodded sagely and smiled, showing a set of perfect teeth which could only be dentures. 'No, it was before you all came,' she said clearly. 'Len was the only one already in bed. His wife had been away, hadn't she? Lucky she popped in, now, with what's happened. They say the dying wait until their loved ones have said goodbye.'

Sara regarded Vera, who was looking around and frowning slightly as though confused. It must be hard to constantly forget things, then remember other things with such clarity. 'Vera, was Len awake or asleep when his wife came?'

Vera's eyes brightened. 'Oh, awake I think, dear. But he still couldn't speak.' She winced politely. 'I think she was leaving a note. She had a pen in her hand.'

Sara sucked her lip. 'Are you sure it was her and not one of the nurses?' She suddenly remembered the dried drop of blood on his arm, as if he'd been pricked with a needle, and the nurse with her bottles of pills. She didn't even know what medications he'd been on.

'Yes, dear. She was wearing that nice red coat she often wore. I rather fancied it myself.' She laughed softly.

Sara remembered Mum had said she'd loaned her coat.

'Thanks, Vera, I'd better go. Get well soon.'

There was a little sign at reception: *Back in five minutes*, and a form with a yellow post-it note stuck to the top with Sara's name on it. The form confirmed all personal effects had been collected for a resident.

Sara signed and then dropped the paperwork onto the desk. She glanced at the visitor registration book and leafed back through to the date of her dad's admission. She found Elena Hamilton written in. She turned the page.

Sara's attention caught on a familiar name the day after Dad's admission. Slowly, she kept turning pages, but didn't see it again, just her mum's name every day until she went away. Sara then found the date of her dad's second stroke and scanned the names. No visitors up until the time she and Mum had arrived for final farewells.

'All okay?'

Sara looked up, smiled at the receptionist, then closed the book. 'Yes. Just checking I'd put in a time. Bye, thanks for everything.'

'I'll get the door for you.' The receptionist pressed a button.

A man in a suit holding wilted flowers used the opportunity to walk through the doors. Sara stood for a moment, considering how easy it was to come and go when the doors were supposedly designed for the patients' safety.

Sara called Mum's flat to see if she was home.

Her mum answered immediately.

'Mum, which jacket did you lend out?'

'Ah,' Mum sounded like she was putting effort into something, like lifting shopping bags onto the bench. 'The red one. Why?'

'Who'd you lend it to?'

'I leant it to Lillian. I feel bad about asking for it back, but I've had it for years. It's my favourite.'

With a jolt, Sara remembered Lillian standing outside the chapel at Dad's funeral. She'd been wearing a red coat. Initially confused to see her, Sara had thought it made sense when Robbie had gone over to her.

Just days before, Lillian would have found out it was Dad who had buried Alec's missing belongings. Why would she attend his funeral?

Sara's scalp tightened. 'When did you give it to her?'

Something clicked, and the sounds of the kettle and then cupboards indicated Mum was probably making tea. There were a few moments of silence that made Sara listen even more carefully. 'I saw Lillian outside Blooms the day you found Alec's things. She'd just found out what had happened to Alec. It was a very difficult conversation, as you can imagine. She was shivering with cold, probably shock too.'

'You went to see Dad?'

A few moments passed. 'Yes,' said Mum. 'Just after I called you, I made Bruno pull in at Blooms. I think I just wanted to ask Len about what he'd done. But once we got there, I didn't want to go in. Then Bruno took his blood sugar, and we couldn't find the new insulin pen. He had to go and get some more. I said I'd walk home.'

'Was that when Lillian arrived?'

'Ah, shortly after. Poor woman.'

Sara's pulse quickened. 'Mum. When you left, was Lillian still there?'

'Yes. I felt bad leaving her so distressed. Told her to call a friend so she wasn't alone. She didn't have a coat, so I gave her mine.'

As Sara ended the call, she remembered the name in the visitors book the day after Dad had been admitted: Lillian Stynes. Then she remembered Lillian at Dad's funeral as she stood by the roses, a peaceful look on her face.

## Chapter 72

As she drove up to Lillian's house, Sara could see sealed cardboard boxes around the front door. She remembered Lillian in a pretty dress at the dance all those years ago, the way Dad's little smile had sent her out the door. Then she remembered the bite mark in Lillian's lip when Sara had asked her if she'd ever met anyone.

Lillian emerged in overalls and a pink jumper, shading her eyes with one hand.

Sara cut the engine and climbed out. 'Hi, Lillian. You're leaving?'

Lillian smiled, looking at the array of boxes. 'Yes, I decided it was time to go.'

Sara nodded, understanding. 'I can't imagine what this must be like for you.'

Lillian inhaled and looked away. 'Thank you for working out where Alec's jacket was. At least I know what happened now.'

'That's okay.' Sara smiled. 'Actually, Lillian, it was a jacket I wanted to speak to you about. Mum's red one.'

Lillian nodded and held Sara's gaze, but Sara could tell she wasn't going to volunteer anything.

'Mum gave it to you outside Blooms, the night my father died?'

'Yes, she did.'

'It must've seemed like such strange timing, Dad dying the same night that I found Alec's coat.'

'He was a sick man,' Lillian said softly, watching her foot as she made an arc in the dirt with her toe.

'You visited him?'

'Once,' said Lillian without looking up.

'I had to pick up Dad's belongings. I didn't want to, but it spared Mum doing it. When I was there, one of the patients told me that Dad had a visitor before he died. A woman wearing a red coat.'

Lillian frowned slightly and folded her arms. Sara waited before she went on.

'Mum filled Uncle Bruno's script for a new insulin pen, but then they couldn't find it,' said Sara.

Lillian squinted. 'I wouldn't know about that.'

'Was there something you wanted to tell me, Lillian?' said Sara.

Lillian lifted her chin and a tension seemed to ease from her. She looked up at the complacent sky, breathed out for a long time and closed her eyes. 'I guess so,' she said quietly.

Sara waited.

The sound of the day grew into their silence. A tractor's tireless drone so common, so unchanging, it wasn't there until you listened for it. A truck engine in a low gear growled as it went down a hill.

'When you came over the other day and asked about the letter, I was expecting you to ask about something else,' said

Lillian. Her eyes half-closed, she seemed to be enjoying the sunshine on her face. When she finally looked over, Sara saw what she'd hoped for. The slight tension and brightness people get before they tell you a secret. 'I remember the day I met Len. He put out a grass fire near my house.'

'I remember,' said Sara. She recalled that he was late home, too.

Lillian frowned slightly. 'He was quite helpful. Concerned. At first.' Lillian swallowed. 'I moved down here to be close to Mum, try and get ahead because I'd taken out a loan to pay for Alec's tuition.' She pressed her lips together. 'I knew with the cheap rent and bookkeeping, I could pay it back, even though the interest was ...' She lifted her eyebrows. '...steep. But then I had a car accident. No one was hurt, but my car was written off. I couldn't work without it, so I bought a good second-hand one. I was determined that Alec wouldn't miss out on his dream, just because I couldn't sort myself out.' She closed her eyes for a moment. 'But it meant another loan.' Lillian's gaze settled on Sara for a minute. 'I didn't use a bank for either loan. I hadn't had full-time work in some time. The people who organised the money were threatening. The repayments were ... unmanageable. I told Len everything.'

Sara tried to imagine her father listening to Lillian, their new and very beautiful neighbour, as she told him her story. Her skin tingled. 'What did he do?' Sara asked, almost scared to hear the answer.

'He paid the full sum for me. He told me just to pay the interest until I was back on my feet.'

Sara nodded slowly.

Lillian swept her hand across her eyes. 'But I could barely even make the interest ... however, with some extra cleaning,

I was able to do it. Then Mum needed some new medications. I couldn't pay Len anything for a couple of weeks.' Lillian looked off at the sky, and her lip quivered. 'He'd begun coming over on a Friday night with a couple of beers. He said he was supposed to be at the pub, but he preferred my company. I felt unable to say no. Then one night, he kissed me.'

Sara swallowed. 'I see,' she said nervously, and her pulse quickened.

'I wasn't interested, and we had this awkward moment. Then he just ...' She shook her head slightly. 'Told me he was just a man who needed a kiss, and now he was embarrassed, and he thought I'd be grateful .... Said that the money had been for his family's annual holiday. Kept going on and on and on!' Lillian held up her hands. 'I just wanted him to stop. So ... I gave him a kiss.' She covered her face with her hands.

'We didn't have an annual holiday.'

Lillian snorted regretfully and dropped her hands. 'I knew he was manipulating me, but the more I couldn't pay anything, the more pressure he put on me, until I felt I had no choice.' She chewed her lower lip.

Sara had a flash of memory. It was not of Lillian but of Dad. With his arm around Mum on a Saturday morning. Cheerful. Unusually nice to Mum.

'You had a relationship with my dad?' Sara asked quietly. She shaded her eyes as the sun dipped lower.

Lillian pursed her lips tightly. 'I wouldn't call it that. He wouldn't take no for an answer. I felt like ... having sex with him was paying *interest*.' Lillian exhaled heavily. 'Then Alec found out. He started coming on Fridays to deter Len. Len got annoyed. Alec said that he'd told Robbie about the debt, and that Robbie was going to help out.'

Sara remembered her brother calling Dad a hypocrite, and Alec meeting with Robbie.

Lillian smiled slightly as she shook her head. 'Robbie came over one day and said he didn't need his motorbike, so he'd sold it. He gave me a cheque.' She looked at her hands. 'He had one condition. That I told no one and paid him back when I could. I was desperate. I took the money.'

'The motorbike,' said Sara. She nodded as she remembered how he'd sold his bike because he was saving for something. A car. Then he'd left home and raided the money tin. Sara realised he must've had nothing after giving it all to Lillian.

Lillian smiled. 'The lump sum I was able to pay took Len by surprise. It took the heat off me, and I started saying no. He still drove over and parked in the pines sometimes, but he stayed in his car. I could see him from my window. I suspected it was him who locked my gate and flicked the power off a few times, but I was too embarrassed to say anything. I knew he'd go away eventually. Then, when Alec was killed, he didn't come over again.'

Sara remembered Dad removing the empty cans from the Hilux shortly after Alec was found dead. She could imagine Dad watching Lillian as he drank beer in his ute, furious that a divorcee, and single mother, no less, had refused the mighty Len Hamilton after he'd generously loaned her money.

A wave of something dark rose in her. Dad's actions had forced two teenaged boys to try and help a vulnerable woman. One was dead and the other, her beautiful brother Robbie, had suffered for years. She felt a surge of understanding for the woman in front of her.

Lillian looked down and rocked back on her heels. 'I didn't see Len until a few weeks ago. It gave me a shock when he turned up here. He just stood there in front of me and said, "Lillian, it was an accident." I asked if he meant Alec. He nodded and then got a dazed look, turned around and stumbled to his ute like a drunk. I was angry. I wanted to know more but when I ran over, Len was slumped in the driver's seat, confused. I quickly called an ambulance, gave his address and drove him home.'

Sara nodded as she remembered how the ute had been parked nose in.

'I heard where he was, so I went to Blooms to ask him more, but he couldn't answer.'

Sara focused on some currawongs carolling nearby. When she looked back, Lillian was watching her. Sara flinched internally, unsure if she wanted to hear what Lillian was going to say.

'I'm proud to say that I repaid Robbie in full a couple of years ago.' Lillian frowned slightly. 'He took some finding. He wasn't well.' She glanced at Sara. 'He accepted the money and said he'd book himself into a clinic because he wanted to get clean.' She smiled. 'I'm so proud of him. He looked amazing the other day.'

Sara swallowed when she remembered Anne had said Robbie changed his life around, a couple of years ago. She realised Lillian's repayment could have been the thing that helped him.

'He's a wonderful person,' Sara said quietly, her throat too thick to say more.

'Sara.' Lillian looked her right in the eye.

Sara blinked and then nodded.

'After I left Blooms, I felt like I'd been turned inside out. Your mother told me that Alec's shoe had been in the bag Len buried. I knew then that it was him who'd been here that night. He had to have been right behind Alec when his shoe came off. I believe that's what Len had meant when he said it was an accident. Maybe he didn't mean for Alec to run out in front of a car, but that's what happened. He chased my son to his death.' Lillian pressed her lips together. 'I'm sorry to be the one to tell you that.'

'I'd worked it out,' said Sara, softly. 'I'm sorry too.'

Lillian smiled sadly. 'I'll go and get that jacket for you.' She turned around.

'Just a sec,' Sara said, almost stuttering at the sudden direction change. 'Was there something else you wanted to say? Did you go inside Blooms with Mum's jacket on?'

Lillian shook her head and frowned slightly. 'After that one visit, I never saw him again.'

Sara, having been so sure it was Lillian whom Vera had seen, wasn't able to speak for a moment. 'So, why did you come to Dad's funeral?'

Lillian shrugged. 'Closure, I suppose.'

Sara remembered Lillian in red. It had almost seemed symbolic.

Lillian was standing there waiting.

'Did you find anything in the pockets?' said Sara.

'No,' said Lillian. 'It was nice of your Mum to lend it though. Please tell her thank you.'

## Chapter 73

**A few weeks later**

Ryan returned from the city, where he'd helped organise a lawyer for Rachel. He had brought Dereck back to the farm and tidied up the Workers' House. He'd thrown old furniture onto a pile with some dead branches, ready for a winter bonfire, then fixed the kitchen and bought a new fridge. Rusty started following Dereck around, and soon she was never more than a metre from him until he went inside. Then she'd sit on the doormat until he came out. Except for tradesmen coming and going, the main house wasn't often occupied, so this made Sara happy.

Sara always brought lamb offcuts to the farm when she'd been home to the Blue Mountains. She'd sit on the doormat next to Rusty and tell her how life was going. That her hands didn't tremble when she woke in the mornings, and that she was talking to someone about her episodes.

Ryan was a witness at Rachel's trial and could face his own charges of failure to report. Back and forth between

Sydney, the farm, and a local lawyer would be Ryan's normal for a while.

When he came down without Dereck, they organised to have dinner together. Afterwards, they walked over to the Workers' House. Sara took Ryan's hand.

'Stay for a bit?' he asked when they reached the door. She hadn't wanted to rush anything and had avoided being alone with Ryan down here.

This time, she nodded and followed him inside.

'Are you going to move down here permanently with Dereck?'

Ryan shrugged. 'I don't know. For now, yeah. I can get electrician work anywhere. We need space from the circus around Rachel.'

In the weeks after the funeral, when Ryan and Sara had found themselves alone in the main house, they'd kissed, both leaning to the same side, necessitating a second attempt. 'I feel like I've never done this before!' Sara had laughed. She thought they'd since refined their technique.

'Maybe we should put some music on,' she said.

Ryan got up from the couch. He'd set up a portable stereo near the window. 'Sure. What do you feel like?'

'Jimmy Barnes. It'll take us back.' She wrung her hands, noticed what she was doing and stopped.

Ryan fiddled with a disc and a few buttons.

Distorted electric guitar, hum of bass, gritty metallic, familiar: 'Lay Down Your Guns'.

'Not this one.'

Ryan grinned, hit a button.

Sara heard the familiar big keyboard: 'Let's Make it Last All Night'.

'Actually, I don't think I can handle Jimmy right now.' Sara took a deep breath.

Ryan smiled gently. 'I know. Let's just take it slow.' He turned the stereo off and sat on the end of the couch.

Sara lay back, her head on Ryan's knee, where she could gaze into the fire. The couch was a cheap one Ryan had had delivered, along with two lounge chairs. The original beds were still there. Sara wondered if the double bed was still squeaky.

Ryan stroked her hair back from her face. 'You know, Len would have known I'd find the shoe if I found the jacket.'

Sara closed her eyes. 'Then you'd know he'd been protecting himself that night, too.'

'Yeah, I thought about that,' said Ryan. He traced the cartilage of Sara's ear and thumbed the edge of her jaw. His touch helped to soften the dark things.

'I'd like to believe he wanted closure for Lillian,' said Sara. 'It doesn't make up for what he did, but I wonder if he'd meant to say sorry.'

Sara had told him about Lillian calling the ambulance for Dad. Sara shifted and folded her arms. 'It must be hard for Mum. She won't talk about it.'

Sara was yet to share everything she and Lillian had discussed and wasn't sure she ever would.

'Give her time.' Ryan squeezed her shoulder gently. They watched the flames curl around the wood, the white-hot glow of the embers.

'I don't know if this helps, but Len was good to me,' said Ryan. 'He gave me a chance, taught me a lot. I didn't like seeing him treat your family badly, and I don't understand it, but you know, the meanest people often hate themselves the most.'

Sara turned her head so she could see Ryan's face better.

'Very wise, Mr Finch. Now kiss me. Then I need to get to bed.'

Ryan kissed her for a long time. He chuckled when Sara held the back of his neck and made him kiss for longer. 'I've missed this,' he said when she let him up. 'I mean, laughing with you. We always got along well.'

She grinned. 'We've got some catching up to do.' She then said goodnight and walked across the small house paddock in the moonlight.

When Sara got back to the empty house, she opened the fridge and noticed she was almost out of milk. Mum still lived at the unit, so there was no one to keep an eye on the food in the fridge.

Mum's red jacket hung over the back of a dining chair at the table. She must've left it when she last visited. Sara walked over and smoothed her hands over the fabric. She paused and then slipped her hands into both of the pockets. She had to kneel down to get right to the bottom.

She thought about how she'd suspected Lillian of doing something to harm her father and then felt foolish. A second stroke was common in patients like Dad. Lillian had finally found out what had happened to Alec and could finally move on with her life.

At the bottom of the pocket, Sara's fingers touched something crinkly. She grasped the edge and pulled out a piece of paper.

Sara got up and turned on the light. She realised she was holding a docket. She carefully unfolded it. One purchase; a Novopen. Sara's breath caught. She imagined Mum slipping the receipt into her jacket. She remembered the lost insulin pen. Did mum slip that into her other pocket or...her handbag? Sara imagined Mum sitting outside Dad's room, her handbag on her lap. She felt a tingle all over. A mist of sweat emerged on her forehead. Her heart pounded.

Sara looked over at the fridge and remembered how stupid she'd felt when she realised Dad wouldn't take beer to the pub.

She stood up and walked to the window. She recalled the day she'd given back the heirloom and Mum explained the sound of the tree when it was falling. How she could see beauty now that the monster was gone.

Sara had thought Mum was referring to the tree.

Sara's hands shook as she grabbed the red jacket, and her wallet and keys. She headed for the door.

Sara knew Mum had two levels; the smiling automatic one and, the real one. The one who cried alone quietly and who glared at Dad sometimes before her blank expression returned.

The one who felt *everything*.

Mum had always made happy chatter to hide the bruises. Not because she didn't feel them, but because she held all her wounds inside. Like Sara used to.

As she turned onto the highway and headed for Parkwood, Sara chewed her inner lip.

She remembered Mum crying when they were talking inside her laundry. When Sara had mentioned the time Dad had hit Robbie. Then again after the funeral when Bruno and Anne left, and then, just recently, when she drove away from Robbie, Anne and Sara.

She recalled how Mum's face had been dry the night Dad had died and, she realised with a start, at Dad's funeral.

*Monster?*

Mum had never called Dad anything like that. She was so good at pretending. At giving Dad excuses, like she was convincing not just Sara, Anne and Robbie, but herself.

As she drove, Sara saw, as if it were yesterday, Mum restocking the fridge so that Dad always had cold beer, and anything he wanted, so that he didn't yell.

Mum would have noticed when Dad took beer on his pub nights. No one took beer to a pub. It would be like taking flowers to a florist.

'Monster,' said Sara. Mum's torment didn't finish at bedtime. Sometimes Sara could still hear the deep breathing from the master bedroom in her nightmares. Marital bliss? Sara knew it was far from bliss.

As she turned into Mum's driveway, Sara realised Mum had probably known that Dad wasn't going to the pub. She may have even guessed where he went.

She turned off the car and closed her eyes.

Sara could almost feel Mum's silent fury, her swallowed words. She knew how it felt to force every cell to hide anger and pain. How it felt to count down the days. But Mum couldn't count down. Even after she'd left him, it was as if something glued her to Dad, and she didn't even feel like there was freedom. Even after she'd moved out; even when he was sick, she still wasn't free of Dad.

Until he was really gone.

Sara knocked on Mum's door. 'Just me, Sara.'

Sara gave Mum the jacket and followed her inside. She could smell tomatoes and garlic. Mum could cook whatever she wanted now. As Mum hung the jacket on the back of a chair, Sara noticed that she looked different. *Taller?* No, she looked straighter. Her shoulders weren't as rounded.

Sara let Mum make her a cup of tea and then waited for her to sit down.

They sat facing one another.

Mum's smile slowly faded. 'What is it, honey?'

Now she was here, Sara struggled to start. She pulled the receipt from her pocket and slid it across the table.

Mum unfolded it and then squinted. Sara had seen her pull out reading glasses when she read the back of food packets.

Mum looked up. 'I see,' she said.

Sara noticed her face had smoothed.

'Where did you find it?' Sara asked, her voice stronger than she felt. 'The insulin?'

'Inside the jacket,' said Mum. 'Bruno had already driven off to get more.'

Sara looked into Mum's green eyes like they were a mirror. 'You told me you didn't want to go inside when you stopped at Blooms. An old lady saw you by the bed, with a pen in your hand. She thought you were leaving a note.'

Mum nodded. A few expressions flickered across her face but were gone before Sara could decide what Mum was feeling.

'After Bruno left, I went for a walk in the park near Blooms. I was devastated about what Len had done. Everything came back.' She shook her head. 'Everything.'

'Oh, Mum.' Sara covered Mum's hand with her own.

'When I put my hand in one of those deep pockets, I found it.' Mum shrugged.

Sara hardly breathed.

Mum went on, her voice quiet and clear. 'I realised that Len wouldn't be able to stand trial. After what he'd done; and the pain, the years and the lies.' Mum took a deep breath. 'I saw the entrance of Blooms where he was being cared for. Staff at his beck and call. I had that pen in my hand. I felt ... calm.'

Sara remembered Mum outside Dad's room. How quiet

she'd seemed.

Mum squinted as though trying to recall something elusive. 'I hardly remember walking in, I just know that he stared at me.' Her eyelids closed. 'Those cold blue eyes. I knew I'd never see them again if I kept turning the dial and pushing the button until it was all gone.'

It was a moment before Sara could speak. 'When did Lillian arrive?' she said.

'Just after I got outside. Once I'd given her my jacket, I walked home.' Mum frowned slightly. 'When they called me back in and told me Len had died, I thought someone would ask me about it. I had the pen in my handbag. I wasn't hiding it. But no one asked. They said he'd had a stroke.'

Sara had a flash of memory. Mum's handbag on her knees.

'Mum,' said Sara.

Mum blinked as though she'd drifted away, like Sara used to do when Dad was yelling. 'Yes?' she said.

'What did you do with the empty insulin pen?'

'Nothing. It's still in my handbag.'

## Chapter 74

### A few months later

Sara had been back to the Family Counselling Centre and let them know of her plans to leave. She liked the idea of studying psychology, but she wasn't fully decided. They invited her to a small morning tea. The staff fawned over Nellie, who accepted their attention with dignity.

Daryl was there.

Sara gave him a long hug. 'Keep writing your poetry,' she said near his ear. 'It's a beautiful way to remember someone you loved.'

Alone in a public toilet outside her old workplace, Sara dropped the empty insulin pen into the safety lid of the sharps disposal unit. Since Mum had handed it to her that night in her unit, Sara had kept it in the glovebox of her car. She was relieved when she heard the little rattle of all the other needles or glass or rubbish, covered in all sorts of DNA. She imagined the container being collected for incineration and everything disappearing in the inferno. Just like a cremation.

## Chapter 75

Ryan, visiting on his way to Sydney, opened the passenger side of his car and stepped back as Sara climbed out. While he let Nellie out, he looked over towards the thick oak and pine trees across the road. Nearby, a decorative arch in a stone fence led into the Cliff's Edge Motel.

Nellie moving in with Sara had meant some changes. A different routine. Treats and dog food in the shopping basket, extra eggs, and a pink collar and lead. When Sara got back to her apartment, she had wiped the whiteboard clean, intending to make a new list, but as she stood with the black marker in her hand, the bare expanse reminded her of the big sky after the removal of the tree. She decided to buy a print of the ocean or forest or desert – something beautiful, vast and edgeless. She walked out onto the balcony, gripped the railing and then slowly looked down. She controlled her breathing. A few moments later, she stepped back from the edge. *Better than last time.*

The back of Cliff's Edge was painted sandy pink. Around the front, facing the valley, were deep ravines, woodland, densely forested hills, and cliffs of soaring heights and dangerous drops; the view tourists travelled for.

Ryan held out his hand. 'Ready for this?'

'Absolutely.' Sara took his hand. 'I have my heart set on the red velvet cake. I have no idea how many calories are involved.'

Ryan grinned. 'Thought we were here for the view.'

'I'm not keen on heights. I guess this is part of the desensitisation thing I'm doing now. Anyway, I like cake.'

At the entrance to the café, Nellie bumped into Sara's leg, a habit she had if she was somewhere unfamiliar. Sara squatted down and stroked the pad of her thumb between Nellie's eyes, and then backwards between her ears. 'We must try new things, Nellie. Don't worry, I've asked if you can come onto the veranda. They're going to give you a little bowl of your own.'

Nellie looked up and whined quietly. Questions, love or blankness shone from Nellie's warm brown eyes. She wagged. It was love, Sara decided.

Sara had phoned Pene for the first time in months and was glad of her friend's voice. She told Pene about Nellie and even arranged a catch up. Nellie seemed to make it easier for Sara to talk to people. They'd promised to have dinner before Pene's new baby arrived.

Sara also had a weekend planned with Anne and an invitation to Robbie's home.

When she'd last seen Mum, Sara remembered to pass on Lillian's message. 'Before she left, Lillian said to say thanks. For lending your jacket.'

Mum nodded. 'Hm.' Then she smiled. 'She'll be happier with a fresh start. She deserves to be happy.'

'So do you, Mum,' said Sara. 'You don't have to worry

anymore.' Mum's gaze flickered as though she registered what Sara meant. Sara thought Mum was going to cry but she swallowed and nodded, and then a moment of understanding passed between them.

At a table closer to the building than the railing, Ryan and Sara had barely sat down before they were approached by a waitress holding a notepad and pen.

'Red velvet cake and a pot of tea, please,' said Sara.

'And you, sir?' The waitress sparkled as though Ryan emitted fluorescence.

'Um, I'll have the chocolate brownie. And a flat white, thanks.' Ryan smiled.

The waitress beamed. 'Warmed with ice-cream?'

'Sure. Love ice-cream,' said Ryan.

Sara bit her lips to stop herself from laughing.

With a puzzled frown, Ryan leant forwards onto his elbows. 'Sara, you're blushing.'

Sara shook her head. 'You know Toby has a date with the manager of Blooms? I thought I saw a bit of eye contact between them.'

'Good for him.' He sighed. 'You know, it's taken us a long time to go on our first date.'

'It's never too late,' said Sara, but then she thought about it. 'Maybe we don't have as long as we think we do. Are you busy this afternoon? I think one of my light switches is broken.'

'Sure.'

Sara then took Ryan's hand and leant towards him. She explained the ice-cream reference quietly in his ear.

As she drew back, his eyes were wide. He frowned suddenly and checked his watch. 'Gosh, look at the time. I should check that switch for you now.'

Sara laughed. 'Not so fast.' She looked out where the land fell away into the forest. A situation which would usually send her close to panic. 'Can you believe that view?'

## *Acknowledgements*

One of the best parts of writing a book is discovering how brilliant your friends are. I am awed by the generosity and talents of my family, colleagues, and friends. Their support and guidance were crucial.

I thank everyone for their faith and trust, passion and expertise.

The honour roll:

Hans and Wendy Stroeve – for school memories, enthusiasm, and local plant knowledge.

Rich – for determining local bird calls.

Kirby and Teleah – for listening to endless ideas and still being optimistic and encouraging.

Jemma – for colour, for being an on-call thesaurus, and for always being open to random brainstorming sessions.

Gerard, a wonderful writer and true legend – for providing invaluable feedback and guidance, and meeting for hours in a coffee shop on a 17-degree day.

Tom and Richard – the eagle-eyes behind the

proofreading.

Michele, Stefan and Tim – for editorial help, professionalism, flexibility, and humour.

Adam – for Law expertise, and a love of dogs.

Bruce – for police help, humour, and storytelling.

Nadene – for the country music collection.

David – for music, inspiration, and for stirring me up.

Tim — my greatest asset and partner in life. For steering the ship during the most intense moments, for honest feedback, and for knowledge in more areas than is normal.

And for my siblings – warriors all.

## *About the Author*

A West Australian, Kamille has a Science Degree, Comprehensive Writing certification and facilitates a prose writers' group at the Fellowship of Australian Writers W.A. Winner of the B.J. Paterson Writing Award 2013, Kamille's various short stories and articles have placed nationally, and been published in print and online.

Kamille's debut novel, A Matchbox Full of Pearls, was voted number one on Goodreads by Blue Ink Review's Best Books of 2022, and included in Kirkus Reviews 2022 'Great Indie Books Worth Discovering.'

Kamille lives in Perth with her family and two dogs.

Visit: kamilleroach.com

Manufactured by Amazon.com.au
Sydney, New South Wales, Australia